Criminal Intent

By William Bernhardt
Published by Ballantine Books:

Primary Justice
Blind Justice
Deadly Justice
Perfect Justice
Cruel Justice
Naked Justice
Extreme Justice
Dark Justice
Silent Justice
Murder One
Criminal Intent

Double Jeopardy
The Midnight Before Christmas
The Code of Buddyhood
Legal Briefs
Natural Suspect
Final Round

William Bernhardt

♦ ♦ ♦

CRIMINAL
INTENT

BALLANTINE BOOKS ♦ NEW YORK

A Ballantine Book
Published by The Ballantine Publishing Group

Copyright © 2002 by William Bernhardt

www.ballantinebooks.com

Library of Congress Cataloging-in-Publication Data

Bernhardt, William, 1960–
Criminal intent / William Bernhardt.—1st ed.
p.   cm.
ISBN 0-345-44173-7
1. Kincaid, Ben (Fictitious character)—Fiction. 2. Tulsa (Okla.)—Fiction. I. Title.

PS3552.E73147 C67 2002
813'.54—dc21   2002066500

ISBN 0-345-44173-7

Manufactured in the United States of America

First Edition: September 2002

10   9   8   7   6   5   4   3   2   1

For Harry and Alice and Ralph.
I have faith in you.

This world is not conclusion;
A sequel stands beyond,
Invisible, as music,
But positive, as sound.
It beckons and it baffles;
Philosophies don't know,
And through a riddle, at the last,
Sagacity must go.

—EMILY DICKINSON (1830–1886)

The term "bad faith" generally implies a design to mislead or deceive another, or a neglect or refusal to fulfill some duty or contractual obligation, prompted by some interested or sinister motive. Bad faith is not simply bad judgment or negligence, but rather implies the conscious doing of a wrong because of dishonest purpose or moral obliquity.

—*Black's Law Dictionary*

Prologue

◆　◆　◆

CHAPTER

1

"FATHER FORGIVE ME for I have sinned.

"Father forgive me for I have sinned.

"Father forgive me for I have—"

Helen's voice broke off. She was breathless. She had murmured the words a hundred times, a thousand perhaps. But it didn't seem to help. Nothing seemed to help.

She was on her knees in the church prayer garden, surrounded by birch trees and flowering plants and multicolored azaleas, a Garden of Eden recreated. Was she Adam, the one who submits to temptation and therefore must be cast out? Or was she Eve, the temptress who leads others to sin and degradation?

"Our Father, who art in heaven, hallowed be thy name. Thy kingdom come, thy will be done . . ."

Her hands were folded and her head was bowed. She was saying the words, chanting them like some arcane ritual. But who was listening? Who would hear the prayers of a woman who had done what she had done?

Had done and been doing for years, she thought, and the sickness took hold of her, sending waves of nausea throughout her body. She doubled over in agony.

At first, what they did had not bothered her. Or perhaps it had, but somehow she managed to suppress the guilt, to bury her true feelings in a morass of rationalization and intellectual posturing. And then one morning, not long ago, she awoke and realized—she was a sinner. A pawn of Satan. What she had done—what they all had done—was worse than mere sin. It was complete and utter corruption. Moral bankruptcy.

It was evil.

"Father forgive me for I have sinned.

"Father forgive me for I have sinned.

"Father forgive me for I have sinned."

She recited the words over and over again, but she obtained no comfort from them. She glared up at the ebony sky, but she found no answer, no release. What was she going to do now? She had gathered some of the others, had talked to them about it. Some had even admitted they shared her feelings. But it wasn't enough. Talking would never be enough. Action was required. She had to do something.

She heard a noise behind her, from somewhere deeper in the prayer garden. The door at the base of the bell tower was closing. But who would be in there at this time of night? Was it the priest? One of the church regulars? An irrational fear gripped her. She didn't want to be seen, not in here, not now, not like this.

"What are you doing?"

She let out a small sigh of relief when she saw who it was. Nothing to worry about there. "I'm just . . . having a quiet moment. Spending some time alone. If you wouldn't mind . . ."

"Could you please help me?"

Helen tried not to frown. This was one of the inescapable realities of being in a church—there was always someone who needed help. An old woman wanting someone to run after her groceries. An Altar Guild guy recruiting help with the cleanup. And it always seemed to come at the least convenient time. "I don't know. . . ."

"Please. I really really *really* need your help."

"What is it?"

"I saw something in the garden, near the base of the tower. Something strange and . . . frightening."

Helen pushed herself to her feet. "Show me."

She followed down the cobbled sidewalk toward the bell tower, in one of the most isolated and secluded parts of the labyrinthine prayer garden. There were two marble benches flanking a small recess planted with honeysuckle and flowered hedges. Many of the parishioners had buried the ashes of loved ones here; a tall marble obelisk behind one of the benches stood as a memorial.

"So? . . ."

"Over there. By the bench."

Helen looked in the direction indicated. Someone had been digging. Signs of excavation were evident; an azalea bush had been all but uprooted.

"My God," Helen whispered. Had someone been digging up . . . one of the graves? She had been at the funeral last week, and she knew this was where Ruth's sister's ashes had been buried. "Why would anyone—?" Helen's eyes widened with repugnance and amazement. "You?"

She turned just in time to see the shovel right before it struck. It hit her on the side of the head, knocking her sideways. The pain was excruciating. She felt as if her brain had been dislodged, her jaw shattered. Her legs crumbled, and she fell down onto one of the benches.

She remained conscious, but just barely. She watched as the shovel came closer, then closer, then closer still.

"But . . . why?" Helen managed to gasp.

"Why not?"

Her assailant's hands clutched her throat with a strong, unbreakable grip. Helen felt her consciousness fading, and she knew that in a few short moments she would be dead. Was this the penance she had been seeking? Was this what it took to make her feel clean again? Her brain was too muddled to make any sense of it. As she felt her life slowly trickling away, her thoughts were not focused on these questions of theology and personal redemption. As she stared into the face of her killer, all she could think was:

I can't believe it's you! I can't believe it could possibly be you!

2

"Mr. Kincaid, please direct your witness to take the stand."

"Sir, my client is on trial. He can't be compelled to testify. The Fifth Amendment—"

"Has absolutely no force or effect here. Please call your client to the stand."

"But sir, it's a fundamental principle of the United States Constitution—"

"The Constitution is not relevant."

"Sir, the Constitution is always relevant. It's the fundamental guarantee—"

"Not today it isn't. Now call your witness."

"Sir, the protection against self-incrimination—"

"Does not exist in this court. Mr. Kincaid, as I think you already know, this tribunal is governed by canonical law, not the United States Constitution. Now please send your client to the stand without any further delay."

Ben Kincaid closed his eyes, trying to mentally regroup. How did he get himself into these situations? After years of practicing law, he had finally managed to achieve some degree of competence in Tulsa's criminal courts. So what on earth was he doing at an ecclesiastical trial conducted under the auspices of the Episcopal Church of the Diocese of Oklahoma?

Losing, that's what he was doing.

Father Holbrook leaned forward, crinkling the flaps of his black robe. "Again, Mr. Kincaid, I must ask you to call your client to the stand."

Holbrook was an Oklahoma City priest who had been appointed to preside over the trial as judge. Fortunately, he had some legal experience; even though the Constitution was not the controlling law, the Federal Rules of Evidence were followed. The jurors were clergy and lay people elected at the annual diocesan convention.

"And again, sir—" Ben couldn't bring himself to call the man *your honor*, even though he was, technically speaking, a judge. "—I must insist—"

Ben felt a tugging at his arm. "It's all right. I'll go."

Ben peered down at the gray-bearded face of his client—and priest—Father Daniel Beale. "I don't think that's wise. Do you know what could happen to you up there?"

"Of course I do." There was a small but discernible tremble in his voice. Though he was in his mid-fifties, at the moment, he looked much older. "But the judge carries the weight of canonical authority, and he has called me to speak. I must comply."

"I don't think that's a good idea."

"The whole reason I submitted to this process was to clear my name. I can't very well do that by refusing to take the stand."

"But you don't know what will happen. I don't know what will happen."

"Then I'll just have to have faith."

Ben held him back. "Father, if you go up there, I can't promise you a good result."

A slight smile crossed the priest's lips. "Ben, you're a fine lawyer, but when I spoke about having faith, I wasn't talking about you."

Ben started to protest, but Beale was already on his feet and heading toward the folding chair at the right hand of the dais of adjudicators.

While Beale was sworn in, Ben's partner, Christina McCall, leaned across the defense table. "Isn't there anything we can do about this?" she whispered.

"You're the legal scholar. You tell me. Haven't you been reading up on the Episcopal Constitution and Canons?"

Christina brushed her flowing mane of strawberry blond hair

behind her shoulders. "Yes, but for all its two hundred and eighteen pages, it doesn't say all that much. Compared to the rules and regulations governing federal courts, it's nothing. I think it's intended to leave the presiding judge great discretion. Here in the ecclesiastical courts, the judge can do pretty much whatever he wants. And usually does. *Folie de grandeur.*"

"Which means Beale is going on the stand, whether we like it or not."

"Think he'll hold up?"

Ben shrugged. "Keep your fingers crossed."

Christina arched an eyebrow. "Wouldn't it be more appropriate to say a prayer?"

Beale lowered himself into a chair that was obviously too small for him, adding to his already evident discomfort. Father Holbrook was just to his left; flanking him on the other side were the stenographer, the jurors, and the Canon of the Ordinary, otherwise known as the bishop's assistant, Harold Payne.

Father Beale seemed worried, and with good reason. A man of God since he was twenty-two, it must have been an unprecedented shock to Beale's system to find himself sitting before a bishopric tribunal on the charge of Conduct Unbecoming a Priest. The evidence that had been adduced already by previous witnesses was substantial and, at times, shocking: Malice toward parishioners. Public denial of the virgin birth. Questioning whether Jesus rose from the dead. Allowing radical political groups to meet at the church.

And there was another memorable allegation of Beale's conduct unbecoming a priest. Murder.

"When did you last see Helen Conrad?" Father Fleming asked. Fleming was a stout, basso profundo lawyer-priest from Kansas City who had been brought in to represent the complainants; in effect, he was the district attorney.

"In the prayer garden," Father Beale answered. "Sprawled across a stone bench, the right side of her face covered with blood. A dirty dishrag wedged in her mouth. Her skin a ghastly gray. Flies buzzing around her corpse."

Father Fleming ran his fingers across the top of his head, as if brushing back the hair that had not graced his scalp for many years. "I mean, when did you last see her alive?"

"At the vestry meeting. The night before."

As Ben had learned, the vestry was the governing body of St. Benedict's Episcopal Church, where Beale was currently priest and Ben was a member of the choir. The vestry, led by the senior warden, oversaw all the administrative aspects of the church. The murder victim, Helen Conrad, had been on the vestry for years and was expected to run for senior warden the following year.

Ben glanced over his shoulder. Most of the surviving members of the vestry were seated in the folding chairs that made for a makeshift gallery in the parish hall of the church. Some of the rank and file parishioners were in attendance as well—many faces he recognized, as well as some he hadn't seen in the entire seven months he'd been attending this church. Apparently a priest on trial was more exciting than your average Sunday service.

"And is it true, as we heard earlier, that you engaged in a heated dispute with Ms. Conrad during the vestry meeting?"

"Yes. I'm afraid it is. Of course, I engaged in a heated dispute with almost everyone who was there."

"What was the nature of the dispute?"

"The vestry had just learned that I have been allowing a gay and lesbian group to hold meetings at the church. In the parish hall. Without the approval of the vestry."

"And for how many months has this been going on?"

Beale drew in a deep breath before answering. "Over three years. Since I transferred to the church."

Although he worked hard to maintain his serene unflappability, this had apparently caught Father Fleming by surprise. "You are aware, I suppose, that the Diocese of Oklahoma does not recognize homosexual marriages or permit practicing homosexuals to act as priests. Opinions regarding the validity of the homosexual lifestyle are sharply divided."

"I am aware of that."

Ben felt he had to intervene, if only to give his client a momentary respite. He rose to address the judge. "Sir, the purpose of this tribunal as I understand it is not to debate theological issues but to determine whether Father Beale should be removed from his position as rector of this church."

Payne, the bishop's assistant, answered on the judge's behalf. "The charge of which Father Beale has been accused is conduct unbecoming a priest." Payne was a short, slight man in a dark suit and white shirt—probably as close as he could come to looking like a priest without being one. In many ways, however, he was Father Holbrook's opposite—not only physically, but in the down-to-earth attitude that sharply contrasted Holbrook's more cerebral approach. "If Father Beale was acting in opposition to canonical law, then he engaged in conduct unbecoming a priest."

Father Fleming resumed his examination of the witness. "Was that the only topic discussed?"

"No," Beale replied. "There were many others. Helen criticized my Christmas homily—"

"Would that be the sermon in which you suggested that the virgin birth of our Savior was a myth?"

Ben could see Beale steeling himself, preparing to do theological battle once more. "We are told that God was made man in the person of Jesus. That he was one of us. But if he was not conceived as human beings are conceived, if he was conjured up through some . . . some mystical magic trick, then he was not one of us, was he? How could he be called human if he was not born of man and woman?"

Fleming made no comment, but his disdain for Beale's argument was obvious. "Was this also the homily in which you challenged the resurrection of Jesus Christ?"

Beale cleared his throat. "No. That was for Easter."

"How appropriate."

"And I didn't challenge the resurrection. I said it didn't matter."

Fleming's small green eyes were fairly bulging. The reaction from the adjudicative panel was no less dramatic. "You said that the return from the dead of Our Lord—didn't matter?"

"I said that what is important is Jesus' teaching, his words, his guidance. That's what gives his life validity. That's why we follow him. We don't need a grandiose bit of abracadabra. We don't need the bribe of life after death. We should follow his teaching because it's the right thing to do, not because we expect to get something out of it in the end."

"And what, may I ask, happens to the blessed sacrament of communion if the priest disavows the resurrection of Christ?"

"Communion is a symbol, a public and spiritual avowal that we are at one with the teachings of Christ. That we draw strength from His presence in our hearts and minds. That we want to do right. That we want to believe."

Back at the judge's bench, Ben observed an infinitesimal pursing of Father Holbrook's lips—a sure sign of his disapproval of the views espoused by the priest on the witness stand.

"We have also been told that the issue of abortion rights was discussed at the vestry meeting, in rather loud and angry words."

"That is true. Helen Conrad was a member of a local organization founded by another vestry member, Ernestine Rupert. It's a pro-choice group. They wanted to meet in the parish hall on Thursday evenings. I gave them my permission. But some of the vestry members—the ones who are pro-life—objected."

"Interesting. Interesting," Fleming said, tapping his lower lip with his pen. "But none of this explains why you were shouting at Helen Conrad."

"She was not the only member of the vestry with whom I had . . . problems. I also had protracted discussions with Kate McGuire. Susan Marino."

"Did you shout at them, too?"

"I used forceful words, but I hope I did not shout at—"

"I have four affidavits from eyewitnesses," Fleming said, shuffling the papers before him. "All four describe your conduct as shouting or bellowing. One witness was able to hear you clearly even though she was in the nursery at the opposite end of the church."

"It was an intense discussion, sir."

"And a violent display of temper, according to these affidavits."

Ben rose to his feet. "Father Holbrook, I must object to the use of affidavits rather than live witnesses. I can't cross-examine an affidavit."

"Mr. Kincaid, this is not federal court."

"No, but this tribunal is supposedly governed by the Federal Rules of Evidence. And there's no way you could do this in federal court, not when the testifying witnesses are available."

Holbrook lowered his chin. "Mr. Kincaid, our goal here is not a flamboyant display of legal skills. Our goal is to arrive at the truth so that we can best serve the needs of the parish."

"I understand that. But I still must insist—"

"Your objection is overruled, Mr. Kincaid."

"Sir, with all due respect—you know that in the eyes of the law, I'm right."

"Perhaps," he answered. "But in the eyes of God, you're wrong. Please sit down."

Thank you, sir. May I have another one, sir? Ben sat down.

Fleming resumed his questioning. "Father Beale, is it true that you said—or rather shouted—that Helen Conrad, the woman who was later murdered, did not deserve to be a member of the vestry?"

"My point was simply that if she could not open her mind to new—"

Fleming's voice rose for the first time in the entire proceeding. *"Did—you—say—those—words?"*

Beale's head bowed slightly. "I'm afraid I did."

"Did you also say that you would not allow her to—quote—bring the whole church down to her small-minded level—end quote?"

"Tempers were high, sir. Words were flying—"

"Did you say it?"

"I did, sir. I did."

"And did she respond by telling you she was going to report you to the bishop? That she would have you removed from the church?"

"She did."

"And how did you respond?"

Father Beale did not immediately reply.

"I have the words right before me, Father," Fleming continued. "But I would like to hear it from you."

When Father Beale's voice finally returned, it was but an echo of what it had been before. "I told her I would not allow her to destroy thirty-four years of ministry. That I would stop her."

"No matter what it took?"

Beale closed his eyes. "No matter what it took."

The silence that filled the parish hall spoke more clearly than all the testimony that had gone before. It was as if a collective chill shuddered down the spines of those present. Ben thought that by now he should be immune to such things, but he felt it, just the same.

Without being obvious, Ben checked the expressions on the faces of the church members who had turned out to witness this event. Ben had hoped for more of a grand jury approach—no spectators allowed—but Payne had decided that since this action directly concerned the parish, and since the action was in fact being brought by the parish, he could not exclude them.

Ben could see at a glance which of the spectators still supported Father Beale—not many—and which were of the clique that wanted him ousted. But even those who backed Beale seemed shaken by this horrible threat.

"It was an inexcusable flash of temper, sir," Beale said. "I know that."

"It was a breach of faith, Father Beale. With your own parish."

"I know. And I have apologized and asked their forgiveness."

Fleming frowned. "After you shouted these threats, you left the meeting?"

"Yes. I was—quite agitated."

"And the next time you saw Helen Conrad—"

"She was dead. Asphyxiated."

"Who found the body?"

"A young woman from outside the parish. She apparently came to the prayer garden early in the morning to visit the remains of her grandmother. She found the body and, since the doors to the church were still locked, she called the police from her car phone."

"When did you find out?"

"When I arrived at the church, perhaps five minutes later."

"What was your reaction?"

Beale lifted his head, staring at Fleming as if his question had exceeded all bounds of propriety. "I was grief-stricken, of course. I was shocked and horrified. A member of my flock had been slain, in a cruel and heartless manner. And on holy ground."

"And yet, the woman had been a thorn in your side. A thorn that was now very conveniently removed."

Beale's lips trembled. His teeth clenched tightly and the lines of his angular face deepened. "I don't know what you're suggesting, sir, but if you imagine that I had anything to do with what happened, or even that it secretly pleased me, then you know nothing about me. I was her priest! Yes, we had disagreements. Yes, I felt she should be removed from the vestry, she and all the others who are so mired in the past they can't see the future. But I never wanted this—" His voice broke on the last word. He jerked his head around abruptly, trying to maintain control. "I would never cause or wish violence on any person. It's contrary to everything I believe."

Fleming was unmoved. "Were you questioned by the police?"

"Yes."

"You were a suspect."

"Most of the members of this parish were questioned. No charges were ever brought. Against me or anyone else."

And Ben knew why. By picking the brain of his good friend, Major Mike Morelli of the Homicide division, he had learned that Father Beale was indeed the police department's top suspect. His collar didn't grant him any immunity from their inquiry. An unveiled threat followed by a violent death was simply too incriminating to be overlooked. The reason no charges had been brought was that there was simply no evidence. Motive, yes, but proof, no. No fingerprints, no footprints, no evidence of any kind. The woman had apparently been clubbed on the head then strangled shortly after nightfall, but it had rained in the early morning. Since the prayer garden was exposed to the elements, whatever trace evidence may have once existed had washed away.

"Not by the police," Fleming continued. "But what about the vestry?"

"On the Sunday following Helen's murder, the vestry formally requested that I resign."

"They believed you had committed the murder."

"They didn't specify their reasons."

"But it was understood—"

"Most of them had been wanting me out for a good long while. This development gave them the perfect excuse."

"Was that what they said?"

Beale pursed his lips. "They said I had engaged in conduct unbecoming a priest."

"But you declined to resign."

"Of course I did."

Which is why we're all here now, Ben thought. He had counseled Father Beale that the simplest thing would be to simply resign and start fresh somewhere else. But Father Beale wouldn't hear of it. He had been sent here by the bishop, and he wouldn't give up—especially not now, when his resignation would be seen as a tacit admission of his complicity in a murder. When he refused to submit to the wishes of the vestry, however, they convened an ecclesiastical trial to resolve the conflict.

"That's all," Fleming said. Ben waived cross. "You may step down."

Father Beale did as he was bid, his legs considerably more wobbly than they had been before.

Father Holbrook addressed the gallery. "I think we've heard everything we need. I want to thank everyone who took time to present evidence to this tribunal." He glanced across the room. "Mr. Kincaid, do you have anything you would like to say before we recess?"

"Yes, sir, I do." Ben had no idea whether he could do any good here, but he certainly hadn't been much use so far, so he felt honor-bound to try. The evidence connecting Father Beale to the murder was tenuous and circumstantial, but as had been made clear to him repeatedly, the criminal court rules—including the standard of reasonable doubt—did not apply here. All they had to do was find him guilty of conduct unbecoming a priest, and if they suspected he had anything to do with the murder, they surely would.

Throughout this trial, Ben reasoned as he approached the judge's station, he'd come up second-best—because this was a court of God, not a court of law. But maybe now he could use that to his advantage.

"Perhaps it's just because I'm used to being in the criminal courts," Ben began, "but I can't help but believe that all these theological and doctrinal issues are a blind. The only reason this proceeding exists is that a tragic murder occurred. And some people believe—or want to believe—that Father Beale did it."

"The charge against him," Payne said, interrupting, "is conduct unbecoming a priest."

"I know. But I still think this court would never have been convened and none of us would be here but for the murder. True, Father Beale has some unorthodox beliefs. Is that news to anyone? He's an independent thinker, and has been his entire career. People who don't like it go somewhere else. Similarly, his temper flare-ups at the vestry meetings are regrettable, but who among us has never lost his temper? Would we even consider removing a priest from his parish for that? No, the reason we're here today is that a murder happened, and there is some superficial, circumstantial evidence that suggests Father Beale could be a suspect."

Ben paused, turning slightly toward the gallery. "And that scares people. People want to love their priest—it's only natural. They want to place their faith in him. But how can they do that when a little voice in the back of their heads is whispering that he might be a murderer?"

"Are you speaking on Father Beale's behalf, Mr. Kincaid?" Holbrook asked. "Because it certainly doesn't sound like it."

"I am, sir, and here's my point. If you remove this man from his office now, for whatever reason, everyone will assume it was because you believe he is guilty of the most heinous of crimes. No one will remember the theological debates, the temper spats. You will have convicted him more surely than a jury of twelve could have done—and on considerably less evidence."

Holbrook's hands parted. "We must do what's best for the parish."

"That's right, sir. And that includes the leader of the parish. Father Beale. Remember, there is a reason he was not charged by the police. There was no evidence against him. Rumor, yes. Gossip, certainly. But they won't condemn a man based on gossip alone. Will you?" He looked sharply at each member of the adjudicative panel. "Will you remove a man from his parish based upon that? Will you taint the rest of his life, his entire career, past and present, based on . . . innuendo? Is this a proper fate for a man of God?"

Ben held their attention a few more moments, forcing them to consider his words. "His future now rests in your hands, ladies and gentlemen. Will you be the one to cast the first stone?"

WHILE THE PANEL deliberated, Ben situated himself in the narthex, the connecting foyer between the church sanctuary and the parish hall. It was a crowded area; no one wanted to go home until they'd heard what the panel was going to do.

Ben kept mostly to himself, avoiding eye contact. He knew this was as stressful for the other parishioners as it was for him. They undoubtedly felt some obligation to be cordial to a fellow church member. At the same time, he was defending the priest many of them were trying to oust, a priest who had become extremely unpopular.

How had he gotten into this mess? It was Christina's fault, of course. Wasn't it always? She was the one who kept urging him to get out, to be more social, to join civic organizations. When he learned that his childhood priest had transferred to St. Benedict's in Tulsa, only a few miles from the boarding house where he lived, it seemed only natural to check it out. In no time at all, Father Beale had Ben singing tenor in the adult choir, and Ben was actually enjoying it— until a corpse turned up in the prayer garden.

On the other side of the narthex, Ben spotted a group of women huddled together chatting. They were all in their thirties or forties. One of them he recognized as Kate McGuire—the woman who had been mentioned during the trial as one of Father Beale's opponents. If he wasn't mistaken, the blond woman beside Kate was Susan Marino. They were both on the vestry; Kate was senior warden. He couldn't tell what they were discussing, but given their extreme agitation, he could guess. Father Beale.

"Excuse me. You're Ben Kincaid, aren't you?"

Ben looked down and saw two teenage girls—about fourteen or fifteen, he judged—standing before him. The one speaking was tall and thin with short black hair. Her companion, who stood a half-step behind her, was somewhat shorter and heavier and had long curly brown hair.

"I mean, I know you are. I should know, shouldn't I? I used to see you all the time. I just wanted to introduce myself. I mean, I'm sorry if I seem brash, but I think if you want to meet someone, you should just walk up and meet them. Why stand around until someone introduces you? I mean, it's not like we're in the eighteenth century or anything, you know what I mean?" She thrust her hand forward. "My name is Judy. Judy Jacobson." Ben took her hand and shook. "My friend here's name is Maura. Maura Hubbard. She doesn't talk much. That's why we're such a good pair. She's shy. I'm not."

Ben smiled. "Nice to meet you, Judy. And Maura."

"Am I turning you off? Because if I am, you can tell me. I know some men don't like women who are too aggressive."

"Not at all. You remind me of a very good friend of mine."

"Really? Cool." She jabbed her friend Maura. "Did you hear that? I remind him of a very good friend of his!"

Maura giggled.

"Have we met before?" Ben asked. "Because you said you used to see me all the time."

Judy laughed. "Oh, I meant on television. When you were trying the Wallace Barrett case."

Ben restrained himself from rolling his eyes. That again.

"I was home that summer, and I thought your trial was a lot more interesting than soap operas."

"Quite a compliment." Ben's defense of Wallace Barrett, then Tulsa's mayor, who was accused of murdering his wife and two daughters, was his highest-profile case to date. The media coverage had been extensive.

"I used to watch you every day on Court TV. Man, you were so good. I couldn't believe everything you got people to admit on cross-examination. And your closing statement—it sent chills down my spine. Watching you made me want to be a lawyer."

"My apologies."

"After the trial, I went on the Internet and read everything I could about you. I even bought that book you wrote, on the Kindergarten Killer."

"Ah. You were the one."

"I've followed all your big cases. I even cut out articles about you in the newspaper and put them in a scrapbook."

Maura's voice was a whisper's whisper. "You're her hero."

Judy jabbed her again, rather more roughly than before. "Anyway, I know you're busy. I just wanted to say I think it's a great thing you're doing in there for Father Beale. I mean, other lawyers talk about taking unpopular cases, especially when they're getting paid a lot of money, but you really do it, and half the time you don't get paid anything at all. I think that's really wonderful."

"Yes, so does my staff."

"I mean, I know you're going to lose this one—the panel almost has to remove Father Beale, don't they? When half the church is up in arms against him, and the man maybe even committed a murder?"

She giggled excitedly at the prospect. "But I think you did everything you could for him in there."

"Girls, girls, girls. I hope you're not bothering Mr. Kincaid." An elderly woman wedged herself between them, pushing the girls back. Her face was familiar. Ben knew he had seen her around; she was one of the women in charge of ECW—the Episcopal Church Women's group. But what was her name? Ruth something. Carter? Conner?

Bingo. "Not at all, Mrs. O'Connell. We're just having a nice chat."

"Well, it's very good of you to spend your time with two silly girls." Judy shot her a look that could have leveled a city. "Shouldn't you two be folding robes or something? Remember, an acolyte's work is never done."

Judy somehow managed to flash a smile that lacked even the slightest trace of warmth. "Yes, Mrs. O'Connell." The two girls skittered away.

"Oh, hello, Ernestine." Ruth was greeting a woman of similar age who was decked out with enough jewelry to stock a Tiffany's. Ben couldn't help but notice the honking big diamond ring on her finger and the diamond-studded bracelet rattling around her wrist. Ben didn't know anything about gems, but he knew those baubles had to be seriously valuable. He'd heard rumors that Ernestine Rupert, a widow, was extremely wealthy, and that her tithe alone made up half the budget for St. Benedict's. With those doodads dangling in his face, he couldn't doubt it.

"Ben," Ruth said, "I just wanted to tell you, on behalf of the entire ECW, that there will be no hard feelings against you when this trial is completed. We just want to put the whole chapter behind us. Let bygones be bygones. And once Father Beale is removed, we'll be able to do that."

"Well, that's . . . very kind of you."

"You mustn't feel that you've failed, either, dear boy," Ernestine added. "The panel really has no choice, does it? And in some respects, you've been part of the process that helped resolve the matter. You shouldn't come down too hard on defense lawyers, that's what I was telling Ruth. They're a necessary evil."

"How kind."

"Well, remember what I said. I expect to see you in the choir next Sunday." She wiggled her fingers and passed on.

Ben felt Christina sidle up beside him. "Looks like you have some admirers."

"What, the old ladies?"

Christina crinkled her freckled nose. "No, the girls."

Ben glanced to the side and saw that Judy and Maura were still watching him. As soon as his eyes met theirs, they giggled and ran off.

"The taller one used to watch me on TV," Ben explained. "Now she wants to be a lawyer."

Christina made a *tsk*ing sound. "Corrupting the minds of youth. Isn't that why they made Socrates take hemlock?"

"I might take hemlock, if it got me out of here."

"That seems a bit extreme."

Ben felt a rush of air behind him. Harold Payne had entered the narthex. "Please reassemble in the parish hall. The panel has reached its decision."

FATHER HOLBROOK SETTLED his considerable weight into the chair behind a table draped with a purple cloth. His face was long and his expression flat.

"First of all," he said, "I want to make it clear to everyone present that neither I nor the jurors take any pleasure in this proceeding. These internecine conflicts within a parish can do irreparable damage, and inevitably divert our attention from the more important matter of serving Our Lord Jesus Christ. I have a responsibility to my diocese, however, and the charges that have been brought against Father Beale are serious ones—ones that cannot be ignored. Therefore, we have conducted this trial in accordance with the canons of this church, and the panel has reached a decision. They have kindly allowed me to speak on their behalf."

He glanced down at his notes. "Even if we exclude the speculations regarding the unfortunate death of Ms. Conrad, the court has received eyewitness accounts of open hostility toward parishioners, church resources used for improper or immoral purposes, and heretical teachings diametrically opposed to the true faith of the Episcopal Church. These offenses simply cannot be overlooked."

Ben laid his hand on Beale's arm. "I'm sorry, Father."

"At the same time, we must reflect that when this church brought Father Beale from Oklahoma City to be the shepherd of this flock, it made a contract. Not only with Father Beale, not only with the diocese, but with God. If, as we believed then, God called Father Beale to this church, what right have we to work against His wishes?"

There was a stirring in the audience. Heads turned. Voices whispered.

"We are also concerned about the suggestions that Father Beale might be involved in the murder of Helen Conrad, based on the flimsiest of circumstantial evidence. Although the evidence was clearly insufficient to warrant criminal prosecution, it is true, as his able counsel noted, that Father Beale will surely be tried and convicted in the minds of most people if we remove him from his sacred office. Therefore, we decline to do so."

The whispers Ben heard over his shoulder grew louder. "No!" "Is he kidding?" "This can't be!"

"The documented instances of misconduct by Father Beale are serious, however, and therefore we are directing Father Beale to take a two-week leave of absence from this church to be spent at the St. Michael's retreat, where he will undergo an extended period of meditation and, we hope, rededication to his vocation. We are also directing him to enroll in an anger management course at the earliest opportunity. But we will not remove him from his calling. What God has made, let no man rend asunder. This court is adjourned."

Usually, after the rendering of a surprise verdict, there was such an upswell of noise and activity that Ben could hardly hear himself think. Not this time, however. After the initial shocked responses had been uttered, most of the audience sat in stunned silence, barely moving, not saying a word.

"Congratulations," Ben said, clasping his client on the arm. "You've won."

"Yes," Father Beale said gravely. "But what have I won?"

"You've won your freedom," Christina answered. "If you want to stay at St. Benedict's, you can. If you'd rather start anew somewhere else, you can. Whichever path you follow, it will be because you chose to follow it, not because you were hounded by enemies or haunted by horrible accusations. The long nightmare is over."

But Christina was wrong, as would become apparent to the three of them, and to the entire church, altogether too soon. The long nightmare was just beginning.

A Question of Faith

◆ ◆ ◆

1

The Gospel According to Daniel

I AM NOT normally given to introspective writing, to self-immortalization, having throughout my career preferred to devote my time to others rather than myself. Moreover, given my current circumstances, this hardly seems a time conducive to starting new projects. I take this pen in hand now, however, at the urging of my attorney. He tells me I should write down everything, just as I remember it, from the very beginning of this protracted ordeal. For myself, I can think of nothing more dreadful, more unbearably harsh. But given my present situation, I must do what my counsel bids, no matter how unpleasant.

I cannot conceive of why this has happened to me, what possible purpose it could serve. True, God tested Job, but Job was a great man, a true servant of God. I've been nothing but a parish priest in a mid-size church, and at times, not a very good one. True, our Savior was tested for forty days in the desert, but he was the Son of God. Satan needs no elaborate ritual to tempt me; I have succumbed far too often, with no malicious imp to blame for my own failings. In the dark of night, I am still tormented by secrets, things I have told no one, and hope to God I never shall.

Do I deserve the misery that has befallen me? I cannot believe that I do. I would not wish this on the vilest of sinners, the most heinous of infidels. I pray at night, when I am alone and no one is watching, as my Savior prayed before me, *Father, let this cup pass from me.* But I know in my heart that there will be no divine intervention. The sad truth is that my fate now rests in the hands of lawyers and judges—a considerably less divine and more fallible audience.

I have titled this document, perhaps in a moment of self-pity or would-be martyrdom, "The Gospel According to Daniel." The word *gospel*, of course, was originally derived from Greek words meaning *good news*. It is familiarly linked with another important word—*truth*.

I just pray to God that this is. I'm not sure I know what the word means anymore.

BEN SAT IN the jailhouse cell facing his new client. "Eric, because you can't afford an attorney of your own, the court has appointed me to act as your attorney with regard to this criminal charge. You may rest assured that anything you tell me will be held in the strictest confidence. Do you understand what I'm saying?"

Eric Biggers was a big man; he outweighed Ben two-to-one. His broad and brawny chest was so large it fairly rippled out of his prison jumpsuit. "Sure, I got ya."

Ben laid three forms on the table between them. "If you're agreeable to having me represent you in court, then you need to sign these. That will demonstrate to the court that you have accepted me as your legal representative." And will also allow me to get paid—no small matter.

"No problem."

"Now, according to the information provided to me, you've been charged with assault and battery with a deadly weapon. Do you know what that means?"

"Sure, sure. I know."

"And it also says—that the victim was your father."

Biggers hunched forward, his chin drooping, his eyes sad. "Mr. Kincaid, I want you to know, I really regret what happened."

Ben found himself warmed by this honest expression of remorse—something he saw all too rarely. "I'm sure you do, Eric."

"I mean that, truly. I really regret hitting my daddy over the head with that gun."

Ben nodded. This was good. The man had made a mistake, but wanted to make it better. This was why he was a defense attorney, Ben told himself. So he could help men of this caliber. "Well, Eric, I know sometimes temper gets the best of all of us—"

"I mean, it was a real nice gun. I loved that gun."

"Uh, what?"

"It was a great little pistol, pearl-handled and everything. But I got blood and hair and guts all over it. Now it ain't worth a damn."

Ben drew in his breath, then slowly released it. "Just sign the papers, Eric. I'm late for a wedding."

JONES PUSHED BACK his French cuff to check his wristwatch for roughly the three thousandth time. "Where is he?"

"Relax, he'll be here," Loving replied, glancing into a nearby mirror and adjusting his bow tie. "Doesn't the Skipper always come through?"

Jones paced up and down the length of the small dressing room adjacent to the church sanctuary. "For petty criminals, yes. For his office manager, no."

Loving spread his arms expansively. He was a big man, with a chest as broad as the Grand Canyon, especially by comparison to Jones's slight frame. "Now you're not bein' fair, Jones. Didn't Ben make all the arrangements for this weddin'? Didn't he get it all squared with the church and rent all the mornin' suits and everythin'?"

"Yeah, yeah."

"The Skipper always takes care of his own." Loving straightened the lie of his vest. "You know, there's a certain symmetry here, Jones. He's takin' care of your weddin', jus' like he took care of my divorce."

"A charming comparison." Jones began wringing his hands. "I can't understand why Ben isn't here. The best man should be at the church on time. He's got the ring! We can't go on without him. You're a private investigator, Loving. Can't you go . . . sleuth around or something?"

"He'll show up, Jones. Just you wait."

"Wait until when? The honeymoon? He's supposed to be here now!"

The door cracked open. Jones rushed forward—but it wasn't Ben. The white-bearded face of Father Beale appeared through the opening. "It's almost time. Has he arrived yet?"

"No," Jones growled, looking even more agitated than before. "He hasn't."

Beale frowned. "Keep me posted."

As soon as the door was closed, Loving jabbed Jones in the stomach. "Was that him? Was he the one?"

"The one that what?"

"You know. The one they say killed that—"

"Ben says he didn't do it. We won that case, remember?"

"Yeah, but still. Kinda creepy, isn't it? Bein' married by a guy who—"

"Would you stop already!" Jones looked as if he were on the verge of a total meltdown. "Where the hell is Ben?"

Loving wrapped a burly arm around Jones's shoulders. "Don't fret, little buddy. I'm here. I've been through this before, and I know that you're not really worked up about Ben. You're worried about gettin' married, whether you're goin' to be happy or whether you're makin' the biggest mistake of your life."

"Oh God, you're not going to get psychological on me, are you?"

"Paula is a wonderful woman, Jones. You two are a perfect match. You're gonna be very happy together." He paused. "And if you're not, you know where you can get a divorce cheap."

Jones removed Loving's hand from his shoulder. "Loving, you're supposed to be an usher. Go ush."

AT THE OPPOSITE end of the sanctuary, in a small dressing room barely bigger than a closet, Christina and the bride-to-be, Paula Connelly, were huddled together with two elderly representatives from the ECW, Ruth O'Connell and her friend Ernestine Rupert. One of the women was adjusting the bride's headdress while the other was messing about with her train.

"There, there," the woman with the big white bouffant said as she adjusted the headdress a micro-inch. "I think that looks better, don't you, Ernestine?"

"Ever so much better, Ruth," replied the one with the blue hair and the expensive jewelry. "I'm having a bit of trouble with this train, though."

"Here, dear, let me help." Both women grabbed an end of the white lace train and started tugging herky-jerky.

Paula was staring straight ahead, her eyes wide and fixed. "I will not break down. I will not break down."

Christina tried to intervene. "Excuse me, ladies, but I think it might be best if we left Paula alone for a bit."

Ruth was not deterred in the least. "Oh, my—no, dear. This is Paula's special day. We want everything to be perfect."

"I want to be left alone," Paula muttered.

"Seriously," Christina said, gently tugging at the ladies' elbows. "Let's give Paula some quiet time. Let her meditate a bit, so she can get in a serene and bridelike state of mind."

"Oh, very well." Ernestine brushed her hands together. "Do you have something blue, dear?"

Paula blinked. "Excuse me?"

"Blue. You must have something blue."

"I thought white was the traditional bridal color."

"Well, of course it is," Ruth explained. "But a bride needs more than just a dress. You need something old, something new, something borrowed, and something blue."

"Why?"

"Well . . . you just do. It's traditional. All the great brides of literature did it. Don't you ever read?"

"I'm a librarian," Paula said. Her voice had acquired a decided edge. "I have, on occasion, read a book, yes."

"Well then, you must understand. Most brides come equipped with something new—their dress. And they usually have something old, even if it's just their skivvies. Something borrowed is easy to come up with, but something blue can be tricky. So I wanted to make sure you had something."

"Well, I don't. We'll just have to do without."

"Nonsense." Ernestine opened the door to the sanctuary a crack. "Bruce!"

A moment later, Ernestine's nephew, Bruce Ashour, entered the tiny room, decked out in a gray pinstripe with a red carnation on the lapel.

"Bruce? We need something blue. Quickly."

Amazingly, Bruce appeared to have no problem comprehending this request. "Are you wearing your turquoise necklace, Ruth?"

The elderly woman shook her head no.

"Aunt Ernestine, what about that cerulean lapel pin?"

"Not wearing it."

He turned his attention to Christina. "What about you? Are you wearing anything bluish?"

"Sorry, no."

"Are you sure? What about undergarments?"

Paula's face grew taut. "I am not wearing someone else's underwear!"

Ruth snapped her fingers. "Hair ribbon." She reached inside her purse and removed a blue bow.

"Look," Paula said, trying unsuccessfully to maintain some semblance of composure, "I've just spent three hours at the beauty shop getting my hair fixed. It is perfect. Impenetrable. Bulletproof. I am not messing it up with a blue ribbon!"

"I'll pin it to the underside of your dress," Christina said. "No one will ever see it. Now please, ladies, I think we should all—"

The door opened again. A mustached man in his mid-thirties leaned in. "I need to talk to someone about the music."

"Who is *he*?" Paula said, fairly ranting now.

"Organist. Choirmaster," Christina whispered. "Paul Masterson."

Masterson entered the room. As soon as he did, Christina saw Ernestine remove a small book from her purse and rifle through the pages.

Masterson was a tall man, thin and ascetic in appearance, but when he entered the tiny dressing room everyone was forced practically nose-to-nose. "I've seen the play list that was submitted, and I have some serious objections to some of these music selections."

Paula's eyelids closed. "What's he talking about, Christina? I don't know what he's talking about. I can't take much more of this."

Christina grabbed Masterson by the shoulders. "Look, you're going to have to find Ben Kincaid. He chose all the music."

"I looked for him in the other dressing room. They said he hasn't arrived yet."

"He hasn't arrived?" Paula squealed. "The best man hasn't arrived?"

Christina tried to calm her. "That's just Ben's way, Paula. He's never early. But he'll be here. I'm sure . . ."

As if on cue, the door opened again. Ben stepped through the opening. "Is this where—?" An instant later, he realized he had stumbled into the women's dressing room. His cheeks turned bright pink. "Oops. Excuse me." He ducked back out again.

All six people crowded into the dressing room spoke at once. "*Wait!*"

Ben reopened the door a crack. "Ye-es? . . ."

Christina yanked Ben in, stuffing the tiny room to its limit.

"Can you breathe?" Paula asked, her face ashen. "Because I can't really breathe. . . ."

"Ben," Christina said, "the music dude has problems with your play list."

"It's the wedding march. From *A Midsummer Night's Dream*," Masterson said, sniffing. "It's an offensive piece of music, inappropriate to the sacred sacrament of marriage. I won't play it."

"What's he talking about?" Christina asked.

"He's talking about 'Here Comes the Bride,'" Ben explained. "The wedding march everyone knows and loves is Mendelssohn's incidental music for the play. It's used in a farce wedding scene—some people say it makes fun of the marriage ceremony. So highbrows and snobs refuse to play it. But the reality is, almost everyone expects to hear this song when the bride walks in, and as long as *we're* not making fun of the marriage ceremony, what does it matter what music we play? Most people don't know where the tune came from."

"I know," Masterson said. "I find it offensive. How can I pour my heart into a performance when I find the music reprehensible?"

"I can't take it," Paula muttered, pounding her head against the wall. "I just can't take it anymore." She would surely have fainted, if there'd been anywhere to faint.

Ben started to speak, but Christina intervened. "If you don't mind, Ben, I think this is more up my alley." She stood on her tiptoes—it was hard to appear commanding given that she was barely five foot one—and revved up the volume. "Now listen up! All of you! Paula needs some quiet time before this wedding starts, and she's going to get it." She turned toward the two older women. "You've been very helpful. Now scram." She jabbed a finger into Masterson's bony chest. "You're going to play the Wedding March, and you're not going to give us any grief about it."

Masterson tucked in his chin. "Yes, ma'am."

"Now get lost! All of you!"

Ben raised a finger. "Christina, I still need—"

"After the wedding, Ben. Go!"

* * *

BEN WALKED IN circles around the narthex, trying to remember where the other dressing room was. Sad to say, even though he'd been going to this church for months, he still got lost sometimes. Not that the church was so large—it wasn't. But Ben's navigational abilities were severely limited. Christina said he needed a GPS navigator just to get from his living room to the kitchen.

As he passed down the large corridor that flanked the Sunday school classes, he heard a commotion at the far end.

"I'm telling you, this is not the place!" he heard a familiar voice say.

"It never is with you. You're always trying to buy time."

"I'm performing a wedding, Kate. It's not appropriate—"

"I've had it with your excuses! This has got to end! I can't go on like this anymore. It's wrong. It's—it's evil!"

Ben peered around the corner. Father Beale, decked out in his ministerial robes, was staring at a woman in her mid-thirties—Kate McGuire, he thought. She was the senior warden and had been in attendance during the ecclesiastical trial.

"It is not evil. You need to open your heart, broaden your mind—"

"Don't lecture me, you sixties throwback."

"It is not evil."

"Well, let's see what the bishop says about that, shall we?"

Beale's eyes hardened. "Are you threatening me?"

Ben glanced over his shoulder. By now, the fight had attracted an audience of five or six parishioners. He needed to break this up and fast.

"Excuse me," Ben said, strolling toward them as if nothing unusual had been taking place. "Can you tell me where the men's dressing room is?"

Beale slowly took a step back from the woman. "This isn't over," he said. Then he turned and escorted Ben to the proper door.

AGAINST ALL ODDS, the wedding was beautiful. Even Ben was moved by the formal yet warm Episcopal ceremony. Father Beale gave a lovely homily about the meaning of the marriage covenant and the service concluded with a full Communion, although Ben did not participate. Cynical as he might be about the "blessed sacrament of marriage," as Ben watched his longtime office manager stroll off with his librarian sweetheart, he couldn't help but feel a certain tugging at his tear ducts.

The reception was held in the parish hall, which was decked out with streamers and wall hangings following a fuchsia and lime green color scheme. Undoubtedly Christina's design, Ben mused. Still, it was a pleasant contrast to Ben's last visit to the parish hall, when he'd been handling Father Beale's trial.

Ben skipped the reception line and scored a piece of the groom's cake—chocolate, not white, thank goodness—and a cup of some pink, ginger ale–based punch.

At a table in the corner, Ben spotted the two teenage girls he had met during the trial. What were their names? Judy and . . . Maura, that was it. They appeared to be industriously cutting the bride's cake and pouring punch.

One of them, the quiet pudgier one—Maura—nudged her friend. "It's him," she said breathlessly.

The other, Judy, looked up. Her eyes immediately brightened. "Mr. Kincaid!"

"Call me Ben." He watched as they poured a liter of Seven-Up into the punch bowl. "Did Christina put you up to this by any chance?"

"Is she the redhead?"

Ben nodded.

"Yeah. How did you know?"

"Just a hunch."

"Ben!" A slim, middle-aged woman dressed in a print dress and sensible shoes approached. "Just the man I need."

"Andrea. Good to see you." Andrea was Father Beale's wife and had been for more than ten years. During the time Ben was working on the ecclesiastical trial, they had gotten to know each other well.

"You too. Got any turpentine?"

Ben patted his suit pockets. "Darn it, I guess I left my turpentine at home. Also my thinner, my shellac, and my WD-40."

Andrea grinned. "I've got glue all over me."

On closer inspection, Ben saw that her hands did appear to be covered with glue and Scotch tape and bits of colored construction paper. "You helped with the decorations, I surmise."

"No, but I cleaned up after those who did. A priest's wife's work is never done." She wandered off toward the nearest rest room. Ben found an empty seat and concentrated on finishing his cake.

"Isn't this the most romantic thing you've seen in your entire life?"

Christina had found the folding chair beside him. She was still wearing her pink maid-of-honor dress. Ben had heard that love is blind, and judging by most of the bridesmaid dresses he had seen, it was true.

Ben shrugged. "I've been to weddings before."

"Yes, but these are our friends," Christina enthused. "We watched the whole courtship. You were with Jones for their first face-to-face date."

Actually, Ben had *been* Jones for their first face-to-face date, but the less he was reminded of that, the better. "Nice turnout, anyway." He gave her a quick glance. "By the way, I don't think I mentioned it before, but . . . you look lovely."

Christina's eyes brightened. "Really? You think so?"

"I do."

"You're just saying that because I'm wearing this bridesmaid getup."

"For you, it is somewhat . . . conservative."

"Boring, you mean. But of course, you like boring. Compared to my usual wardrobe, this outfit is pretty uninteresting."

"Compared to your usual wardrobe, nudity would be pretty uninteresting."

A small balding man with thick black spectacles slid into the chair on Ben's other side. "Can you believe what a mess they've made of this place?" he muttered.

"I'm not sure what you mean," Ben replied.

"All this grotesque pink and puke rubbish. A revolting display. Who's responsible for this catastrophe?"

"That would be me," Christina said, smiling.

The man's chin dropped. "Oh." He winced. "Open mouth, insert foot." He tentatively held out his hand. "I'm sorry. I'm Alvin Greene. Head of the Altar Guild. And church bookkeeper."

"Ah," Christina said, taking his hand.

"You'll have to forgive me. I just transferred over from St. John's to fill the staff opening. I don't really know many people."

"You must be responsible for cleaning this place up after we're all gone."

"I'm afraid that's true."

"In that case, you're forgiven. I might be grumpy about this decorating job if I had to take it down."

"Still . . ." The man seemed to be having trouble removing his eyes from Christina's face. "I should've kept my mouth shut."

"Tell you what," Christina said. "I'm not doing anything tonight. How about if I hang around and help clean up?"

Greene's eyes widened. "Would you really? Oh, that would be— I mean, not that you should—but if you would—that would be—I mean—that would be—"

Ben frowned. It appeared Christina had another admirer, and not just for her dress, either. Which shouldn't bother him . . .

"Oh, Bruce, wait. I want you to meet someone."

Ben recognized the voice—unfortunately—before he spotted her face. Ernestine, the *grande dame* of St. Benedict's. She was being squired by a middle-aged man with a soft face who Ben remembered from the ladies' changing room.

"Bruce, this is Ben Kincaid." She lifted her brows knowingly. "He's the lawyer, you know."

The man extended his hand. "Hello. I'm Ernestine's nephew."

"Pleased to meet you. Are you—"

"Bruce, do be a dear and fetch me a piece of wedding cake," Ernestine said, interrupting. "Not too large a piece, please. Must watch my figure, you know. All right? There's a good boy."

"Yes, Aunt Ernestine." Bruce obediently fluttered away.

"Ben, I am so pleased that I've been seeing you in the choir every Sunday," Ernestine said. "It gives me great satisfaction to see you there in the loft, singing your heart out. You have a lovely tenor voice."

Ben wondered how she could possibly distinguish his voice from the eight other lovely tenor voices, but a compliment was a compliment. "You're very kind."

"I'm so pleased that you took what Ruth and I told you to heart. I know that after all that . . . unpleasantness, you must've wondered whether you would really be welcome here at the church. I wanted to make it clear to you, on behalf of all of St. Benedict's, that you are."

Ben wondered if all of St. Benedict's knew Ernestine spoke on their behalf. Presumably, when you were the church's leading benefactor, you could get away with that sort of thing.

"Here's your cake, Aunt Ernestine."

Ernestine looked askance at the plate he proffered. Crinkles formed around the corners of her mouth. "Bruce, dear boy, I didn't mean the groom's cake. I couldn't possibly eat chocolate. I need the white cake."

Bruce appeared to be used to this sort of thing. "Yes, Aunt Ernestine."

"And please find a piece a bit larger than that. I'm not diabetic, for heaven's sake."

"Yes, Aunt Ernestine." Bruce disappeared again.

"He's a dear boy," Ernestine said, with a small sigh. "But not much up here," she added, tapping the side of her skull. "I don't know what he'd be like today if he hadn't had me to take care of him."

Probably a lot happier, Ben suspected, but he kept his thoughts to himself.

"Oh, Ruth! Ruth!" Ernestine waggled her fingers at her elderly friend. "I was just about to discuss our problems here at the church with Ben."

"Oh, my," Ruth replied. "These last few weeks at St. Benedict's, ever since the trial, have been such a strain. Many families have left us, you know. And the ones that have remained have been very disappointed."

Their disappointment, Ben assumed, being that they hadn't been able to oust Father Beale, despite their best efforts.

"I think it will all blow over," Ben opined. "You just need to give everyone a little more time."

"I hope you're right. But if this church is to survive, there are going to have to be some changes. Father Beale must recognize that he can't simply go on doing whatever pleases him. He has a parish to consider."

"Of course."

"In fact, I think I'll find Father Beale and talk to him on that very subject. I wonder if he's in his office?"

For Father Beale's sake, Ben hoped he wasn't. Ruth left, Ernestine departed in a different direction, and Ben managed to return his attention to his cake, which for wedding fare, was not half bad. A few minutes later, he felt Christina giving him a gentle nudge. "Have you been watching the woman with the blue hair?"

Ben scanned the parish hall. "That doesn't quite narrow it down."

"Ernestine. Ruth's friend."

"Not in the last ten seconds. Why?" Ben spotted her at the other end of the room, chatting with George Finley, another member of the vestry. "What about her?"

"That's the third man I've seen her approach. And every time she does, the man gives her something. And then she takes that little notebook out of her purse. For that matter, I saw her get that out back in the dressing room, when the minister of music came in. What do you think it is?"

"Who knows? She's probably lining up volunteers for a bake sale or something."

Christina's eyes narrowed. "I don't know. My great-aunt Bettie used to have something like that. It was her account book. She made a record of every penny she ever earned or spent, right down to the last postage stamp. She was seriously tight."

"Must be that Scots blood."

"Quite possibly."

"There she is!" Paula came running toward them, still decked out in her bridal regalia, her full-length train trailing behind her. "Come on, Christina. It's time for me to throw the bouquet."

Christina jumped out of her seat. "You don't have to tell me twice." She raced to the center of the parish hall.

Paula reared back with a full fastball windup, then released the bouquet into the air. Several arms reached for it, but Christina sprang into the air with a leap that would've made Michael Jordan proud and snagged it.

"I got it!" Christina crowed. "I got it!"

"All right," Jones announced. "Time for the garter."

Ben began looking for an exit.

"Wait a minute, Boss." Jones blocked his path. A moment later, Loving had a hammerlock on him and dragged him into the center of the parish hall, where several other mildly embarrassed males were waiting.

Ben tried futilely to escape. "This really isn't my—"

"Shush," Loving said. "Don't spoil it."

A moment later, Jones was at the front, garter in hand. He pulled it back on his thumb like a slingshot and let it fly—directly toward Ben's face.

"You caught it!" Loving cheered, slapping Ben on the back.

"As if I had a choice," Ben muttered.

Loving jabbed his knuckles into Ben's rib cage. "And you know what this means, Skipper?"

"You're all fired?"

"It means you're gonna be the next to get hitched. You and—"

"Calm down, Loving. We don't want to scare the boy off." Paula stepped between them and placed her hands on Ben's shoulders. "I have something for you, too."

"No more undergarments, hopefully."

"Hopefully is an adverb. You mean, No more undergarments, I hope." She smiled. "But no. Just this." She leaned forward and kissed him on the cheek. "Jones and I would never have gotten together if it hadn't been for your kindness. Thank you."

"Nonsense. I had nothing to do with it."

Paula shook her head. "You're a wonderful person, Ben. Even if you don't know it." She stepped away and took Jones's hand. "And now, my love, I think it's time you and I—"

Her words were cut off by a piercing scream. Half the people in the room jumped at the earsplitting sound. Plates and punch glasses crashed to the floor.

"What on earth?" Jones whispered under his breath.

Paula shook her head. "We'd better go see."

Ben held them back. "You two go on your honeymoon. I'll see what's happening."

Jones and Paula nodded, then headed toward the rear entrance. Ben started in the direction of the scream.

By the time he'd left the parish hall and walked down the long corridor, a crowd had gathered before him. They were blocking the entrance to the glass-encased area where all the church employees had their offices.

"I went in looking for Father Beale, and I found her there, just like that." It was Ruth O'Connell, near hysterical, rambling to no one in particular. "I had no idea! I walked in and there she was, sprawled across the desk!" She covered her face.

Ben pushed his way through the crowd to one of the inner offices, the one farthest from the entrance.

"She's the one," he heard someone say quietly.

"Guess there's going to be another vestry election," said another.

Apparently Ben's status as *the lawyer* gave him some official sanction in the minds of the gathering crowd; they parted like the Red Sea as he approached.

Ben stepped inside the office—and gasped. A woman's body was sprawled across the desk, her skirt hiked up to her waist, her legs contorted in an unnatural position. The right side of her head was covered with blood. Her tongue was black and her face was an eerie, translucent blue.

He didn't have to get close to know that she was dead. Very dead.

It was Kate McGuire—the woman he had seen earlier in the corridor, arguing with Father Beale.

On a sudden impulse, Ben glanced at the nameplate on the door.

This was Father Beale's office.

Ben staggered out, suddenly overcome with a sickness rising fast from the pit of his stomach. Never eat wedding cake when you're about to view a corpse, he thought, trying to comfort himself with sick humor. He pushed through the crowd, hoping he could make it to the restroom in time. Throwing up all over the spectators would certainly betray his cool demeanor.

"Someone call the police," he grunted. And as quickly as possible, he found the nearest men's room and rushed inside.

Someone was already there.

Father Beale stood at one of the sinks, the water from the faucet running fast. There was blood all over his hands. And like Pontius Pilate before him, he was doing everything he could to wash it off.

2

BEN WATCHED FROM a distance as the various white-coveralled technicians back-and-forthed over the crime scene. To an untrained eye, it might seem like chaos in action, so many different people criss-crossing one another's paths in the tight, enclosed space of Father Beale's office. To Ben's more practiced eye, however, it was like watching scores of ants passing through the many-tiered tunnels of a complex ant farm, each drone performing his unique and specialized task. The fingerprint team scanned and dusted, the hair and fiber team scrutinized every surface with magnifying glass and tweezers, the serology team scraped, the coroner's team sniffed, and the detective's team interrogated. From the sidelines, the videographers recorded everything.

And beside the body, supervising every one of these complex and multifaceted operations, was Major Mike Morelli, Tulsa PD's top homicide detective, not to mention Ben Kincaid's former brother-in-law.

More than an hour after the police arrived, Mike left Beale's office for the first time ("Isn't there any coffee in this church?") and Ben was able to grab his ear for a few moments when he stepped outside for some fresh air.

"Congratulations, Ben," Mike said, once he finally had some caffeine in him to calm his nerves and amplify his wicked sense of humor. "Once again, you're in the middle of some major nastiness. And on the side of the nasty."

Ben ignored the gibe. "Any word on the cause of death?"

Mike strolled down the sidewalk parallel to the parking lot. Most people would be drawn to the prayer garden, particularly lovely this time of year when the flowers were blooming. But Mike avoided it. Too many unsettling memories, Ben supposed, of the last time he'd been to this church—also to take charge of a corpse. "Oh, you know how coroners are. They don't want to say anything useful until they've had three weeks to write reports and run every test known to man."

"What have you learned about the victim?"

"Name's Kate McGuire. By all accounts a lovely mild-mannered young woman. Member of the vestry—senior warden, actually—which I'm told was greatly at odds with Beale and had been trying unsuccessfully to have him removed. And—get this—she was engaged to be married for the first time." Mike paused, then stared up at the sky. "She was in love. But that marriage will never happen." He took another deep breath, as if he needed some oxygen coursing through his system. "For the sword outwears its sheath/And the soul wears out the breast/And the heart must pause to breathe/And Love itself have rest."

"Very lovely. But what do you think? About the murder."

"You know perfectly well what we think. What does everyone think?"

"Listen to me, Mike. I've known Father Beale since I was a kid. He wouldn't do this."

"Yeah, that's what you told us the first time someone turned up dead here."

"I was right then and I'm right now."

Mike shook his head and inhaled another gulp of the coffee. "Well, I can tell you this, pal. It doesn't look good for him."

"I noticed you haven't arrested him yet."

"Give us a minute. This is going to be a very high profile case. Before we bring charges, we want to make sure we can make them stick." He took another swig of java, then crumpled the Styrofoam cup in his hands. "Still, at least half a dozen witnesses tell me he had an altercation with this woman just before the wedding. Two witnesses saw him after the wedding with blood on his hands. And the body was in his office."

"Which is a good point in his defense."

Mike chuckled. "Only a lawyer with your imagination could turn that into a good point in his defense."

"Seriously, Mike, think about it. If he planned to kill the woman, why would he do it in his own office?"

"I don't think he *planned* anything. From what I've been hearing, he has an uncontrollable temper. Explosive and sometimes violent. I'm told he was ordered to get some therapy. I figure the woman came to his office to continue the argument, and he lost his grip and did her in."

"You can't prove any of that."

Mike thrust his fists into the pockets of his trench coat. "Not yet, my friend. But give me a couple of hours."

"You really want Beale, don't you?"

"What I want is the same thing I always want, Ben. You remember what Shakespeare said in the thirtieth sonnet?"

"Oh, stop waving your English degree in my face and just tell me."

" 'All losses restor'd and sorrows end.' In other words, justice." He shrugged his shoulders. "Is that so much to ask?"

ONCE EVERYONE HAD been thoroughly questioned, names and addresses had been taken, and all had been cautioned not to leave town, most of the guests and the wedding party disappeared. No speed was too great when one was escaping a horror of this magnitude, Ben supposed. Only a few of the church diehards remained; some who had been at the wedding, and a few, Ben noted, who showed up as soon as they heard about the new tragedy. Ben thought he should stay as long as Father Beale did, in part, to lend his support, and in part, to make sure the man didn't say anything he shouldn't.

To suggest that Beale was not at his best would be a pitiful understatement. He was shaken, spiritually ruptured, to a degree that was immediately evident to anyone who came near him. In that condition, Ben knew even the most innocent man might say something foolish that would haunt him ever after—especially on the witness stand.

"Ben," Beale said at one point, away from the ears of the police officers, "we—we need to talk."

"You're right," Ben answered. "But not here and not now. Tomorrow morning, in my office."

Beale's lips moved slowly, as if finding each word was a major struggle. "I—have a vestry meeting tonight."

"You're not still planning to go through with it!"

"I have no choice. The bishop's review council arrives tomorrow and—and—" He turned away, his head trembling. "We have to appoint someone to replace Kate."

Ben placed his hand on the troubled man's shoulder. "Come on."

Ben found Father Beale a quiet room in the rear of the church where he could try to get a grip on himself, somewhere he would be safe from prying eyes and probing questions. Then he returned to the crime scene, hoping he could overhear some of the remaining interrogations.

Ben spotted Ernestine Rupert, once again on the arm of her nephew.

"Truly, Aunt Ernestine, we should leave. You shouldn't be subjected to this macabre business. Let me take you home."

Ernestine slapped his hand away. "Don't be a ninny, Bruce. I can't leave now, not with all this trouble about. I have a responsibility to the church."

And besides, Ben thought, you might miss something good.

"But Aunt Ernestine, you shouldn't be associating with all these police and—"

"Balderdash. The church needs me. I am becoming a bit parched, though. Would you fetch me a club soda?"

"They don't keep club soda in the kitchen, Aunt Ernestine."

"The convenience store down the street will have it. Please hurry, dear boy."

He let out a long sigh. "Yes, Aunt Ernestine." And disappeared.

Ben spotted two of Mike's lieutenants quizzing Paul Masterson, the choirmaster. He appeared to be quite agitated about something. Probably attributing the murder to the fact that he was forced to play the Wedding March.

Not far away, he saw Christina, and clinging close behind her, Alvin Greene, the Altar Guild guy. Was this love at first sight, or was he just making sure she didn't forget she promised to help clean up?

Ben grabbed Christina's arm and tugged her aside. "Learn anything useful?"

She shrugged. "Lots of church gossip. I don't know how useful it is. But there certainly seems to be a lot going on here at St. Benedict's."

"We'll compare notes later. Jones and Paula?"

"Halfway to Eureka Springs by now."

"Good. I didn't want this to spoil their honeymoon. I'm sure it already spoiled their wedding."

"Oh, I don't know. They're certainly going to have some interesting stories to tell their grandchildren." She smiled. "So what do we do now?"

"Unbelievable as it may seem, there's a vestry meeting tonight, and it isn't being canceled. I have to be there with Father Beale. God only knows what will happen. Why don't you start seeing what you can dig up about Kate McGuire?"

"Anything in particular?"

"Yeah. Why someone might want to suffocate her."

"Ben." Christina gave him a concerned look. "You realize that to most people . . . this looks like an open-and-shut case."

"That's why God invented defense attorneys, Christina. So people wouldn't be convicted on 'looks.' "

"Still . . . are you sure you're entirely . . . impartial on this one? After all, Father Beale was your childhood priest. And technically speaking, still is."

"As a matter of fact, I'm not impartial. I'm totally partial. In his favor. Which is what a defense lawyer is supposed to be, remember?"

"Yes, but—" She reached out tentatively. Her fingers brushed against his hand. "I just don't want to see you get hurt."

"Don't worry about me, Christina. Worry about Father Beale. He's the one who has problems."

"Of course." She slowly withdrew her hand. "It was a lovely wedding, though, wasn't it? While it lasted?"

"If you like that sort of thing."

"I do," she said quietly. "Don't you?"

He shrugged. "It had its moments. But the murder wasn't one of them. Get me the scoop on Kate McGuire, okay?"

"Of course. I live to serve. Anything else I can do for you?"

"Well, now that you mention it . . . do you suppose there's any of that groom's cake left? . . ."

3

MANLY TRUSSELL SAT at the darkest corner of the long conference table, silently stewing. He hated meetings. And this had to be one of the worst. A lot of people sitting in uncomfortable chairs in a dark basement in a Unitarian church pontificating from ignorance.

These ecumenical committees were always abysmal wastes of time. Why had he ever agreed to be on this one? Perhaps because they were drawing talent from churches all over Tulsa, he thought this would be different? Perhaps because he had allowed himself to be deceived by the fact that it was called an *action* committee? The term was an oxymoron. All committees ever did was sit around and talk. And talk and talk and talk . . .

"What's your take on the Sapulpa situation, Manly?"

Hearing his name jerked him back to earth. "What situation is that?"

"Haven't you been paying attention?" The man at the head of the table drummed his fingers. "There's a new rumor that a doc out at that free clinic is performing abortions."

That was his idea of a new rumor? Another reason this committee never went anywhere—the chairman was a blithering idiot. Manly had first heard that rumor months ago. "I think it's a lot of baloney, Craig."

"You don't think it's true?"

"If I believed it, I wouldn't be sitting here."

One of the men on his side of the table laughed. "That's our Manly. The original Danger Boy."

A woman on the opposite side didn't seem as amused. "What are you saying? That if you thought it was true you'd go out there with an AK-46 and blow him away?"

Manly leaned slowly back in his chair. "An AK-46 would be overkill, I think."

The woman flipped. "I can't believe this. I mean, is he serious?"

Chairman Craig smiled. "Manly's Manly, that's all, Pamela."

"I don't think this is something we should just shuck and grin about." Pamela, an anorexically underweight brunette with long tapered fingers, was not prepared to let it go. "Our goal is to represent the entire Christian community. To create a perception of spiritual unity. One loose cannon like this could destroy our credibility. It could undermine our entire purpose."

Manly ran his tongue along his bottom row of teeth. "And what exactly is that purpose, ma'am?"

"What we're trying to do, for your information, is to unite the community behind the pro-life cause. We're joining hands to educate and enlighten people on an important issue. We're accomplishing an important goal through nonviolent means."

Manly fanned the air with his hand. "Sounds like a load of crap to me."

Veins stood out in Pamela's neck. "I think we have a problem here. A serious problem. In some people's minds, pro-life is already associated with dunderheads and backwoods bullies. Religious paranoids—those who think it's acceptable to kill a doctor and call it pro-life."

"I don't think people should be criticized for taking action in support of their beliefs."

"That depends on the action, doesn't it?"

"When a doctor commits an abortion, he takes a life. That's murder, pure and simple."

"I don't argue with that, but I do argue with—"

"Is it a crime to stop a murderer before he murders again?"

"It's certainly a crime to shoot a doctor in cold blood when—"

"Doesn't the Bible say 'an eye for an eye'? Isn't that what it says?"

Pamela tumbled back into her chair. "Oh, please. Here we go again."

"Don't duck the question. Doesn't the Bible say 'an eye for an eye'?"

"And 'vengeance is *mine*, sayeth the Lord.' That's the end of the quote, the part people like you always leave out. Retribution is for God, not man. We were told to love one another. Which you can hardly reconcile with shooting a man down in cold blood!"

"You know what I think?" Manly shouted back. "I think you're a coward, that's what I think. All of you! You don't have the courage of your convictions. You don't have the strength to do the hard jobs. You can talk the talk, but you can't walk the walk!"

"Oh, sweet Jesus." Pamela pressed her long fingers against her forehead. "Craig, I can't work with this. I just can't."

The chairman cleared his throat. "I think perhaps if we stick to our agenda . . ."

"I'll tell you where you can stick your agenda!" Manly bellowed.

Pamela's eyes rolled. "Seriously, Craig. This kind of talk—much less action—could undermine everything we're trying to do. How can we be taken seriously as a force for peace if we're represented by a neanderthal wannabe murderer?"

"Are you talking about me?" Manly asked.

"If you could both please just calm down!" Craig glared across the table, as if challenging anyone to say another word. "We have work to do, people, and this isn't getting it done."

"I won't let this go, Craig," Pamela muttered under her breath.

"I'm calling a ten-minute recess," Craig announced. He banged his little gavel on the tabletop. "Go get a drink and cool off! Both of you! When you return, I expect to get back to work!"

MANLY STEPPED OUTSIDE, but the ten minutes stretched to fifteen, then twenty, then more. Almost an hour passed before Chairman Craig emerged from a side room to talk with him. It was obvious he wasn't looking forward to saying whatever he had to say. He didn't sit down with Manly; in fact, he couldn't even look him in the eye.

"Manly, we've been having a little impromptu meeting in there. I'm very sorry, but—"

"I'm out, aren't I?"

Craig rubbed the back of his neck. "I wouldn't put it like that.

The committee just feels that our goals and . . . methodologies are radically different and that we will never be able to work together as a team."

"Work? Who ever said anything about work? All you people do is talk. That's all you ever will do."

"Still, we feel that it would not be mutually beneficial to continue—"

"You're afraid I'm gonna go lop off some abortion doctor's head, aren't you?"

"No, no, nothing like that—"

"Well, you should be," Manly said, pushing himself onto his cowboy boots. "Because I just might."

"Manly—"

"You people make me sick. You go on and on, talking about how ethical and righteous you are. But not a damn one of you has the guts to put your money where your mouth is."

"We don't feel that the most politic approach—"

"Did Christ care about politics?" Manly bellowed. "No, sir. He did not! He put his life on the line. Upset a lot of people, too. But he did what he knew was right."

"He never killed anyone."

"He tossed the money-changers out of the temple. He fought back the madding crowd."

"Look, we're never going to agree. And we're never going to be able to control you. You're not a team player, Manly. So we have to sever the relationship. We can't have you on this committee. I'm sorry, but we just can't."

Craig hurriedly stole back to the conference room, leaving Manly to sit and stew. Goddamn cowards. Self-righteous dilettantes. What do they know about what it takes to get anything done in this world? Not a damn one of them has ever accomplished anything in their entire lives. They stroke themselves and tell themselves what a wonderful contribution they're making to the world, but the truth is they never do a damn thing!

Manly was so absorbed in his thoughts that at first he didn't notice the stranger's approach.

"You're upset, aren't you?"

Manly glanced up. "Damn right I'm upset. Don't I have every right to be?"

"Far as I'm concerned. All I wondered was . . . what you're planning to do about it."

"And what makes you think I'm going to do anything about it?"

"Instinct. I can tell just looking at you. You don't belong on some committee chewing doughnuts and bulleting action items. You belong on the front lines."

"Front lines? Is there a war?"

"I think there is, yes. Don't you?"

"Maybe." He rolled his tongue around inside his mouth. "So what do you want?"

"I'd like to propose a mutually beneficial relationship for both of us. A win-win situation. You get what you want, I get what I want. We both fight for the causes we believe in. Sound good?"

"Couldn't say. Don't know what you're talking about."

"Well, you will. Soon enough. The great work has begun, you know." The visitor's eyes darkened. "But there's still much to do. Ever so much more to do."

CHAPTER

4

BEN SAT AT the darkest corner of the long conference table, silently stewing. He hated meetings. And this had to be one of the worst.

"This is supposed to be a house of God, not a house of horrors!"

"And we're supposed to be loving Christians, not back-stabbing assassins!"

"How can we behave as Christians when we're living in the third circle of hell?"

"Should I be putting this in the minutes?"

Ben had known having a vestry meeting tonight, so soon after the discovery of another murder, would be a mistake. But no one would listen to him—not even his client, Father Beale. The work of the church must go on, he insisted. And the vestry must select someone else to lead it, now that Kate is gone. So the meeting was convened, and Susan Marino, a thirtyish woman who appeared to Ben much too nice to even be on this vestry, was chosen to lead it. And from the moment the senior warden position was filled, the meeting had been nothing but an acrimonious succession of accusations, backbiting, and venom.

To her credit, Susan managed to keep her voice calm and even. "Father Beale, surely you can see why many people think this would be an appropriate time for you to step down."

"Yes, I certainly can. Politics." Beale seemed badly shaken, both by the discovery of the body in his office and the battering he'd endured in this meeting, but it hadn't quelled his vigor. "This latest tragedy involving poor Kate is nothing but an excuse to accomplish what you people have been trying to do for months."

"I think we have valid reasons," said Ernestine.

"As you did before," Beale replied. "If you'll recall, the matter was subjected to a full-blown trial. And you lost. And after the trial, you were instructed to give it up. Except apparently none of you were listening, because now, here it is again."

Ruth, the vestry secretary, talked while simultaneously taking notes. "That is not precisely what Father Holbrook said." She would be the one who knew, Ben realized. Probably had the man's every word scribbled down somewhere. "Moreover, he specifically said that he would revisit the matter in six months and that his ruling was contingent upon Father Beale's compliance with the conditions laid down by the adjudicative panel."

"There have been some rather extenuating circumstances since the trial," Ernestine replied. Her bearing and manner were, as always, upper-crust and domineering. She had not put her name forward for senior warden, but Ben suspected she considered herself the true leader of the vestry regardless of who sat in the end chair. "When tragedy mounts upon tragedy, it's only natural for people to want . . . change."

"What are you saying?" Beale asked.

Ernestine pressed her hand against her bosom. "I'm only saying that given the circumstances—"

"You're saying I killed Kate, aren't you? And Helen?"

A deathly silence fell over the parish hall. No one spoke. No one even moved.

"Well, listen up, people. I did not kill Kate. I did not kill Helen. Or anyone else. And I will not be railroaded out of this church based on these false—and damned convenient—accusations."

Ben cleared his throat, even though at heart the last thing on earth he wanted to do was to attract attention at this little get-together. "Father Beale, as your legal representative, I must caution you again not to comment in any way on the murders."

"I am an innocent man," Beale insisted. "Why shouldn't I say so?"

"Believe me—it's for the best. Don't refer to the murders at all."

After another moment of silence, Susan reasserted herself. "Let's

approach this matter from a different direction." Ben had learned Susan was a divorced mother of two who worked full-time as an accountant for WorldCom. A stressful situation, but possibly good
training for conducting this meeting. "St. Benedict's has always supported the Episcopal doctrine of lay leadership. As a member of the
vestry, and now acting senior warden, I also support lay leadership."
Her eyes rose. "Do you, Father?"

"With all my heart and soul."

"Then how can you . . . persist in this refusal to step down, when
it is perfectly apparent that the majority of the vestry believe you
should resign?"

"I believe in lay leadership as to administrative matters of the church.
You decide when services start and who teaches Sunday school. You
can hire and fire janitors and select the menu for Lenten dinners. You
can do basically anything—except oppose the will of God."

"Are you suggesting that you are the embodiment of the will of
God?"

"Don't be absurd. What I'm saying is simply that God called me
to this church and his representative in this diocese, the bishop, installed me here. The vestry does not have the authority, legal or
moral, to undermine those appointments. You've tried everything
possible, and it has all been unavailing."

Another member spoke, a slender young woman Ben had seen
teaching Sunday school classes. Carol Mason. "Father, all we're trying
to do is find some peace and harmony for this church."

"No, what you're trying to do is use rumor and false witness to accomplish a political goal—getting rid of me."

"Speaking for myself, Father, I would never accuse you of anything." Despite her agitation, Carol was quite lovely, with delicate
features and gorgeous blond hair. Ben felt his heart beating faster just
watching her. "But I do think it might be best for the church if you
resigned. Best for everyone. Including you."

"Do you believe in the doctrine of divine commission?"

Carol stuttered. "W-well—of course."

"Then you believe God calls people into service?"

"Ye-es . . ."

"As do I. I believe God called me to be a priest, and I believe he
called me to St. Benedict's. Come to think of it, Ruth, I recall you

saying the same thing when you were on the search committee that first issued my invitation to come to St. Benedict's. Do you recall that?"

Ruth nodded, not looking up.

"Then please answer this question for me: If God has called me to this church, what right do we have to thwart His desire?"

"Father . . ."

"It's a serious question. Either you believe God has a plan or you don't. And if He does, if I was brought to this church for a reason, how can we unravel His design?"

"We can't," said Masterson, the organist, who Ben knew had been at St. Benedict's much longer than Father Beale. "At the same time, we don't always know His design. We thought God called you to this parish. But obviously we were wrong. We made a mistake."

"You're still sulking about All Saints' Day."

"Does this relate to the murders?" Ben asked. An embarrassing question, but he didn't even know when All Saints' Day was, much less to what incident Father Beale was referring.

"No," Father Beale answered. "This relates to our choirmaster pouting like a five-year-old because I instructed him to play 'I Sing a Song of the Saints of God' on All Saints' Day."

"It's a children's song," Masterson said, "trite and imbecilic, and it may be appropriate for Sunday school or Children's Chapel, but it has no place in the worship service."

"It's a lovely little tune," Beale rejoined, "and while it may be simplistic, it is liturgically correct and many parishioners, including me, look forward to hearing it during the All Saints' service."

Masterson made a sniffing noise. "Music should be left to those who know something about it."

"Excuse me, but that's exactly wrong. The Book of Common Prayer says the rector is in charge of the service and the other members of the staff take instruction from him. End of story." Beale turned back toward Ben. "Could there be a clearer proof of what's going on at this meeting than this? This dispute has nothing to do with murders. The deaths are just an excuse for excising a rector who has become inconvenient."

Beale paused, and all at once the air seemed to go out of him, like a punctured balloon. He fell back into his chair, looking tired and unsure. "I know I've made mistakes. I know I haven't handled my-self . . . appropriately in all instances. I've done some things that—that I shouldn't have done. I know that. And I know I have a foul temper. I'm working to get it under control. Everyone makes mis-takes. I've learned from mine. I'm confident that if we can just get past all this—this—*hate,* this unkindness, I can make a success of this. St. Benedict's has some wonderful people. We could be an out-standing church, the best in the diocese, leaders in outreach. But we can't do that when we're still trying to hurt one another. We can't do that until we're willing to let the past be the past and join hands to work together."

The parish hall fell silent. Ben couldn't tell whether Father Beale's speech had hit home with any of them or whether they were just too tired to argue.

"Look," Ben said, his voice almost inaudibly quiet. "I'm a lawyer. I don't know much about this church stuff, I admit. No one ever comes to a lawyer for moral guidance."

"You can say that again," Masterson grumbled.

"But I did grow up in an Episcopal church," Ben continued. "And I have known Father Beale for a long time—longer than any of you, I think. And I can tell you this. He's a good man. A very good man. Sure, he's flawed, just like the rest of us. But he tries to do the right thing. Isn't that what it's all about?"

Susan turned her head away. "He may have tried, but he made grave errors. Some of which you . . . know nothing about."

"He's admitted that," Ben said. "Who among us hasn't made mis-takes? The point is, he wants to make good here. Can't we let him? Can't we forgive his errors? Come to think of it, isn't that what Chris-tianity is all about?"

Ben gazed across the room, trying without much luck to read the faces.

"I'm speaking to you now, not as a lawyer, but as a member of this church. We haven't passed the point of no return, the place where our differences become utterly irreconcilable. Let's put an end to this un-pleasantness before we do. Let's give the man another chance. Let's let him stay at St. Benedict's and continue God's work."

"A noble sentiment," said a familiar voice from the rear of the hall, "but I'm afraid that isn't going to be possible."

Ben knew the speaker even before he turned. Major Mike Morelli, Homicide.

Two uniformed officers stood by the door as Mike calmly crossed the parish hall. To Ben's dismay, he saw that Mike was walking, not to him, but to Father Beale. "Daniel Beale, it is my very unpleasant duty to take you into custody immediately."

Beale appeared stricken. "B-but—why?"

Mike's face remained unexpressive as he gave what Ben knew was the only possible answer. "Sir, I'm afraid I'm under orders to arrest you on the charge of murder. Murder in the first degree."

5

The Gospel According to Daniel

IT MAY SURPRISE some to learn that this was not the first instance in my less than illustrious career when I had been incarcerated. For a time, the jailhouse and I were close friends, although those days now seem like distant reflections barely visible through the cracks of memory. But I grew up in the sixties, after all, and I came to view civil disobedience as a moral duty, an imperative no thinking man could deny.

When I first emerged from seminary, I still had that youthful desire to make a difference and the unquestionable certainty that I could. Now I can see my past self with a certain detached irony, but at the time, I marched out into the world with unquenchable enthusiasm, certain I could make the world a better place. I protested against the proposed Black Fox nuclear plant and won; I protested in favor of the passage of the ERA and lost. And both those activities got me thrown in jail.

Of course, in those days there was a certain radical chic to being the liberal activist priest. I was the Oklahoma version, but there were others like me all across the country, many of whom got far more press than I did, a fact which privately never failed to irritate me. We were the New Wave of religious leaders, men and women who were more interested in this world than the next, who found politics and religion inseparable. To me, "Onward Christian Soldiers" was more than a Sunday school song; it was a rallying cry. The Episcopal Fight Song, if you will.

But those days are long past. Nowadays, if you see a man of God mentioned in the papers, it's because he's been caught with the choirboys or because he's bilked his followers out of another million dollars. Too much of the enthusiasm that spilled out of my youthful soul was squelched long ago, suffocated by the weight of the world and the seeming impossibility of bringing about any permanent change. Yes, we can improve our institutions, we can make our society more progressive. But people remain the same. Human nature, it seems, does not improve. The ego of man, the breadth of his folly, is without limitation. No matter how democratic our government, no matter how sophisticated our technology or how advanced our medicine, people remain people—at times noble, but more often petty and selfish and closed-minded.

But I digress. My attorney asked for a record of the case, not a whining jeremiad. The most ironic detail is that, at this point, I still expected the crisis to blow over. I didn't know what had inspired the police to arrest me, but I never doubted for a moment that they eventually would see the error of their ways. I would be released, all would be forgiven, and I would go on about my holy business.

As I said before, the ego of man, the breadth of his folly, is without limit.

"MORNING, MURRAY."

Murray Plimpson, startled, jumped up behind his desk and tried to act as if he hadn't been asleep on the job. "Uh, m-morning, Ben."

"Is it too soon to see my client?"

"N-no, no. Not at all." He fumbled in his pockets for his keys. He had looked peaceful a few minutes before, but now looked utterly wretched; Ben began to feel guilty for having disturbed his sleep. Murray was the night/morning shift superintendent for the downtown county lockup and had been for years. All the local criminals came here after they were arrested and remained until they were transferred to more permanent quarters. "You here to see that kid who clobbered his dad?"

"Clear out the cobwebs, Murray. I bounced Eric Biggers yesterday. Suspended sentence."

"You got that scumbag back on the street with a suspended sentence?" Murray shook his head. "Man, you must be good."

"It's a gift." Ben passed him the file he'd gotten from the desk clerk downstairs. "Actually, I'm here to see Daniel Beale."

Murray's eyes widened a bit, droopy as they were. "You got the killer priest?"

"Accused killer, Murray. He didn't do it."

"Yeah, that's what they all say." Murray glanced over his shoulder toward the cells. "Literally."

Murray opened the thick double-bolted steel door and led Ben down the main corridor of the downtown lockup. The grill floor rattled thunderously beneath their feet, notifying all present that a visitor was approaching. Ben knew his suit and tie immediately identified him; Murray might as well have announced, "Lawyer on the bridge!"

A scabrous man in a cell on the right reached his long arm through the bars. "Hey, lawyer! I shouldn't be here. I didn't do nothing!"

Another man on the other side shouted, "Me too! I'm totally innocent, man. I was framed!"

Murray gave Ben a sideways glance. "Whaddid I tell ya?"

Murray led Ben to the last cell on the right. Inside the dark, tiny room, Ben saw a hunched figure on the floor before his metal cot. He was on his knees.

Praying.

Murray turned the key in the lock. Father Beale heard the noise and looked up. Ben stepped inside.

"Let me know if you need anything," Murray said.

"I will. Thanks." Ben approached Father Beale. It was hard to think of him as Father Beale, dressed as he was in the standard issue orange jail pajamas rather than a black suit with a white collar. He didn't look like a man of God. Sadly enough, he didn't look like anything except another criminal, no different from any of the other poor souls who had proclaimed their innocence as Ben made his way down the corridor. His eyes were red and tired; he probably had not slept well. His back was slightly bent, even after he rose to his feet.

"How are you holding up?"

"Well enough," Beale said. "When do I get out of here?"

"I don't know," Ben replied. Better to be honest than to disappoint.

"I've been in jail before, you know. Civic protests, that sort of thing. But I was never behind bars for more than twenty-four hours."

"This is a capital murder charge," Ben said. "This is . . . different." He took a seat on the edge of the cot, since there were no other options. "We've got an arraignment set for tomorrow morning where I'll ask the court to set bail. But I have to tell you, Father—Oklahoma judges almost never grant bail to capital murder defendants."

"But surely in my case—where the evidence is entirely circumstantial—and I'm a priest, after all."

"Believe me, Father, I'll be playing every card I have. But it's still a long shot."

"Then I could be stuck here—until the trial?"

Ben nodded. Or longer, he thought, but did not say.

"But who will look after the church? Who will take care of my parish?"

"Father—realistically, I have to assume your arrest will give the vestry the ammunition they wanted to have you removed. Even the bishop will be hard-pressed to back a priest who's currently residing in the county jail."

"A man is innocent until proven guilty. Not only in law, but in the church as well."

Ben popped open his briefcase and took out a legal pad. "You have more faith in the system than I do, I'm afraid."

"Faith is my business. Do you have any idea what possessed the police to arrest me?"

"Unfortunately, yes." Ben removed a small file from his briefcase. "I've had a nice long chat with Mike—Major Morelli. In Homicide. They found a large acrylic paperweight in your office covered with blood."

"The murder weapon?"

"Not exactly. They say the woman was suffocated. But she was struck by the paperweight. That's what caused the wound on the side of her head."

A shudder passed through Beale. "That's horrible. Poor Kate."

Ben showed him a photo of the paperweight, an irregularly shaped clear object about the size of a football. "Do you know what it is?"

"Of course. That's my St. Crispin's award."

"And that is—?"

"It was given to me fourteen years ago by the Episcopal Council of Churches. In recognition of my humanitarian work. So is this why I've been arrested? Because my award was used by the murderer?"

"I'm afraid there's more to it than that. They've found your fingerprints on the thing."

"Well, of course my fingerprints were on it. It's mine! It was on my desk. I probably touched it every other day!"

"Yes, but you see . . . your fingerprints were on it . . . and no one else's. If the award was used by another person to club Kate over the head, that person's prints should also be on the award, in addition to or obscuring yours. But there are no other prints. No partials or smudges. Nothing. Except yours."

"Perhaps the killer used gloves."

"A good theory. Except that no one on the premises was wearing gloves. Not even the bride."

"They could've been hidden."

"The police were on the scene less than five minutes after the body was found, and they searched the premises and everyone present before they were allowed to leave. No one had any gloves."

"Then maybe it wasn't gloves. Maybe they covered the award with a cloth or rag or . . . or something."

"Perhaps. But anything used in that manner would've been covered with blood. And the police didn't find anything. No rag, no cloth, no torn shirt, nothing."

Beale's eyes turned down toward the stone-cold floor. "Looks bad, doesn't it?"

"I'm afraid so. I mean, the killer might've washed his hands. But I don't think he could've done his laundry."

Beale did not look up. "You think I did it, don't you?" he said quietly.

"No," Ben said firmly. "On the contrary, I know without a doubt that you did not do it. But it looks like we're going to have a hell of a time proving it."

"You saw me, didn't you? In the bathroom. Washing my hands."

Ben nodded. This time he was the one who didn't make eye contact.

"About ten minutes after the wedding concluded I went to my office and found Kate lying across my desk. I rushed to her side, praying she was still alive. I held her in my arms and felt the side of her neck for a pulse; that's when I got the blood on my hands."

"That makes sense."

"But then Ruth O'Connell came along and screamed, and all those other people arrived, and I knew the police would be along shortly, but—but—that still wasn't really the problem. I can't explain it. I had to get that blood off my hands. I couldn't stand it."

"That's perfectly understandable, Father."

"To you, maybe. But what will a jury think?"

"We'll cross that bridge when we get to it." Ben paused. He'd much rather skip the next topic that had to be addressed, but he couldn't. And if they had to talk about it, it was better to do it now than later. "Father—I must tell you. I saw you talking to Kate just before the wedding started. You appeared to be having . . . well, a rather strong disagreement. And I wasn't the only one who heard."

Beale's shoulders sagged. Each new development seemed to bring him lower. "It's true. We were fighting. She threatened me and . . . and I got angry."

"I have to ask what you were arguing about."

"It was a . . . theological disagreement."

"I heard her saying something about . . . evil. She said something you were doing was evil."

Beale's eyes darted up, then quickly looked away. "She was referring to my permitting a gay and lesbian group to meet on the church premises. She's from the old school; she considers homosexuality an aberration, a sin against God. Evil. She thought that by allowing the group to meet I tainted the whole church with their sin."

"I see. Do you have any idea why anyone would want to kill Kate?"

"I can't imagine. I mean, sure, we had philosophical disagreements. She was on the vestry, and they all want to be rid of me. But people don't commit murder because of philosophical disagreements. Do they?"

"Who knows why people commit murder? I've seen more than my share, but I still find it unfathomable." Ben glanced toward his briefcase. "There's more evidence, but the forensic teams are still working. Apparently they found a hair on the body, and they'll try to link that back to you. They'll probably come up with a few more tidbits before trial. They usually do." He looked through his papers for a few more moments, then closed the lid on his briefcase. "Anyway, that should about cover it for now. We'll talk again after the arraignment. We'll know better where we stand. Anything I can do for you in the meantime?"

"Yes. Please tell Andrea everything you've told me."

Andrea. Of course. Ben had been so concerned about Father Beale he'd forgotten about his wife. She must be worried sick. "I'll do that. And she can come visit you, if she'd like."

"I don't know how she'll feel about that. It might be . . . more stress than she wants. Or needs. But do keep her informed."

"I will. Anything else?"

"Yes. I want you to know that I appreciate everything you've done for me, ever since these troubles started. But this is different. This is a murder trial, and it's probably going to get a lot of play in the papers. I'm sure most of what they say about me will be negative, and that's going to reflect on you. Much as I appreciate your help, speaking as your priest, I think it would be best if you stepped down and let another attorney handle my case."

"No chance."

"Ben, I'm serious. You're a great lawyer—and a fine human being, I might add. But you don't need this. Step down."

"No."

"You're not thinking this through."

"The answer is no."

"Ben . . . I know what you do. In many ways, your law practice is *your* ministry, and you do important work. I don't want to see that come to an end."

"I am not going to resign from your case."

"Ben—"

"Are you firing me? Because if you are, then I have to go. But I will not resign."

"Ben, consider what your—"

"Do you remember the stained glass window?"

A small smile played on Father Beale's lips. "It's been a while. But of course I do."

Ben nodded. "You were there for me. I'll be here for you."

Beale leaned back, letting his head touch the hard stone wall behind him. "It's been good having you in church these past few months, Ben. Particularly since I know you've been a church absentee ever since you left home."

"It's been good for me, too."

"Masterson tells me you've been a valuable addition to the choir, and that you help him out at rehearsals by playing the piano. You've done a fine job with the Old Testament readings." He paused. "But I notice you never go up for communion."

"Nothing gets by you, huh?"

"That's my job. So, what's the story, Ben?"

Ben thought for a long moment. "I don't know. I suppose I'm still not . . . totally comfortable with this church stuff. I mean, I enjoying the singing, and the fellowship, and all that. But to take communion—" Ben stared at the stone walls, searching for words. "To get down on your knees and take the cup, that's like saying, *I believe.*"

"No, you're wrong," Father Beale replied. He stretched out on the cot and closed his eyes. "That's like saying, *I want to believe.* There's a difference."

6

SOMEONE IS IN my apartment, Ben realized as he approached the door. If I were in a horror movie, this would be a sure sign that I'm about to die. And even though danger is obviously afoot, I would plunge on in and get eaten or dismembered or whatever.

Happily, he recalled, I'm not in a horror movie, although some of my trials come close. His apartment had been broken into before, however, and the locks in this building were not what they should be. If he were smart . . .

But somehow, he was not inclined to call 911. Most of his friends had keys, and they used them with impunity. This could be Mike, raiding the icebox, or Loving, wanting to watch the football game on Ben's big screen (nineteen inches).

Or Christina. "What on earth are you wearing?" he said as soon as he passed through the door.

Which was, of course, a rhetorical question. He could see what she was wearing. He just couldn't believe it. A black leather skirt and black Metallica T-shirt with a sleeveless fleece vest and high black leather boots.

"Goth?" he asked.

Christina grinned. "It's not just for kids anymore."

Ben tossed his briefcase onto the coffee table. "I thought you were going to try to dress more . . . um . . . conservatively."

"When I'm working, yes. Am I working?"

"Beats me. What are you doing?"

"Nothing in particular. I just thought I'd bring some sunshine into your dreary little existence."

"Gee, thanks." His eyes scanned the perimeter of his apartment. Something was very wrong. "Forgive me for asking this—I don't want to offend you—but, have you been cleaning?"

"What do you know. I was wrong. You did notice. What was your first clue? The fact that you didn't trip over your entire wardrobe on your way through the door?"

"No. The smell of Lemon Pledge in the air. It reminds me of my mother's house."

"Believe me, Ben, there's no comparison between this dive and your mother's house."

"What on earth possessed you—?"

"Much as I would like to take credit for spiffying up your perpetually unkempt dwelling place, I can't. Thank Joni. Or blame her, depending on how attached you were to the squalor."

Ben hung up his coat and sat in the overstuffed chair opposite Christina. "She didn't need to do that."

"No, but she wanted to."

"She should be concentrating on her schoolwork, not mucking about in my apartment. This was a total waste of her time."

Christina puffed out her cheeks. "Ben, when are you going to get it through your thick little head that you have friends who care about you? This wasn't a waste of her time. This was something she wanted to do. And something that seriously needed to be done."

"Still, she's in college now—"

"Only because of you. You've been her mentor, in more ways than one. You took a dizzy teenager and turned her into a responsible human being."

"Oh, nonsense."

"It's true. Her whole life now is centered around other people. Care giving. And today she decided to give some care to your apartment. So be grateful." She grabbed a file out of his briefcase and started thumbing through it. "What happened in the Beale case?"

Ben filled her in on all that had occurred since the arrest, including his visit with Father Beale.

Christina let out a long whistle. "Boy, Jones is not going to be happy."

"Is he ever?"

"Well, no. But this case has *Loser* written all over it. And I'm assuming the good priest doesn't have deep pockets."

"He's innocent, Christina."

"You really think so?"

"I know so."

"How can you know?"

Ben hesitated. "I suppose Father Beale would say it's a question of faith. I have faith in him. And I have to stand by him. No matter what."

She looked at Ben curiously for a moment, then let it pass. "I'll get cracking, then. First thing in the morning. I've already uncovered a few interesting tidbits about the victim."

"I want a team meeting right after the arraignment. Tell the others."

"Already did. Efficient, aren't I?"

"That's why I pay you the big money."

"In your dreams."

"Got any plans for dinner?"

"Actually, yes. Three invitations from well-heeled suitors, plus a pot roast in my freezer that really needs to be cooked." The corners of her lips tugged upward. "But I'd rather share that leftover pizza in your fridge."

He grinned. "If you insist."

CHRISTINA STAYED UNTIL almost nine-thirty, filling Ben in on all the latest and greatest gossip in the legal world. She'd been a full-fledged attorney for less than a year, and she was already much better connected than he could ever hope to be. She knew all the latest scuttlebutt—which judge was sleeping with which lawyer, which lawyer was being investigated by the bar committee, which firm was teetering on the verge of bankruptcy. And she clued him in on what was happening in his own office—Loving's latest conquest, the honeymoon reports from Jones and Paula. They talked about anything and everything—except the Beale case. After several hours of this, Ben was beginning to wonder if she would ever leave.

Until she did. And then he was alone again.

And maybe five minutes after that, he started kinda sorta wishing Christina was still around.

This wasn't the first time this had occurred. Christina was such a vibrant, vivacious, unstoppable force that he supposed it was only natural she would leave a gaping hole in her wake. But she had other fish to fry—friends, colleagues, social groups. And he had . . . he had . . .

A cat, Giselle reminded him, as she shoved her black furry nose in his face. He had an overweight, utterly indulged cat. And he only had the cat because Christina gave her to him and insisted that he keep her.

And beyond that? he wondered, as he stroked Giselle's soft silky fur. He had friends, of course. A few, anyway. Colleagues. He had a mother on the other side of the state. He had a sister so estranged he didn't even know where she lived. And a nephew he hadn't seen in months and months.

In the course of his many years on his own in Tulsa, he had managed, slowly but surely, to teach himself to be a decent lawyer. He had even managed to learn to get tough and forceful when necessary. But he hadn't learned how to be . . . friendly. He was awkward in social situations. He could barely speak to strangers. He froze up at parties. In his heart of hearts, he was still the bespectacled ten-year-old geek with a speech impediment no one wanted to play with. Or so he saw himself, anyway.

He heard a scritch-scratch sound coming from the vicinity of the front door. He craned his neck in time to see a white envelope slide under the door.

He jumped up, sending Giselle flying off his lap. He scooped up the envelope. It had to be a rent check. *Yes!* Glory hallelujah!

He flung the door open. A tall woman in her fifties was quietly creeping down the stairs.

"Joyce!"

Joni and Jami's mother slowly pivoted. "Oh . . . hello, Ben. I'm sorry—I didn't mean to disturb you."

"Not at all." He glanced down at the envelope and grinned. "Believe me, receiving rent money is never a disturbance. Especially after all the unexpected maintenance expenses we've had this month."

"Ye-es," she said slowly. "I was pleased to see the central heating back."

"You and me both. Would you like to come in for a moment?"

"Uh—oh—my—" She couldn't have acted more awkward if he'd asked her to strip off her clothes and perform the dance of the seven veils. "I—no—the girls—"

"Sure, I understand. Well, I really appreciate this."

"Ye-es." She took a short step backwards down the stairs.

"I mean, another day or two and I would've had to mention it to you, and I just hate that. The worst part of being a landlord is hassling people for the rent money."

"I'm sure."

"It's a real relief to not have to do that, you know?"

"Ben . . ."

"Yes?" Something about her expression finally tipped him off that all was not as he supposed. He took a closer look at the envelope, then opened it.

There was not a check inside. It was a note written in an awkward block-letter scrawl. SORRY, CAN'T MAKE ENDS MEET. WILL GET YOU NEXT MONTH. JOYCE.

Ben slid the note back inside the envelope.

"I really meant to pay you this month," Mrs. Singleton said. She was speaking much more quietly than before. "But with Jack gone and Joni in college—I can't tell you what a strain it's been."

"I thought we had your finances straightened out. You had a budget."

"We did. But then Jami wanted to get her teeth whitened, and Joni needed these expensive textbooks for some class she's taking, and the boys need school clothes, and—" She tossed her head from side to side, seeping embarrassment and pain like water from a sponge. "I just don't know what to do anymore."

Ben took a step forward. "You did the right thing, Joyce."

"I know we owe you money. You've been so good about letting us stay even though we haven't made a rent payment in, what, four months now? And I—"

Ben cut her off, hoping to minimize the pain. "You take care of your family, Joyce. That's your first priority."

"But the rent—"

"You'll catch me next month."

"But—"

He gave her shoulder a squeeze. "You'll catch me next month."

"Thank you." She turned away, then all at once turned back, leaned forward, and kissed Ben on the cheek. Then she scurried down the stairs.

Ben reentered his apartment and closed the door behind him. Well, he'd just have to find another way to pay the bills, that was all. True, the repairs had way overextended his budget, but maybe if he cut back to the bare essentials and didn't—

He felt something warm and wet and furry tickling his ankles.

Giselle? Meeting him at the door? Now this was a first.

He stretched out his arms and, a second later, Giselle jumped into them. Ben pulled her close, scrunching her up against his face.

Why, you old sweetie, he thought as he rubbed his nose against hers. You do love me, after all.

He smiled, then made his way toward the kitchen. As long as I feed you, anyway.

CHAPTER

7

WHEN BEN ENTERED Antony Canelli's closet of an office on the fourth floor, he found the assistant DA behind his desk kneeling, prostrate against the desk.

"Praying?" Ben asked. "I've heard the thought of going up against me in court strikes terror in the hearts of DAs, but I hadn't realized it was enough to drive them to religion."

"Ha ha," Canelli said, looking up. "I dropped a pencil." He was a tall man, six foot four, which made him almost a foot taller than Ben. He was buff and muscular and exceedingly handsome—professional-model handsome. "Don't worry about driving me to religion. Sister Mary Theresa and twelve years of Catholic school beat you to the punch."

"Mind if we talk about the Beale case?"

"Is there any point?" He glanced at his watch. "The arraignment's in fifteen minutes. Once your boy gets denied bail and pleads we'll have a better idea where we are."

"That's what I'd like to avoid." Ben plopped himself down in the nearest available chair. He hadn't been invited to do so, but in his experience, DAs rarely invited defense lawyers to get comfortable. Might be bad for their reputations. "If we go to arraignment, there's going to be an enormous amount of publicity. Which is going to make you look really lame when you lose. You know your case is weak. Cut Father Beale loose now before you get embarrassed."

"Our case is weak? You must be kidding. Our case is sensational."

Ben waved a hand in the air. "I know about the fingerprints. It isn't conclusive."

"How'd you find out about that? You been talking to your brother-in-law?"

"Ex."

"Lemme tell you, Kincaid—the fingerprint evidence is just the tip of the iceberg. It's good, but possibly not good enough to get a conviction. Happily, we've got much much more."

Ben felt a gnawing in his chest. "Like what?"

"Hmm, let me see, I'm thinking back to law school." He tapped the side of his face with a finger. "Do I have to tell you everything I know before the arraignment? Wait—no! There's not a case yet. After the arraignment, after you file your motions, then, maybe—"

"Give me a break, Canelli."

"Why not? I got a memo from the boss just the other day saying, 'Tony, start giving the defense attorneys a break, okay?' " He gave Ben a long look.

"Have I mentioned that I find this new predilection for sarcasm most unbecoming?"

Canelli pressed a hand against his heart. "You have no idea how much that wounds me. I live for your approval."

"C'mon. At least give me a hint."

"A hint? Fine. Be sure to ask to see all trace evidence discovered on the body. You'll be glad you did."

"I would've asked for that anyway."

"I know. Why else would I tell you? And be sure to check the witness list, especially the long parade of folks who saw your boy threaten the last victim. And the veritable horde who saw him stumbling around with blood on his hands."

"That can be explained."

"And I'm looking forward to reading the briefs in which you attempt to do just that. I love fiction."

"You are really in a mood today."

Canelli lowered himself into his chair. "Yeah, I guess I am at that."

"I was kinda hoping you might be inclined to . . . go a little easy on this guy. Cut him some slack."

"Because, after all, he's only killed two people."

"No. Because he's a man of God."

"Jesus and Mary." Canelli slapped his desk, hard. "You have got to be kidding."

"I'm not. Be sensible. It's not like we're dealing with some crack-addicted gang member here. He's a priest."

"Yeah. And you know what? I think that makes it worse." Canelli swivelled around. "I can occasionally muster some sympathy for a poor kid who's grown up in a crappy neighborhood with sorry excuses for parents, dumb as a post, who makes a mistake. I can at least understand that. But this man was a priest. A *priest*, for God's sake. He had a responsibility to the people in his parish. More than that— he owed them a sacred trust. And he betrayed that trust. In the worst possible way."

"You're assuming he's guilty of the murders."

"I *know* he's guilty of the murders, but even if he isn't, from what I hear, this man has been betraying his collar for a good long while."

Ben didn't like the sound of that. "What do you mean?"

Canelli cocked an eyebrow. "You don't know?" He eased back into his chair. "I think you need to a have good long sit-down with your client, Ben. The sooner the better. Because your client offends me, you know what I'm saying? He offends me at the most profound level. I want him behind bars—at the least."

"You know, Canelli, I love it when you get feisty. You've got that great tough-Italian-kid thing working for you and I go for it in a big way. Gives me shivers."

"Laugh all you want, Kincaid. I'm serious."

"You're more than serious. You're starting to sound like some kind of zealot."

"Maybe I am. Maybe I should be. A man like that, hiding behind a clerical collar. That's depraved."

"Don't be so cynical. You have to have a little faith in—"

"Don't you dare lecture me about faith!" Canelli's hand shot out across the desk, finger extended. "I know what faith is. My whole life is about faith—faith in the justice system, faith in God. What have you got faith in, Kincaid? Your ability to put killers back on the street?"

"Canelli—"

"I'm a lifelong Catholic, Ben. Always have been, always will be. I know what faith is. Don't get me wrong, I got nothing against the Episcopal Church. I mean, I think Episcopalians are Catholics who don't have the guts to go into the confessional, but that's got nothing to do with this case. This case is about a man who was charged with the most valuable treasures human beings possess—their souls. And he betrayed them."

"Canelli, calm down so—"

"That's a horrible crime, Ben. Absolutely horrible. Worse than murder, or rape, or incest, or anything else you can conjure up. Beale committed a crime against his parish and against God. And you want me to cut him some slack, basically because he speaks the Queen's English and scrubs up nicely."

"Be reasonable."

"I am being reasonable. I'm being perfectly reasonable. And you can just forget it. There will be no deals this time. Don't even bother asking. This man must be punished. And I believe—I have *faith*—that he will get the punishment he deserves."

MASTERSON SAT ON one end of the organ bench, in such pain that tears nearly rolled down his cheeks. No, he was not suffering an internal distress, nor was physical discomfort being applied. This pain was an aesthetic one, or, one might say, a spiritual one. He was listening to one of his private students play the organ. And it was the godawfulest noise he'd heard in his entire life. Since his last private lesson, anyway.

"Listen to me, Tom," he said, when at last the hideous caterwauling ceased, "the organ is not like the piano. It doesn't matter how hard you strike the keys. The volume is controlled by the pedal your right foot is perched upon."

"Yeah, yeah," the kid said. "I know." He was thirteen and in all likelihood hadn't the slightest desire to play the organ. Lessons were the kid's mother's brilliant idea, not his.

"And go a little easier on the pedal keyboard," Masterson added. He was doing his best not to scream: And get away from my organ, you bloody heathen! And never come back! "All it takes is a slight depression. You don't have to kick them into submission."

"Sorry, Dr. M. Guess it comes from playing soccer."

Soccer. Now there was a worthless occupation of time much more suited to this abominable brat's talents. Or lack thereof. "Why don't we try it again from the top"—he couldn't believe he was saying it even as he did—"and this time remember that this is a hymn, not a marching band tune."

The boy repositioned himself to give it another try. Before he began, however, Masterson detected the presence of a third person in the church. He couldn't explain exactly how—it was less than a throat clearing, and yet more than nothing. Like a disturbance in air currents. Or the spiritual discomfort that attended being in the presence of evil. He knew someone was there. He knew who it was, too.

"Just a moment, Tom." He excused himself from the organ and walked to the back of the sanctuary.

Ernestine Rupert was waiting for him.

"Do I need to ask why you're here?"

The elderly woman didn't say a word. She just stared at him, one hand holding her purse, the other clenching her little blue book.

"I suppose you know I haven't been paid this week. The vestry is in such chaos that nothing's getting done."

Ernestine didn't blink. Masterson was beginning to wonder if the blue-haired bitch ever blinked. Maybe she didn't have eyelids. Like a snake.

"If you could just wait until next week, it would make a world of difference. Seriously." He heard his voice crack. He sounded stressed, desperate. Goddamn it but he hated this. "All the difference in the world."

Still no reaction. And no sign of sympathy. Or mercy.

"I mean, it's not like I haven't been regular in the past, is it? I'm probably your most dependable customer."

He attempted a small laugh, but it fell flat. Ernestine didn't smile. Not even a smirk.

"Damn you, anyway." He reached into his pocket and whipped out a twenty. He slapped it into Ernestine's hand. "Will that do you?"

Ernestine's hand remained outstretched.

"Damn!" One after another, Masterson slapped four more twenties into the palm of her hand. When he was finished, she slid the money into her pocketbook, then made a notation in her blue book in a tiny, crimped hand.

"Thank you so much," Masterson said, his voice dripping with contempt.

"And thank you," Ernestine replied. She pivoted on her orthopedic heel and disappeared as silently as she had come.

Heartless hag, Masterson thought. Can't stand her. Can't *stand* her! But at least it was over, for a while anyway. It was over, and now he could relax and try to soothe—

"Dr. M., do you still want me to play this song again? I've got twenty minutes left in my lesson, and Mom won't like it if I tell her you didn't give me my full hour's worth."

Masterson felt his canines drilling into his molars. Sartre was right, wasn't he? Hell is other people. And St. Benedict's, alas, was full of other people.

"BEN KINCAID FOR the defense, your honor. Waive reading, plead not guilty, request release on bail."

Canelli, standing beside Ben at the bench, snorted. "You've gotta be kidding."

"Is that your legal argument? Because if it is, you need a new research intern."

Judge Pitcock, his eyes busily scanning the arraignment papers before him, ignored the banter. "This is a capital murder case, right, counsel?"

"That's the charge, sir," Ben replied. "At least, until the preliminary hearing."

"Murder in the first degree," the judge murmured. He glanced over at Father Beale, who was sitting at the table behind Ben. He arched an eyebrow. "Bail?"

"Yes, your honor. Absolutely. This is not your run-of-the-mill murder case."

"I hope I never get to the point where I perceive any murder case as run-of-the-mill."

"Of course you're right, your honor. Let me explain." Ben paused, using a deep breath as an excuse to slow down and think. He had to approach this argument carefully. Judge Pitcock, Ben knew, was not your standard issue hardcase war-on-crime judge. He was a reasonable man, a family man, a practicing Mormon. He believed in redemption, both in the church and in the courtroom. Ben liked him and was thrilled when he learned that he had been assigned to the Beale case. In Tulsa, Oklahoma, Pitcock was about as good as it got for defense attorneys.

Pitcock's soft spot, as a general rule, was the sanctity of the family. Over the years, Ben had learned that he had a chance of persuading the man of almost anything if he could couch the argument in terms of the sanctity of the family. As in: Yes, your honor, he stole a loaf of bread, but it was to feed his starving family. Or: Your honor, if you give him the maximum, it will do irreparable damage to the psychological well-being of his six children. Or even: Yes, your honor, he robbed a bank—everyone makes mistakes—but he's a very loving and attentive father. . . .

The present case didn't immediately lend itself to this approach. But Ben had a theory. . . .

"Yes, sir. I'm quite serious about asking for bail. As I'm sure your honor is already aware, we're not dealing with a hardened criminal here. We're not taking about someone who ran a meth lab or hustled prostitutes. We're talking about a priest. A man of God. There's a bit of a difference."

"I have to disagree," Canelli said, predictably inserting himself into Ben's argument. His enormous height advantage made him seem to tower over Ben. "This man committed a murder."

"Accused," Ben inserted harshly.

"Probably two," Canelli continued. "As soon as that happened, he became a criminal, no better than the punk running the meth lab or hustling prostitutes."

"This is not the place to argue guilt or innocence," Ben said. "This is an arraignment, not a trial. And what I'm saying is, the risks that are normally attendant to anyone accused of murder simply do not apply here. Even the prosecution is not suggesting that this man is a psychopath or sociopath. Even viewing their evidence in the most favorable light—which takes some doing—their theory is that he was pressured and pressured and finally lost his temper—hardly a situation likely to occur again. He has strong ties to the community—the strongest possible, I would argue. He is well known and has many friends and connections throughout the city. The risk of flight is virtually zero."

Judge Pitcock nodded thoughtfully. He ran his fingers through his thinning hair. His hair was pure white—prematurely so, given that he was only a few years older than Ben. In most situations, that would have been a detriment, but for a judge, it was an asset. It seemed to give him the sense of seniority, the gravitas, that a young man might otherwise have lacked. "I hear what you're saying, counsel. But still—the charge is first-degree murder and—"

"Let me say one thing more, your honor, if I may."

Pitcock shrugged. "You may speak, but I really don't—"

"I know that in the past we've talked about the importance of the family, and the sanctity of the family unit, and you've very candidly expressed your concerns about what's happening in this modern world, how the family is being torn apart by outside forces that sometimes seem unstoppable and irresistible. Because I know you're sincere in your beliefs, and because I know you're the kind of judge who means what he says, I must urge you to allow bail to issue in this case."

A crease appeared in the center of the judge's forehead. "Is Father Beale a family man?"

Canelli inched forward. "He has a wife, sir. No children."

"Then I don't understand—"

"Your honor," Ben continued, "I would suggest that Father Beale has the largest family, the most important family—and the most threatened family—in our modern community. Because his family is the church. His family is the four hundred and thirteen people that compose the parish of St. Benedict's. These are the people who look up to Father Beale, who love and respect him"—Ben worked mightily to maintain a straight face—"who look to him for spiritual guidance. His family is the family of God. Is there any family more important?"

Canelli looked disgusted. "Oh, puh-lese—"

Ben ignored him. "As your honor well knows, in this modern, seemingly godless world, the church is being attacked from all directions. Assaults on faith—and those who have it—have become so commonplace that we almost don't even notice. Some people have already perceived the arrest of Father Beale—on the thinnest of evidence—as an assault by an atheistic and amoral government on the traditional church. And now, if Father Beale is torn away from his flock at the time of its greatest need, it will do irreparable damage to that little church. It will do irreparable damage to the community of God." Ben stepped forward. "I urge this court—indeed, I implore it, not to let that happen."

Both attorneys stared straight ahead, trying to read the judge's professionally inscrutable face. Seconds ticked by like hours. Pitcock rattled the papers on his desk, read and reread, frowned. He stared across the courtroom at Father Beale, in his orange coveralls, seated at the table behind the attorneys, flanked by two men from the sheriff's office.

Finally he spoke. "Will you wear a collar?"

Ben knew Father Beale would understand what the judge meant; Ben had briefed him on the possibility of being released with the proviso that he wear an electronic tracing collar that would allow the sheriff's office to monitor his location at all times.

Father Beale slowly rose to his feet. "I already wear one collar," he said, with a faint trace of a smile. "Why not another?"

"Good." Pitcock reached for his gavel. "Counsel, I am persuaded by some of your remarks that this case does require special consideration. What's more—I'm moved by your thoughtful and eloquent argument. We are dealing here with a trusted counselor in whom many have invested their faith, and even when faced with charges that seem . . ." He paused, glancing at Canelli. " . . . difficult to believe with regard to the defendant in question, some special accommodation seems appropriate. The court rules that bail will issue in this case, with the requirement that the defendant wear an electronic tracing unit at all times. Any attempt to remove the collar, or to leave the fifty-mile radius of its effective range, will result in the immediate and permanent revocation of bail."

Canelli leaned forward, obviously agitated. "Is there going to be a financial requirement?"

"From a priest?" Pitcock looked at him as if he were some sort of bug. "The court has ruled. This arraignment is concluded. The court is in recess." He banged the gavel, then excused himself out the back door of the courtroom.

As soon as the judge was gone, Canelli whipped around to confront Ben. "I thought I'd seen it all, Kincaid, but this has got to be an all-time low, even for you. Playing the God card."

"I'm just doing my job, Canelli."

"In the sleaziest possible way."

"Don't be a sore loser."

"You'll resort to anything, won't you?"

"I'll use the natural and obvious argument in my client's favor, yes." He turned and began repacking his briefcase.

"You embarrassed me in front of the judge. I won't forget that."

"If you'll recall, Canelli, I tried to work this out with you privately, before the arraignment, but you were too hardheaded to listen. I was trying to talk sense, and you were giving me your I'm-on-a-mission-from-God routine."

"I'm filing a motion *in limine* today, Kincaid. I'm not going to let you drag God into the trial."

"Oh, heaven forbid that."

"This case is going to be tried on its merits. And your . . . your *man of God* is going to pay for his crimes. I'll be damned if I'll let you get away with your little tricks again!" Canelli marched out of the courtroom.

Ben glanced over at the table. Father Beale, of course, had been listening to every word. "I'm sorry you had to hear that diatribe."

"Not at all," Beale replied. He was remarkably calm, given all that had been said about him in the last ten minutes. "I found it most illuminating. Are all prosecutors like him?"

"No. He's one of the better ones."

"In a way, it's very encouraging. Think about it—we put a Catholic, an Episcopalian, and a Mormon in a room together. And we still managed to get something accomplished. And no one was killed."

Ben clicked his briefcase shut. "The important thing is, you're out of jail. You can return to your church."

"Yes." He almost smiled. "Won't the vestry be delighted?"

"No comment." Ben tilted his head toward the door. "C'mon, Father. Let's go pick out your new collar."

8

JOHN PHILLIP CRATER never intended to become a social activist. He was a simple unpretentious man who grew up on a small farm in Muskogee. His family was always poor. One summer their house burned down and the whole family lived in a boxcar. He left home when he was old enough and set out to make something of himself. At first, he took what work he could find. He'd been a truck driver, farmer, ore mine assessor, auto mechanic, Dairy Queen cashier. But he never stopped trying to better himself. Twenty years after he left home he was the senior vice-president of ITT Financial. Then he started his own commercial finance company and was partnering in multimillion-dollar deals with major entertainment corporations. He'd done all right, although you would never hear him say that. He'd taken good care of his wife, Deb, and his three children. He'd made his mark in the world. But social activism? No. That just wasn't part of his life.

Until his next-door neighbor's girl got into trouble. In the classic sense. He hadn't held it against her; these things happened, even to sweethearts like Alison. And when she decided to terminate the fetus, even if he didn't much like the decision, he resolved that he would stick by her, right or wrong. It was her decision.

But no one had the right to do what happened next. Some pro-life organization got a hold of her name and published it in a newspaper advertisement. They held public meetings downtown, flashing her name and others on their roll of "murderers." She was publicly embarrassed and humiliated. She still did what she had to do—although she went to another state to do it—but the toll on her was profound. She had a total mental breakdown. Even now, years later, after she'd been released from the institution in Norman, she wasn't the same. She wasn't the beautiful girl he'd known before. She was something different, and something . . . less.

And he didn't blame the abortion, although that was undoubtedly traumatic enough. It was those zealots who thought they had the right to single out and destroy Alison, just to make a petty point that was already apparent to everyone. Just to deny her the right to decide for herself what to do with her own body.

Two weeks after she'd gone into the institution, John had joined the South Central pro-choice organization, and he hadn't missed a meeting since, regardless of how busy he was, where he was, or how many religious zealots were marching outside, shouting obscenities, showing horrible pictures, throwing blood. He didn't let anything stop him.

Including tonight. But he was running late, he realized, glancing at his watch. Walking, so he could get some air, had been a good idea in principle. But he was going to have to walk a little faster. . . .

"Going to the meeting?"

That broke John's stride. He stopped, looking all around him. It was dark out, and since this part of the apartment grounds was dark and spotted with trees, he had trouble locating the source of the voice. "Is someone there?"

"Oh yeah." A man stepped out of the shadows, someone John did not recognize. He was a thick, sizable man. He looked strong.

"Do I know you?"

"You're about to." The man came close, much too close, especially for someone John didn't know. "You're going to the PCSC meeting, right?"

"As a matter of fact, I am." He tried not to be intimidated, but the man cut an imposing figure, particularly when silhouetted across John's face. "May I ask why this is any of your concern?"

"You're going to meet with the other babykillers."

John felt a chill race down his spine. "Look, I don't know who you are—"

"I'm a friend of the unborn."

John felt his anger rising, and it helped him overcome his growing panic. "We're not going to be intimidated by your bullyboy tactics. I have a right to hold different beliefs than you, and I'm not going to—"

The man shoved him back hard. "If anyone should be accused of bullyboy tactics, it should be you and the rest of your murdering friends. Have you no shame?"

"I don't think this is the place to discuss these complex issues."

"Like what? Like the fact that we want to save lives, and the rest of you want to kill unborn babies? You're murderers, every one of you. You should be punished accordingly."

Okay, John thought, now he was scared. He tried to brush past the man. "Look, let me get on—"

The man grabbed his arm, clutching it so tightly it hurt. "You don't get off that easy."

John tried to shake free—unsuccessfully. "Just let me go. If I don't appear at the meeting soon, they'll—"

"I don't think so." He grabbed John's other arm and squeezed just as tightly. "You're so fond of killing. Let's see how you like it."

The first blow caught John beneath the chin, shattering his jaw. He clutched it with both hands, as if trying to hold himself together. He fell to his knees, but not before the second blow crushed his nose. Blood spurted out, covering his face and hands and neck. He had never been a fighter, not even in grade school, and he lacked even the most fundamental means of defending himself. A quick kick between the legs sent him reeling forward on his hands and knees, broken, like a pathetic oblationer prostrating himself before a cruel god. After that, one kick after another rained down on his ribs and stomach, so fast and furious he couldn't keep track. All he could feel was the immense pain, like nothing he had ever experienced in his entire life. He would have cried out for mercy, if he could have mustered the strength, and when at last he lost consciousness, it was the sweet release for which he would have prayed, if he could still believe that any God would permit such cruelty to be visited upon one of His children.

INSIDE HIS SMALL single-story home, Manly Trussell wiped the blood off his hands and arms. In the fifteen minutes it had taken him to run home, some of it had congealed and matted with the hair on his arms, creating an awful mess.

"Is it done?" Manly's newfound friend had come inside. Not that that was particularly surprising.

"Oh yeah. It's done."

"Good boy. Did you . . . deliver your message?"

"I think he got the point." He grabbed a towel off the rack. "Loud and clear."

"And he'll pass it along to the others?"

"If he lives." He winced slightly as he scraped the blood off his hands and face.

"You seem . . . disturbed."

"A little, yeah."

"Surely you're not losing your nerve. After all that time belittling those who would talk but wouldn't act. Are you going to become one of them?"

"No. I'm not. But still . . . that man was seriously hurt."

His friend considered this for a moment. "Have you studied the Crusaders?"

"Yeah, sure. I'm mean, not really . . ."

"The Crusaders were dispatched to the Holy Land, something like eight hundred years ago, to deliver sacred sites from the hands of the infidels. They were forced to fight, even to kill. Hundreds and hundreds of the Saracen heathens fell before the swords of the Crusaders. And yet, history remembers them as great heroes. There is no doubt that they were doing God's will. And so are you."

"I know." He threw the towel down on the floor. "Still . . . it's hard."

The friend laid a hand on Manly's shoulder. "Of course it is. Which is why not just anyone can do it. Why God needs you. The day of the Crusader has not passed. God still requires soldiers. And he will save them a sacred seat at his right hand in heaven."

Manly's resolve appeared to return. "I was being weak. Indulging myself. It won't happen again."

His friend clapped him on the shoulders. "Good. What next then?"

"Next?" Manly lifted his chin. His eyes glistened as he pressed one strong fist against the other. "We carry on God's work."

9

"YOU HAVE GOT to be kidding me!" Jones paced around Ben, etching a well-worn circular track into the office carpet. "I don't believe it!"

"Take a chill pill, Jones," Ben replied. "It's just a case."

"Just a case? Just a case?" He pounded his forehead with the palm of his hand. "I was gone for four days. Four lousy days! A guy can't even go on his honeymoon without someone torpedoing the firm while he's away!"

"I think you're exaggerating. . . ."

"Do you? Do you really? Did you even consider the financial ramifications of this case before you accepted it?"

"Well . . ."

"I thought after that disaster with the Blackwell parents we had an agreement. No one was going to accept any unduly risky or expensive cases without it being put to a vote of the entire staff."

Ben squirmed. "I don't see this case as being all that expensive . . ."

"Oh, this is going to be one of our bargain-basement capital murder defenses? Have you mentioned that to your client?" He threw his hands up into the air. "Nothing personal, Boss, but as my grandmother used to say, you don't have a lick of sense. Which is why I'm the office manager. And you're not."

"I also don't see the case as being particularly risky. . . ."

"You don't? Well, let me explain it to you." He swiveled Ben's chair around to face him. "Your client is the chief suspect in two murders. He's already been crucified in the press. Everyone in town thinks he's guilty, including the prospective jurors, whoever they may be. He was seen arguing with the last victim minutes before she turned up dead. He was seen with her blood on his hands. His fingerprints were found on the murder weapon." He grabbed Ben's shoulders and shook them. "Does this case sound winnable to you?"

Ben shrugged. "I've seen worse."

Jones pounded his head against the chair. "I've already heard the flak on the streets. Every lawyer in town thinks you're going down in flames."

"Then everyone in town is wrong. Father Beale did not commit those murders. And we will get him off. We have to."

"And may I ask how this priest, whose salary is even punier than mine, is supposed to pay our fees?"

Ben coughed. "Well . . . I was really perceiving this case as more of a . . . a . . . more of a pro bono thing. . . ."

"Aaaargh!" Jones threw himself against Ben's desk. "Why am I not surprised?"

"I am hoping he'll be able to cover some of his expenses."

"Oh, well, wouldn't that be dandy?" Jones stared at the carpet. "I can't stand it. I just can't stand it!"

At that opportune moment, Christina sailed through the front office doors. She took one look, then spoke. "What's wrong?"

Jones lifted his head. "Christina, is there some kind of twelve-step program for attorneys addicted to unwinnable cases?"

She smiled. "Welcome back, Jones. We missed you."

"We missed you? What is that? Some kind of patronizing remark? Why do I get the impression that no one is taking me seriously?"

"I can't imagine." She patted him on the head. "Now you run along and play. Mommy needs to talk to Daddy."

Jones threw up his hands and stomped over to his desk.

Ben pushed himself out of his chair. "How did the oral argument in the Wooley case go?"

"Well, at least we managed to avoid summary judgment. We'll be going to trial. But it still looks like my man breached the contract."

"Have you got a defense?"

"Yup. Bad faith."

Ben nodded. As every first-year law student knew, a contract can be voided if one of the parties acted in bad faith, by making misrepresentations or failing to disclose material facts. "Made the house sound a bit nicer than it really was?"

"No. Failure to inform. The roof suffered a lot of hail damage between the final showing and the closing. Seller forgot to mention that." She tossed a newspaper down on the desk. "Read about the guy who got beaten up on his way to a pro-choice meeting?" She shook her head. "Is it just me, or do there seem to be more creeps, scumbags, and psychopaths out there every day?"

"It's not just you. But at the moment, we have to focus on uncovering the creep, scumbag, or psychopath who killed Kate McGuire."

Out of the corner of his eye, Ben saw some movement at the front door. He greeted Father Beale and his wife, Andrea. Beale was in his usual priestly regalia, black suit with white clerical collar. Ben knew that somewhere under all that he was also wearing another collar—an electronic one—but happily, it didn't show.

Andrea fidgeted with her hands and seemed nervous. That was not altogether surprising; most people were when they visited a lawyer's office for the first time.

Ben shook her hand. "Thank you for coming, Andrea. I can imagine how hard all this must be for you."

She did not disagree. "Daniel wanted me to be here."

"I wanted you to be here, too," Ben said. "But I didn't know if I would get my wish. Sometimes I think criminal prosecutions are harder on the spouses than the defendants."

Again, the woman did not disagree.

"Nonetheless, I'm glad you could come."

Her head nodded slightly. She glanced quickly at her husband, then back at Ben, then answered, simply, "I didn't have any choice."

FIVE MINUTES LATER, everyone was assembled in the main conference room—Ben, Christina, Jones, Loving, and Father Beale and his wife. Ben decided to plow right into the heart of the matter. Difficult though it might be, this was not the kind of occasion that lent itself to icebreakers. The best he could hope for was to get the work done as efficiently and painlessly as possible.

"I still haven't been able to get the straight scoop on the forensic evidence," Ben reported to all present. "But I'm convinced they have more that they've said—or think they do, anyway."

"Can't you file a motion to produce?" Christina asked.

"Already done. And they will eventually answer. But not any sooner than is absolutely necessary. They know the trial date is fast approaching, and since most of their work is done and ours is just beginning, they know that time is on their side."

"I don't understand," Father Beale said. "Why play games with the evidence?"

Even Loving could answer that one. " 'Cause prosecutors like to win."

"But this isn't a game," Beale replied. "This is a forum of justice. Both sides should work together to arrive at the truth."

"A noble sentiment," Ben said. "But unfortunately, not the way it works. At least not here in the good ol' US of A." He glanced down at his notes. "We do know that they have some compelling fingerprint evidence. And we know they have many witnesses prepared to testify against you. Some of them"—he cleared his throat—"some of them are members of your parish."

"Can't say that I'm surprised," Beale mused. "So what do we do?"

"Well, it goes without saying, the most wonderful thing we could do would be to discover who the killer really is."

"Any chance of that actually happenin'?" Loving asked.

"Not without a lot of legwork. Which is where you come into the picture. And Jones." He glanced at his office manager, who was still fuming. "And Paula, too, if she's got time."

"She has time," Jones said. "And needs extra work. Since her husband will soon be declaring bankruptcy!"

"Where do we start?" Loving asked.

"I hope you'll forgive me for saying this, Father," Ben answered, "but I think we begin at the church. Both victims have been church members—members of the vestry, in fact. All indications, therefore, are that the killer has some connection to the church. We have to start our investigation there."

"Got it," Loving said. "Any idea who the likely suspects are?"

"Not really. But I've made a list of the most prominent names— the other members of the vestry, the leaders of the various departments and committees. It's a starting place, anyway. You're going to

have to talk with everyone, see what they think, see what you can uncover. That goes for both murders. The DA has only charged Father
Beale on the second murder, because that's where they have their evidence. But common sense suggests that they're connected. So if we
can learn something about the first one, we may also learn something
about the second. Problem is—I know these people. I'm not objective, and they probably wouldn't talk to me openly, anyway. So I'm
going to have to pass the buck to you."

"I'll get right on it," Loving said.

"And I'll help," Christina added.

"That's fine." It was more than fine; Christina was a good inter-
rogator and had an instinctive understanding of most people she met.
"But I'm going to need your lawyering skills, too. There will be countless motions and oral arguments and discovery hassles before this case
is completed."

"No problem. I specialize in multitasking."

"Marvelous." He turned his attention to the other end of the table. "Jones, I'd like you and Paula to do some deep background
checks, both on the church itself and the parishioners. Start with the
two victims and the names on my list."

"What am I looking for?"

"How should I know? Anything suspicious. Any dark secrets. And
especially anything that might give someone a motive for murder."

"We'll do our best. And after that?"

"Well . . . don't get too excited. But I think this may be another
case where you actually need to get out into the field and do some
legwork."

Jones's eyes widened. "Me? Really?"

"Absolutely." With Paula at your side, he thought, to keep you
from getting yourself killed. "There are too many tangled webs in
this case. Loving can't possibly unravel them all."

"I agree that we may need some outside help on this one, Skipper," Loving said. "Do we have a budget for additional investigators?"

"Well . . ." Ben tried not to look at Jones. "Do whatever you need
to do."

"I could use an intern on some of this legal briefing," Christina
said. "Especially if I'm going out in the field during the critical pretrial period."

"Get whoever you need."

"That's just great," Jones said. "And since our budget is unlimited, maybe we could fly in a team from the Mayo Clinic to take DNA samples from the communion cup!"

Ben's neck stiffened. "Look, we will do anything we can to win this case."

Father Beale edged forward. "You sound as if you may have some idea what really happened."

"I wish I did," Ben replied. "But I don't. Suspicions, yes. But facts, no. That's what we have to remedy. The fact is, we have more than just two murders taking place in a church here. We have two murders committed in such a way that it was inevitable that you would become Suspect Number One. I know I've asked you before, Father, but—do you have any idea why anyone would want to frame you?"

Beale shook his head. "Granted, I know there are many people who want me out of the church. But to resort to this—"

"It's politics."

The two words, though spoken barely louder than a whisper, riveted the attention of everyone in the room. It came from Father Beale's heretofore silent wife, Andrea.

"Excuse me?" Christina said.

"It's all politics. Religious politics, true. But it's still politics. These people have been trying to get Daniel out for months. They're willing to do anything—anything at all. So when ordinary means didn't work—they turned to extraordinary means."

"You're sayin' they killed two people just to get a new man behind the pulpit?" Loving scowled. "Sorry, but I have a hard time buyin' that."

"You wouldn't, if you'd been married to a priest as long as I have. People have been murdered for much stupider reasons."

Ben found himself shocked to hear such strong words—about churchgoers—coming from the previously subdued woman. "But these people, let's remember, think they're doing the work of God. They consider themselves crusaders, fighting evil for a holy cause. The God of the Old Testament never hesitated to spill a little blood to get what he wanted. Why should they?"

"Still," Ben said, "that seems an extreme reaction to doctrinal disputes."

"Does it really? Think about it. Daniel has been active in every major social issue since the sixties—and that has seriously ticked off a lot of people. Daniel marched with Dr. King in Selma—did you know that? He was at the forefront of the Oklahoma ERA movement. Now he's gotten himself involved in the gay rights movement—and how many Oklahoma rednecks have committed acts of violence against gays? How many murders have been committed by pro-life crazies? Face it—many people take these issues to heart—and are willing to commit murder in support of their beliefs."

"Do you have anyone in particular in mind?" Ben asked.

"Where to begin? I think at least half the vestry would be capable of it. Especially that superzealot, Susan Marino. She'd do anything to get rid of Daniel. She'd kill her own mother if she thought it would help."

Father Beale frowned. "Andrea. I don't think—"

She ignored him. "And what about that witch, Ernestine Rupert? She thinks she owns the church and everyone in it. Probably figures she has the right to murder anyone she wants."

Again Beale interrupted. "Ernestine is in her late sixties."

"Then she would hire someone to do it."

"Really—"

"Oh, stop it, Daniel. She's a horrible person, and you know it as well as I do. The only restraint on her willingness to swing her money around like a club is that nephew of hers, and he can't do much, scurrying around like her indentured servant. I know you like to think the best of everyone—or act like you do, anyway—but this is serious. You're on trial for your life."

Ben moved quickly to cover the awkward moment. "Anyone else you think is a possible suspect?"

"As I said, the list is too long to mention. Don't forget that egomaniac music minister. He's been at odds with Daniel since we came to St. Benedict's. Probably still nursing a grudge because Daniel wouldn't let him sing 'Amazing Grace' at the Christmas service or something. And what about the rest of the vestry? These are magnificently petty people, all shouting *Peace be with you* while they plot to get rid of their priest!"

Beale took her hand and squeezed it. "Andrea. Please."

She yanked her hand away. "I'm not going to let them do this to you without a fight, Daniel. And I'm certainly not going to let them throw you in jail—or worse—without giving your lawyers the information they need to fight them."

"I appreciate your candor," Ben said. "Any time you have information you think might even conceivably be of use to us, please don't hesitate to let us know."

She settled back and folded her arms across her chest. "I've been married to Daniel for over ten years. Some of those years have been better than others. There have been things I—I—didn't exactly enjoy. Or approve of. But I don't—I—I can't conceive of a life without him."

Ben tried to sound reassuring. "We're not going to let it come to that, Andrea."

"Absolutely," Christina echoed.

"Your husband did not commit this crime," Ben said. He broadened his gaze, bringing everyone at the table into view. "And we are not going to let him be convicted. We will win this case." He paused, then looked at each of his staff members in turn. "We will."

10

The Gospel According to Daniel

As a theologian and a former philosophy major, I'm aware that most of the great minds of human history have written about "home" at one time or another.

Robert Frost: "Home is the place where, when you have to go there, they have to take you in."

Thomas Wolfe: "You can't go home again."

And, of course, the greatest of them all, Dorothy Gale: "There's no place like home."

But today, as I sit down to write a few words on the subject, I find I have mixed feelings—and mixed definitions—regarding the elusive word. Most people would assume that the house Andrea and I shared on Sandusky would be my home, but to me, in both my heart and mind, home was St. Benedict's. It was there I felt most relaxed, most comfortable. It was there I did my most important work. The house on Sandusky was chosen by a Realtor; my home at St. Benedict's was chosen by God. St. Benedict's—during the good times— gave me a sense of contentment and fulfillment far more intense than the ambiguous signals that often attended the tiny cottage on Sandusky. At St. Benedict's, I felt closer to myself, and as a result, closer to God.

Therefore, despite all that had gone before, and some might say, despite all common sense, I looked forward to my return to St. Benedict's after my brief all-expenses-paid sabbatical courtesy of the Tulsa Sheriff's Department. I naively thought that with the worst behind us, we could begin to rebuild, to do God's work. I saw it as a fresh beginning.

Alas, I was the only one. None of my detractors had altered their opinions in the least; to the contrary, their animosity had intensified, something I would not have thought possible. Even those who had previously been my supporters did little to welcome me back; they seemed weary of the fight, more than ready to admit defeat and end the protracted power struggle. Indeed, more than one of my most ardent advocates suggested that it might be best for all concerned—for me and the church—if I resigned. Why protract the misery? they would say. Why involve the church in a high profile criminal prosecution? Everyone seemed convinced that this was the time when I should finally throw in the collar and call it quits.

Except me. I wouldn't hear of it. I have been called to this church, I must've said a million times. The bishop installed me here to do God's work. Who am I to say that His will should not be done? Did Job quit when he was persecuted? Did Christ? Of course not. They survived their tests—for that is what this surely must be— and went on to do great work. To be cherished messengers of the Word of God. I would do the same. I would not betray my divine commission.

That was my thinking at the time, at any rate. Now, looking back on it after so much has happened, I wonder if my reaction had more to do with ego than religion. No doubt the role of the Christian martyr appealed to me subconsciously, particularly when there was so much trauma in my life. It was all a matter of where I mentally pictured myself, of what I called home. Did I prefer to locate myself in the cottage on Sandusky, with a wife who had never really accepted the lifestyle I adopted—we adopted? Was it in the political arena of St. Benedict's, arguing with the vestry and disputing even the most minor points of theology and liturgy? Or was it on the cross, suffering with my Savior? What would I choose? What would anyone who perceived himself as a man of God choose?

Viewed through the refracted light of memory, my choices made a sort of irrational sense. But now, after all I have seen and experienced, and in the light of the tragedy that has befallen, I can see myself for the fool I was. And am.

*   *   *

BEN FELT AS if he must be carrying a magnetic charge, because as soon as he stepped through the front doors of the church, everyone began to gravitate toward him.

Ernestine, being squired as usual by her puffball nephew, reached him first. "If you're looking for your client," she said sniffily, "he's in his office. Alone."

"Thanks. But I'm just here for choir practice."

Alvin Greene, the Altar Guild man, rose up behind Ben. "Is it true? Is he going to stand trial?"

"It's true," Ben said ruefully.

Ruth O'Connell tottered beside Ernestine. "Isn't there anything we can do to end this?"

"No, I'm afraid—"

"Do you mean end the trial," Ernestine asked, "or the occupation of our church by this priest?"

"Now, Aunt Ernestine," Bruce said, patting her hand. "Let's not be testy."

"I'm sixty-seven years old," she said sharply. "I can be testy if I want to be. Go fetch me some lemonade."

"Aunt Ernestine, I—"

"And hurry. My throat is dry."

"Yes, Aunt Ernestine." He slinked away down the corridor.

The questions continued to fly. "What evidence do they have against him?" "Do you think you can get him off?" "Is the DA seeking the death penalty?"

Ben was reminded of the "Heal thyself" crowd Jesus had to bust loose from. He held up his hands, backing away. "Please," he said. "I'm not here to be a lawyer. Or to hold a press conference. I'm just here for choir practice."

"I don't see that it hurts you to answer a few questions," Ruth said.

Ben didn't care. He was already halfway down the corridor, scrupulously not making eye contact with anyone he met. He passed Father Beale's office and could see through the glass windows that he was in. He was seated in the chair behind his desk, all by himself. He didn't appear to be working or reading or anything. Just thinking. Staring at the wall and thinking. Ben couldn't guess what he might be thinking about—and didn't want to. The possibilities at this point were all too painful.

Ben continued down the corridor, ducked inside the choir room, and closed the door behind him.

Practice had not yet begun; most of his fellow choristers were standing around chatting. Masterson, the minister of music, saw Ben and headed his way.

"We have two new members tonight," Masterson whispered. A small smile danced on his lips. "And I believe I have you to thank for it."

Ben's eyes swept across the room, searching for the newcomers. It didn't take long. Two pink painted fingernails waggled at him in front of two tightly braided pigtails.

Judy. With her friend Maura.

"A little young for the adult choir, aren't they?" Ben asked.

"Not really," Masterson answered. "I've always welcomed teenagers. I just never got any. Until now. Thanks to you."

"I doubt if I had anything to do with it."

"Oh? Then why are they both insisting on singing in the tenor section?"

Masterson wandered away to his piano and began pulling out bolts of sheet music. Judy skittered down from the back row, Maura close at her heels.

"Ben! Ben!" Judy leaned forward conspiratorially. "Everyone in the church is all abuzz about Father Beale and the trial."

"I'm sure it will blow over soon enough. I'd recommend you concentrate on more interesting subjects."

"Are you kidding? This is the most exciting thing that's happened to this church since—well, ever. Have you been investigating?"

"Well . . ."

"When you investigate, do you wear disguises? Or do you prefer to stake people out?"

If only a lawyer's life was as exciting as it seemed to a fifteen-year-old girl, Ben mused. "I have a private investigator who does most of that sort of thing," Ben explained.

"Does he use disguises?"

"Oh, yes," Ben said, trying not to laugh. "And accents and wardrobe. He has eighteen different ways of limping. He's a veritable Laurence Olivier."

"Way cool. Can I go on a stakeout with you sometime?"

Ben shook his head. "I don't think your mother would approve of that."

Judy snorted. "I don't think she'd ever notice."

"I hardly think—"

"I want to help you, Ben. I feel it's my duty to uncover the truth, being a member of this church and all."

Maura giggled. "She just wants to get close to you."

Judy jabbed her hard enough to leave a bruise. "I'd like to see you in the courtroom. I mean live, in person. It would be good experience. Like I told you, I want to be a lawyer someday."

"Then the best thing you can do is read good books and concentrate on your schoolwork. Going on stakeouts won't get you there."

"But I need field experience!"

"All in good time." Over her shoulder, he saw that Masterson had approached his music stand and was ready to begin. "We'd better get into our places."

"All right," Judy said. "But don't forget. Next time there's a big stakeout, I want to go!"

"I'll make a note."

MASTERSON, TO HIS credit, managed to get through the rehearsal without so much as a mention of the murders or the trial. He did announce that they would be able to sing certain favored tunes that previously had been unavailable—no doubt an oblique reference to the fact that Father Beale had other things to do at the present than police the hymn list. But that was it. He took them through the songs in his usual professional manner. They ran through all the hymns for next Sunday's service, then practiced the anthems they would sing during the offertory for the next three weeks. Next Sunday's was one of Ben's favorites—a tune called "The Gift of Love," based upon the traditional Celtic folk melody "The Water Is Wide." It was so beautiful it gave Ben chills, although the closing passage contained some high Fs and Gs that were out of his range, as well as that of most of the other tenors. Happily, tonight they had two teenage sopranos in the tenor section.

About three quarters of the way through the practice, Ben saw

Ernestine slip quietly out the door. An odd thing for a devoted cho-
rister to be doing, he thought. She had a determined expression on
her face; Ben felt certain she wasn't just going to the water fountain
or the bathroom. Something else was going on.

Thirty seconds later, he was out the door, too.

He stayed well behind her, out of sight. Fortunately, there weren't
many places to go in a church building that wasn't that large, so it
wasn't necessary to keep her in sight at all times. Given the direction
she was headed down the corridor, she could only be moving toward
the parish hall, the kitchen, or the Altar Guild office.

Ben casually eased over to an open door, hoping to get close enough
to hear what was being said without attracting undue attention. He
couldn't see them, but he could hear most of what they were saying.

Alvin Greene was speaking. He sounded agitated. "You have to
give me more time."

"I've already given you too much."

"But I need more!" Alvin was begging like a baby. "You don't
know what it's been like at home. Everything's been in turmoil. Joel
practically totaled his car, Julie got braces, our roof leaks. Pam has
been a wreck."

"I know something that would make her even more upset,"
Ernestine said quietly.

"Please!" Alvin said. "Please!"

But it did no good. Nothing was forthcoming. Except cold dead
silence.

"Oh, all right. All right!" The man was weeping now. Ben heard a
rustling denim sound; he guessed Alvin was pulling something out of
his pocket. More rustling, followed by a decided click.

"I'll be back for the rest," Ernestine said.

Alvin was still in tears. He could barely speak. "M-Maybe—
maybe next week—"

"I'll be back tomorrow."

Ben heard a squeaky heel that informed him Ernestine had made
a sharp pivot. He scrambled down the hall and around a corner. Rather
than be caught halfway down the corridor headed in the wrong direction, he reversed himself so she would meet him as soon as she rounded
the bend.

Which she did. "Is choir practice already over?" she asked.

Ben shook his head. "Not yet. I'm . . . not feeling well." He pointed toward the men's room.

She nodded, then passed brusquely by him, but not so quickly that Ben couldn't see that she had her little blue notebook clutched tightly in her right hand. Ben wondered how many names of the members of St. Benedict's appeared in that book. Because unless he was very mistaken, this woman was running a money-lending racket that would put Ebenezer Scrooge to shame.

11

LOVING HAD A strong hunch that talking to the two giggling girls in the parish hall was not going to accelerate his investigation, but no one else seemed to be around at the moment, and when you had a list of suspects to interview as long as the one in Loving's pocket, every second counted.

As he approached the table where they were folding acolyte robes, the giggling intensified. What? he wondered. Do I have something in my teeth? Is my fly unzipped?

"Maura likes your muscles," Judy explained, after the introductions were completed. "She thinks you're a hunk."

Maura slugged her hard enough to crack a rib. "Do not."

"She does. She's lusting after you. She wants to have your children."

"At least I'm not lusting after the lawyer," Maura retorted. "He doesn't have any muscles."

"Girls, girls," Loving said, suppressing a grin. "This is flatterin', but I'm a confirmed bachelor-type. Always have been."

"Maybe since your divorce," Judy replied. "Not before, obviously."

Loving did a double-take. "Now how on earth do you know about that?"

"Got it off the Internet," Maura explained. "She's read everything about Ben Kincaid and his friends and coworkers. She's head over heels about the guy."

Loving looked incredulous. "About the Skipper?"

"She is," Maura continued, being surprisingly garrulous. "She follows all his cases. She'd have his poster up over her bed, if he had one. Frankly, I don't see the attraction."

"Maybe I just prefer someone with brains over some big dumb hunk of muscles!" Judy said.

Loving tried not to take offense.

"Maybe I think there's more to love than a physical attraction!"

Maura was unimpressed. "Maybe you're afraid that if there isn't, you've got no hope!"

Loving frowned. "Now that seems kinda harsh."

"Oh, I don't mind," Judy said. "Normally Maura doesn't say anything at all. She's just talking now because she's desperate to impress you because she wants to be your love puppy."

"Judy!"

Loving held up his hands. "Girls, please! Personally, I love all this Truth-or-Dare stuff, but I'm kinda busy right now. Could either of you tell me where I might find Alvin Greene? He doesn't seem to be in the Altar Guild office."

Judy checked her watch. "It's after five. I'd try the White Swan."

"What's that? Some kind of prayer meeting?"

Judy laughed. "It's a bar. Well, a pub, technically. Very British. As you may know, all Episcopalians are closet Anglophiles. They love all that Old World steak-and-kidney-pie fake accent stuff. Of course, they don't like to admit that's the real reason they're Episcopalians, but honestly, why else would anyone want to be an Episcopalian?"

Loving decided not to engage in this dubious theological discussion. "Can you give me directions?"

"Of course." She grabbed a piece of scrap paper and started to draw. "By the way, stick with the Bass Ale. That Guinness stuff is really nasty."

Loving peered down at the fifteen-year-old girl. "And how would you know, may I ask?"

Judy winked as she handed him the map she had drawn. "Oh, I get around. I'm very worldly."

THE WHITE SWAN was, as advertised, the spitting image of a British pub. The walls bore a dark wood finish, decorated with pictures of soccer matches and fox hunts. The dining room was furnished with cozy little round tables, all laden with bottles of vinegar and HP Sauce.

Loving passed quickly through the restaurant area to the real center of action. The bar was a big brass affair, imported from a Manchester saloon dating back to the 1870s, according to a plaque on the wall. The room was packed and then some; almost all the seats were taken, and at least twenty more people were standing. The room was thick with smoke, the only drawback from the otherwise charming image. Loving didn't like to admit it, because it didn't go with his rough-and-tumble rep, but he hated smoking. He didn't do it (anymore), and he didn't like to be around people who did. For that matter, he wasn't that crazy about bars. There had been a time . . . but why think about that? He'd made a whole new life for himself since he linked up with the Skipper. It was a good arrangement, because it had come at the right time and Loving liked and needed it.

He grinned. And Ben sure as hell needed him.

Well, he was burning daylight. He took a deep breath and plunged into the smoky fray. The sacrifices I make for the Skipper, he mused, not for the first time.

He saw several people he believed were members of St. Benedict's. Some he recognized from the wedding, some not. And he saw at least a dozen strong young men wearing matching jerseys—a soccer team, if he wasn't mistaken. And in the far corner, sitting by himself, was Alvin Greene.

Against all odds, there was an empty chair at his table. Apparently no one wanted to sit with Alvin this evening. After taking a look at the glum expression on the man's face, Loving could see why.

Loving introduced himself. Alvin didn't seem exactly pleased to see him, but he didn't chase him off, either. When you worked for an attorney, that was almost as good as an engraved invitation.

"Look like you've seen better days," Loving observed. Not exactly a probing question, but Loving conducted interviews a little differently than the Skipper—especially when they took place in bars. If he could loosen the guy up a bit, both verbally and liquidly, he was far more likely to get some useful information. "Money problems?"

Alvin looked up slightly. "How'd you know?"

"Aww, you've just got that look on your face." That, plus he read Ben's report on what he'd overheard at choir practice. "I've been there."

"Yeah?" This time Alvin's eyes remained off the table. "I never thought it would happen to me."

"It'll get better. It always does."

"Well, it sure as hell couldn't get much worse."

"Laid off?" Loving asked.

Alvin nodded. "Two months ago. And I've got three daughters and a son to support. Lost my wife to cancer a year back. Now one daughter needs braces, the other wants to go to Mexico for spring break, the boy wrecked his car . . ." He waved his hand in the air. "I just can't stand it."

"Got any prospects?"

"Not really. I came over from St. John's so I could fill this book-keeper vacancy. It pays a little, but I need a real job or I'm going straight down the tubes."

"Can you borrow?"

"Who'd lend money to me?"

"I know a guy," Loving answered. "Downtown. Mark Sloan. He's a good ol' boy. We're not talkin' Mafioso or usury rates. He's a straight shooter. And he likes to help good people who've just gotten themselves into a little trouble. I could put in a good word for you, if you want."

"Really?" Alvin sat up straight for the first time. "Man, that'd be great. I don't need much. Just something to get me through the next few months."

"I'll call my friend first thing in the morning. I'll bet you can work somethin' out."

Loving scribbled an address on the back of a napkin and Alvin took it. "Man, I didn't think there was a chance anyone would ever loan me money again."

"Why's that?"

"Oh, I just . . . I don't know. . . ."

" 'Cause you still owe Ernestine Rupert?"

Alvin's alcohol-impaired eyes seemed to gain their focus. "How do you know about that?"

"Hey, I'm an investigator. It's what I do."

"I didn't think anyone knew about that. Except Ernestine, of course."

"So she loaned you some money, and now she's callin' in your marker?"

Alvin hesitated a moment. "Something like that."

"The old bat leanin' on you pretty hard?"

Alvin wiped his hand across his forehead. "Like you wouldn't believe. She's done everything but send out some boys to break my thumbs."

"Sounds miserable."

"It is. Especially now, on top of everything else."

Loving waved at the bartender. A minute later, two pints of Bass Ale were headed their way. "You're talkin' about all the trouble at the church, right?"

Alvin took a deep swallow. "Yeah."

"What's your take on the murders?"

"I don't know. I just don't know."

Well, at least he didn't immediately blame Father Beale, like every other witness to whom Loving had spoken. "You know anybody who'd have any reason to kill those women?"

"No, I don't. I can't imagine. It doesn't make any sense. Kate was a lovely woman. Lovely. We went out a few times, after my wife died. Did you know that?"

"No, I didn't."

"Yeah. And you probably don't believe it, now that you've heard. A beautiful woman like that going out with a homunculus like me? Doesn't seem right, does it?"

"Oh, I don't know. . . ."

Alvin waved it away. "Don't bother. I know what I am. They were probably more pity dates than anything. Still . . . a man can't help but hope . . . even if he knows how unlikely it is." His eyes seemed to drift somewhere far away from the bar. "She let me kiss her, the last time. Only on the cheek. But still . . ."

"You musta been pretty torn up when she was killed."

His eyes remained fixed. "You could say that. Yeah."

"What about the other woman? Helen Conrad."

"Aw, I never dated her. She was married."

Loving almost smiled. "Do you know anyone who might've had a reason to kill her?"

"No. Makes no sense to me."

Loving would have to agree with him on that score, but he'd seen some strange things in the time he'd been working at the Kincaid factory. "So you don't think the murders had anything to do with the church?"

"Oh, I never said that."

"But then why—?"

Alvin seemed to withdraw back into himself. "I told you. I don't know."

"Alvin . . ."

"Don't hassle me."

"Alvin, you know somethin'. Somethin' you're not telling me."

"I don't. I don't know who the killer is."

"But you know somethin'! What is it?"

Alvin glanced back over one shoulder, then the other. "I've already said too much."

What the hell was going on here? "Gimme a hint, Alvin. Is it about some religious thing? Abortion? Evolution?"

"No, nothing like that."

"Then what?"

Alvin looked away. "I can't tell you. It's . . . secret."

"Secret? Churches aren't s'posed to have secrets!"

Alvin scoffed. "Don't be naive. All churches have secrets."

"They don't all have murders!"

Alvin pulled out his wallet and tossed some bills onto the table. "I have to go. I've said too much already."

Loving held out his arm to block the man's passage. "If you think I'm going to let you tease me and then just disappear, you've got another think coming."

"Let me pass."

"I can get your butt subpoenaed."

"Won't matter. I won't say anything."

"Alvin, tell me what you know!"

"No. Let me pass."

"No!"

"I have friends in here!"

Loving gazed at the man's stony face. This was a loser situation, of course. He had no way to make the man talk, especially not in a public place. He could only come out of a confrontation looking stupid. Like it or not, he would have to back down.

He reluctantly lowered his arm.

"Thank you," Alvin said. He began to walk away.

"I still can't believe it," Loving muttered, to himself as much as anyone. "I can't believe a church could have some secret so big no one will talk about it. Even after two people have been murdered."

Alvin paused. He stared down at the floor. And just before he plunged into the smoke and far away from Loving, he whispered: "You wouldn't believe what's going on in this church. You wouldn't believe it."

12

CHRISTINA LIKED TO think of herself as a paragon of feminine grace, but as she approached the front porch of Apartment 10B at 2952 South Peoria, she had a near-collision of a distinctly ungraceful nature. Just as she neared the front door, a tall woman wearing sunglasses and a hoodlike scarf came barreling out at about three times Christina's speed. A last-minute sidestep avoided a collision, but the woman was thrown off balance. She teetered sideways onto the steps, turned her ankle, and tumbled.

Christina knelt beside the woman, who was sprawled across the concrete walkway. To her credit, the woman had not cried out in pain, but the expression on her face suggested that her landing hadn't been all pillows and marshmallows, either. The fall had knocked off her sunglasses, and her face was familiar, but Christina couldn't quite place her. She was someone Christina had seen at St. Benedict's, though—someone she'd seen the day Kate McGuire was killed.

"Are you all right?"

The woman ran a quick inspection of her immediately accessible body parts. "Nothing broken, anyway."

"I'm sorry. I'm so clumsy sometimes."

The woman shook her head. "Not your fault. I was moving too fast."

Which was true, Christina was forced to admit. And which also raised a question: Why was the woman leaving the apartment of George Finley—the vestry member who supposedly lived alone—in such a hurry, her face hidden behind shades and scarf? At eight o'clock in the morning.

The woman struggled to push herself up.

"Let me help you," Christina said.

"No, no. I can manage," she replied, but Christina helped her just the same. "I need to be moving along."

At eight A.M.? On a Saturday? "Are you sure you shouldn't come inside and sit for a moment? Just until you've collected yourself?"

"No, really, I must be—"

"Susan?"

George Finley was standing in the open doorway. "Are you all right, Susan?"

Susan. That was it. Christina remembered now. This was Susan Marino, the new senior warden, now that Kate McGuire was dead.

"I'm fine, George."

"You don't look fine." He took her arm and steered her back toward the door.

"I'm okay. Really," she insisted, but George kept a firm hand on her arm. He turned and, for the first time, his eyes drank in the fact that there was a third person on the sidewalk.

"I'm Christina McCall," she said, extending her hand. "I'm the legal—the lawyer who called yesterday." It still required a conscious effort to keep from calling herself a legal assistant. Of course, she'd been a legal assistant for almost a decade and a lawyer for less than a year. "You said I could talk to you."

"Right," George said slowly. "I guess I wasn't expecting you quite so early."

No doubt, but Christina had learned it wasn't necessarily a bad thing to catch people when they weren't expecting you, as this morning was proving, big time. "Sorry. I have a lot of people to talk to, and only a little time till the trial begins."

George frowned, but accepted her story. "Very well. Come inside." He maintained his grip on Susan's arm and led both women into his apartment.

George's place was nice enough, for what it was—basically a modest-size midtown two-roomer. The furniture was adequate, if not extraordinary. Christina suspected he had probably taken the apartment prefurnished. The room was tidy—no underwear on the floor or thick layers of dust. Surprising, really, for a man his age who lived alone. If he did in fact live alone.

"How can I help you?" George asked Christina as he led Susan to the couch.

"As I told you on the phone," Christina said, seating herself in a nearby chair, "I'm working on Father Beale's defense. My associates and I are talking to all the prominent members of the church, trying to learn anything we can about what happened."

"I see," George said quietly.

"What can you tell me about the murdered women?"

George almost shrugged. "I think Father Beale killed them."

"But why?"

"Kate McGuire was his fiercest opponent in the church," Susan explained. "And she was the leader of the vestry. What's more, she was a strong, very effective, capable businesswoman. He knew she would eventually boot him out of the church."

"She hadn't had much luck so far."

"But she would. She hadn't been senior warden long, remember. She was a forceful woman who knew how to get what she wanted. It was just a matter of time."

"So you're saying he killed her—just to keep his job?"

"I'm not saying it was planned or anything," George explained. "The man has a temper like the wrath of God. He was seen fighting with her at the wedding, you know. I think his temper got out of hand. He lost control and grabbed the paperweight and killed her."

"What kind of person was Kate?"

Susan answered first. "Serious. Hardworking. Efficient. She was an accountant for Helmerich and Payne. Had been for years. She was doing well."

"What about her social life?"

"I think she spent most of her time at work, which probably cost her her marriage."

"Was she engaged in church politics?"

"Obviously. She was senior warden."

"What about church social activities?"

George and Susan exchanged a look. It was brief, but not so brief that Christina couldn't catch it. "She did . . . some of that," George answered.

"Bake sales, Lenten dinners, prayer meetings, that sort of thing?"

"Yes. That sort of thing."

Christina paused. Something was going on here—something they weren't telling her. Ben often rattled on about what keen instincts Christina had, but instinct could only take you so far. Right now her instincts were telling her something was up, something hidden that she needed to uncover. But how to do it?

She tried a shot in the dark. "Wasn't Kate on some committees? Other than the vestry?"

"I think so," George muttered. He looked to Susan for help. "Didn't she head up the Stewardship committee?"

"No," Susan said. She had been staring at the door. She didn't like being here, Christina was certain of that. But why? Did she really have somewhere else she needed to be? Or was there something more? "Ernestine headed Stewardship, then and now. But Kate was on the committee. She and Ernestine worked together. On many things."

Christina frowned. This interview was nowheresville. She wasn't going to get anything out of these two—at least not until she had enough information to force them to tell the truth. "Anything else you can tell me about Kate? Or Helen? Or Father Beale?"

"The man's a menace," George said emphatically. "He's devastated our little church. Despite what Beale says, this is not a dispute over politics. It was always more than that. Beale has been . . ." Again he looked at Susan. " . . . a—a moral disaster. He's hurt this church in—in more ways than you can imagine. We've lost half our members in the past year—did you know that? People are sick of the controversy, sick of him. Afraid that if they hang around, they'll be his next victim. Is it any wonder our church is a shadow of its former self?"

"As vestry members," Susan explained, "we're charged with preserving and protecting this church. And we've tried everything possible to expunge this monster. But no matter what we do, he keeps coming back, like Jason or something. Every time we think he's finally gone for good—he isn't."

"Did you know," George added, "that the minute that insane

judge granted Beale bail, thirteen more families turned in their requests for transfer of membership?"

"No," Christina answered. "I didn't." She folded up her notepad. "Well, I've taken enough of your time." She walked over to Susan. "Sorry again about the head-on collision on the doorstep."

"Forget it. I feel much better." She rose. "And I must be going, too."

"How long have you two been dating?"

George and Susan stared at one another, their faces frozen. After a few beats, Susan smiled, but it struck Christina as forced. "We're not . . . dating. I'm married."

"Oh, I'm sorry," Christina said. "I just assumed . . . since you were over here so early . . ."

"Susan and I were discussing church business," George said. "Kind of a planning session for the next vestry meeting. They've become so overwrought and complicated that . . . well, if you hope to get anything done, you need to start early."

So he said, but Christina had read the expression in his eyes when he first saw Susan sprawled out on the sidewalk, and it convinced her that their relationship was something more than professional. Susan had insisted that they were not dating, though. And if they were, she would've surely heard about it by now. Wouldn't she?

Christina let George lead her to the front door, then walked to her car, still pondering all she had seen and heard. There was something strange going on here. Christina had no idea how to get to it. But she knew they had to, and quick, before the trial. Because if she had learned anything from her years in the law, it was this: When you went to trial without all the facts, the price was always high. And in this case, the price might well be Father Beale's life.

CHAPTER

13

"YOUR HONOR," BEN said, "clearly in this case the evidence of past crimes is more prejudicial than probative."

"I disagree," Canelli responded, as if this might be a surprise to someone. "It's crucial that the jury know that the defendant is a repeat offender."

"Repeat offender? We're talking about a man who was arrested at an ERA sit-in. Not exactly Charles Manson."

"A crime is a crime. And the jury has a right to know who they're dealing with."

"I agree," Ben rejoined. "That's why we have witnesses testify. But the jury won't be aided by the minor detail of a past conviction. It will, however, give the assistant district attorney something he can distort and misuse at trial."

Canelli glared at Ben. "I resent that remark!"

"Resent, or resemble?"

Ben turned away, avoiding Canelli's wrath. For all his movie-star looks, Canelli had been anything but suave and debonair at this hearing. Ben didn't know if it was some weird Catholic-Episcopalian thing, or what. But something definitely had his dander up.

Judge Pitcock, on the other hand, was his usual cool, collected self. If anything, he seemed somewhat amused by the sputtering of the attorneys and perhaps more than a little pleased to see so many members of the press in his courtroom.

Ben was also impressed by the number of newspaper and even television reporters in the gallery—far more than had been in attendance at the preliminary hearing. Of course, the preliminary hearing had been a foregone conclusion. Everyone knew Beale would be bound over for trial, so Ben had no incentive to reveal any of his case strategy or theories. This pretrial hearing was different. The outcome was not preordained, and if Ben could keep some of the prosecution's evidence out of the trial, it would be perceived as a major success for the defense.

"Mr. Canelli," Judge Pitcock asked, "are you suggesting that the defendant's prior arrest and conviction—which I note took place many years ago—are somehow related to the present case?"

"Not as such, your honor. But there's a pattern here."

"A pattern? How so?"

"A pattern of . . . disregard for the law."

Pitcock cocked an eyebrow. "Well, I suppose we could say that about any conviction, couldn't we?" He drummed his fingers. "Explain to me how the fact that he was previously arrested during a social protest is probative on the issue of whether he murdered a woman in his church?"

Canelli hesitated. "It shows that he . . . that he . . . he is subject to strong feelings. Temper. That leads him to commit criminal acts."

Ben looked at the judge. "This no doubt explains the outbreak of mass murders on Greenpeace boats."

That one got a hearty laugh from the gallery. Judge Pitcock frowned at the disruption, but unless Ben was mistaken, he was forcing back a grin himself.

"I'm sorry, Mr. Canelli," Pitcock said, "but I'm not buying this one. I don't think you need this evidence. I don't think it helps you. Frankly, I think you may be better off without it."

Ben had entertained similar thoughts himself. Defense attorneys always tried to keep out past crimes to prevent the jury from being negatively biased. But in this case, if he drew the right jury, it might actually be helpful. It would make clear that Father Beale was a man of convictions, a man who cared deeply about causes and people. Or in other words, the last person on earth you would expect to commit a murder.

"Your honor," Canelli said, "may I expand on my argument?"

"No, I think I've heard enough on this one. The defendant's motion to suppress evidence of past crimes will be sustained."

Out the corner of his eye, Ben saw the reporters in the front row of the gallery breaking out their pencils. That's right, Ben thought, keep score for all the people out in newspaper land. Kincaid, one; Canelli, zero. And be sure to spell my name right.

"Have you got anything else, Mr. Kincaid?"

"Yes, your honor. I've also moved to suppress evidence regarding my client's political beliefs."

Pitcock scrunched up his face. "Why would a man's politics ever be relevant to the question of whether he committed a murder?" He paused. "Unless, of course, the victim was a Democrat."

Ben blinked. Did the judge make a funny? My, but he *was* in good spirits. Ben should bring an entourage of reporters with him every time he entered the man's courtroom.

"It's not remotely relevant," Ben answered. "It's just another attempt by the prosecution to prejudice the jury."

"That's not true," Canelli said. As tall as he was, he hovered over the bench. "The defendant's political beliefs—and his political activities—were a major cause of the disharmony between Father Beale and many members of his church. It is our belief that this conflict eventually led to the murders."

Ben looked at him harshly. "My client has only been charged with one murder!"

Canelli looked contrite. "Murder," he corrected himself.

"People were discussing politics in a church?" Judge Pitcock asked. "That doesn't seem right. Church and state are separate. And for a good reason." Ben wondered if the judge's Mormon background was influencing his thinking. The Mormon church had a long tradition of resisting government interference. "Bound to cause trouble."

"And it did," Canelli said, pouncing. "Of the worst kind."

Pitcock did not appear enlightened. "I'm still not getting it, gentlemen."

"That's because we're both dancing around what we're really talking about," Ben explained. He checked over his shoulder to make sure the reporters were still listening. They were going to love this. "We're not talking about nuclear proliferation here, judge. We're talking about gay rights."

Pitcock pursed his lips. "Indeed."

"Father Beale was and is a strong supporter of gay rights. He

believes gay people should be allowed to be Episcopal priests, he believes Episcopal priests should be allowed to marry gay couples and
he has allowed a gay activist group to meet at the church for some
years."

"Without the knowledge or consent of the governing body of the
church," Canelli couldn't resist adding.

The judge nodded. "And you believe this plays some part in the
intrachurch disharmony that provides your theory of motive?"

"Exactly so, your honor. That's what we intend to argue."

Ben couldn't contain himself. "Does anyone in this room believe
that Father Beale knocked off a vestry member because she disagreed
with him about gay rights? Give me a break."

"It does seem a bit tenuous," Judge Pitcock agreed.

"Your honor," Canelli insisted, "we have considerable evidence
that—"

"Give us some credit, Canelli," Ben interrupted. "We all know perfectly well this has nothing to do with motive. The only reason you
want this evidence in the trial is because you know that even with half a
million people in the metro area, Tulsa is still basically a big small town,
and we have our share of rednecks and mental midgets who don't like
gays and don't like people who like gays, either. You're hoping to play
on homophobia and ignorant prejudices to help you get your conviction. It's totally improper. More than that—it's disgraceful."

Canelli's handsome face turned stone cold. "Your honor, I very
much resent defense counsel's remarks. He's insinuating that I'm acting pursuant to an improper motive."

"I don't think he's insinuating," Judge Pitcock said laconically.
"He pretty much came straight out and said it."

"Well, it isn't true!"

Behind him, Ben saw the pencils were back in action again.
"There's no other rational reason for trying to admit such grossly improper evidence."

"There's nothing improper about informing the jury of the true
facts of the case!"

"Calm down, gentlemen," Pitcock said, pushing air with his hands.
"These histrionics are not necessary."

"Your honor," Canelli said, "I want to assure the court that I'm
acting in good faith. Let me restate my argument."

"Don't bother," the judge replied. "There's no way I'm letting this evidence in at trial."

Canelli looked as if he'd been sideswiped by a truck.

"Regardless of your motive theories, this is grossly prejudicial evidence. Even if I believed it might be probative—and I don't—I still wouldn't let it in. It's much too inflammatory. Let's move on."

Ben resisted the temptation to give himself a high five. Two for two! And the reporters were getting every word of it. Now if he could only score on the third item on the agenda—the one that really mattered.

"Your honor," Ben said, "our third motion to suppress relates to an acrylic award that was found by the police in my client's office. And, of course, the fingerprints that were taken from that award."

"Your honor," Canelli said. "Now he wants to suppress the murder weapon!"

"And with good reason. The award was discovered and seized pursuant to an illegal search."

"There was nothing illegal about it," Canelli insisted. "The police were called to the premises. The award was near the body at the scene of the crime."

"That is not precisely correct." Ben removed Mike's SOC report from his notebook. "The victim's body was found at the church, in Father Beale's office, atop his desk. The award was in a desk drawer. But, as the report of the chief officer on the scene makes clear, the drawer was closed." Ben looked up at the judge. "I will grant you that the police had the right to be in that office, and they probably had the right to examine anything that was in plain sight. But they did not have the right to open the desk drawer. For that, they needed either the permission of Father Beale or someone in charge of the premises, or they needed a warrant. They had neither. They had no business rifling through my client's desk. The search was improper; therefore, all evidence uncovered as a result of the illegal search must be suppressed."

Judge Pitcock rubbed his forehead. "These are very serious charges, Mr. Canelli. Do you have a response?"

"Yes, your honor," Canelli replied. "My response is that this argument is absurd."

Judge Pitcock rose slightly out of his chair. His calm exterior was betrayed by a flash of anger. "Mr. Prosecutor, let me assure you that there is nothing stupid about the Fourth Amendment protections against unlawful search and seizure. I take the Constitution very seriously, and so does the Supreme Court, and their decisions, may I remind you, are binding on this court. Now, if you don't want to see your case crumble right before your eyes, you'd better explain what your officers were doing in that desk drawer!"

Canelli frowned, then took a step back from the bench. "They were looking for a pencil."

"Excuse me?" the judge said.

"They were looking for a pencil. There was no intentional misconduct. No one expected to find the murder weapon. But the homicide detective on the scene—Major Morelli—likes those fancy fountain pens, and his ran out of ink and he needed something to write with, so he naturally opened a desk drawer. And there it was."

"And that's your story? That he was looking for a pencil and stumbled across the murder weapon?"

"That's it. Major Morelli's affidavit is on file."

Pitcock turned toward Ben. "You agree with that?"

"Up to a point, sir. Major Morelli's affidavit is uncontested. He's a straight shooter, and I have no doubt that he was doing what he says he was doing. But the absence of improper intent doesn't alter the fact that it was an unauthorized search, contrary to Constitutional guidelines."

"Actually, it might." The judge already had one of his law books out and was thumbing rapidly through the pages. "The Supreme Court has ruled that intent is relevant as to the propriety of unwarranted searches." He flipped through some more pages till he found what he was searching for. "Yes. *State versus Pezzoli*. Inadvertent discovery of evidence while looking for something else unrelated to the case. As I recall, the officer found a vital piece of evidence while searching for a bathroom. Anyway, the court ruled that since there was no intent to conduct an illegal search or seizure, the evidence did not have to be suppressed." He looked up from his book. "Sorry, Mr. Kincaid."

"Your honor," Ben implored, "think of the precedent. If you allow this, every time a police officer conducts an illegal search, he'll claim he was looking for a pencil. Or something like that."

Pitcock pondered. "True, this does have potential for abuse. I hate to take us down a slippery slope."

"Your honor," Ben urged, "consider the impact on the sanctity of the home. Of the family." Cheap, Ben knew, but when you're dying fast you have to pull out all your guns. "Can the family survive in a world without privacy? When personal space can be invaded by any officer who claims he's looking for a bathroom?"

Judge Pitcock thought a long while before answering. "Your argument is not without merit, Mr. Kincaid. I don't like improper searches any better than you do. But the case law is clear, and I am bound to follow it. If you'd like, I'll grant you leave to take an interlocutory appeal."

"Taken," Ben said, but he knew it would make no difference. The Court of Criminal Appeals would follow the Supreme Court's prior ruling.

"Very well. In the meantime, your third motion will be denied. Is there anything else?"

"No, your honor."

"Good. This court is now dismissed." He rapped his gavel and disappeared into chambers.

Canelli grabbed Ben on his way back to counsel table. "I don't appreciate what you said back there, Kincaid."

"Oh, go model some underwear or something."

"You know what I mean. Suggesting that I was playing dirty tricks. That I wanted to railroad your client."

"Forgive me. Prosecutors never want to get convictions, right? And your boss doesn't care at all whether you win this incredibly high profile case. What was I thinking?"

"I'm warning you, Kincaid. If this happens again, I'm asking for sanctions."

"Ooh. Please stop. You're giving me shivers again."

"You know, it doesn't have to be like this, Kincaid. I'm not attempting anything improper. The only thing I want to do is put away a murderer."

"Then get a new defendant!"

Exasperated, Canelli marched off to his own table. Ben sat down beside Father Beale.

"So how'd we do?" Beale asked. "When you lawyers start lawyering, I can't tell what's going on."

"We won two, lost one."

"Which one was most important?"

"Which do you think? We knew trying to get the murder weapon suppressed was a long shot. Christina found the *Pezzoli* case days ago; we tried to distinguish it from this case in our brief. But I figured Judge Pitcock would feel compelled to follow it."

"What are our prospects at trial?"

"Oh, about the same as they always were. Maybe slightly better, now that we don't have to worry about any gay-baiting tactics. We're in good shape. Really."

"Glad to hear it." He paused. A thin line creased his forehead. "You know, before, I was only in jail overnight. But I didn't like it. And the thought of being in prison, perhaps for years and years—or worse . . ." He shook his head. "I just don't think I could survive it, Ben. Not now. Not at my age."

Ben clasped him on the shoulder. "We're not going to let that happen, Father."

Beale nodded, but Ben could tell his words of reassurance were useless, because when all was said and done, words were just words, and words could never combat the greatest demon of them all—fear. Not even for a man of faith.

14

"WOULD YOU LIKE another cup of tea, Mr. Loving?"

"Yes, ma'am. Please."

"Digestive biscuit?"

"Yum."

Loving sat in a violet overstuffed chair with a demitasse, saucer, cookie (which the ladies insisted on calling a biscuit), and a little lace doily that he thought was supposed to serve as his napkin. Not the usual look for Loving; it was rather as if the Selfish Giant had dropped in on Alice's tea party. Just as well, he mused, that he'd come alone. If Jones or the Skipper got a look at this, he'd never hear the end of it.

"Chamomile, or Earl Grey?" Ernestine asked.

"Um . . . yes, please."

Ernestine hesitated a moment, then began pouring the Earl Grey. "A strong man like you needs a strong drink." She used a tea towel to catch the last stray drop from the teapot. "I'll save the chamomile for my nephew."

Over his shoulder, Loving saw Bruce, the nephew, wince.

Loving sipped his tea and tried to act as if he enjoyed it. Tasted basically like hot water to him; he was used to drinks of a somewhat stronger nature. Still, it seemed to give the ladies, Ruth and Ernestine, pleasure to have him join them. And he didn't want to disappoint. He only hoped the feeling would be mutual.

He'd come by Ernestine's home hoping to interview her about the murders. Finding Ruth here was a stroke of good fortune; her name was also on his list, which was already far too long. And to make it even better, Ernestine had her nephew Bruce in tow. Now he could kill three birds in one throw, so to speak, and interview them all without a lot of running around. It could be a great break for him—if he could get any of them to talk about something other than tea.

"I do so love a good cuppa in the early afternoon," Ernestine said, putting on what Loving thought was a faint trace of a British accent. "Don't you, Mr. Loving?"

"Oh, yeah," he answered enthusiastically. Especially if it's laced with a little Jack Daniel's.

"Ruth and I go to England every year or so to take the waters, don't we, Ruth dear? Of course, I love Oklahoma, too," Ernestine said, and an almost melancholy twinge entered her voice. "But I do feel that England has . . . well, just a bit more culture than we have here, don't you think, Mr. Loving?"

"I think we've got culture here, too," Loving answered. "It's just diff'rent."

"Of course you're right. Still, in England, everything is so much more . . . civilized, somehow."

She paused wistfully, which Loving took as his invitation to move on to subjects of considerably greater interest to him.

"Did you know the most recent victim?" he asked. "Kate McGuire?"

"Mr. Loving, I've been a member of St. Benedict's for over forty years. There isn't anyone I don't know."

"Did you know her, Ruth?"

Ruth nodded silently.

"Do any of you know of any reason anyone had to kill her?"

The ladies exchanged a meaningful glance. Ruth took a deep breath, then spoke slowly and regretfully, as if it were an unpleasant duty. "Mr. Loving, I realize you're working for Father Beale, so you may not want to hear what we have to say."

"You think he did it?"

Ruth stopped stirring her tea. "I know he did."

"And how d'ya know?"

She paused reflectively. "I suppose it's because I'm a lifelong student of human nature. I have an instinct—it's a gift, really. A fundamental understanding of how people behave."

"And that tells you Father Beale's guilty?"

"It takes a certain kind of man to commit a murder. To kill a woman, no less. Most couldn't do it. But Father Beale could. I've seen the look in his eye when he loses his temper. I've seen how his fists clench, how his arms and legs tremble. The man simply loses control."

"And you think that's what happened?"

"Yes. Twice. He lost control and strangled those poor women."

Loving turned toward Ernestine. "What about you? You agree?"

Ernestine checked her friend, then nodded. "I can't think of any other explanation."

"This last victim was on the vestry, wasn't she?"

Ruth answered. "She was. As was the previous victim, Helen Conrad."

"Is it possible that they were killed 'cause of some . . . vestry problem? Some church-related thing that didn't involve Father Beale?"

"Such as what?"

"I dunno. Maybe someone wanted to rub out their votes. Maybe someone wanted them dead so someone else would become senior warden."

"I think that unlikely in the extreme."

Well, so did Loving, but he had to explore every possible explanation. "What about . . . some kind of rivalry? Some infighting."

"There has been strife in the past between those who support Father Beale and those who do not, but frankly, at this point, he has so little support that I don't think the conflict exists anymore. Everyone now seems to agree that—guilty or not—it would be best for the church if he left. Everyone except Father Beale, of course."

"Maybe it didn't have anythin' to do with church business. Maybe someone got mad for some other reason. Maybe some guy thought somebody was slee—er, showin' too much attention to his wife."

"I haven't heard anything like that," Ernestine said primly. "And I would've."

"What about money?"

"What about it?" Ernestine replied. "Your question is a bit vague."

"I know. Because I'm just fishin' around. But I have been doin' this work long enough to know that, more often than not, these things come down to money. And churches usually have money, right?"

Ernestine cleared her throat. "Well, ours is a small parish—

getting smaller every day Father Beale remains. But we have been fortunate enough to receive financial gifts and legacies that are . . . far beyond what you might expect from a church of this size."

"Really?"

"Thanks to my aunt Ernestine," Bruce explained.

"Ah," Loving said, nodding.

"Please, Bruce," Ernestine interjected. "Don't let's be vulgar."

"Aunt Ernestine, there's nothing vulgar about—"

"Oh, Bruce, please don't be tiresome. Fetch us some more of these cinnamon scones, would you?"

"Aunt Ernestine, I don't—"

"Please, Bruce. Now."

"Yes, Aunt Ernestine." He drifted off into the kitchen.

"Poor Bruce," she said, shaking her head, after he was gone. "He never played sports, you know. Preferred to stay inside and read books all day long. I tried to talk to his parents, God rest their souls, but they wouldn't listen to me. 'If he keeps reading all the time, he's going to turn into a book,' that's what I said. But no one listened."

Loving's heart went out to Bruce. How long had he been putting up with this?

"And you see what the result is," she continued. "The man is in his forties, and what is he? Nothing. Oh, he's nice enough, in a puppy-dog sort of way. But he's got no job, no family. And to think this man is the last surviving member of my family. My sole heir." Her eyes brightened, as if by sudden inspiration. "You know, Mr. Loving—I think Bruce could learn a great deal from a man like you. Perhaps you two could . . . spend some time together."

Gee whiz, maybe I could teach him to play catch! "That's sounds nice, ma'am, but I'm afraid I'm very busy just now."

"Oh, I should've made it clear—I would expect to compensate you for your time, of course."

Loving could see she was a woman who thought she could get anything if she came across with enough money. Which made him all the more determined to decline. "I'm sorry, ma'am, but I'm spendin' all my wakin' hours on this case, at least until trial."

"Perhaps if I just gave you a little something up front."

Ernestine popped open her handbag and a large wad of bills tumbled out. Ernestine scooped them up quickly, but not so quickly Lov ing couldn't see there was a seriously large amount of cash in there. More than you would expect an elderly lady to be carrying around.

"Mind if I ask why you're carryin' so much scratch?" Loving asked.

"It's not—I just—" She seemed flustered. "I have some bills to pay."

In cash? Come on, lady . . .

"If you'll excuse me," Ernestine said, "I have an appointment."

Why was she in such a hurry to leave all of a sudden? Loving started to get up, but Ernestine waved him back down. "No need for you to leave. Ruth has keys. She can lock up when you've all finished chatting. I apologize for leaving so abruptly, but as I told you on the phone, I have some . . . errands I must attend to." Without giving anyone an opportunity to object, she ambled toward the front door and closed it behind her.

Bruce returned with more of the cookies, and Loving dutifully wolfed down a few. They seemed fairly tasteless to him, but he supposed he should be grateful they weren't serving little bitty cucumber sandwiches.

"Can either of you think of anythin' else that might help this investigation? Anythin' that might relate to the murders in any way?"

Both of them appeared to be trying, but no one offered any assistance.

Ruth was the one who finally spoke, but she wasn't answering the question. "Will you be seeing Father Beale today?"

"I dunno. Maybe. Why?"

"Would you please talk some sense into him? This business of hanging on as priest at the same time he's being tried for murder—it's destroying St. Benedict's. It makes a mockery of everything we do. Our membership has been decimated. Who wants to take the sacrament from a murderer?"

"I heard Father Beale say he was brought to St. Benedict's for a higher purpose. He thinks he was called by God."

"Delusions of grandeur."

"Maybe." Loving slapped his thighs and began clearing away all the tea paraphernalia. "But if the man thinks he's takin' his instructions from God, far be it for me to interfere."

"But he's a murderer!"

"Ben says he isn't. And in my experience, he's usually right." Well, two times out of three, anyway. "Thanks for talkin' to me." He shook Bruce's hand. "Thanks for the cookies."

"Digestive biscuits," Ruth corrected.

"You can call 'em whatever you want, ma'am," Loving said amiably. "But a cookie is still a cookie. And God willing, always will be."

JONES AND HIS new bride, Paula, sat in the front seat of his blue Volkswagen Beetle parked on a side street off Lewis.

"Have I mentioned how much I love you?" Jones asked.

"Yes," she replied, coiling her brunette hair around a finger, "but as a newlywed, I think I'm entitled to hear it several times a day."

"More than the moon and the sun. More than the stars in the sky."

"How Elizabeth Barrett Browning." She giggled. "You give me chill bumps when you get all poetic like that."

"Your eyes are diamonds. Your hair is silk."

"Do tell."

"You're a beauty like the world has never seen before."

"Such as."

"Excuse me?"

Paula twisted around in the car seat. "A beauty *such as* the world has never seen before."

Jones frowned. "Why did I marry a librarian?"

Her fingertips danced across his chest. "I'll remind you."

About a minute later, their lips finally parted. "Wow," Jones murmured breathlessly, in a wobbly, slightly drunken sounding voice. "Don't quit on my account."

"I'm not. Our target is on the move."

In the rearview mirror, Jones saw that Ernestine Rupert had left her house. She was on foot, heading toward Lewis.

"Let's go," Jones said. He started the car but stayed out of sight, a good distance behind. Jones knew for a fact that the elderly woman was nearsighted, even with glasses, so the chances of them being spotted were remote.

About ten minutes later, Ernestine approached a modest white-walled house with an extraordinary garden out front. A middle-aged man of slight build was working diligently in it, pulling weeds and putting down mulch.

"Do you recognize him?" Paula asked.

Jones nodded. "Alvin Greene. Altar Guild. I'm going in closer."

Paula held tight to his arm. "Loving said to just follow. See where she goes."

"Because he was afraid that if I tried to do anything more, I'd screw it up. I want to hear what they're saying." He slid out of the car and quietly ran to the next house down, crossed through the unfenced backyard, then slowly crept into the area between the two houses. He was still out of sight, but he could pick up some of the conversation.

"I know what day it is," Alvin was saying. "But I just can't do it."

Was Ernestine replying? Jones wondered. If she was, he couldn't hear it.

"Please. If you could only give me a little more time. There's been so much turmoil and chaos and—and—"

Jones couldn't see his face, but it sounded as if the man was sobbing.

"Please, I'm begging you. Pammy is still sick. Jenny has so many needs."

The despairing quality in Alvin's voice was tearing Jones apart. What on earth was that woman doing to him?

"Fine!" Alvin shouted. Jones didn't need to be nearby to pick that up. It was probably heard in the next county. "Take your goddamn blood money! I hope you rot in hell!" Jones heard sounds of movement, then nothing but Alvin's pathetic crying.

He crept to the other end of the house in time to see Ernestine walking back toward the sidewalk, clutching a small blue notebook in her hand. He ducked back behind the hedge till she was gone. Then he made his way back to the Beetle.

"Did you get anything?" Paula asked.

"Oh yeah. Did you read the Boss's report? He thinks Ernestine's been lending money at usurious rates and demanding repayment."

"And? Didn't you tell me Ben is usually right?"

"About legal matters, sure. But about people?" He shook his head. "This is a situation where Ben's naïveté clouds his judgment.

He's blinded by the woman's age, her blue hair, her grandmotherly face."

"So what's the sweet old biddy doing? Organizing a renegade sewing circle? Setting up an unauthorized Scrabble tournament?"

"Not quite." He fished the keys out of his pocket and started the ignition. "Hold on to your hat, sweetheart. That sweet old biddy is no moneylender. She's a blackmailer."

15

CHRISTINA WALKED BRISKLY down the carpeted steps of Phil-
brook Museum, thinking, Would they never stop changing this place?
It was originally the private Italian-villa style mansion of Frank Phillips, oil baron extraordinaire and founder of Phillips Petroleum. After
it passed out of the family hands, it became a tourist attraction and
locus for traveling art exhibitions. Then the big change—millions
were spent adding wings to create a museum, with room for a permanent collection, traveling shows, a restaurant, and, of course, a gift shop.
Personally, Christina thought the mansion got somewhat lost, now
that it was buried under all these additions, even though it was lovely
having another great art museum in Tulsa.

And now they've updated the restaurant, she noted. Spiffy modern metal chairs and matching tables, and an all-new California-style
menu. It seemed a bit antiseptic to Christina, but she supposed it
hadn't really been designed with her in mind. They were presumably
going for the ladies-who-lunch crowd, of which Christina was definitely not a member.

Andrea Beale, however, was. She was on her second or third glass
of white wine by the time Christina arrived. Christina detected a change
in Andrea's manner almost immediately. Some of the fire she had dis-
played in the office had fizzled. There was a disconnected look in her
eyes. A fuzzy wall between her and the rest of the world which, alcohol-
induced or not, Christina sensed Andrea preferred to have surrounding her.

"Thank you for inviting me to lunch," Christina said, taking her seat at the table. "I think this is a much friendlier environment than the office."

Andrea shrugged, a minimalist gesture. "Beats eating alone."

"I suppose your husband is busy preparing for trial. I know Ben is."

Andrea took a sip of her wine. "Daniel never takes lunch with me. He's too busy. Always on the go. Lots of projects. Saving the world."

Even if Christina had been sloshed herself, she could not have missed the note of irony. "Ben's told me about some of his political and social work. I was impressed."

"Oh, yes. Everyone is." The waiter appeared at her side. "Glass of wine, Christina?"

"No, thank you. I have so much work to get done today. I'll have the flavored tea, please."

Andrea smiled slightly and ordered another glass of wine for herself.

Christina scanned the menu. It was all too *haute cuisine* for her taste. She knew the portions would be too small and everything would have too much goat cheese or sun-dried tomatoes. After some deliberation, she went with the Caesar salad. Andrea ordered some sort of pasta.

Once the waiter brought Christina her raspberry tea and Andrea her next glass of chardonnay, Christina decided to start the questioning.

"I want you to know that Daniel is in good hands," Christina said reassuringly. "Ben is a great criminal attorney. The best, I think."

"He seems rather young."

"That's just because he's slim and baby-faced. Trust me, he's got more experience with murder trials than anyone I know. And he's very smart. Fast on his feet."

Andrea nodded. "And cute, too." She eyed Christina carefully. "I think he's cute, anyway. Don't you?"

Christina cleared her thoat. "I've been working with him so long, I hardly notice those things anymore."

"Indeed."

"But I know he's determined to win this case. And so am I." She readjusted herself slightly. These metallic chairs might be stylish modern art, but they were damned uncomfortable to sit in. "Do you have any theories about what happened?"

"I'm not sure what you mean."

"At our meeting last week you said you thought it was all politics. That Daniel's enemies at the church were out to get him. At trial we'll need some alternative explanation for the murders, and we may well use that one, if we can come up with some evidence in support. But to blame the church is a little nebulous. It would be better if we could name an individual or individuals who could have been behind the killings."

"So you can call them to the stand Perry Mason–style and try to browbeat a confession out of them?"

"So we can raise doubt in the minds of the jurors as to Daniel's guilt. That's what it's all about for the defense, remember. We don't have to prove who did it. We just have to establish that there's reasonable doubt about Daniel."

"I hope you'll do more than that. Daniel shouldn't have this hanging over his head for the rest of his life. Some people will always assume he was guilty, even if he gets off. Unless you discover who the murderer really was."

Christina nodded. Andrea wasn't telling her anything she didn't already know. But at this juncture, their first priority had to be getting a not-guilty verdict—regardless of what other people thought. "We'll do our best."

"I really couldn't single anyone out. I don't know who might be a murderer. I mean, I can tell you who the ringleaders of the anti-Beale movement were. Both of the dead women. Susan Marino. George Finley. And of course, Ernestine Rupert."

"Hard to imagine that elderly lady strangling two young women."

"Well, she wouldn't do it herself. She'd hire someone. Ernestine believes she should be able to buy anything she wants—including control of the church. Daniel was able to hold her at bay for a time, because he supported that pro-choice organization she founded and still chairs—the PCSC. But after a while, that wasn't enough for her. She wanted him gone. And she had full vestry support."

"Have you seen anything at the church—or elsewhere—that you think might possibly be connected to the murders? Something . . . suspicious? Something unusual?"

Andrea shook her head. "I'm sorry. Nothing comes to mind."

"Has anyone said anything out of the ordinary? Made any threats?"

"Well, almost everyone in the church has threatened to do one horrible thing or another if Daniel doesn't resign. Which he won't."

"And what's your take on that? Why won't he go?"

"He's too proud," she said flatly. "He won't admit defeat. Ego."

"Not that he thinks he's been called to the church by God?"

"They're the same thing. How could any man ever believe he was doing the work of God unless he had a little ego? How could any man cling so tenaciously to his position unless he believed he was doing the right thing? Believe me, most priests—probably all other priests—would've resigned long before it got to this point. But not my Daniel. The stronger the storm, the more resolute he becomes. He's like a character out of the Old Testament." She laughed bitterly. "I'll bet Moses' wife had a hard time of it, too."

"What's your take on why Daniel has had so many problems at this church?"

"Well," she answered thoughtfully, "Daniel is a child of the sixties. And the members of the vestry are children of the nineties. The 1890s."

Christina smiled.

"Churches have different personalities," Andrea continued. "People don't realize it, but it's true. The members create a group mind—a gestalt, if you will. Back at St. Gregory's in Oklahoma City, the largest slice of the membership was composed of raised-in-the-sixties liberal activists—or would-be activists. Daniel was a perfect fit. But the transfer to St. Benedict's was a mistake. Suddenly he was confronted with a group of people who voted for Reagan and carry NRA sharpshooter certificates in their wallets. It was a disaster from the get-go."

"I don't normally think of religion as being so . . . political."

"Well, religion isn't. But churches are. Oh, don't get me wrong. Daniel had some supporters, at least at the outset. But not many. Not enough."

Something about the tone in her voice inspired Christina to take the conversation down a side road. "What about you? Were you a supporter?"

Andrea's eyes flickered upward. "I'm his wife."

"Come on, Andrea. Don't give me that Pat Nixon my-husband-right-or-wrong stuff. Did you support him?"

"I've known Daniel since the sixties. We didn't get married until much later. I was an activist in my own right. The day we both marched with Dr. King in Selma—that was also the first day we kissed. In fact, in those days, I was probably more active than he was."

"So you knew what you were getting into when you married him."

"Of course. It was part of what made me fall in love with him." She paused. "I've always supported his political activities."

"Is there something else, then? Something you don't support?"

Andrea hesitated. Her body seemed to retract, to withdraw into her chair, just as she had done back in the office. "I have always been a supportive wife. Free-thinking. Open to new ideas. But some things . . . some things are just . . . wrong. Worse than that. Evil."

Evil? According to Ben, it was the same word Kate McGuire had used with Father Beale. Just before she was killed. "What are you talking about, Andrea?"

"N-nothing in particular. I was just speaking generally. . . ."

"Don't give me that. There's something you're not telling me."

"No, really . . ."

"Tell me, Andrea."

"I—don't—" She spun her head around, as if hoping the waiter might come to her rescue. "Let's talk about something else."

"Andrea, listen to me. Ben and I are Daniel's attorneys. We're trying to help him. But we can't do our job if there are important things we don't know. It's absolutely crucial that you tell us everything—*everything*—that might relate to these murders. If we know about it now, we can prepare accordingly. Minimize the damage. If we get bushwhacked at trial, the damage could be irremediable."

"It has nothing to do with the murders," she insisted. "It has nothing to do with anything. I was just—just—" She gasped slightly. "Nothing." She picked up her wineglass and downed at least half of it in a single swallow. "Where's my pasta, anyway?"

Christina tapped her fork against the table. Rarely had she felt so frustrated during an interview. She was certain this woman knew something she and Ben needed to hear about before trial. She was also certain this woman was never going to tell her what it was.

"All right," Christina said, trying another approach. "We'll avoid the specifics. But—is it something that might've turned some of the church members against Daniel?"

Andrea's head was trembling. "It's—possible. I mean—I don't really know what you mean—I don't—I—"

"Is it something that turned *you* against him?" Christina knew she was pushing—probably too hard. But the questions had to be asked. "Tell me the truth, Andrea. Is it something that turned you against him?"

"It's . . . so . . . hard . . ." Christina felt as if Andrea were squeezing each word out of a narrow toothpaste tube. "I'm his wife. I mean—that's what I am." She spread her arms wide, her face strained, as if she was trying to explain the most complex matter with a hopelessly insufficient vocabulary. "I will always be his wife, no matter what. And we've shared so much—there was so much I could put up with. Effortlessly. So much I could tolerate, with barely a shrug."

Her voice broke down. Her head hung low, barely hovering over the table. "But there comes a point when it's more than just disappointment. More than just . . . obscenity. There comes a point when it is . . . betrayal. Betrayal of everything I hold most dear. And that's the one thing I could not forget. Or forgive." Tears sprang out of the corners of her eyes. She took her cloth napkin and wiped her face. "Not then. Not now. Not ever."

16

MANLY CROUCHED DOWN among the azaleas, waiting for his prey.

His friend had informed him that there was some sort of meeting on Wednesday night; all the doctors and their staff would be there. All who played a part in the mindless murder of babies. So he just needed to be patient. And he could do that. Willingly. Because he knew what he was doing was important, that it mattered. He was defending the martyred, fighting for a holy cause. It was only right to expect to make some sacrifices. Like the sacrifice of time. To boredom.

His boredom didn't last long. After waiting barely half an hour, he saw a tall, slender woman in a midlength skirt moving past him. He was glad; women in skirts were always more vulnerable. They knew it and felt it. It would make what he had to do all the easier.

She must've parked in the north parking lot. By the faint blue glow emanating from a street light, he saw chestnut-colored hair, slim hips, ample bust. It was Dr. Laurie Fullerton, if he wasn't mistaken. The chief of staff at the clinic. The abortion doctor.

His eyes glowed with excitement. He'd scored the jackpot.

He waited until she was just past his hiding place, then pounced. He knocked her forward, face first. Her chin thudded into the concrete, stunning her. Before she had a chance to react, he rolled her over onto her back. Straddling her, he stuffed a dirty sock into her mouth.

"Listen to me, bitch," he said, his hand clutched tightly around her throat. "We can do this easy, or we can do this hard. It's not gonna be pleasant for you, either way. But if you try to make any noise, try to scream or shout, it's gonna be so much worse you'll wish you were dead."

Dr. Fullerton was still conscious. Her eyelids fluttered and her chin was bleeding, but she was awake, alert, aware.

"I got a message for you. And I want you to carry it back to all your buddies at the clinic. Stop killing God's children! Got it?"

Fullerton nodded her head.

"I'm on a crusade, lady. I'm trying to save four thousand babies a year, while you and your friends get paid to be their executioners."

Some muffled noises were audible beneath the sock. Fullerton was trying to do something—to protest, to deny, to plead for help. Whatever it was, no one heard it.

"Now I'm going to have to hurt you," Manly growled.

Fullerton twisted her head furiously back and forth.

"It's not something I want to do. It's what I have to do. What I'm called to do. We don't like violence, but sometimes it's necessary. Just as the Crusaders had to slaughter the Saracen hordes."

Fullerton continued shaking her head, faster and faster. Her face was transfixed with fear. Tears welled up in her eyes.

"Don't look at me like that!" Manly bellowed. He brought his hand back and slapped her hard across the face. "It's your own fault! You have no one to blame but yourself!"

The tears flowed faster now. Fullerton was pleading, begging for mercy, in every possible way except verbally. But it didn't help. Manly brought his arm around, this time fist clenched, and smashed it down on her jaw.

Even with the sock stuffed in her mouth, her cry of pain was audible. Her eyes clenched shut. She writhed and twisted under his weight. But he was far too heavy for her. She was powerless.

"It's going to get worse now," Manly muttered. "I can't let you off with just a warning."

No, no, no! Fullerton screamed behind the gag.

"Did those four thousand babies get a warning?" Manly asked. He pressed his knees down into her chest. "Did anyone give them a second chance?"

Fullerton mustered all her strength, trying to break free. But she didn't even come close.

"Time to pay for your sins," Manly said. "You, and everyone like you." He reared back with his fist, this time even higher than before. He tightened his muscles, readying himself to make the maximum impact. He leaned back to get more height. . . .

And the instant he reduced the weight pinning her down, Fullerton whipped out her right hand. She was holding something; it made a hissing sound. A second later, Manly felt an intense burning in his eyes.

He clutched his face, reeling backwards. Pepper spray! Where did the murdering bitch get that?

Fullerton scrambled out from under him. Not a second later, he felt a sharp kick in his groin.

This time, he was the one who cried out. He lurched toward her, but she was already running full tilt toward the clinic. He knew he had no chance of catching her; he could barely see. The smartest thing he could do was get out of here fast, before she returned with friends.

He limped away, heading toward the side street where he had parked his car. Damn everything! How could he let her get the drop on him? And what was he going to say when he got back home?

One thing was certain. His friend would not be pleased.

"YOU STUPID BASTARD!" Manly's friend slapped him across the face. "Couldn't even keep control of a woman?"

"I didn't know she had the spray," Manly mumbled. "I didn't see it comin'."

"You couldn't handle one lousy piece of ass in the dark. You probably outweigh her by two to one."

"She was fast. She must've had it in her purse."

"That's no excuse!" Another slap, then another, and then another. "Do you think Jesus made excuses when he went to Gethsemane? Did Abraham make excuses when he was told to sacrifice his son?"

"You don't know what it was like."

"And I don't want to know, you sorry sack. Don't make your excuses to me. Get down on your knees and pray to your God." Manly's friend shoved him downward.

Manly did as he was told. He folded his hands and prayed for his soul. It was a full five minutes before he got up again.

"I'm so sorry," Manly said, hanging his head low.

"That much is certain."

"Will you forgive me? Will you still help me?"

"I shouldn't, you know. I should find someone else. Someone competent."

"Please!"

His friend considered for a long moment before speaking. "One more chance then. But this will absolutely be the last one. I will tolerate no more failure!"

"I understand." Manly looked up expectantly, like a naughty puppy who still hoped to be stroked. "I'll go back out tonight."

"Don't be a fool. They'll be looking for you."

"Then—?"

"Don't worry. I have a plan. A target." The friend's eyes darkened, contracting to tiny points of light. "One even better than what you've had before. One no one will be able to ignore."

17

BEN CRAWLED ON his hands and knees close behind Dr. Masterson. It was dark in here; the light from Masterson's flashlight provided the only illumination, and it wasn't enough, at least not as far as Ben was concerned. The air had a musty, heavy smell—not unusual for attics, he supposed. Neither were the cobwebs, but they were atmospherics he could've lived without.

"Almost there," Masterson said.

They crawled on. The levers and hoses overhead were so low that Ben was forced to go down on his elbows and practically slither forward. And why did he have to choose this morning to wear his new suit?

"I didn't even know this place existed," Ben said, making conversation. "Dark, convoluted, inaccessible. This could be a perfect hiding place."

"I suppose it could at that. Here we are." Masterson laid the flashlight on the wooden planking beneath them, opened a metal panel, and went to work.

This was the first time Ben had been in the St. Benedict's organ chambers—and the last, he resolved. He had never considered himself claustrophobic—look where he lived—but this place might change all that. He hadn't wanted to come up here at all, but Masterson insisted he had to work on the organ electronics right now, and Ben was somewhat pressed for time himself, so it was talk now or never.

"What exactly is it you do up here, anyway?" Ben asked.

"Oh, these pipe organs require a lot of maintenance," he explained as he worked. "Just general stuff. Checking the wiring. Tuning the reeds. Making sure everything is behaving as it should."

"For this you got a doctorate degree in music? Seems like there should be someone else who can handle this sort of thing."

"Like I'm going to let some boob from the Altar Guild mess with my organ? Think again." He tightened something with a pair of pliers. "Now a trained professional, sure. That would be permissible. But it would also be expensive. And given the current sorry state of St. Benedict's financial affairs after losing half its members . . . well, it's best I attend to it myself."

"Where'd you learn how to do this, anyway?"

"Juilliard, believe it or not. It's not all just singing and dancing up there, you know. Sometimes we actually learned something practical."

Ben was impressed. "You went to Juilliard? I didn't know that."

"Well, I don't have it engraved on my business cards the way some of my colleagues do. But yes, I went to Juilliard. Got in when I was fifteen."

Ben whistled. "That's impressive." Impressive—but also somewhat incongruous. "And then when you got out, you took a position with the Church?"

Masterson made a coughing noise, deep in his throat. "No. Not exactly." He reached for another tool. "My initial goal was to be a concert musician. I played piano on a per-service basis with the Cleveland Orchestra. And the Boston Symphony."

"Really?"

"I even played Carnegie Hall. Not alone, of course."

"That's tremendous. And then you . . . I mean, and after that you . . ."

"You're searching for a graceful way of saying, What the hell happened to you? Right?"

"Well . . ."

"Yeah. Don't worry about it. It's a sensible question to ask." He gritted his teeth, applying force to a stubborn connection. "Have you ever known anyone who worked as a musician?"

"I've worked as a musician," Ben answered. "In college. And again, not too long ago. Played the piano. Sang a little."

"Indeed. I didn't know we had a former professional in our little choir. What kind of music do you like?"

"Well, I played jazz, in a club down in Greenwood. My personal taste leans more to folk music."

Masterson's voice became quizzical. "A folk pianist?"

"Yeah, well, that was the problem."

"Who are your favorite folk musicians?"

"Classical or Celtic or modern?"

"Whatever."

"Well, big picture, no one was ever better than Oklahoma's own Woody Guthrie. Modern? I liked Harry Chapin. I'm still crazy for Christine Lavin. Janis Ian."

"Mmm." Masterson made a swooning sound. "Janis Ian. She's got to be one of the greatest songwriters of our time, don't you think?"

"You know her work?"

"What, you thought I just listened to church music all day long?"

"Well . . ."

"You thought I just listened to stuffy boring classical music." He chuckled. "Well, I suppose I deserve that. I'm a bit uppity about my music at times. So how long did you play in this club?"

"About six months. I eventually returned to practicing law."

"Couldn't live without the big bucks, huh?"

Ben snorted. "Yeah, that's it. Big bucks."

"Well, my story is much like yours, only in reverse," Masterson said wistfully. "You probably know what's been happening to symphony orchestras lately. Funding dries up; the community doesn't support serious art. They try to limp along doing those embarrassing pops concerts—which is a nice way of saying they're playing drivel to make money—but it doesn't last long. I don't know how the Tulsa Philharmonic has survived as long as it has. Anyway, to make a long story short, I got laid off."

"So that's when you started playing in churches?"

"No. That's when I became so thoroughly disgusted that I gave up music altogether. I managed a bookstore in a Boston suburb. Had nothing to do with music for three years."

"But you eventually came back."

"Yes. I remember one of my professors at Juilliard saying, in essence, that you have to leave music for a while to find out if you really have what it takes to spend your life there. I guess I learned that I did, or at the least, that I couldn't live without it. But no one was hiring in the concert halls. So a friend steered me toward an Episcopal church near Boston that needed an interim organist. I took the job—and loved it. The parishioners were highly educated; they appreciated quality music. The rector was a delight. He let me do my job without interference. It was a pleasure."

"But it ended."

"Yes. As I knew it would. It was only an interim position. I managed to work at a series of different churches. And each one, if you'll forgive me for being blunt, seemed to be smaller and more ignorant than the one before. Until finally I ended up here."

"St. Benedict's is a long way from Juilliard."

Masterson made a grunting noise. "No comment." And he went right on tightening.

"Still, it isn't the worst church in the world."

"You mean, it wasn't," Masterson corrected him. "That's true. In the early days, before Father Beale arrived, it was a nice place. Small, of course, and filled with hicks, but nice. Didn't pay me squat. I was forced to moonlight, taking teaching jobs at ORU or filling in at special events downtown. Playing the celesta for the *Nutcracker* every Christmas. Now there's an insipid piece of pabulum if ever there was one. But I made ends meet. I was fine." He paused. "Until Father Beale arrived."

"You don't like Father Beale much, do you?"

"I have no personal feelings for him one way or the other," Masterson insisted. "But he's been a horrible rector. Look what he's done to this church. I realize he's your friend and client, Ben, but let's be honest—he's torn this place apart."

"I'm not sure everything that's happened can be blamed on him."

"I am. I saw disaster coming the first day I met him. And I was right."

"What do you mean?"

"I've been around enough priests to know when trouble is brewing."

"But what exactly did Father Beale do wrong?"

"It's not really what he did, Ben. It's who he is. Whether you care to admit it or not, the man is a raging egomaniac. I mean, all that save-the-world folderol, with the protest marches and equal rights and gay rights, et cetera. What is that, when you get right down to it, but egotism? 'If only the world was as truly holy as I am.' "

"Did you have trouble working with him?"

"Always. And without exception. And I am mindful of the fact that the church canons say the rector is the boss. But any sensible rector, anyone with a modicum of respect for other people's work and talents, would not constantly interfere."

"But Father Beale did?"

"He was always overruling me, choosing different hymns, vetoing anthems. And he didn't have the foggiest idea what he was doing. Some of his selections were flat-out tasteless. He favored trite familiar hymns to anything interesting or of quality. He would choose too many hymns too similar, instead of giving the congregation some variety. It was an artistic outrage."

"I'm sure he was trying to do what he thought best for the church."

"I don't think so. I think he was trying to show his total and utter contempt for me. He was trying to prove that he was the boss. That this was his church so he could do anything he wanted. It was egotism, pure and simple."

"So . . . you were hoping that . . . somehow . . . he would leave the church?"

Ben could not see, but could hear, the grin on Masterson's face. "Trying to find a motive, are we?"

"Can't blame me for trying." Ben wondered how much longer they were going to be in this cramped attic. Both his legs had fallen asleep. If he was here much longer, he probably wouldn't be able to move at all.

"I didn't frame him for murder."

"Can you think of anyone who might've done it?"

"Ben, virtually everyone in this church might've done it. They certainly had cause. But I don't believe they did. Because when all is said and done, to commit crimes of this nature, horrible crimes, requires an anger, a . . . a *meanness*, that no one here has. No one but Father Beale."

Ben sighed. He'd heard this story far too many times. "What

about the two women who were killed? Do you know of any reason anyone might've had to do that?"

"Other than the strife in the vestry regarding Father Beale? None whatsoever. They were both lovely women. Treasures. I knew them both and loved them both. What happened to them was an atrocity."

"Ernestine Rupert suggested to my investigator that Kate McGuire might've been in some sort of trouble."

"Ernestine Rupert." The words dripped with contempt. "Well, she would know, of course."

"You don't like Ernestine?"

"Let's move on to another subject."

"Why don't you like Ernestine?"

No answer. Masterson was ignoring him. So of course, he plowed right on ahead. "Was she blackmailing you?"

Masterson dropped his wrench. "What has she told you?"

"She hasn't told me anything. But my assistant thinks she's blackmailing . . . someone else, and judging from the thickness of her little blue book, I'm guessing he's not her only source of illicit income. Am I right?"

Masterson's voice became hard. "I told you, I don't want to talk about it."

"Okay, let me ask you a slightly different question. Why was she blackmailing you?"

"I don't know what you're talking about. And if you don't drop this line of inquisition immediately, I'll toss you out of my attic. Headfirst."

Ben let it pass. Whatever it was, Masterson obviously didn't want to talk about it, or he wouldn't be paying hush money. It probably wasn't germane to the murders, and Ben was in no position to browbeat Masterson, with his legs fast asleep and his nose pressed against the floor. "I've noticed that you talk about the importance of music and the purity of the selections, but you never actually seem . . . oh . . ."

"Devout?" Masterson said, completing the sentence.

"Yeah. Are you an Episcopalian?"

"Got bad news for you, Ben. I'm not even a Christian. Not in the organized religion sense, anyway." He slapped his hands and closed the metal panel. "Oh, I am on paper. But after all I've seen . . ." He shook his head.

Ben was stunned. "Isn't that sort of like . . . a requirement for being a minister? Even of music?"

"Nope. All they ever quiz me about are my musical credentials. They assume religion from the fact that I work in churches. And to be fair, I do consider myself religious. But as for all this kneeling and bowing and such—forget it. I mean, it's pretty medieval, isn't it? With the robes and the candles and incense and all. Primitive. And rather creepy. Don't you agree?"

"No, I don't."

"You say that, Ben, but I don't see you up at the communion rail Sunday mornings."

"Well . . . that's different."

"You know what the difference is?" Masterson squirmed around on his elbows until he was facing Ben. "The difference is—I'm honest about it. I don't believe in all this hocus-pocus, and I won't pretend that I do. I won't put on a show for the audience. I don't hedge my bets with heaven just in case I'm wrong. I try to be intellectually honest. And I don't make exceptions. Not even for God."

18

BEN WAS SITTING at the piano in his apartment, trying to learn a Janis Ian tune called "Hopper Painting," when he heard a knock on the door.

"Who is it?" he asked.

"Lasagna," came the reply.

Ben flung open the door. Joni Singleton stood on the other side, cradling a baking pan in her arms.

"Lasagna who?"

She smiled. "If this is a joke, I don't know the punch line. Make way, Benjamin. I fixed you dinner." Without waiting for an invitation, she pushed past him and made her way to the kitchen.

Ben checked his watch. "Isn't it a little late for dinner?"

"What, like you're going to tell me you've eaten already? You've been banging on that piano since you came home." She peered down at an open box of Cap'n Crunch on the coffee table. "Honestly, Ben, you eat like an eight-year-old."

"I like to keep my life simple."

She opened the cupboard and began removing plates and silverware. "You need someone to take care of you, Ben. In the worst way."

"I beg your pardon. I think I get along quite nicely."

"For a sad-sack thirtysomething who isn't married and as far as I know isn't even dating regularly and lives alone and thinks dip made from onion soup mix is a gourmet treat, yeah, you're getting along great."

God save me from twenty-year-old college students, Ben thought.

"Well, it's a treat, anyway," Ben corrected her. "It's only a gourmet treat if you wash it down with chocolate milk."

Joni cringed. "Don't make me barf, Ben, okay? I'm trying to fix a meal here."

Ben watched quietly as his tenant and part-time handyman (handywoman?) set the table. She was looking good these days. Of course, she always had, but even more so tonight. Ben suspected she'd been visiting the gym, although how she fit that in with going to TU full-time, working part-time, and helping her divorced mother manage her much-too-large family, Ben couldn't imagine.

When she was finished, Joni fluffed her curly hair behind her head, took a seat at the table, and instructed Ben to take the one opposite. Ben picked up his fork and started toward the lasagna.

"Who's going to say grace?" Joni asked.

Ben froze. He made a coughing noise. "Uh . . . perhaps you . . . should. . . ."

"Fine." Joni bowed her head and clasped her hands. "Good bread, good meat . . . good God, let's eat." She giggled. "Amen."

Ben cocked an eyebrow. "I'm not familiar with that particular catechism. Did you learn it in Catholic school?"

"Oh, yes. But not from the sisters."

Ben scooped up a large helping of the lasagna. He wasn't remotely hungry—Cap'n Crunch is deceptively filling—but he knew Joni had gone to a lot of trouble for him.

"This is excellent," Ben told her. "Is this an old family recipe?"

"Yes, but I'm the only one who makes it anymore. Mother just buys the frozen lasagna tins at Sam's. It's sad, really."

"Agreed." He took a second helping. "So, how's school? If you don't mind my asking."

"Mind you asking? If it weren't for you, I wouldn't even be there. And I'm doing great. But that's not what I wanted to talk about." She paused. "I've got a favor to ask."

Uh-oh. Was this where he paid for the pudding? "And what would that be?"

"You remember me telling you about Milo?"

Ben nodded. "New boyfriend. Very intellectual. Likes to rattle on about Kierkegaard and the works of William Faulkner."

"Yeah. Well, see . . . he's got this sister. . . ."

"Ye-es? Some people do."

"Yeah. Well, her name is Brita and she's very nice and smart, too, and Milo has been wanting to double-date with her 'cause there's this play they're doing at Theatre Tulsa they want to see, except she doesn't have anyone to go out with right now. . . ."

Ben put down his fork. "Ye-esss?"

Joni drew in her breath. "So, we were wondering if you would maybe come with us. Just to make it a foursome."

He gave her a stern look. "Joni Singleton. Are you trying to fix me up?"

She waved her hands in the air, a bit too energetically. "No, Ben. Nothing like that. It's just that there's this play we want to see, and I know you like plays and all that cultural stuff. . . ."

"Uh-huh."

"And she's older than Milo, so she's actually closer to your age."

"How much older?"

"Like . . . almost two years."

"So, I'd only be, say, a decade older than her?"

"Well, a little more than that, actually, but what does it matter? It's just a play." She giggled nervously. "So what do you say?"

"You want me to go out with a woman who's barely old enough to drink?"

"She can drink chocolate milk, so what do you care?"

"I don't think so, Joni."

"Why not?"

"Because I'm too old for her. I might as well be dating you."

He had meant it as a joke, but for some reason, the instant he said it, the table conversation went dead. Joni coughed into her hand. Ben wiped his mouth with his napkin. They avoided one another's eyes.

"Now that really *would* be ridiculous," Joni said finally, her voice a bit warbly. "But like I said, Brita is older than I am."

"Joni," he said, "The Beale trial starts Monday morning. I'm very busy right now."

"Busy with work, yeah. But you can't spend your whole life working. You never spend any time hanging with girls."

"That's not true. I hang with girls all the time."

"Like who?"

"Well, Christina, of course. And . . . and . . . well, Christina takes up a lot of time."

"There's Christina, and there's me. And unless I'm missing something, you're not dating either one of us."

"Forgive me, Joni, but this is none of your business."

"I know it's none of my business, Ben. But I care about you. I'm sorry, I know that sentimental stuff makes you uncomfortable, but I do. You've done so much for me. I just wanted to do a little something for you, you know?"

"Like cleaning my apartment?"

"More than that."

"I'm perfectly able to meet women on my own."

"Oh, sure, I know you are. In theory. But I also know that you tend to be a little shy and backward—"

"Backward?"

"I mean, not mentally. Not that you're stupid, exactly. But, like, socially. You tend to be a little . . ."

"Backward?"

"You know what I mean." She slapped her hands down on the table. "So what do you say, Ben? I really wish you would come. I think we'd have fun."

Ben chewed his lower lip. He could think of about a thousand reasons to decline, but somehow, when he peered into Joni's big brown eyes, he couldn't make himself do it. "If I can get away from work, I'll join you."

"Yippee! Oh, Brita's going to be so excited. I've told her all about you, how smart you are, and talented, and erotic—"

"Excuse me?"

"Okay, so I improvised a little. But she's going to be so happy!"

After Joni cleared the table and wrapped up the leftover lasagna, of which there was enough to last Ben a month, which was probably Joni's plan, they set a tentative date. Joni glided out of his apartment.

As he fed Giselle some of the leftover lasagna, his mind inevitably drifted back to what Joni had said. Backward? Was she right? Was that why he was still alone? Was that why he wasn't seeing anyone seriously? Why he really hadn't seen anyone seriously for any length of time—since Toronto and Ellen?

Ellen. She used to haunt his dreams. And now she haunted his nightmares. He could never forget. No matter how hard he tried.

Was that the problem? Or was it just his natural reticence? His wariness of other people. Because after all, other people were nasty. Could be, anyway. He smiled when he recalled where he had first heard that. Because, against all odds, he had first heard it long ago, when he was not yet even a teenager.

And he had heard it from a priest.

FATHER BEALE, THE much younger, beardless version Ben had known twenty-three years before in Oklahoma City, tried to counsel him. They were sitting in folding chairs set up in the back of the sanctuary for the choir. It was just the two of them; no one else was around.

Father Beale peered down at the twelve-year-old boy. "So, you're saying you don't want to participate in acolyte training?"

"No," Ben replied quietly. "I don't."

"And may I ask why?"

"Because I don't want to be an acolyte."

Father Beale tilted his head. "Flawlessly logical."

"Why does everyone think I have to be an acolyte, just because I'm twelve?"

"It's traditional. A time-honored rite of passage in our church."

Ben squirmed. "Well, I don't believe in all that church stuff, anyway."

Beale's forehead creased. "Are you telling me you're an atheist?"

"No," Ben replied. "I'm a nihilist. There's a difference."

"I see. A twelve-year-old nihilist. Interesting."

"I hope you won't repeat that to my parents."

"Of course not. Priest-communicant privilege."

"Good. I'm not sure they'd understand."

"Probably not." Beale's eyes turned toward the rafters. "Especially not your father."

"What's that supposed to mean?"

"Oh, nothing really. Except that I've noticed that you and your father are . . . well, what's the phrase? Not exactly a perfect match."

"That's one way of putting it."

"I've noticed in church that sometimes he'll put his hand on your shoulder and you . . . sort of cringe, don't you? You pull away."

"I don't mean to."

"I'm sure." Father Beale locked eyes with Ben. "I've also noticed more than once the bruises on your arms. Your legs. That black eye you had last winter. A lot of injuries for a boy who doesn't play sports."

Ben fell silent. He looked down at the floor tiles.

"That's what this is all about, isn't it?" Beale continued. "You don't want to be an acolyte—because you father *does* want you to be an acolyte."

"I don't know what you're talking about. I just don't believe in all that mumbo jumbo."

"I expect I've got a lot of acolytes who don't believe in all that mumbo jumbo, but they're still happy to be acolytes. If for no other reason, it's fun. Lighting the candles, wearing the robes. Hanging out with the other kids." He batted his lips with a finger. "But that doesn't really speak to you, either, does it?"

"I just don't want to be an acolyte, okay already? Are you going to make me?"

"No, Ben, I'm not going to make you. I think it would be good for you. I think God wants you to do it. But you have to come to Him willingly, or it's meaningless. Don't you agree?"

"I agree that it's meaningless."

Beale grinned. "I like you, Ben. I really do. You're a rebel, just like me. And we need more rebels in this world." He stretched out in his chair. "I do think it would serve you well to have some friends, though."

"I have friends."

"What? Books? I'm talking about the other kids in this church. Why aren't you out in the back shooting the breeze with the other boys your age?"

Ben's voice was soft and halting. "I don't really . . . get along with the other boys. They always talk about . . . weird stuff."

"Like sex?"

Ben's eyes widened. "How did you know?"

"For starters, I was twelve once. In my experience, the conversation of twelve-year-old boys principally deals with bodily functions. Sex being the most popular."

Ben looked down at the floor. "I just can't . . . follow all that dirty talk."

"Dad hasn't had the chat with you yet, huh?" He sighed. "Well, your father is a busy man. Tell you what, Ben. I've got a book I'm going to lend you. You like books, right? It should solve some of the mysteries. But, uh . . ." He tugged at his collar. "You don't necessarily need to tell your parents I lent it to you. In fact, I don't think they need to know you have it at all. We'll just make it our little secret. Okay? That shouldn't be a problem for a twelve-year-old nihilist."

"Okay. Cool."

"Read it through a few times. Then you should have no trouble conversing with the other boys on this all-important subject."

"But—even when I know what they're talking about . . . they talk so dirty. They make fun of me 'cause I don't talk like them."

"Well, other boys can be nasty. Other people, actually." Father Beale pondered a moment. "May I make a suggestion? Another one that your father probably wouldn't approve of?"

"Sure."

"Next time you see the other boys, just say *fuck* a few times."

Ben gasped. "Wha—wha—"

"You heard me. Just say *fuck*, loud and clear. It's a very flexible word. An Anglo-Saxon classic. You can use it, or a form of it, as a noun, a verb, an adjective, or an adverb."

Ben gaped. He'd never in his life heard any grown-up use that word. Especially not a priest.

"Just do it and get it over with. God won't hold it against you, I promise. And once you've done it a few times, you'll be in the club. You'll be one of the gang. And," he added emphatically, "you won't have to do it any more thereafter. Understand?"

Ben nodded.

"Good. Now run along. I'll tell your father we're doing some soul-searching, and we'll put off this acolyte decision for a while, till you've had more time to think about it. I want you to join—I want you to feel that you're dedicating your life to a higher cause—but it's something you have to come to on your own."

"Okay."

"And be sure to admire my new stained glass window on your

way out of here. It's a beaut, isn't it? I've waited eight years to put something that exquisite in this church."

Ben did admire the new window, a full-length, multicolored portrayal of a dove rising above a rainbow. The conclusion of the Noah's Ark story. He could see why Father Beale was so proud; it was positively breathtaking.

What he did not know then, what he could not possibly imagine, was how that window—and Father Beale—would change his life forever.

CHAPTER

19

The Gospel According to Daniel

MY FIRST SERVICE after my release from jail was not, I would have to say, a rousing success. I had feared a boycott, but when the parishioners began to arrive in their usual numbers, I was lulled into the false belief that all was well, that they were willing to give me another chance. No one spoke to me, true, but that in itself was not unusual before a service, when both they and I are in a contemplative and prayerful state. They took their seats in the pews and all proceeded as usual. The choir sang, the readers read. I preached a sermon on the importance of forgiveness. I'm sure many in attendance thought I had chosen a self-serving topic, but in fact I had based my homily, as I always do, on the gospel reading for that Sunday prescribed by the lectionary. Whatever their thoughts, everyone sat quietly and listened. I was elated.

Until it came time for communion. At St. Benedict's, as at many Episcopal churches, we take communion at every Sunday service. I went through the usual procedures, breaking the bread, blessing the wine, singing the Sanctus and the Agnus Dei and so forth. But when I opened my eyes, the congregation was not moving forward to take the sacraments of Christ. One by one, they were moving in the opposite direction. They were leaving.

My people would not take communion from me.

Like Christ in the Garden, I stood alone.

That afternoon I cried like a baby. Cried and cried and cried. Cried to myself, cried out to God. Why would he visit this upon me? I still believed I was following his calling, that he wanted me to be at

St. Benedict's. But if that was true, why was he punishing me so?. For a shepherd to watch his own flock walk out on him—that went beyond testing. That, it seemed to me, was pure cruelty. But I did not—I could not—believe that my God was a cruel one. I do not believe that God causes tragedies to test us, that he kills tiny children to bring about some greater scheme. So why then was this happening? Either God truly was cruel, or God was powerless to stop the chain of events that had ensnared me. There seemed no other possible explanations.

And I did not know that I could live with either of those.

"ALL RIGHT," BEN said to all those gathered around the conference table, "this may be our last chance, so if there's anything you've learned, anything you've suspected, anything you haven't told me yet, this is the time. The trial starts Monday morning at nine A.M., and I intend to be ready."

Despite the fact that it was a Sunday afternoon, Ben had his whole staff gathered in the office—Christina, Loving, Jones, and Paula, just for good measure—as well as Father Beale. Everyone was trying to put a brave face on it, since the defendant was present, but Ben knew they were all conscious of the same omnipresent fact: The prosecution had a lot of evidence against Father Beale, and they had come up with precious little in his defense.

"What about all the people from St. Benedict's you've interviewed, Loving? I've read your reports. Is there anything more? Any suspicions you couldn't quite nail down? Any possible theories or motives?"

"I keep comin' back to the fact that Alvin Greene dated the last victim, Skipper." The large man shifted his weight uncomfortably in a chair that was much too small for him. "And that no one else in the church seemed to know anythin' about it. Seems suspicious to me."

"Alvin Greene?" Christina said. "That sweet little Altar Guild guy? He couldn't harm a fly."

"Yeah, that's what they said about Ted Bundy. Looks can be deceivin'. I know this guy is hidin' somethin'. He practic'ly admitted it to me, but I couldn't pry it out of him, come hell or high water."

"You think it has something to do with the church?" Ben asked.

"I know it does. The question is—what?"

"Maybe he was hinting about Ernestine's blackmail racket," Jones suggested.

Father Beale did a double-take. "Ernestine Rupert? A blackmailer?"

"Like I said," Loving grimaced, "looks are deceivin'."

"Now there's a woman," Jones said, "who strikes me as being capable of doing just about anything."

"Like hirin' a hit man?" Loving suggested.

"I don't know if I'd go that far. But she's a strong-willed woman. And even if it's just gossip, everyone seems to think she's quite wealthy."

"Fabulously wealthy would be more like it," Paula said. She opened a red folder and slid a report across the table. "I went onto the Internet and researched all our suspects. She's loaded."

"How rich is fabulously rich?"

"Well, she's not quite up there with Elizabeth II, but it's impressive, just the same. Her estate is around eight or ten million."

Ben whistled. "That could buy you a few hit men."

"Yes. And anything else you wanted."

Jones frowned. "If this woman is so wealthy, why is she blackmailing people?"

"Greed," Loving suggested. "Coupled with fundamental meanness."

Ben addressed his client. "Did you know how wealthy she is?"

"I knew she had a lot. I knew it because she reminded me of it constantly. Reminded me what an outsize proportion of the St. Benedict's budget comes from her annual tithe. She frequently implicitly threatened to withdraw her support if I didn't give her what she wanted."

"And did you?"

"More often than not. Though not often enough to please her. We have a lot of wonderful, warm, giving people in our church—but few who have any money to speak of. The truth is—if Ernestine withdrew her pledge, I don't know if we'd survive."

"What about her nephew?" Ben asked.

Loving grinned. "Now there's someone who really couldn't harm a fly. Though I suspect he'd like to. But he's totally under his aunt's thumb."

"You can't see him slipping away to cause a bit of mischief?"

"When would he have time? He's too busy fetchin' his aunt's slippers and stirrin' her tea."

"I talked to Paul Masterson yesterday myself." Ben turned toward Father Beale. "He's got a few axes to grind with you."

Beale stroked his beard. "The man is a consummate musician, but unfortunately, he suffers from a huge inferiority complex. I have suggested that he try some counseling, but of course, he was not receptive."

"He says you overrule him and change his hymn selections for the services."

"That's true. Did he tell you why?"

"Not really."

Beale tried to explain. "Selecting a hymn is more than just picking a pretty song. Masterson is untouchable when it comes to musicality—but he sometimes forgets that there is more to a hymn than an interesting tune. There is a text, too. They're little homilies. Short sermons. The Book of Common Prayer sets forth our scriptures for each service—chooses our topic, if you will—and the hymns should be coordinated with that topic. When Masterson forgets to do that—or does it poorly—I intervene."

It sounded rational enough to Ben, but he had a hunch Masterson might have a rebuttal. "What about you, Christina? Did you find anything out from George Finley or Susan Marino?"

"Well, I told you, I think they're very close."

"Are we talking romance here?"

She shrugged. "They denied it. But there was definitely something between them. Some tension or uneasiness or . . . something."

"More secrets," Loving mused. "How many can this church have?"

"We need all the information we can muster in that courtroom," Ben said. "I can't cross-examine people effectively when I don't know what's going on."

"We know, Skipper," Loving said. "We're still lookin'."

"Good. I need Christina with me in the courtroom. But the rest of you—keep investigating. Follow these people. Talk to their friends. Dig around on the Internet. The most trivial detail might turn out to be important."

Jones nodded. "Got it, Boss."

"I know we've been in tight scrapes before. And there have

probably been cases where we went into trial with less information, too. But this is different." He tried to avoid looking at Father Beale. "This time we know the prosecution has a strong case. We know public sentiment has already tried and convicted our client. We know there are secrets no one is talking about." He paused. "We know the odds are stacked against us."

He took a deep breath. "But we can't let that get to us. No matter what—we have to win this case. We—we—" His voice broke. He turned to Father Beale. "We will win this case. That's a promise."

AFTER THE REST of his staff departed, Ben remained in the office with Father Beale. Beale had uncorked a bottle of merlot, and he and Ben were sharing a drink.

"Hope you don't mind," Beale explained. "But I know this trial could go on forever, and I know once it starts, drinking will not be an option." He winked. "So I wanted to get in a few good gulps while the getting was good."

He swirled the burgundy liquid around in his glass. "I do love red wine, don't you?"

"Well, I've learned how to drink it," Ben answered. Not a cool response, he supposed, but you can't lie to your priest. "I'm not much of an aficionado."

"You should be. It's smart and relaxing and—in my opinion— even holy. Benjamin Franklin said beer was proof that God loves us." He smiled. "It's all part of making the most of what God has given us. Taking comfort from his treasures. While we can."

Ben arched an eyebrow. "Excuse me, but are you promoting the consumption of alcoholic beverages?"

"Well, I am a priest, aren't I?" He took a deep swallow. "And speaking of religion—"

"Do we have to?"

"I noticed you still didn't take communion last Sunday. It would be hard to miss—since virtually everyone else in the sanctuary walked out on me."

"I'm sorry about that, Father. I thought that was nasty and . . . and inexcusable. Regardless of the circumstances."

"Yes, but don't change the subject. When are you going to stop toying with religion and really commit yourself? Take a leap of faith?"

"I'm not twelve anymore, Father."

"Do you have to be a child to believe?"

"Father, if you'd seen some of the things I'd seen . . ."

"Oh, please."

"Look, I've got too much to do at the moment, Father. More than I can handle, what with this trial and everything."

"Have you asked God for help?"

Ben's neck twisted. "You see—that's what I dislike most about religion—the power-of-prayer bit. People say, God answers prayers, so pray for what you want, and you'll get it. Unless you don't. Then it means God said no. Which is pretty convenient, isn't it?"

"We can't begin to understand why God answers some prayers and not others."

"I mean, it's really like a celestial Santa Claus. You make out your list and send it up. If you get some of it occasionally, it proves Santa exists. Except, of course, that he doesn't."

"But you're so wrong, Ben," Beale said. "Santa does exist. If you don't believe me—ask a five-year-old. Santa is the spirit of Christmas."

"Oh, don't give me that 'Yes, Virginia' rot."

"But it's true. You have to realize—just because things don't have tangible reality, that doesn't mean they don't exist. Ideas are just as real as people and property. Ideas have changed the world, profoundly, to an extent most people never approach. The idea of Santa—the spirit of Christmas—is very real and wonderful."

"I think you're stretching a point to win an argument."

"You can't ask me to explain the unexplainable, Ben. Some questions simply have no answers. It was meant to be that way. If we could prove empirically that God exists—what would be the point? That wouldn't be faith. That would be . . . science class. True religion requires an act of faith—that's what defines it. That's what makes it important."

"This is all sounding pretty mysterious to me, Father."

Beale settled back into his chair. "I've talked to your partner, Christina. I like her a lot."

"Everyone does."

"Including you?" He grinned. "Never mind. None of my business. But she tells me that you're very good at solving mysteries."

Ben shrugged. "I've gotten lucky a time or two."

"Well, then," Father Beale said, wrapping his fingers around the silver cross dangling from his neck, "isn't it time you tackled the greatest mystery of all?"

CHAPTER

20

BEN ALMOST MISSED it, in the early twilight, as he crossed the parking lot to get to his car. A plain piece of paper, folded over once, and tucked under the driver's side washer blade.

He looked all around. As far as he could tell, no one else was present. Of course, he'd been in the office almost all day. This note could've been left at any time.

He unfolded it. The short message was spelled out in block capital letters: MEET AT SHED BEHIND CHURCH AT NINE. WE MUST TALK.

He crumpled the note in his hand. He knew the place—a storage shed where they housed seasonal decorations and gardening equipment and anything else that didn't fit in the church itself. But who was it from? And what did his correspondent want to talk about?

He knew one thing for certain—if Mike were around, he would tell Ben that under no circumstances should he make this rendezvous. It could be anyone—someone who thinks Ben knows too much, someone who hates lawyers, someone who's convinced Beale is guilty and wants to take it out on his attorney.

But there was also the possibility that the person who wrote the note knew something about this case, maybe something he or she couldn't say on the record. Something that might help Father Beale. And if there was any possibility of that . . .

His throat dry, Ben slid behind the wheel and started toward Seventy-first. This was probably stupid—possibly even dangerous. But he had no choice. He simply had no choice.

* * *

As Ben entered the north parking lot at St. Benedict's, he was surprised to see several other cars already there. Had other people gotten mysterious notes under their windshield wipers? he wondered. Or was something else going on here?

Up ahead, passing by the prayer garden, Ben spotted Father Beale heading toward the church. That was odd. He'd given his client strict instructions to go home and get some rest—because once the trial started, he would have little spare time and even less rest.

Ben ran up behind him. "Father Beale? What are you doing here?"

Beale stroked his snowy white beard. "Vestry meeting," he said, without much enthusiasm.

"You're kidding!"

Beale shook his head sadly. "It is Sunday night."

"I told you to go home and relax. A vestry meeting is about the most unrelaxing thing I can imagine."

"I am the rector of this church," he replied evenly. "I can't miss the vestry meetings."

"But what's the point? You know how those people feel about you."

"I am the rector of this church," he repeated.

"I need you to be one hundred percent tomorrow, not all strung out from some aggravating, traumatizing meeting."

"I have to be there," he said simply.

Ben let him pass, but he was not happy about it. The last thing on earth they needed was another angry confrontation fueling the prosecution theories. Most of the vestry members were on Canelli's witness list. This would only give them one more horror story to relate to the jury.

Inside the church, Ben saw Dr. Masterson and George Finley and Ruth O'Connell and several other vestry members in the parish hall, waiting for the meeting to begin. They looked about as enthusiastic about this as Father Beale did. Ben toyed with the idea of getting on his cell phone and calling in a bomb threat, just to break up the meeting. Illegal, true, but it would be a mercy to all concerned.

Carol Mason, the gorgeous Sunday school teacher, met Father

Beale at the door outside the parish hall. "We have to talk," she said quietly. She took Father Beale's hand into her own and held it, leading him away. A surprisingly intimate gesture, Ben thought. He wondered if he was the only one who noticed.

Behind him, outside the parish hall, Ben heard voices—angry voices. He turned quietly and followed the sounds. They were coming from the nursery, of all places, but they were not the voices of children. Two adults were in there, one male, one female. He pressed up against the wall just outside the door and listened.

"Hell, yes!" the man said. "Of course I knew the trial started tomorrow. But I didn't expect to be subpoenaed!"

"It's just a precaution," the female assured him. "Standard procedure. To make sure you'll be there when they need you."

"Maybe so, but I still don't like it. What if they call me to the witness stand and start asking a lot of questions?"

"Like you thought you'd be one of those witnesses they didn't ask any questions?"

"You know what I mean."

There was a protracted pause, long and deadly.

"There's no reason why it should even come up. It has nothing to do with the murders."

"Susan, I don't know that."

There was another pause, even longer than before. Ben took the opportunity to quietly inch his head toward the door, just enough to see who was in there. As he surmised, the woman was Susan Marino, current leader of the vestry. And she was speaking to George Finley.

"A little late to be having second thoughts, isn't it, George?"

"How did I know it would come to this?" he said, his voice escalating. "How did I know people were going to be murdered?"

"You didn't, George, and you still don't. You don't know anything."

"Susan—I'm warning you. I do not want this to get out."

"Then keep your head together and your mouth shut. Look—it's almost nine. Let's go to the meeting."

Ben crept away from the door and segued into the hallway. Bad enough to be eavesdropping; he certainly didn't want to be caught. He drifted into the narthex and talked to other members of the vestry, but didn't learn anything of interest. After a few minutes, he gave it up. The meeting was getting ready to start, and he had no desire to experience the acrimony that was sure to follow. Besides, he had a rendezvous to make.

He passed through the front doors of the church and walked around to the back. About fifteen feet away from the south wall of the church was the barn-shaped storage shed.

The door was open, just barely.

Slowly, Ben crossed the darkened yard to the shed. Twilight had given way to night, and there was no moon out, or if there was, it was hidden behind heavy cloud cover. A little light spilled out of the top windows in the back of the church, but not much. If the shed had been any smaller, he might not have been able to find it.

The wind was cold on his cheek; rain was coming, if he wasn't mistaken. It gave him a shiver. Or something did, anyway.

He took the doorknob in hand and slowly pulled it open. The door creaked like something out of a haunted house, or so it seemed, there in the chilling darkness.

He stepped inside. It was much too dark to see anything. He knew from previous visits that the shed was stacked high with boxes and decorations and lawn care equipment, but he couldn't detect any of that yet. Maybe in a moment, after his eyes adjusted. Although what they were going to adjust to, he didn't know, because it was just as dark outside as it was in here.

"Hello?" he said into the darkness.

There was no response.

Maybe this was a mistake, he thought, staring out into the void, goose pimples crawling across his flesh. A killer had already struck twice at this church. Maybe for once he should play it smart and get out while the going—

He heard something. A rattling noise, something moving ever so slightly.

"Is someone in here?"

Still no answer. Ben's pulse was racing. He was breathing harder and deeper and his knees were beginning to shake.

He was terrified, but it wouldn't do to let that show. He tried to sound tough. "Look, if you have something to tell me, let's get it over with, okay? Otherwise, I'm out of here."

There was a sudden rustling sound in the rear of the shed. He heard footsteps fast approaching. And some kind of muffled shuffling or murmuring or—

Giggling? Did he really hear giggling?

All at once, the overhead light flashed on and Ben saw two small figures standing before him. Two teenage girls.

"Judy! Maura!" His eyes flashed red with anger. "What in the—?"

Control your language, he told himself. Not in front of the children. "What do you think you're doing?"

"Only having a little fun," Judy said. She was grinning from ear to ear. "Didn't you think that was exciting? And mysterious?"

Ben could still feel his heart thumping in his chest. "You don't want to know what I thought it was. Did you put that note under my windshield?"

Judy nodded her head guiltily.

"Judy, do you understand that I'm starting a murder trial tomorrow morning? You shouldn't be telling me you need to talk if you don't."

"But I do need to talk to you," she said. Both eyes and voice dropped a notch. "I—I've been needing to for a long time."

"Why? What is it?"

For once, Judy appeared to have lost some of her brashness. "I . . . wanted to ask you something."

"Yeah, yeah. What is it?"

"I wanted to ask . . ." Her eyes roamed all around the shed. "I wanted to ask if you'd like to go out to dinner with me."

Ben's lips parted. "You're kidding me. You brought me here—to ask me out on a date?"

"She's been wanting to ask you for weeks," Maura said, piping in. "She has the most gigantic crush on you."

"Maura," Judy said out the corner of her mouth, "clam up."

"Well, it's not like he doesn't already know. She worships you. She doodles your name in the margins of her papers with little hearts all around it."

"I do not!" Judy turned back toward Ben. "She's so immature sometimes. So what do you say?"

"What do I say? You mean—about going out with you?"

"Sure. Why not? I checked with your investigator, and he said you're not seeing anyone."

Remind me to give Loving my thanks, Ben thought silently. "Judy, you're a charming girl with a lot of energy, but you're—how old? Sixteen?"

"Fifteen. Sixteen in July. But I'm very mature for my age."

"Granted. But I still can't be dating someone who's two decades younger than I am."

"I don't see why not. Lots of men marry younger women."

Shades of Joni. Why was everyone trying to fix him up with teenyboppers? "Not fifteen-year-olds. Besides, what would your parents say?"

Maura made a slashing gesture across her throat, but too late.

"I haven't seen my father for years," Judy said quietly. "He doesn't live with us anymore. And my mother is much too busy with the new baby and the rest of her brood to even notice that I'm alive."

"I'm sure that isn't true."

"It is. She hates me. She thinks I ruined her life because she got pregnant with me and then she had to get married and she's been screwed up ever since."

It was amazing how in a few short strokes you could get a complete picture of where someone had come from and why they were what they were.

"Look," Ben said, "you're a great girl, but you're just fifteen and I can't date you."

"Fine," she said quietly.

"But I'm thinking this summer, when school lets out, I am going to have to hire a clerk for my law office."

Her head turned up. "Seriously?"

"Seriously. And I can't think of anyone who'd be better for the job than you. Since you're an aspiring attorney and all."

Her face was transformed by an unrestrained grin. "Seriously? And I could work with you on all your important life-or-death cases and stuff?"

"Well . . . in some capacity."

"And you'd pay me and everything?"

"Of course." He couldn't wait to see the expression on Jones's face when he heard about this.

Judy was bouncing up and down, bubbling with excitement.

"Maura! He's going to let me come to his office and work with him and be part of his elite dream team!" She stopped suddenly. "But what about Maura? Could you find a job for her? Maybe she could mop the floors or something."

"I don't mop," Maura said flatly.

"I'm sure we could find something for you to do, Maura. If that's what you want."

"Oh, I'm so excited!" Judy said, bouncing again. "Thank you so much!" She plunged forward and, before Ben could avoid it, wrapped her arms around him. "Thank you."

"You're welcome. Now get home, both of you."

He watched as the two girls skittered out the door, talking excitedly as they went. Well, it would be fun to have some new blood in the office, come summer. And they could use an extra hand or two, particularly during trial crunch times. Although, if Christina and Judy ever got together, they might create an elemental force unstoppable by mortal man.

Well, he'd worry about that in June. For now, he had a trial coming up. He needed to get home and—

A terrifying scream pierced the darkness, splitting the night apart. Ben froze.

"Judy! Maura!"

If anything, the night seemed even darker than it had before. The lights in the church were out. Ben saw two shadowy figures about ten feet away, in the direction of the street, huddled beneath a river birch. He ran toward them.

"Judy? Maura? Was that you?"

"It was Judy." Closer now, and with the faint glow of a street light somewhere on Seventy-first, he could barely make out their faces. "She got scared."

Judy was sitting on the ground, her hands pressed against her face, breathing hard enough to induce hyperventilation.

"Take it easy," Ben said, crouching beside her. He put his hand on her shoulder and tried to calm her. "You're okay. What happened?"

"I—don't—know," she choked out between gasps. "I guess I panicked."

"Why?"

"We—we were walking toward the street, and suddenly the lights in the church went out, and I felt something on my shoulder and—and—I guess I just freaked." Her eyes were wide and teary. "I guess it was just the tree branch, but I thought I was dead. I thought—I thought—"

"I know what you thought," Ben said. After two murders, who could blame her? He looked over his shoulder, back at the church. Sure enough, the lights in the top windows were now out. "Can you walk okay?"

"I—guess so," Judy said quietly.

"Good girl. Now both of you—get out of here. Don't stop till you're home."

Judy and Maura linked arms and started back toward the street. Ben headed for the back door of the church.

Inside was even blacker than out; all the lights appeared to be dead. He could hear movement and whispers in the parish hall.

"Is everyone all right?" Ben asked, shouting at figures he could barely perceive.

"How the hell should we know?" someone replied—George, Ben thought. "I can't see a damn thing."

"What happened?"

"The lights went out," replied an older female voice. Ruth? Ernestine? He couldn't be sure. "We were conducting our meeting, having the usual titanic shouting match with our priest, and then suddenly everything went black."

"Father Beale? Are you there?"

There was no answer. Ben felt the short hairs rise on the back of his neck. Where was he?

"Father Beale?" Still no answer. Clinging to the wall to guide himself, Ben entered the main corridor. "Father Beale?"

The response came as a thunderclap of shouts and ear-piercing screams. The tumult sideswiped him like a knockout punch from a prizefighter. He reeled, trying to figure out from which direction it came. How many times had he heard screams in this church? he asked himself as he raced down the corridor. How many times had his flesh crawled and his knees knocked, dreading what he might find?

He was one of the last to make it to the utility area behind the parish hall. Most of the vestry were already there, and one of them—George—had managed to locate a flashlight. Courtesy of the illumination of the narrow beam, Ben could see that the room was in disarray—folding chairs fallen and scattered on the floor, overturned tables. The breaker box was hanging open.

And Susan Marino's upright body was in the center of it all, the side of her head covered with blood, her eyes lifeless.

She was dead. Ben could see that in an instant. And he could also see how she managed to remain upright.

Father Beale was behind her, cradling her in his arms.

Two

The Gospel Truth

◆ ◆ ◆

21

The Gospel According to Daniel

As we posed there in the darkened room, transfixed like some twisted version of the pietà, I could only think, *My God, my God, why hast thou forsaken us?* Is this the twelfth plague, a visitation from the Angel of Death? Yes, God works in mysterious ways, but he's not normally sadistic about it. If ever there was to be a time when my faith might waver, this was it.

And it did, in my heart at least. True, I did not run, but I certainly considered it. I knew what this latest tragedy would mean—more infamy, almost certain revocation of bail, perhaps even defrocking. The temptation to run—to let this cup pass from me—was great. In another world, in another time, I very well might have done it.

But not here, not with Susan. One instinct overcame another. I took her into my arms and cradled her, hoping to bring some comfort to her passing, if she was not dead already. I gave her unction, performed the last rites. *Requiescat in pace.* And I did not run. I trusted God to take care of me.

Dear, dear Susan. At one time we had been close, we had held one another and it had meant something to both of us. And now there was nothing left. Not of us. Or of her.

The police were as shocked as I was to see that it had happened again. Few words were spoken. I was taken into custody, read my rights. My attorney did his best to intervene, arguing about my readiness for the impending trial, but there was no point. I had blood on my hands again—literally—and even I could see it would be gross misconduct for the police to do anything other than what they did.

And so, like Paul in Rome, I was once again imprisoned, if not for my faith, then certainly because of it.

If I were one to believe in omens, I would have to think that this new murder, on the eve of trial, was not a good one. Forces were at work that seemed determined to see me punished, humiliated. And yet, as they led me from my cell to prepare for court, I thought that as hideous as the night had been, as ghastly as the trial was sure to be, I at least had the comfort of knowing that it was coming to an end. It could not possibly get worse. Nothing could happen that could be any more horrible than what had already occurred.

In retrospect, my naïveté seems pathetic. The trial, not the legal trial but the spiritual trial, was just beginning. The worst was yet to come.

BAIL REVOKED.

The notice was waiting for Ben when he arrived in the court-room. It was no surprise. As it stood now, Judge Pitcock looked like a fool for having granted bail in the first place, when Father Beale was a suspect in two murders. Now he was a suspect in three, if not virtually convicted in the minds of most, and the only act Pitcock could take to save face was to revoke bail as fast and fully as possible.

Ben crumbled the notice and tossed it into the nearest waste-basket. He was tired. He'd had less than an hour's sleep. He'd spent the night dealing with Mike and the rest of the homicide department, who questioned Father Beale well into the wee hours. They wanted to interrogate everyone immediately, before memories faded, before Beale had a chance to concoct a story or have one fed to him. But Ben fought it all the way. He's going on trial for his life, tomorrow morning, Ben argued. To deny a man sleep on the eve of his trial was a violation of the fair trial provisions of the Constitution.

Ultimately, they compromised. Mike questioned Beale for an hour, then said he would continue it the next night—and as many nights thereafter as it took to get it done. After Beale was in bed, Ben went through the usual motions he made for the newly incarcerated, including an all but preposterous request that he be released on bail.

Outside the courtroom, in the hallway, Ben heard the buzz rise among the huddled throng of reporters. Beale was on his way.

The hallway was jam-packed with press, more than Ben had seen in his entire career, even when the city's mayor was on trial. Sadly enough, by the time a case went to trial, it had usually been bumped from the top of the news list. Not this time. With a fresh victim only the night before, this was the story of the day. It was taking on the tone of a tabloid soap opera—exactly the kind of story reporters seemed to love most.

As soon as Ben was back in the hallway, questions started flying his direction.

"Is it true God told him to kill that woman? Or Satan?"

"How can you explain the blood all over him?"

"How many women does he have to kill before he gets the needle?"

"Are you going to make a deal with the DA?"

Although he normally assiduously ignored the press while a trial was in progress, Ben felt he had to answer that one. "No deals."

Accurate, if somewhat uninformative. Ben had in fact visited Canelli this morning to discuss the possibility of a deal. Canelli told him to go climb his thumb.

"Why no deals?" one reporter followed up.

"Because Father Beale is innocent!"

Ben's statement was met not only with disbelief, but outright laughter. The reporters seemed to think it humorous that a lawyer would so tenaciously argue the innocence of someone who so clearly wasn't. A bad sign. Because those journalists would be sharing their opinions, however subtly, with their readers and viewers. Or to put it another way—the jury pool.

Ben wished Christina was here, but he knew she was in the clerk's office prepping for jury selection. Christina got along well with the press; many of these reporters were her friends. Not so he. Ben knew he should be more open-minded about people who did, after all, fulfill an important role in a democratic system, but he'd seen too many cases screwed and too many jury pools tainted by reporters trying to boost their ratings or to get a scoop on the competition.

Ben spotted the two marshals escorting Father Beale down the hallway. At Ben's insistence, he was out of the orange coveralls and into a suit and tie, shaved and groomed. Choosing his clothes had been a bit of a problem. Beale wanted to wear his clerical collar; he always did, at least when he wasn't in prison. But Ben worried that the jury would see it as putting on a show, trying to shove his holiness down their throats. Beale finally agreed to wear a blue suit, with a regular button-down collar. Ben was relieved. No one would ever have an opportunity to forget that he was a priest; he didn't need to be costumed for it.

Ben put his arm on Beale's shoulder, careful to act friendly and unafraid. Those potential jurors were probably watching; it was important that Ben indicate that Beale was someone he liked, not just someone for whom he worked. And the importance of seeming unafraid was obvious. Since everyone else in the hallway was acting just the opposite.

"Get any sleep?" Ben asked.

"Cot was a bit lumpy," Beale replied. "Think you could get me one of those cushioned orthopedic numbers?"

"I'll work on it." Ben peered at his face. For a man who had been through everything he had endured in the last twelve hours, he didn't look half bad. "Ready to go?"

"Would it change anything if I said no?"

" 'Fraid not."

Ben pushed open the double doors and stepped inside the courtroom. The room was packed; there wasn't an empty seat in the house. Again, Ben was not surprised. The third murder had made this trial a major draw for fans of murder and mayhem. Ben saw some familiar faces, including many people from St. Benedict's—Ruth, Ernestine, Alvin, and several others. He also spotted Andrea, in her reserved seat at the front, just behind the defense table. That was important—Ben wanted the jury reminded that Father Beale was married, and to see that she was here supporting him.

Ben and Father Beale walked down the aisle to the front of the courtroom. The marshals remained at the rear. Ben pulled out a chair at the defense table, but instead of sitting in it, Beale knelt beside it.

Ben leaned in close and whispered. "What are you doing?"

Beale's eyes were closed. "I'm praying."

"Well . . . stop it."

"I always pray for God's support and guidance before I do anything important."

Ben's forehead creased. "But people are looking at you."

"And? You think they'll be surprised to see a priest praying?"

"They'll think you're putting on a show. For the prospective jurors."

"I can't help what people think."

"I can. It's my job." He tugged at Beale's arm. "C'mon. If you have to pray, at least do it sitting in a chair."

"It's not the Episcopal way."

"Consider it an order."

"But—"

"Remember our discussion last night? As soon as we stepped through those double doors, I became the boss. So do what I tell you."

Beale reluctantly allowed Ben to pull him into the chair. He continued to pray, head down, hands folded, like Ben had done as a child saying grace at the dinner table.

What a great job this was, Ben mused. The life-enriching work of a defense attorney. Today, for instance, his first act had been to tell someone to stop praying. And if he was trying to lead people away from prayer, that would make him . . .

Never mind. Too many people thought that about lawyers already.

Assistant DA Canelli strolled over from his side of the courtroom, towering over Ben with his stratospheric height. "Look, I talked to my boss. I think we've got a slam dunk, but he's worried about negative publicity fallout from nailing a priest, even if we win. So I'm willing to give you life."

"Life?"

"Right. But it has to be on three counts."

"Three? You haven't even charged him on the first and third—"

"We have now."

Ben ground his teeth. "When were you planning to tell me?"

"I gave the papers to your partner—the redhead."

"Right before trial?"

"Sorry, but everything has happened so fast. I didn't plan a new murder the night before trial, but I had to deal with it."

Ben supposed that was probably true. "Give me second degree and I'll take it to my client."

"No deal. I'm saving you from the death penalty, and I think that's gift enough for a three-time serial killer. Take it or leave it. Personally, I want to go to trial."

Ben glanced down at Beale, who was shaking his head vigorously. "No deal," Ben answered.

Canelli did not appear surprised or disappointed. "See you in the funny papers," he said, flashing his uncommonly handsome smile.

Christina appeared, her arms loaded down with paper. "Got the drivers' licenses." Which was her way of saying she'd obtained a copy of the rolls of prospective jurors—who were selected at random from drivers' license records.

"Good. Keep an eye on them. You're my people person."

She beamed. "Because of my sunny personality?"

"Because . . . I'm not."

Judge Pitcock entered the courtroom from chambers. He couldn't possibly be unaware of the enormous number of reporters in the courtroom, but Ben thought he was doing a fair job of not playing to them, at least not obviously.

"This court is now in session," he said, rapping his gavel. "First on our docket today is the State of Oklahoma versus Beale, Case CJ-02-78945P. Murder in the first degree. Are all the parties ready?"

Both Ben and Canelli indicated that they were.

"Very well. Let the trial begin."

22

As BEN WELL knew, an old trial lawyer bromide held that there are only two subjects on which you absolutely could not quiz jurors during voir dire. You could ask them about their personal lives, even their sex lives, if need be. You could ask what they watch on television, what they read, what they eat, where they work, how they like their steak cooked, how often they go to the bathroom, whether they have an innie or an outie. But there were two subjects you could not touch, two areas so sacrosanct the judge would shut you down in a heartbeat if you even tried to address them: politics and religion.

Unfortunately, this voir dire necessarily involved both.

"I'm sure most of you, like me, tend to automatically treat a religious man with a little more respect than the average joe," Canelli said, addressing the first eighteen drivers' licenses called to the jury box. "It's kind of automatic. And that worries me, of course, because in this case, it's important that you treat Daniel Beale no differently than you would any other defendant. No special privileges. Just fairly."

But not too fairly, right? Ben thought.

"Do you think you can do that?" Canelli asked. He polled some of the prospective jurors, starting with older men who were less likely to be traumatized by being called on individually. "Do you think you could treat the defendant just as you would anyone else charged with a capital crime?"

Well, honestly, Ben thought, what were they going to say? Ben scrutinized the men and women giving the answers, and he saw no indication that the defendant's priestly status was going to give him any great advantage. In fact, he wondered if it might not be just the opposite.

An elderly Hispanic woman on the second row shifted her weight slightly. "Act'lly, sir, I do have a problem with that."

Even Canelli seemed surprised. He was making a rhetorical point, not really expecting an affirmative answer. "How so, ma'am?"

"I just don't think I could ever do anything that would hurt a priest."

"Even if I proved that he had committed a horrible crime?"

"Well . . . maybe. But I think—he's the strong right arm of God. He goes where God wants him to go."

Including the state pen? Ben wondered.

"Ma'am, are you saying you couldn't convict this defendant even if his guilt were proved beyond a reasonable doubt?"

Again she did not directly answer the question. "I'm not saying that. I just can't see myself doing any harm to a man of God. A man who has devoted his whole life to Christ. I grew up in a Catholic school, and I was taught that a priest is special."

"I understand," Canelli said patiently. "I must ask you to answer—"

"I mean, doesn't he deserve some extra consideration? We're talking about a man who has agreed to give up everything. Money, worldly possessions, even women!"

Canelli cleared his throat. "Uh . . . actually, ma'am, Daniel Beale is an Episcopal priest. They don't . . . uh . . . you know, swear an oath of chastity. He's married."

"Episcopal? Oh." She slid back into her seat. "Well, that's different."

Canelli nodded slowly. "So . . . do you think you could judge him just as you would any other defendant?"

"Oh, sure. No problem."

Ben glanced at his client. Beale should be distressed by this about-face, but Ben could tell he was working to suppress a grin. Nice that he could still see humor in the horror.

"Many of the witnesses Daniel Beale may call to the stand will also be religious men and women," Canelli continued. "Members of the clergy, members of his church. Again, of course, their testimony should be treated no differently than anyone else's. You should watch what they say and how they say it just as you would anyone else, trying to determine whether you're being told the truth—or a lie."

Ben poised himself to rise. He preferred not to object during voir dire, because he knew the jury didn't like it, but Canelli was pushing this about as far as Ben could tolerate.

"It's even possible," Canelli continued, "that a member of his church or a professional colleague might feel they have an obligation to a man of the cloth, that their duty to God created a duty to his representatives, and that might cause them to say things that are . . . um . . . not, strictly speaking, true."

That was it. Too far. "Objection," Ben said, rising. "This is becoming argumentative."

Judge Pitcock nodded. "Sustained. Stick to examining the jurors' qualifications, counsel."

"Of course," Canelli replied. He ran through most of the obvious subjects—looking for personal connections to any of the players, deep-rooted biases against law enforcement—anything that might hamper his case. He previewed some of the political issues that had been subjects of disagreement on St. Benedict's vestry. He made sure the jurors would all be willing to deliver the death penalty, if the evidence called for it. Then he finished, after not quite four hours—a surprisingly short interrogation for the prosecution in a capital murder case.

"Go get 'em, tiger," Christina said, giving Ben a little push.

Ben flashed a wry smile. He hated voir dire, as they both knew. He had tried to get Christina to do it. After all, she was the one who was good with people. But Christina insisted that she was better able to evaluate the venirepersons if she didn't have the distraction of having to ask questions and field answers. If she were free to watch and listen, to look for the subtle cues, the twitch of an eye or the turn of a head, that ultimately told her far more than the spoken answers did.

Ben started with some softball questions about their jobs and their families. Stuff that was marginally relevant, but was really being asked to give them an opportunity to adjust to Ben's style and warm up to him. There was a certain rhythm to a good voir dire, Ben had learned, but sometimes it took a few questions to find it. After about twenty minutes of that sort of thing, he redirected himself to the main topic—the forbidden one.

"How many of you folks go to church? At least occasionally?" Even Canelli hadn't been this brash, but Ben thought it was important.

All but two raised their hands.

"How many of you belong to Episcopal churches? Or have in the past?"

No hands rose. Ben wasn't surprised. Oklahoma was fundamentalist country—Southern Baptists, Methodists, that sort of thing. He also knew, unfortunately, that some retro-Protestants still harbored long-seated prejudices against those on the other side of the communion cup.

"The defendant, Father Beale, as you already know, is an Episcopal priest." Ben had noticed that Canelli always referred to him either as the defendant or as Daniel Beale, so as not to remind them of his clerical status. Ben, of course, would do just the opposite. "Is that going to influence anyone? I mean, negatively. I know some people are raised in a certain way, or maybe they have a bad experience early on, and for whatever reason they end up not liking people of other religious faiths."

This wasn't going to work. Who was going to admit to being a religious bigot? Ben had to try something else.

"Doesn't mean you're necessarily a bad person or anything." Sure, you could be one of those friendly bigots. "But sometimes things happen, and we don't know why exactly. We just are what we are and think what we think."

Still no takers. Ben kept pushing.

"Take asparagus, for instance. I hate asparagus." Several of the jurors chuckled. "It's not rational, I know. Lots of people love asparagus. Consider it a delicacy. My mother makes wonderful asparagus—or so I've heard. I've never tried it myself, and I never will. Because I hate the stuff. Don't even like the way it smells."

Ben let his smile fade, then brought them back to the serious subject at hand.

"But I have to keep asking about this—because it's so important to this case and my client getting a fair trial. I have to ask if anyone out there has similar negative feelings about . . . people who worship differently. Go to different kinds of churches. That sort of thing."

Apparently he had finally struck the right chord. A burly man in the back row, probably in his fifties, raised his hand.

The man spoke slowly and with a touch of a drawl. "I suppose mebbe I've got a little of that in me."

"You mean—about other religions?"

"Yeah. I mean, I ain't proud of it or anythin'. But I grew up on a farm, out in the western part of the state. Near Kingfisher. And some of the folks out there, my pa for instance—well, they just thought different. You know how it is. We almost never saw any Catholic or 'Piscopal types. So most of the things we said about them weren't too kind. Kneelers, that's what we called 'em."

"And . . ." Ben broached it gently. " . . . do you still feel that way?"

"I get a little uncomfortable when I see a grown man in a black dress or with one of those funny backwards collars around his neck. Kind of gives me the heebie-jeebies, if you know what I mean."

"Sure. So, given all that—do you think you'll be able to judge the case fairly? To treat Father Beale as you would anyone else?"

"I'd sure try but—well, I guess to be honest, I don't really know."

"I understand. Thank you for your candor, sir." Ben glanced over at the judge. It was a brief look but a meaningful one. It said: *Don't make me do it.*

Judge Pitcock nodded. "Mr. Graves, I would also like to thank you for answering these questions fully and fairly. And this is no reflection whatsoever on you, but I think it would probably be best for all concerned if you did not serve on this particular jury."

"I understand, your honor."

"Good. You're excused."

The bailiff called a replacement for Mr. Graves, and voir dire continued.

But not for that long. Ben eventually uncovered two other prospectives who possibly harbored some form of prejudice against Catholics or the pope or nuns or whatever, but nothing so strong or self-confessed that he could expect the judge to remove them as he had Mr. Graves. Ben touched on a few other important areas, including some of the political issues involved, made sure they all understood what the words *reasonable doubt* meant and what a high standard it was, then sat down.

Both sides removed five jurors, which required calling replacements, who in turn had to be questioned from scratch. Ben removed both men he suspected harbored some religious prejudice, then removed three women, basically because Christina told him to. She thought two of them seemed harsh and judgmental—thus more likely to convict—and she thought one of them was lying about her background, or at least holding something back. Good enough for Ben. He used all his peremptories expunging them.

Canelli removed the Hispanic woman from Catholic school. Despite her assurances that a mere Episcopal priest was no great shakes, he apparently thought it was a risk he didn't need to take. He removed four others for reasons that totally baffled Ben. Did he find them too kind and generous, thus unlikely to convict? Did he not like the way they looked at him? Did he not like what they were wearing? Ben had no clue, and Canelli was not likely to explain his case strategies to him, either.

It was a long day, but they managed to get the jury selected before five, which meant the trial could get under way first thing in the morning.

"Opening arguments at nine," Judge Pitcock said, rapping his gavel. "Court is now in recess."

The reporters flanked the exit, poised like rattlesnakes, which made Ben all the more content to hang about in the courtroom.

"Nice job," Christina said.

"Are you being facetious? Canelli is much better at voir dire than I am."

She shrugged. "Canelli is a people person. You're a . . . a . . ."

"A non–people person?"

"You're more reserved," Christina settled on. "Which makes all the more impressive what you accomplished. I mean, you got a guy sitting in a room full of people to admit he still carried around negative religious baggage from his childhood—without embarrassing him or causing him and everyone else to clam up. How many lawyers could've managed that?"

"I was impressed, too," Father Beale chimed in. "Although I was dismayed to see how much of that still exists. I thought we had all but rooted that out by working together, forming these interfaith and ecumenical committees. I liked to think all that backwoods Protestant-Catholic enmity was a thing of the past." He shook his head. "I guess I've been a fool."

Ben gripped him by the shoulder. "Well, Father, if that were a crime . . . I'd be doing life."

23

THE CRIME SCENE teams were still hard at work when Ben drove by the church about eight o'clock that night. Most of the hardest work had been done—the pictures were taken, the site had been combed for physical evidence, the body had been removed. But that was just the start of the process; Ben knew it would be days before the police pulled out entirely, and weeks before the church was able to return to any semblance of normalcy.

He was surprised, however, to see Mike's shiny silver TransAm out front. He parked and strolled inside.

Mike was in his usual rumpled trench coat, even though it wasn't remotely cold, barking orders and marching his underlings through their paces.

"Didn't I tell you to get those bloodstains off the wall?" Mike bellowed. He was nose-to-nose with some poor unfortunate baby officer.

"Y-y-yes, sir. I did that, sir."

"And how, may I ask? Did you lick it up?"

"N-n-no, sir. I used a rag."

"A rag and what?"

Ben heart's bled for the poor chump. He looked as if he were about to pass out. "Water, sir."

"And where, may I ask, did you get this water?"

"I—I found a sink. In the sanctuary, sir."

"That wasn't a sink, you dunderhead." Mike leaned into his face. "That was a baptismal font! You just scrubbed the walls with holy water!"

"I—I—I—oh, I'll refill it—"

"I've been informed they have that water brought in all the way from the river Jordan in the Middle East."

The young officer's mouth formed a broad *O*.

"And you just used it to moisten your Comet!"

"I—I—I—don't know what—"

"Get out of my sight, Sergeant. Finish your job!"

"Yes, sir. I will, sir."

"And this time get the water out of the bathroom!"

The young man scurried away, obviously relieved to escape the senior homicide detective's wrath.

Mike spotted Ben standing at the door. "Returning to the scene of the crime?"

"So to speak. Being a bit harsh, weren't you?"

Mike shoved his hands deep into his coat pockets. "It's good for them."

"Oh, no doubt. Sort of like verbal shock therapy." He grinned. "I thought you were supposed to mellow as you got older."

"Seems to be having the opposite effect on me."

"That's because you spend too much time around murders."

"No, that's because I spend too much time around lawyers. So what brings you here? Didn't your big case start today?"

"Yup. But I wanted to see what was going on here. See if you learned anything."

"Like what?"

"Like maybe—who did it?"

Mike gave him a withering look. "Give me a break, Ben. I'm not on the jury."

"Mike . . . Father Beale did not commit this murder. Or any of the others."

"You're in deep denial, Ben."

"I'm serious. I have a strong feeling about this."

"Do I need to catalog all the times your feelings have turned out to be dead wrong?"

"I'm not wrong this time. I know I'm not."

Mike shook his head. "I think it's best we change the subject. Before I have you arrested for aggravated stupidity."

Ben took the hint. "Is this killing consistent with the previous two murders?"

Mike's head tilted slightly. "There are a few minor differences, but I still—"

"What are they?"

"This is probably like feeding a piece of the sky to Chicken Little, but the MO is somewhat altered here. The previous two murders involved some kind of blunt instrument. But this time the killer used a knife."

"Meaning it's a different killer."

"Or, more likely, that the killer is becoming more bold, more bloody. Needs a little gore to keep it exciting."

"Have you found the knife?"

"Unfortunately, no. But we will."

"Time of death?"

"Of course, the coroner hasn't made any official pronouncements, but the inside scoop is that it could've been anywhere from five minutes to an hour before the body was found."

"No way. I heard Susan Marino engage in a heated discussion with George Finley maybe half an hour or so before we discovered the body."

"You saw her alive?"

"Well, I didn't actually see her. But I heard her voice."

"Who's this George?"

"Another member of the vestry. One of the few remaining." He glanced over Mike's shoulder, toward the utility room where the body was found. It was roped off with yellow tape; several technicians were still buzzing around. "I assume the killer shut off the lights."

"Well, you'd think so. But here's the interesting thing." He held up a thick palm-size device. "Know what this is?"

Ben squinted. "Isn't that one of those gizmos people use to turn their lights on and off while they're on vacation?"

"You win the Daily Double. Since St. B's here has a rather old, if not antiquated breaker box, someone was able to plug this doohickey in and use it to shut off the lights—at a predetermined time."

"So the killer didn't have to be in the utility room when the lights went off?"

"You got it. The lady was probably already dead when everything went black. Which enlarges our pool of suspects from the handful of people on the premises when the body was discovered to, basically, everyone on earth."

Ben's lips tightened. "That's just . . . dandy."

"Yeah. Well, I've got work to do."

"Mike, if you learn anything important—please call."

"I doubt if Mr. Canelli would appreciate me helping out his sworn adversary."

"But you will anyway, right?"

Mike sighed. "I suppose. But do me one favor, okay?"

"What's that?"

"Stop inviting me to visit your church. This place is way too dangerous for me." He pushed his fists into his pockets and headed back toward the utility room. "Half a league, half a league, half a league onward, All in the valley of Death . . ."

24

CANELLI'S OPENING ARGUMENT began, no surprise, with a gory, no-holds-barred description of the death of Kate McGuire. It was a well-established fact, or so prosecutors believed, that if you can make the crime seem vile enough, the jury will vote to convict, basically, anyone. What did surprise Ben was how often Canelli managed to work Father Beale's name into what was supposed to be a nonargumentative recitation of the facts.

"Daniel Beale was officiating at the wedding. Daniel Beale argued with Kate McGuire minutes before she was killed. The body was found in Daniel Beale's office. Her blood was on Daniel Beale's hands. Ladies and gentlemen, there is no question about what happened. The only question is—what are you going to do about it?"

Getting a bit argumentative, Ben noted, but it was too soon to object. It's not like he was telling the jury anything they didn't already know. The prosecutor wants you to convict. Big surprise.

"We will call to the stand numerous witnesses," Canelli continued, "both inside the church and outside, who will testify about the enormous anger and enmity Daniel Beale had for all members of the vestry, but especially for Kate McGuire—anger which revealed itself in repeated displays of temper. Threats were made, violent promises. Promises that were ultimately fulfilled in the most heinous way possible.

"We will also call to the stand expert witnesses—the police officers who investigated the scene and the forensic experts who tested the evidence. Each of these witnesses will tell you the same thing. That Daniel Beale committed this crime. That it was him and could have been no other. That the violent promises he made were fulfilled with deadly certainty."

Getting a bit poetic on us, Mr. Canelli? Apparently he'd put some extra time and effort into this opening. A bad sign for the defense. Because if he put this much time into the opening, Ben could only imagine what he'd planned for the rest of the trial.

Canelli finished at the end of the predetermined half hour, and Christina rose and introduced herself to the jury. Ben had assigned opening to her, in part to save closing for himself, and in part because he knew she would get the defense off to a good start with the jury. People trusted Christina; she came off friendly and honest—because she was. They recognized that her job was to defend the accused, but they also got a strong sense that she believed what she was saying—an all too rare circumstance for criminal lawyers.

"Most of what the prosecutor has told you is true," she said, right off the bat. "He's exaggerated and melodramatized it, but his facts are essentially accurate. But does the fact that the body was found in Father Beale's office prove he's the killer? Of course not. Doesn't look good, but it doesn't prove he committed murder. Certainly not beyond a reasonable doubt. The evidence presented in this courtroom will demonstrate that there are many other possibilities, and most important, that Father Beale did not commit this horrible crime.

"The prosecutor has made much of the fact that the body was found in Father Beale's office, but consider—if you're going to kill someone, is it smart to do it in your own office? On a day when literally hundreds of people will be in the church? Though the prosecutor wants you to believe Father Beale is a killer, he has never suggested that Father Beale is stupid. But let's face it—that would be a stupid thing to do. It only makes sense if the killer was someone else. Someone who wanted to throw suspicion on Father Beale."

Ben couldn't help but take pride in what a good job Christina was doing. Not that he had anything to do with it. She'd been around lawyers for so many years, it was only natural that she'd pick up a few skill points. Still, he couldn't help but feel a bit of a surge when he saw what an outstanding presentation she was making. Straightforward but not boring. Effective but not overreaching. Damn near perfect, really. And she'd had her license less than a year.

"The prosecutor talked about Father Beale's horrible temper, suggesting that this murder might've been the product of his rage. But the evidence will show that at no time did Father Beale, even in the most heated of arguments, strike anyone or harm them physically. There's a big difference between having a shoutfest at a meeting and strangling a woman over your desk. No witness called by either side will ever testify that he was physically violent. Sure, he had disagreements with the governing body of the church. Some of them serious. Frankly, that's not unusual. Is it a credible motive for murder? Do we believe someone would kill a woman just to silence her opinion about church matters? I couldn't believe that of the lowest life-form on earth. And I certainly can't believe it of Father Beale."

She turned slightly, compelling the jurors to look at the defendant. "We're not going to be asking for any favors based upon the fact that the accused is a priest. But we will ask you to consider the man, the person who sits at that table. As the evidence will show, he has no history of violence. To the contrary, he has only a history of selfless devotion, both to the world and to God. He has given most of his life to projects benefiting others, important social and religious causes. And we're supposed to believe that man suddenly became a cold-blooded killer—over some church dispute? Is that credible?"

She was, of course, doing exactly what Canelli had tried to circumvent, arguing—He's a priest! Therefore, he's a good guy, not a bad guy. But she was doing it so intelligently, and weaving in so much legal jargon, it was impossible for the DA to object.

"My partner will talk to you about this later," Christina continued, "and so will the judge, but it's worth reminding you, while we talk of possibilities and probabilities, that you have not been called here to guess about what happened. You have been called to listen to the prosecution's theory, to hear their evidence, and to answer one question—Have they proved their case beyond a reasonable doubt? If not, if doubts remain, then you must vote to acquit. It is not optional. The burden of proof is entirely on the prosecution. And if they do not meet it, then you must vote not guilty."

She stepped closer to them. "But I don't think it will come to that. Because the prosecution's case, as you will see, is full of holes. And Father Beale is not a murderer. My partner and I know that.

And at the conclusion of this trial, I believe you will, too. That's why you'll vote not guilty."

Christina took her seat. Father Beale looked pleased; Ben gave her an under-the-table thumbs-up.

Judge Pitcock banged his gavel. "Mr. Canelli, you may call your first witness."

And so the trial for Father Beale's life began.

25

The Gospel According to Daniel

IT IS A strange phenomenon, hearing people you know, people you love even, talk about you as if you were not present, even though they know perfectly well that you are. It is strange—and painful—watching them studiously avoid making eye contact, even as they say your name and talk about you at length. One always likes to imagine that one's acquaintances think well of them, and that when they are not present, they make warm and heartfelt compliments on your behalf. One fantasizes about being present at one's own funeral, like Tom Sawyer, and seeing friends and acquaintances, prostrate with grief, declaring the deceased to be "the finest man I have ever known."

My experience in court was somewhat different.

I was aware, of course, that many of my parishioners would be testifying for the prosecution, and I did not take it personally. I knew they had been subpoenaed, in the main, and that they would only be providing bits of circumstantial evidence, telling what they had seen and heard, and letting the prosecutor run with it as he would. They were fulfilling their duty to the state, just as I fulfilled my duty to God, I rationalized. No harm could come of that.

Again, I was a fool.

I knew there were strong feelings about me at the church, and I knew that many of them were unkind. I had heard impassioned arguments at meeting after meeting. I had watched in tears as almost every member of my congregation rose and walked out of the sanctuary, refusing to take communion from me. But to say these things in a public forum—in a court of law, no less—where their priest is literally on trial for his life? That was a development for which I was unprepared. Nothing could possibly have prepared me for that.

Perhaps optimism really is a disease, as Nietzsche suggested. Perhaps I was infected, and deep down I believed, or wanted to believe, that it would be my own flock that saved me. Whatever the reason, I simply wasn't prepared for it when they appeared, not in the role of saviors, but of executioners.

"HOW WOULD YOU describe the defendant's disagreements with the vestry, ma'am?"

"I would describe them as murderous." Ruth O'Connell clutched at her handbag. "Many a time I thought to myself, if that man had a knife in his hand, he'd kill every one of us."

"Objection!" Ben said rising to his feet. "Move to strike."

"The objection will be sustained," Judge Pitcock said. "Mr. Canelli, please instruct your witness to stick to factual matters. Without elaboration."

"Yes, your honor. Of course. Sorry."

Despite his words, Ben saw very little regret in the prosecutor's countenance. He'd managed to get his witness to use the *M* word, a prosecution victory by any measure.

"Could you give us an example, Mrs. O'Connell?"

"At one vestry meeting, he became so enraged at Helen Conrad that he rose out of his chair shouting, his face flushed red with anger, banging the table and threatening."

"And what exactly was the threat?"

"He said that if she didn't stop making these petty attacks, he'd stop them himself." She paused meaningfully. "Of course, only a few weeks later, she—"

"Objection, your honor," Ben said. "Are we going to have a mistrial this early in the game?" The judge had declared before trial that, since this case was concerned with the murder of Kate McGuire, there would be no mention of the murder that came before, or the murder that came after.

"No, we are not." Pitcock looked at Canelli sternly. "Counsel, if you can't control your witness, I'll excuse her from the courtroom."

"Yes, your honor. Of course. Again, I'm sorry." Canelli spent the next two hours eliciting sordid stories from Ruth about Father Beale's hot-tempered relations with the vestry. She cataloged every perceived grievance, every run-in with any member of the church. Canelli drew it all out with fervor. They were like two old gossips at a sewing bee; they acted as if every little tidbit pained them, but they told them all, just the same. Ben objected time and again, on grounds of hearsay or lack of foundation or whatever, and most of his objections were sustained, but Canelli still got the gist of the matter across to the jury. And the gist was—Father Beale had a serious temper, and he frequently vented it on the vestry.

At long last they came to the afternoon of the murder.

"I was at the church on behalf of the ECW," Ruth explained. "To help with the wedding. I assisted the bride with the preparation of her attire, just before the service began."

"And what did you do after that?"

"I walked down the main corridor toward the staff offices. But before I got there, I heard a thunderous voice I knew all too well."

"And who was that?"

"Father Beale, of course." She glanced at the jury. "He was arguing with Kate McGuire."

"What did they argue about?"

"I couldn't tell. Frankly, I was all too used to it. I just couldn't stand it anymore. Mentally tuned it out. But I could tell he was angry. And he was threatening her."

"How so?"

"I heard him say he wasn't going to allow her to get in his way, or something like that."

"And what did you take that to mean?"

"Objection," Ben said. It was getting wearisome. Canelli was forcing him to object, which would make him the bad guy "suppressing the truth" in the eyes of many jurors. "She's on the stand to provide facts, not characterization."

Judge Pitcock nodded. "The objection is sustained."

"Were you the only one who witnessed this fight in the hallway, Mrs. O'Connell?"

"Not even close. There were many people watching—including Father Beale's lawyer." She pointed at Ben. "He saw more of it than I did."

Ben felt the heat of collective eyes turning on him. Thanks so much, Ruth.

"Very interesting." Canelli made what Ben knew was a meaning-less check mark in his outline, just to accentuate the moment for the jury. "What did you do after the argument?"

"I returned to the sanctuary for the service."

"Did you know the couple being married?"

"No, but I knew Dr. Masterson would be playing from Widor's Fifth, and I love that piece. So I took a seat in the back and listened. After the service, I wandered out of the sanctuary."

"Did you see anything of interest?"

"Oh, yes. Just a minute or two after the bride filed out, I saw Fa-ther Beale entering his office. At the other end of the corridor. I thought nothing of it at the time, but it later became significant. Af-ter we found Kate's dead body in the very same office."

"Yes. Very significant indeed. Thank you, ma'am." Canelli glanced at Ben. "Your witness, counsel."

Ben rose to his feet, thinking as he walked to the podium. He had decided not to touch the subject of the strife with the vestry. Those bad feelings existed, as even Father Beale would admit; there was no point in denying it. For that matter, there was no point in denying that Beale had a temper, or that he argued with Kate McGuire shortly before the wedding. But it was just possible he could do something with that last attempt to place Father Beale at the crime scene at the very moment the forensic experts would later declare to be the time of death.

"Mrs. O'Connell, are you sure the person you saw enter the office was Father Beale?"

"Of course I am. I think I should recognize my own priest."

"Were you wearing your glasses?"

Her head twitched a jot. "Glasses?"

"That's my question. Because, as you pointed out to the jury, I was there, and I don't recall seeing you wear them. In fact, I don't re-call ever seeing you wear them."

She drew herself up. "I don't need glasses. You shouldn't assume that just because a woman is elderly—"

"Mrs. O'Connell, I have here a copy of your drivers' license records." He glanced up. "Good record, by the way. No tickets for the last thirty years. But they do mention that you're supposed to wear corrective lenses when you drive."

"Well . . . that's different. When I'm driving, I do wear—"

"So I assume you're nearsighted." She did not answer immediately. "Am I right?"

"I suppose that is . . . technically correct."

"You don't see clearly things that are far away."

"They may get a trifle fuzzy. But I can still—"

"Mrs. O'Connell, how long is the corridor at St. Benedict's that connects the narthex to the staff offices?"

"I don't know. Twenty feet or so."

"It's fifty-five feet, actually," Ben said. "I measured it myself. And if there's any doubt about this in the prosecutor's mind, I can ask the judge to take judicial notice of the floor plans, which my partner Ms. McCall was good enough to bring." He paused. "Now, Mrs. O'Connell. Fifty-five feet—that's a good long ways, isn't it?"

"Well, I don't—"

"If you were driving, would you be able to see clearly something that was fifty-five feet away? Without your glasses?"

"I know what Father Beale looks like. Even if he's a trifle fuzzy."

"You admit he was fuzzy. So when you say you saw Father Beale, what you're really saying is you saw someone you thought looked kinda sorta like Father Beale."

"I wouldn't put it like that."

"I'm sure you wouldn't—and didn't—but it would be more accurate than what you did say."

"Objection," Canelli said. "He's getting argumentative."

Judge Pitcock shrugged. "It's cross-examination. I'll allow it."

Ben continued. "What you're really saying, Mrs. O'Connell, is that you saw someone who you took for Father Beale."

"I know what I saw. The man had gray-white hair and a beard—"

"So it could've been Alvin Greene."

Ruth paused a moment. "I don't—"

"He has gray hair. And a beard. Doesn't he?"

"I don't recall whether Alvin was there."

"He was. As leader of the Altar Guild, he has to be at all major functions, to prepare and to clean up afterward. But you know that even better than I do, don't you, Mrs. O'Connell?"

"I suppose."

"For that matter, on several occasions I've noticed a homeless man sleeping in the prayer garden at St. Benedict's. I'm sure you've noticed him, too, Mrs. O'Connell—since you introduced a motion at the last vestry meeting to have him forcibly removed."

"It's not an appropriate image for a church. . . ."

"Come to think of it—that poor homeless man has gray hair, too, doesn't he? And a beard. Well, stubble, really. But still."

Ruth began to get indignant. "Mr. Kincaid, I could not possibly mistake a homeless man for my priest! Their faces are nothing alike."

"Ah, but you didn't see the face, did you?"

"What do you mean?"

"You testified that you saw a man entering the office. But the front door to the office suite faces north. You were at the north end of the corridor. That tells me that, at best, all you saw was the man's back."

"Well . . . I . . ."

"Come to think of it, Father Beale and Alvin Greene look a lot alike—from the back. Don't they? For that matter, Father Beale and a whole lot of people probably look the same from the back."

"You're wrong. You're twisting—"

"I'm not convinced you even saw a gray head and beard. At that distance, I don't think you could tell whether someone was actually entering the office suite. I think you saw someone's back and subsequently filled in the details to make it Father Beale because, consciously or unconsciously, you wanted to incriminate him."

"You don't know—"

"The truth is, ma'am, you couldn't possibly know with any degree of certainty who you saw, not at that distance with your vision. Studies have shown that eyewitness testimony is inherently unreliable; in controlled experiments, test results from eyewitnesses are barely more accurate than if the witnesses were just guessing. What you've done is called *unconscious transference*. The mind drafts a familiar face to play a role that could not otherwise be cast based upon the available information."

Canelli rose to his feet. "Is Mr. Kincaid giving expert testimony now?"

Ben ignored him. "You only decided the man you saw was Father

Beale—after the murder was discovered—because that's who you wanted it to be. Because, as you told the jury in great detail, you and the rest of the vestry strongly despise him and have been trying everything possible to get rid of him."

"That's not true! I mean, that's not why—"

"So you say, but how else can you explain giving a positive identification from a distance where your vision simply makes it impossible that you could be sure of anything?"

Ruth had no answer. She clutched her handbag and stared at the floor.

AFTER RUTH WAS dismissed and court was on a ten-minute recess, the defense team took its first huddle.

Christina gave Ben a high five. "Nice job, killer. You totally blew that meddling crone out of the water."

Father Beale agreed. "I have to admit, you were quite effective."

"I had to undermine that ID," Ben explained. "It was too convenient, given the time of death the coroner will later establish."

"But I worry about you, Ben," Beale continued. "The position you're in. Your job virtually requires you to humiliate people. To make them look like fools and liars."

Ben felt a burning in his cheeks. "We're trying to get at the truth."

"Right. And Ruth was mistaken in her identification. You made that clear. But at what cost to her personally? Am I to be saved only by destroying others? Is that what Jesus would do?"

"No," Christina said, "but as I recall, Jesus' trial didn't turn out so hot."

"I'm not going to let you martyr yourself," Ben added, "if that's what you're thinking. We'll do everything possible to fight this thing. Even if it means embarrassing a few people on the witness stand."

"I know that," Beale said. "You misunderstand. I'm not concerned about the effect of this trial on me." He turned, adjusting his eyes to meet Ben's. "I'm concerned about the effect of this trial on you."

26

"AND WHAT DID you see when you entered the church, Sergeant?"

The slim, square-jawed man with perfect posture cleared his throat. "A large crowd of people huddled in the foyer just outside a suite of offices."

"And who were these people?"

"As I learned subsequently, most of them were either attending or participating in a wedding."

"What did you do next?"

"I proceeded through the crowd and made my way to the offices. Following the pointed fingers of some of the spectators, I found a large office in the rear. I went inside."

"And what did you find?"

The man's emotionless expression didn't waver, although Ben detected just the slightest tremor in his voice. "I found the body of Kate McGuire sprawled across a desk, her dress hiked up around her waist. Blood was caked and smeared across the side of her face. Her skin was a pale blue. She was obviously dead."

"Was there a name on the door to this office?"

He nodded solemnly. "Father Daniel Beale."

As Ben well knew, Sergeant Cooper had been the first officer on the scene after the police were called. Mike showed up about fifteen minutes later, but before then, it was Cooper's show.

Christina whispered into Ben's ear. "Should we object? He couldn't possibly be certain she was dead just by looking at her."

"To what end? She *was* dead, and everyone here knows it. An objection would only irritate the jurors."

That was the last thing Ben wanted to do, especially at this stage. He had been at the scene, after all, and he knew Cooper had conducted himself and the preliminary investigation in a professional by-the-book manner. Ben didn't like what he knew the man would say next, but making a lot of objections would only highlight it in the jurors' minds.

A few minutes later, Cooper described his first encounter with Father Beale. "I found him by himself, in one of the small Sunday school rooms in the opposite corridor. He was on his knees. His face was red and streaked; he appeared to have been crying."

"What did you do?"

"I lifted the man to his feet, read him his rights, and attempted to question him."

"Attempted?"

"Yes, and not very successfully. He seemed confused, dazed, as if he had just—"

"Objection," Ben said. "The witness is here to provide facts, not to speculate."

Judge Pitcock agreed. "Sustained."

Sergeant Cooper resumed. "I wasn't able to get any clear answers out of him. He was not cooperative."

"Did you notice anything unusual about the defendant at this time? About his appearance?"

"Yes. Blood." Cooper drew in his breath, extending his ramrod back even higher. "He had spots of blood on his robe. Some in his beard. And under his fingernails. He had tried to wash it off in the bathroom before the police arrived. But he missed some of it."

Ben watched as the jurors looked at one another. The importance of that detail was not lost on them.

"Did anything else happen, Sergeant?" Canelli asked.

"Not really. Soon after that, Major Morelli from Homicide arrived and he took over the investigation."

"Thank you. That's all I have for this witness."

Ben strode to the podium. There were few things on earth less appealing than cross-examining a witness you knew was essentially telling the truth. Unlike some defense attorneys, Ben didn't go in for trying to make the police look like bumbling idiots. Still, there were a few points he needed to drive home.

"Sergeant, you are aware, aren't you, that Father Beale told the police he found the victim already dead when he returned to his office after the wedding? That he approached the victim to see if she was dead."

"I heard that, yes."

"In fact, you heard it from Father Beale, that very same day, when he explained the circumstances to Major Morelli, didn't you?"

"Yes."

"Why didn't you tell the jury about that?"

Cooper didn't blink. "I wasn't asked."

"You didn't think it was important?"

"I wasn't asked."

Ben had to hand it to the man; he was a rock. "I suppose the prosecution was being selective about what information they wanted the jury to have."

"Objection!" Canelli said.

"Sustained," Pitcock said. "Counsel, let's have the questions without the commentary, okay?"

"Yes, your honor." Ben resumed questioning. "If Father Beale felt the body for a pulse, perhaps even moved the body, it's certainly possible that he might get some of the blood on him, isn't it?"

"It's possible."

"In fact, it's more than likely, isn't it? It's probable."

"As I said, it's possible."

"Later in the day, you were part of the team that assisted in moving the body to the medical examiner's hearse, weren't you?"

"Yes."

"Did you get blood on yourself?"

"Some. It was mostly dried by that time."

"Did you wash it off?"

"Of course."

"Why?"

Cooper looked at Ben as if he were dumber than ditchwater. "I would wash my hands any time I came into contact with foreign bodily substances."

"Understood. You did the natural thing." Ben glanced at the jury. "And Father Beale did the same exact natural thing when he washed his hands, didn't he?"

"If you say so."

Cooper was too smart to get caught up in an argument he couldn't win. Too bad.

"Now, let's talk about your interrogation, Sergeant. You said you discovered Father Beale on his knees crying, right?"

"Right."

"Is it possible he was praying?"

"His eyes were wet—"

"And he was on his knees. Is it possible he was praying?"

Cooper resisted. "It seems unlikely to me that—"

"That a priest would be praying?"

Cooper released his breath. "Okay. It's possible."

"You complained to the jury that, at first, Father Beale was confused and had trouble answering questions. Of course, the man had just discovered a woman he knew well—a member of his own parish—dead on his desk. Is it really surprising that he might be a bit confused? Not in a chatty mood?"

"It seemed to me he was not being cooperative."

"Sergeant Cooper, if you had just discovered the dead and bloody body of someone you knew sprawled across the judge's bench, do you think you'd feel like playing twenty questions?"

The sergeant's lips pursed. "Possibly not."

"But Father Beale did in fact answer questions shortly thereafter, when Major Morelli was on the scene, right? He answered all questions put to him, several times over, right?"

"As far as I know."

"Thank you. That's all I have."

THE PROSECUTION CALLED several other police officers who had been at the scene of the crime and a few other vestry members from St. Benedict's, but for the most part they just rehashed what had been said before. By the afternoon, Canelli had moved to his more specialized witnesses.

"What did you do when the body arrived at your office, Doctor?"

The young man in the white coat leaned forward eagerly. "I performed a full-length autopsy, as is traditional in cases of violent death."

"Did you notice anything unusual?"

"Other than the fact that she was dead?" He grinned, as if he thought he'd made a rare witticism. "There were two obvious signs of violence—a blow to the side of the head, and strangle marks around the neck."

"So what did you do?"

"I ran a serious of tests, examining the depth and impact of the blow to the head, examining the lungs for air, that sort of thing."

"And what did you determine?"

"The cause of death was asphyxiation."

"And is that your scientific conclusion?"

"Yes."

"To a medical certainty?"

"Yes. I'm as certain about this as I am about death, taxes, and heavy rainfall right after I wash my car."

The medical examiner grinned, but alas, once again his humor fell flat. There just wasn't anything funny about being a coroner, Ben thought, as he watched the hapless performance from the defense table, although Bob Barkley didn't appear to have figured that out yet. Ben still couldn't get over having this geeky, hyper twenty-something (who looked younger) as the state medical examiner. After years of the stern and serious Dr. Koregai, Coroner Bob was a startling contrast. Koregai had always believed forensic science was a pathway to higher truths; Bob seemed to think it was a good way to meet girls.

"Can you offer any testimony regarding the time of death?" Canelli asked.

"Yes, more accurate than in most cases, in fact, since the body was discovered so soon after the murder took place. I measured the internal body temperature and examined the contents of the victim's stomach. I estimated the time of death at about two-fifteen, which I'm told is almost immediately after the wedding ended."

"You mentioned strangle marks earlier. Could you tell the jury what that means?"

"Finger imprints. Deep impressions around the victim's throat. Still discernible, even at the time I got the body in my office. Because the blood stops circulating after death sets in, the bruises tend to linger. They weren't clear enough to take fingerprints or anything, but they were definitely present."

"So the killer strangled the victim by physically applying his hands to her throat? By choking her to death?"

"That's correct."

"That would require a strong man, wouldn't it?" All heads in the jury turned to scrutinize Father Beale's six-foot-two frame.

"I would think so."

"Was the body moved?"

"Absolutely not. There were no indications of movement whatsoever. Not until the police arrived. The victim was DRT, as the cops say. Dead Right There."

"So the murder took place . . . in Father Beale's office?"

"That's correct."

"Shortly after Father Beale finished officiating the wedding?"

"Evidently so."

"Thank you, Doctor." He glanced at the defense table. "Your witness."

Ben gave Christina a little push. "Go for it."

She frowned nervously. "Should I mess with all the technical forensic stuff?"

"Only if you enjoy public mortification."

"Then—?"

"Physical strength."

Christina grabbed her legal pad. "Got it. Anything else?"

He shook his head. "Make your point and sit down. Experts are dangerous."

CHRISTINA SQUARED HERSELF behind the podium. "Good afternoon, Dr. Barkley."

"Hey-ya, Chrissy. I like what you've done with your hair."

"Well . . . thanks."

"Have you got plans Friday night?"

Christina chose to ignore him. "You testified that the murderer would have to be a big man possessed of serious physical strength to strangle the victim to death."

"Well, I doubt if she would just sit still and let someone do it to her for fun."

"But it's possible the murderer held the victim in an awkward position, isn't it? Pinned her down in a way that made struggling impossible."

"I saw no evidence of that."

"If the assailant was hovering over her, and had her pinned against the desk, he or she would have a natural advantage, right?"

"I suppose."

"You also testified that the victim suffered a serious blow to the head."

"That's true."

"Is it possible that the blow came before the strangulation?"

Bob tilted his head. "It seems more likely that—"

"You're not answering my question, Doctor. Is it possible that the blow to the head came first?"

"I can't rule it out."

"And if the blow came first, the victim, a young woman weighing one hundred twelve pounds, might well have been stunned. Even knocked unconscious."

"There's no way I can accurately predict that."

"But it is possible? Someone hits you on the head—you're stunned."

"It's possible."

"At any rate, she wouldn't be feeling her best. In top strength."

"No."

"And if she was somewhat incapacitated, strangling her would be a lot easier, wouldn't it?"

"Yes, though it would still require some strength."

Christina held out her hands and clenched her fists. "Well, I've got a pretty good grip. Could I have done it?"

Bob smiled slightly. "I wouldn't put anything past you."

"For that matter, my twelve-year-old nephew has a better grip than I do. He knocks the baseball out of the park every time. Could he have done it?"

Bob began to squirm. "I suppose if the victim were stunned, it's possible . . ."

"The truth is, under those circumstances, almost anyone could've committed this crime, right?"

Bob shrugged his shoulders. "If the victim was stunned . . ."

"So in fact, this prosecution evidence not only doesn't indicate Father Beale was the murderer, it doesn't exclude much of anyone!"

Canelli rose to his feet. "Is this a question, your honor? Because it sounds a lot like closing argument."

"I'll withdraw it," Christina said. "I think I've made my point. No more questions."

CHRISTINA SLID INTO her seat at the counsel table beside Ben. "How'd I do?"

"Great. Except for the part where you clenched your hands and suggested that you could've been the murderer. You shouldn't give the cops ideas. You were at the wedding, after all, and they hate lawyers."

She blanched. "You think they might accuse me?"

He patted her hand reassuringly. "Of course not. Going after a priest is one thing. But no one's stupid enough to mess with you."

27

By late afternoon, Ben knew everyone, jury included, tended to get a bit sleepy-eyed. For that reason, experienced trial lawyers typically arranged to have their least important witnesses on at that time, or to finish up early so their opponent would be cross-examining when the jury was least attentive.

That being so, Ben was surprised that an experienced trial hand like Canelli would call an expert witness this late in the day. Perhaps Canelli's theory was that establishing an expert witness's credentials was so boring the jury might as well be catching a few *z*'s while he went through this tedious but legally necessary procedure.

And thus the afternoon was graced with the wit and wisdom of Dr. Miguel Valero—prosecution hair expert.

Christina listened to his professional history with amazement. "He's spent fourteen years studying . . . hair?" she whispered.

Ben nodded. "A tough job, but someone's got to do it."

Her forehead crinkled. "Why?"

Valero was a heavy-set man with florid, fleshy face. He wore solid black—shirt, slacks, coat, and tie. During direct, he established that he had a degree in forensic sciences and that he had devoted the majority of his professional career to the scientific examination and classification of hair, its characteristics and identifying traits. According to him, he had spent ten thousand hours over the past decade and a half studying hairs and was considered one of the leading experts in the field.

"Dr. Valero," Canelli asked, once his credentials were finally established, "would you please explain to the jury how you became involved in this case?"

Valero cleared his throat and shifted around in the smallish wooden chair. "One of the hair and fiber crime scene techs discovered a stray hair on the victim's body—in the wound, actually—that did not appear, on visual analysis, to have come from the victim. So I was asked to investigate."

"And did you?"

"Of course."

"Could you please explain how you go about your analysis?"

Valero turned slightly toward the jury. "Well, the first thing I do is get the hair under a microscope. To the naked eye, a shaft of hair is so thin it's difficult to discern any identifying characteristics. Under the microscope, however, a shaft of hair is two inches wide. That's a whole different ball game. At that magnification, you can start classifying and identifying."

"What do you do first?"

"The traditional first step in hair classification is to determine which racial group the hair came from—Caucasian, Negroid, or Mongoloid. This is a relatively simple procedure. Next we establish what part of the body the hair came from—scalp, pubis, or limbs. That's not much harder."

"And after that?"

"Then the work gets a bit more complicated. We consider color, thickness, texture, and any other available characteristics of identification. In this case, I had a hair exemplar that was taken from the defendant after he was arrested. I was able to put it under the microscope and compare it with the hair found on the victim."

"And did you reach a conclusion?"

"I did. The hair taken from the victim is consistent in all respects with the hair taken from Daniel Beale."

"In other words," Canelli summed, "the hair on the dead body came from the defendant."

"That would be the obvious conclusion, yes."

"Thank you. I pass the witness."

*   *   *

BEN PLACED HIS hand on Christina's shoulder. "I'll take this one."

"Suit yourself. Don't you hate experts?"

"I'm looking forward to this one."

Father Beale leaned sideways to whisper into Ben's ear. "Am I to be convicted based upon the testimony of a hair?"

Ben gathered his CX papers. "Not if I can help it."

"This is right out of the Gospel According to Matthew. 'But the very hairs of your head are all numbered.' That's what it says. I never understood what it meant, though. Until now."

Ben crossed to the podium and launched right in. "Dr. Valero, you weren't involved in the initial gathering of evidence, right?"

"That's true."

"And you don't know how that hair got on the victim, do you?"

"Well, the obvious way would be when the killer—"

"I didn't ask you to speculate, Doctor. I asked if you know."

"No, of course not."

"Isn't it possible she picked up the hair from the desk? I mean, she was on Father Beale's desk."

"I think it unlikely that—"

"How much hair does the average person shed in the course of a day?"

"Well, it's hard to say precisely—"

"But it's a lot, right? People shed hair constantly. There might have been dozens of his hairs on that desk."

"That's true. But may I remind you that the hair was found on the front of her neck, in the wound? She was lying on her back. Any hairs from the desk would've been found on her back."

"All you know is that she was on her back when she died. You don't know how many other positions she might've been in *before* she died, right?"

"The coroner said the body was not moved."

"If Father Beale approached the body, say, to feel for a pulse, or to administer last rites, he might've left the hair then, right?"

"I think that unlikely. The hair was in the wound."

"But you can't eliminate the possibility."

"I can say I think it unlikely in the extreme."

"But you can't eliminate the possibility."

"I suppose it is remotely possible. Remotely."

Ben turned a page in his notes. "Let's move on to your so-called identification. Dr. Valero, let's be honest with the jury. Hair identification isn't what you would call an exact science, is it?"

"I don't know what you mean."

"Well, it isn't the same as fingerprints or DNA, right?"

Valero appeared puzzled and mildly miffed. "Again, I'm unsure . . ."

"If you match fingerprints, that's a positive identification. But hair analysis is a good deal more . . . squishy, isn't it?"

"Not in my opinion."

"Isn't it true that hair characteristics are not uniform?"

"There are occasionally some variances."

Ben lowered his chin. "Dr. Valero. Let's talk turkey. Isn't it true that two hairs pulled from the same head still might not match one another?"

Valero squirmed slightly. "It is possible. Especially among older subjects."

"Like Father Beale, who is fifty-seven. Isn't it also true that some people have so-called featureless hair that is very hard to distinguish?"

"Yes, but the defendant is not one of them. His hair had many identifying characteristics."

"Such as?"

"You want a list?"

"That would be dandy."

"Well . . . that could take some time."

"I'm not going anywhere, Doctor. I think we're all interested to hear what you say. Because to me, and to most people, a hair pretty much looks like a hair."

Valero cleared his throat. "Well . . . the hair found on the victim was Caucasian."

"Okay. That narrows the suspect pool down to half a billion people or so."

"And there is color, of course."

"You're telling me you identified this hair as coming from Father Beale based upon the color?"

Beads of sweat glistened on Valero's forehead. "As I recall, there was also a distinctive curl."

"Excuse me, Doctor. Did you say *curl*?"

"Yes."

Ben cranked his voice up. "Are you telling me you identified my client as a killer, that you publicly accused him of murder, based on a curl?"

"That wasn't the only . . ."

"What percentage of the population has this so-called distinctive curl?"

"I couldn't really say."

"Because there's no reliable library of information on curls, right? Because no objective expert would ever suggest that a shaft of hair could be traced back to its source by its curl!"

"There was also the color."

Ben didn't let up. "So you're saying you made this brilliant ID based upon the gray color and the curl. Tell me, doctor—how many people have gray hair with a little curl in it? Couple hundred million or so?"

"I couldn't say . . ."

"Because you don't care, right? You just took two flimsy similarities and turned them into a positive ID."

"I only said that the hairs were consistent."

"When you get right down to it, you didn't say much of anything, did you?"

Canelli rose out of his chair. "I object, your honor. This is becoming abusive."

"I agree," Ben replied. "But the abuse is being perpetrated by the prosecution. They're trying to buttress their weak case with junk science."

"That is not true!"

Judge Pitcock glared at them. "Both of you, approach. And don't say another word until you're up here."

At the bench, Ben lowered his voice, parked his righteous indignation, and continued the argument. "Your honor, this hair evidence is flimsier than Kleenex. This does not meet the standard set forth by the U.S. Supreme Court in *Daubert versus Merrill Dow Pharmaceuticals.*"

"I've already briefed this," Canelli said wearily.

"Right," Ben continued, "but how could we possibly evaluate your arguments until we heard how weak your evidence really was?

Your honor, the Supreme Court left it to trial judges to act as gate-keepers, barring entry to junk science. If we allow baloney like this in the courtroom, how can we expect jurors to distinguish between real science like fingerprints and this sort of bogus poppycock? This whole line of testimony should be excluded."

"I am concerned about the reliability of this evidence," Pitcock said, fingering his lower lip.

Excellent! Ben thought silently. And I didn't even have to whine about the sanctity of the family.

"But I'm not prepared to exclude it altogether."

"Your honor," Ben said, "this is a lot of hooey!"

"Which you're doing a rather good job of pointing out on cross-examination. Tenuous as it is, I think it does meet the *Daubert* standard, and you can and will point out any failings in methodology during your cross. Let's continue, gentlemen."

Close, but no cigar. Ben returned to the podium and relaunched his attack. "Dr. Valero, isn't it true that even amongst so-called 'hair experts,' there is no consensus on the criteria for making comparisons such as the one you just made under oath to this jury?"

Valero's expression grew more pensive. "It seems you've done your homework, Mr. Kincaid."

"I try. So what about it?"

"There . . . is some dispute about methodology and matching criteria."

"In fact, despite several efforts, no one has ever been able to set up a national data bank for hairs—like the ones existing for fingerprints and DNA—because there's no agreement on the criteria."

"I'm afraid that's also true."

"And therefore it's impossible for you to say with any reliability whether a characteristic in a hair is common or rare, right?"

"I have been examining hair for fourteen years. I've examined hundreds of thousands—"

"And you still haven't seen one one-millionth of one percent of all the hairs in this country. Which means you have a grossly low statistical base for drawing any conclusions."

"That's your opinion, not mine."

"Are you familiar with a proficiency testing program conducted by the U.S. Law Enforcement Assistance Administration on hair analysis a few years ago?"

Valero pursed his lips. "Yes."

"That's good," Ben said, opening a folder, "because I happen to have a copy of their report right here. In a controlled and monitored experiment, they sent hair samples to a variety of labs and experts. The error rates on five different samples ranged from fifty to sixty-eight percent. That's an error rate of more than half."

"True."

"In other words, the prosecution would be better off just flipping a coin than getting one of you so-called hair experts to deliver your expert opinion."

Canelli jumped up. "Your honor, I'm offended by that remark."

"You know what offends me?" Ben shot back. "I'm offended by the fact that the prosecution knows this evidence is unreliable, but they try to get it in anyway because they assume the jury won't be bright enough to see it for the junk it is!"

"This is not the time for speechifying, Mr. Kincaid," Judge Pitcock said. "Did you have any more questions?"

"No," Ben said, snapping his folder shut. "I'm done with this witness."

BACK AT COUNSEL table, Ben consulted with his client. "So, did I get my point across?"

"Oh, yeah," Father Beale said. "I think you buried him."

"Like, seriously buried?"

"Like Vesuvius to Pompeii, buried."

Ben settled into his seat. "Well, he made me mad."

Beale nodded. "I can only hope every other prosecution witness makes you mad, too."

28

AFTER COURT ADJOURNED for the day, Ben and Christina began packing up the files that needed to go back to the office. As grueling as a day of trial was, the work did not end when the judge slammed his gavel. Ben knew he'd be up past midnight, reviewing outlines and preparing for the next day's witnesses.

So who could deny him a moment's respite? He knew Charlie at the courthouse snack bar always held back a carton of chocolate milk when Ben was in trial. Maybe after a couple of shots of sugar-enriched calcium he'd be energized enough to—

"Excuse me. You the lawyer?"

Ben stopped. "I'm the lawyer representing Father Beale."

"My name's Marco Ellison. And I saw something I think can help your guy."

He was a young man, maybe twenty or so. He had short, spiky peroxided hair and had rings piercing his ears, nose, lower lip, and tongue. In other words, the ideal witness.

"How did you come by this knowledge?"

"I was at the wedding."

Ben wondered how he could possibly have missed this guy. Maybe he hadn't been pierced yet. "Okay. And what do you know?"

"Well, for starters, I know your guy didn't do it."

Ben edged closer, his eyes widening. He wrapped his hand around the young man's leather-coated arm. "And how do you know this?"

" 'Cause I saw him after the wedding ended. I'm not really into all that 'death us do part' crapola, so I went outside to the prayer garden

for a smoke. And I saw Father Beale come into the garden a few minutes later. He sat for a while. Even got down on his knees and prayed."

"But he didn't go to his office?"

"No way. Not at first, anyway. He was in the garden."

Ben squeezed his arm all the tighter. Could it be—an eyewitness
who could place Father Beale somewhere else at the time the prosecution had established as the time of the murder? It was almost too
good to be believed. "Why haven't you told this to the police?"

"I did."

Ben's eyes opened all the wider. "You *did*?"

"Yup. They didn't seem interested in anything that was going to
help the priest. They didn't even write down my name."

Ben swore silently. "Would you be willing to testify? In court?"

"Of course. That's why I came up here."

"That's great." Ben wanted to hug the kid, but he'd probably take
it the wrong way. "Give me your address and phone number. I'll add
you to the witness list and call you when it's time for us to put on
our case."

"Sure. No problem." The kid gave him the information.

"This is a great thing you're doing, Marco. A great thing. This
could turn the whole trial around." He paused. "I don't want to push
my luck, but—any chance you could lose the jewelry before you go
up on the witness stand?"

"Why? Don't you want me to look my best?"

"Yeah, to my jurors, whose average age is fifty-five. But never
mind. I just want you to be there." He took Marco's shoulder again.
"This could be the most important thing you do in your entire life."

THAT EVENING, BACK at the office, Ben gave his client a recap.

"So the kid says he can positively state that you were not in your
office at the time of the murder."

"Well, I wasn't."

"I know that. But we didn't have a witness to say it. Until now."

"I can say it," Father Beale said, stroking his beard. "I can speak
for myself."

"Father, I've told you this before. I don't like putting defendants
on the stand. It's too risky. Especially in a capital case."

"But I would prefer to do it, just the same. I want people to hear about my innocence from my own lips."

"You don't know what it's like up there, Father. Having the DA pound away at you, accusing you of horrible things, twisting your words around, trying to trip you up."

"I'm an adult, Ben. I can handle myself."

"I know you can. You're probably better spoken and more intelligent than most of the people I've represented. But there are still risks."

"Ben—"

"Father Beale, you agreed that I was in charge of this trial, remember?"

"Yes, and I won't renege on that agreement. But at least think about it, okay?"

"I'll think about it." But with a new witness who could put Father Beale in the prayer garden at the time of the murder, Ben knew there was simply no reason to take that risk.

He said good night to Father Beale and watched as the marshals took him back to his cell at the county jail. It was a horrible thing, seeing a man who had done so much for people, who had done so much for Ben, being treated in this manner. It must be an almost unbearable nightmare for him, Ben mused. At his age, his position in life. There had to be some way Ben could put an end to it, once and for all. Some way he could help Father Beale.

Just as the man had helped him, all those years ago.

ALTHOUGH HE DID not join the acolyte class, the twelve-year-old nihilistic Ben did spend more time at the church after his counseling session with Father Beale. Following the priest's advice, he had managed to integrate himself into the core group of kids his age. Deep down, he might know that Curran and Conner and Landon and the others would never have included him in their set if they hadn't all gone to the same church, but as long as he appeared to be one of the gang, what did it matter? Right?

One Sunday after services, Ben and the others were hanging outside the robing room. For some reason, the male acolytes had changed first; now they waited while the only girl in the class, Valerie Beth McKechnie, wiggled out of her heavy black-and-white Anglican robes. Ben was admiring the new stained-glass window, Father Beale's pride and joy, which he had fund-raised eight years to purchase. The translucent red and blue of the rainbow, the art deco design of the ascending dove . . .

"So, Kincaid. You gonna touch her titties or not?"

Once again, Ben was glad he'd gotten in with a group of kids who were clearly on a higher spiritual plane. "Shut up, Conner. We're in church."

"And so is she, Ben. That's the point."

"I'm not going to do anything like that, Conner. Forget it."

Landon came around on his other side. "C'mon, Ben, you gotta do it. If you wanna be in the club. Everyone else has done it."

"They have?"

"Oh, yeah. Well, not with Valerie Beth McKechnie. But someone."

"Yeah, you probably did it with your sister."

"I don't have a sister, Kincaid, and it's a good thing I don't, or I'd be really pissed off right now."

"Cool down, Landon," Curran said. All three of them were surrounding Ben. "Don't pressure him so much. He just needs some time."

"She'll only be in there another minute or two," Landon said.

"Good point." Curran took Ben by the shoulders and adjusted his lapel. "So, what do you say, Benny-boy?"

"I say, don't call me Benny-boy."

"I mean about Valerie Beth McKechnie."

"I say, no."

"Aw, c'mon, Kincaid," Conner whined. "You wanna be a virgin all your life?"

Thanks to the book Father Beale had given him, Ben was slightly better able to deal with this question than he would've been a few weeks ago. "Feeling someone up in the robing room is not going to make me not a virgin."

Conner's reaction made Ben wonder if he knew as much as he acted like he knew. "Well . . . it's a step in the right direction."

"It's a step I won't be taking. So clear off. My parents are somewhere around here, and if they knew—"

"She wants you to do it."

Ben slowed. He squinted at Landon's grinning face. "What do you mean?"

"Just that. She wants you to do it."

"How do you know?"

"I can tell. She likes you, man."

"Get stuffed."

"No, it's true, she does," Conner said, backing his friend up. "Have you seen the way she looks at you during church? The way she gazes at you during the reading of the gospel?"

"No, I haven't."

"Then you need to pull your head out of your butt and take a look around, Kincaid. Valerie Beth McKechnie is a fox. And she wants your body."

"Even if she liked me, that wouldn't mean she wanted me to—"

"She does, Ben. She told me she does."

"She told you? Why would she tell you?"

"We're friends. Have been since kindergarten. We tell each other everything."

"You're full of it."

"What's the matter? Are you scared?"

Ben squirmed. "I'm not scared. I'm just not—"

"Then what are you waiting for?" He pushed Ben toward the closed robing room door. "This is your big chance. She'll probably get so excited she'll ask to go steady or something."

Ben steeled himself. "And if I do this, you guys'll stop hassling me?"

"Absolutely," they all swore.

"And I'll be in the club?"

"Forever and ever."

"Great." Ben touched the doorknob. Maybe if he just went in quietly and talked to her, she wouldn't mind that, would she? It's not like she's changing her clothes, actually—she's just derobing. Maybe if he got it over quickly. Who knew—maybe she really did like him. She was gorgeous, with all that long chestnut hair and the cute little nose and dimples and—

"So, go already!" Curran opened the door and Landon shoved Ben through it. And closed the door behind him.

Ben tried the knob, but the boys were holding it shut. Great.

"Ben! What are you doing in here!"

Valerie Beth McKechnie stood before him in all her glory. Long hair, cute nose, exposed midriff, and training bra. Apparently she had removed her blouse when she put on her robe—probably so she wouldn't look so bulky—and she hadn't quite gotten it back on yet.

"Ohmigosh." Ben's face flushed and suddenly he felt about ten million degrees Fahrenheit. "I'm sorry—I—I—didn't know you were dressing. I—"

"That's all right. I don't mind." She shrugged, then gave him a wink. "I'll show you mine if you'll show me yours."

Ben felt his mouth go dry. He realized this would be a good time to speak, but somehow, he was utterly unable to make any words come out. He stepped—sort of lurched, really—forward, getting close enough to accomplish his mission without saying anything coherent.

Happily, Valerie Beth filled in the gaps for him. "I think you're cute, Ben. Really I do. I wish the other boys wouldn't make fun of you so much. Boys can be so mean sometimes, don't you think?"

"I—I—I—" That was an improvement over slobbering silence, but still not exactly the suave Cary Grant–like banter he'd been hoping for.

"Why did you come in, Ben? Do you like me? Was there something you wanted?"

Just as Ben thought his knees would buckle, the lights went out. The room was pitch-black.

"Ben Kincaid! Was this your idea?"

Definitely not, but he'd probably never convince her. Curran and Landon at the breaker box, unless he missed his guess. If he was ever going to do this, if he was ever going to be in the club . . .

"I don't have much time, Ben. My parents never stay at the after-church coffee long. If there was something you wanted . . ."

By God, he would never get a better invitation than that. It was dark, they were alone, she had told Curran she wanted him to do it. . . .

He sucked in his gut and lunged.

Valerie Beth McKechnie screamed.

"Ben! Stop that!" She slapped his hands away. "What do you think you're doing?"

"But you said you wanted—"

"I don't mind a little kissing. I like kissing. I don't like being pawed like a dog!"

"But Curran said you wanted—"

"And you listened to him? What kind of moron are you?"

Ben turned and ran. The door was free now; he whipped it open. The light flooded in and, sure enough, there were the Three Stooges huddled outside, pointing and laughing hysterically.

"How'd she like it, lover boy?" Curran asked. He was prostrate with laughter.

"Yeah, Casanova," Landon said. He wrapped his arms around himself and made kissy noises. "Has she had your baby yet?"

Something must've snapped, because not only did Ben come at them, he came at them with enough strength and ferocity to chill them even with three-to-one odds in their favor. The whole group scattered, helter-skelter, with Ben chasing at their collective tails.

After they scattered, Ben had to prioritize. He chose to hunt Curran first—after all, this disgrace was more his fault than anyone's. He pursued the boy outside the church and around the back end of the church, fists clenched, teeth gritted.

"Come back, you coward!" Ben shouted, but apparently, separated from his friends, Curran felt no need to put on a show of strength. He continued running as hard as he could.

Ben knew Curran lived in the apartments on the west side of the church. In other words, if he got much farther, Ben would never catch him.

"Come and fight, you chicken!" he screamed, but Curran did not stop. He didn't even slow. In desperation, Ben picked up a rock and hurled it toward Curran with all his might . . .

Ben didn't have much of an arm, which was why they always put him in the infield during softball games. But the adrenaline rush must've made a profound difference, because when he hurled that rock, it flew forward with the strength and velocity of a major league fastball—

Right into Father Beale's brand-new stained glass window.

It shattered. Big chunks fell to the ground, making a tremendous clatter. Almost immediately, a cry went up from the parish hall where the adults were having their coffee. Through the outer windows, Ben could see Father Beale emerging from his office, rushing to the scene. And that wasn't all.

Further back, Ben could see his own father making his way to the scene of the disturbance.

His fists were clenched.

Ben ran to the window, hoping there was something he could do, but he saw in an instant that the beautiful glasswork was destroyed. He had ruined it.

And his father would arrive at any moment.

29

THE COMBINATION OF narrow hallways outside the courtroom and the press of journalists forced Canelli to pass near Ben and Christina at the courtroom door.

"Ready to call it quits?" Ben asked him.

Canelli checked to make sure the minicams weren't on. "Don't get cocky just because you spun an expert around, Kincaid. This trial has barely started."

Ben shrugged. "Just trying to spare you further mortification, my friend."

Canelli moved in closer. "Make no mistake, Kincaid. Your boy's still going to get the needle for what he did. He's blowfish."

Despite Canelli's bold words, Ben noticed that several announced prosecution "experts" disappeared from the up-next witness list. Thus, they were spared the serology expert, the fiber expert, and the psychiatrist. They would still have to deal with the fingerprint evidence—easily the most damning piece of physical evidence weighing against Father Beale—but Ben couldn't help but feel his burden had been immeasurably lightened. As he stood in the hallway waiting for the trial to resume, he had to admit that the case was going better than he expected. It was early days, to be sure, but if Canelli kept stumbling and he kept scoring touchdowns, he might even get a directed verdict, thus avoiding the inherent risk and uncertainty of a jury.

"Excuse me, Mr. Kincaid. Could I have your autograph?"

Fortunately for his ego, Ben had identified the giggle even before he turned to see who was addressing him. Judy. With Maura, as always, tucked close behind her.

There was something oddly self-conscious about Judy's voice, though it took him a moment to figure out what it was. The red light on the minicam from Channel Eight was blinking in their direction, and she knew it. She was playing for the camera.

"I think you're a fabulous attorney, Mr. Kincaid, the best ever." She gave him a quick wink. "You've been such an inspiration to me. When I grow up, I want to be a brilliant, honest, crusading lawyer just like you."

"Judy, what are you—?"

"You're so amazing in the courtroom, Mr. Kincaid. I think you must be the best lawyer in the Southwest. Probably in the United States!"

"Judy . . ."

"Go along with it," she said sotto voce. "It's free publicity." Then in a louder voice, she added, "I know how busy you are, what with every rich and important person in the country wanting you to be their lawyer, but if you could just take a few moments to sign something for me, it would be the greatest thrill of my life!"

Ben gave her a sharp look. "What is it you want signed, a check?"

"Ben," she said under her breath, "think marketing. This could translate into big bucks." And then, in her stage voice, she added, "Since I want to be a lawyer like you, perhaps we could get together sometime and discuss trial strategies and such. Maybe over dinner."

"Judy, I'm not going on a date with you."

Maura rolled her eyes. "See, Judy, I told you it wouldn't work."

"But I think I would really benefit from your career advice," Judy continued, as loud as before. "And I know you don't like to disappoint your fans."

"Lawyers don't have fans." Ben took her by the wrist and led her away from the cameras. "Shouldn't you be in school?"

"We're out for break," Judy explained. "And we're getting extra credit for observing this trial."

"I don't think this trial is . . . appropriate for fifteen-year-old ears."

"Why? Is there going to be sex?" They both giggled.

Ben rolled his eyes. "Let's hope not. Although that would probably be more fun than the fingerprint expert."

SAMMIE FLYNN WAS pretty calm for a young woman sitting in the interrogation room at the Tulsa county jail. She was smoking a cigarette, her fourth in a row. Her auburn hair was slicked back behind her ears. She seemed relaxed and not at all perturbed by the stark environment or the two unfriendly faces on the other side of the table.

But then, she'd been here before.

"We've got you dead to rights this time, Sammie," said Sergeant Lewis, the older of the two cops interrogating her. "You're going down."

She took a long drag on her cigarette. "I don't know what you're talking about."

"Don't play games, Sammie. You're dead meat."

She blew smoke in his face. "Well, I've been dead before."

"Passing bad checks is a felony, Sammie," said Patrolman Harriman, the younger man at the table. "That's why I had to pick you up."

She was wearing cutoffs and a T-shirt, which she pulled over her knees. She sat lotus-style, on her own bare feet, exposing the numerous tattoos on her upper and lower legs. "It's all a mistake. I thought I had enough money to cover those checks."

"You were short, Sammie," Lewis said. "By about twelve thousand dollars."

She shrugged, a revealing gesture, given that she was wearing no bra and not much of a T-shirt. "I was never good at math."

"Can you count to twenty?" Lewis shot back. " 'Cause that's the minimum you're looking at, sweetie. Twenty years."

She lowered her cigarette slowly. "Twenty years? For passing a bad check? No way."

"Yes way. You're a three-time offender, baby. Minimum sentencing guidelines. Twenty years."

Somehow, she managed to retain her cool demeanor. "You're blowing smoke up my ass."

"You don't believe me, Sammie? Ask your lawyer when you see him."

"I want to see him now. I thought we were having the arraignment or whatever the hell it is."

"We're trying. Courtroom's stuffed to the gills and all cases are backed up. That priest-murder thing is gumming up the works."

"Priest-murder? What the hell?"

"Don't you know, Sammie?" Lewis gave his partner a quick but meaningful look. "Hell, you've been in a cell next-door to the guy."

"Yeah, what's the deal with that? Since when did the jail go coed?"

"It's only temporary," Lewis replied. "We're having . . . space problems. So what did you think of him?"

"That old gray-headed coot? The one who never talks and prays all the time?"

"That's the one."

"He's a murderer?"

"No doubt about it. I understand the DA is having a little trouble scraping together all the evidence he needs, but he's guilty, take my word for it."

Sammie took one last drag from her smoke, then ground it out on the table. "Go figure. Well, once I beat this rap, I'll never have to see the creep again."

Both the officers chuckled. "Beat this rap? Sammie, you're in deep denial. Our case is ironclad. You're hamburger."

"I told you, I thought I had the money. My boyfriend must've made a withdrawal just before I wrote the check. Besides, I never actually passed the thing. I was just thinking about it."

Lewis leaned across the table till he was close enough to smell her. "The bank says no one had withdrawal privileges on that account but you. You've never had a thousand dollars in the bank, much less twelve thousand. And we've got footage from the bank video camera that shows you passing the check." He smiled broadly. "Your ass is grass, Sammie. You're going down."

SAMMIE LEFT THE interrogation room with an astounding degree of calm and reserve. But she was an experienced girl; she didn't panic. Easily. And she had a battle plan that had served her well in the past and would no doubt do so again.

Since the arraignment had to be postponed to the next day, Sammie was given access to a phone to make whatever arrangements necessary. She made four phone calls, then asked for the week's old newspapers, displaying a heretofore unrevealed intellectual curiosity. And then she called her attorney.

"Donald? Yeah, it's Sammie. Yeah, I know. Hey, you gotta get me outta here. I can't do no twenty years."

She paused, twirling the phone cord around her finger. "I don't care what the law says. There's gotta be a way."

She listened intently. Her disposition did not improve. "Well, you're pretty goddamn useless, aren't you? Public defender. More like public menace." She ignored the eruption on the other end of the line. "Yeah, well, I know how you wanna be paid. And it ain't gonna happen again, not unless you find some way to get me outta here."

She listened patiently to another three minutes of insults and excuses. "You really are useless, aren't you, Donald? Well, listen, you big jerk. I've got a way, even if you don't. I've got it all figured out."

AT THE END of the day, Harriman reported back to Lewis. "I had them give her the newspapers, just like you said. And we let her make as many phone calls as she wanted. What's she doing, anyway?"

Sergeant Lewis grinned, then spread his hands. "How should I know? We're not allowed to listen in, you know. Unconstitutional."

"She was actually reading those newspapers. I was surprised. Of course, I was surprised she could read."

"Sammie's a girl of many talents. And amazing resourcefulness."

"You think she's up to something?"

"Couldn't say. How could I know? I'm not her confidant."

"Still . . . I thought maybe you had some idea."

"Far be it for me to try to understand the criminal mind." Lewis's smile broadened. He leaned back in his chair, placing his hands behind his neck. "But I think maybe you've just made a friend of mine in the district attorney's office very happy."

CHAPTER

30

"THIS IS TRIAL by ambush, your honor!" Ben argued vehemently. "Prosecutorial tactics at their sleaziest!"

"I apologize for the last-minute notice," Canelli said. He was doing a better job than Ben of staying calm—and with good reason. "The woman just contacted us last night. What could I do?"

Ben had an answer. "You could tell her to go away and keep her lies to herself."

"Ignore an eyewitness to a confession? I'd lose my job."

"Better you lose your job than Father Beale loses his life!"

"Gentlemen, gentlemen, stop!" Judge Pitcock tried to retake control of the heated discussion taking place in his own chambers. Somehow, being separated from the jury seemed to have given the lawyers leave to turn the volume up about three thousand decibels. "This isn't helping anything."

Ben continued pressing. "This is grossly improper, your honor. Tell me you're not going to allow this woman to testify."

"I don't think I can do that, counsel."

"Your honor, this is a repulsive assault on everything this court is supposed to represent—fairness, ethics—"

"He's wrong," Canelli countered. "His client is the repulsive assault. On human life, religion, safety. Even the sanctity of the family—"

The judge turned his eyes skyward. "Please, Mr. Canelli. I'm a Mormon, not a moron."

"But your honor—"

"Listen up, both of you. This is how it's going to be. I don't like last-minute witnesses, but I've got an affidavit here saying the woman just came forward last night. It's uncontested, so I have to assume its truthfulness. I can't prevent a keenly relevant witness from testifying where there has been no fault on the part of the prosecution."

"But your honor—"

"Mr. Kincaid, this is my turn to talk, not yours. If the defense needs additional time to prepare for cross-examination, I will grant it. But she will be heard."

"But she's a snitch!"

Judge Pitcock looked at him wearily. "Mr. Kincaid, if the prosecution were only permitted to put nice people on the stand, they'd never be able to convict anyone, would they?"

CANELLI HAD THE sense to admit up front that Sammie Flynn had a rap sheet as long as the Isthmus of Panama. He even acknowledged that the prosecution had given her a break in exchange for her testimony. Which was too bad. As Ben knew, if he'd brought those details out on cross, they'd be damaging. By bringing them out himself, Canelli effectively defused the time bombs.

"When did you first meet Daniel Beale?" Canelli asked her.

Sammie had gotten scrubbed and fitted with a pleasant pantsuit that covered most of her tattoos. In the witness box, she looked relatively presentable. "In jail, when I first got brought in on the bad check charge. He was in the next cell over."

"Did he ever speak to you?"

"No. I tried to talk to him a coupla times, but he never said nothing. Well, not to me."

"Did he speak to anyone else?"

"Yeah. God."

"He spoke to God?"

"Yeah. He prayed. Out loud. Down on his knees, like a schoolkid."

"And did you overhear what he said?"

"Objection," Ben said, rising. He was liking this testimony less and less, the more of it he heard. "Hearsay."

"It's an admission against interest," Canelli argued, "as will soon be apparent. Plus, it qualifies as being given under circumstances that suggest truthfulness." He paused, giving Ben a wry expression. "People don't normally lie to God."

"No, they don't," Judge Pitcock said. "I'll allow it."

"What did he say in his prayer?" Canelli reasked.

"He asked for forgiveness."

There was an audible stir in the jury box—and for that matter, throughout the courtroom.

"Forgiveness—for what?"

She drew in her breath, then let it rip. "For killing that woman. Kate McGuire."

The commotion in the courtroom at this point was loud enough to merit a stern warning and a few raps of the gavel from Judge Pitcock.

At counsel table, Father Beale leaned toward Ben and whispered. "This is absolutely false."

"I know."

"I don't pray aloud when I'm alone. And I wouldn't pray for forgiveness for something I didn't do."

"I know."

"Why would she say these horrible things?"

Ben's eyes narrowed as he scrutinized the witness box. "You're her get-out-of-jail-free card."

Canelli continued the direct examination. "Did he say how he'd done it?"

Sammie nodded. "He said he clubbed her over the head with a paperweight, then strangled her."

"And did he say why?"

"He said he became angry. He was tired of the . . . intense dissension . . . in the church."

At counsel table, Ben hastily scribbled a note and passed it to Christina. She read it and then, a moment later, left the courtroom.

"But why kill Kate McGuire?"

"Because she was the main troublemaker. She was the ringleader for all the . . . the . . . what did he say? The theological malcontents."

"I see," Canelli said gravely. "So he killed her."

"I don't think he planned it exactly. He was asking God for forgiveness for his temper. I think he got mad and just went crazy."

How kind, Ben thought. She was sending Father Beale up the river, but she was at least giving him an opening to plead insanity. A generous girl.

"Are you sure you heard this? You didn't misunderstand him?"

"I couldn't misunderstand what he was saying. Our cells were right next to one another."

"Thank you, Sammie. Your witness, Mr. Kincaid."

For once, Ben did not have to feign his anger on cross examination. "You really don't care what happens to anyone other than yourself, do you?"

"I don't know what you mean."

"I mean you're condemning an innocent man to death just to save your miserable butt, and that's about as low as it's possible to get."

"Your honor," Canelli barked. "This is outrageous."

"I'll tell you what's outrageous," Ben snapped back before the judge could speak. "Allowing this kind of testimony in a trial for murder. First we had junk science; now we get junk eyewitnesses. What's next? Testimony from the psychic hotline?"

"Your honor!" Canelli protested.

Judge Pitcock looked at Ben levelly. "Mr. Kincaid, I will not permit this kind of tirade in my courtroom. You will either ask proper cross-ex questions, or you will sit down."

"Very well, your honor." Ben had let the jury know what he thought of the witness; that was the foundation. Now he had to take her apart limb by limb.

Out the corner of his eye, Ben saw Christina returning to the courtroom with a big bundle of newsprint. Excellent.

"Ms. Flynn, how many times have you been arrested?"

She looked bored. "Haven't we been over this already? I've been in jail twice."

"That isn't what I asked. How many arrests?"

She shrugged. "I don't know exactly. Five or six."

Ben pulled the rap sheet out of the folder Loving had brought him as soon as he got the new witness's name. "Actually, it's fourteen. For a variety of low-level felonies. But you've only been incarcerated twice."

"Guess I've been lucky."

"No, you've been busy. How many times have you testified in court, Ms. Flynn?"

"Objection," Canelli said. "Relevance."

"Overruled." Judge Pitcock needed no urging; he knew where Ben was going. "Answer the question."

"I ain't sure," Sammie replied. "A few."

"Five isn't a few, Ms. Flynn." He withdrew another long piece of paper from his folder. "Five is a lot."

"Well, whatever."

"Is it true you're known in the law enforcement community as the 1-800-CONFESS Girl?"

"How would I know what the cops say about me?"

"Your honor," Canelli said, "this is offensive and—"

"Overruled. You may continue, Mr. Kincaid."

"You've testified against five different inmates—three for murder, one for robbery, and one for grand larceny. Correct?"

Sammie frowned. "I'm not good with that legal talk."

"When you got arrested yet again a few days ago and were look-ing at the hard side of a mandatory twenty years, you needed to make a deal in a hurry, right? And with those pesky mandatory sentencing guidelines in place, the only way you could get your sentence reduced or eliminated was in exchange for 'cooperation,' right?"

"I already said we made a deal."

"Yes, but what you didn't say is that you concocted the whole story so you *could* make a deal!"

"That's not true," Sammie said angrily. "It isn't—"

"I think you're an expert in this field, Ms. Flynn. I think once you knew you were in trouble, you walked into the county jail like a shopper in a grocery store. You sized up all the tomatoes, then squeezed them a little to see what you could get out of them. You probably heard the DA's case against my client was hurting, so you called some friends and read some newspapers and got enough infor-mation to offer the authorities a convincing lie. A lie that would con-demn my client."

"I heard what I heard."

"And it's just a coincidence that the district attorney wanted it so bad he offered you complete immunity, right? What a break for you when Father Beale started praying out loud."

"Hey, I didn't make the old man talk."

"I wonder. I think you made up the whole story."

Sammie didn't blink. "You're just saying that because your guy is a murderer and you want to get him off."

"I think you took what little you know about the murder out of the newspaper."

"That's not true!"

"So you're denying it?"

"Yes! I told you what I heard. From that man's own lips."

"Really. Because some of your testimony seemed a little unusual. Like when you talked about"—Ben glanced at his notes—"the 'intense dissension.' Big words for a down-to-earth girl like you."

"What's that supposed to mean?"

"Only that you didn't strike me as sesquipedalian."

"Huh?"

Ben smiled. "Were those your words, Ms. Flynn?"

"No, they were his words. Beale's."

"Then I guess it's just a coincidence"—Ben picked up the top newspaper Christina had brought him and flipped to the front page—"that the *Tulsa World* used the exact same phrase yesterday in its coverage of this case."

She shrugged. "Huh. Maybe they've got a spy in the jailhouse."

"And look," Ben continued, "here's another one of your key phrases. 'Ringleader of a group of theological malcontents.' " He held the paper up so the jury could see. "And they weren't quoting anyone; they were just being prosy. Another coincidence, Ms. Flynn?"

She was beginning to lose some of her sangfroid. "Must be."

"The truth is, you didn't hear Father Beale say a thing, did you? You just read about it in the paper."

"That's bull. You can't prove that."

"Can't I?" Ben laid down the newspaper. "I noticed you described the murder weapon as a paperweight. I'm sure the jury noticed that, too. Isn't that what you said?"

"Yeah. So?"

"So—it wasn't. It wasn't the murder weapon—because the victim died from strangulation—and it wasn't a paperweight. It was an award. Father Beale's St. Crispin's Award."

Sammie was beginning to look as if she could really use a smoke. "Well, whatever. I guess he made a mistake."

"About his own award? I don't think so. But the newspaper did.

Right here." He took another paper from the stack and pointed out the offending passage. "That's where you got the mistake. Not from Father Beale. From the morning newspaper. Your so-called confession is nothing but a tissue of lies."

Sammie's face puffed up. "All I did was repeat what he said. I mean, maybe I didn't get the exact words right. But what I said was what he told me."

"I thought you said he was talking to God."

"No, he—I mean, he was, but—" She was starting to lose it, which of course was exactly what Ben wanted. "You're trying to confuse me!"

"And you're trying to convict an innocent man to save your sorry little butt. The worst of it is—since you've already made your deal, you'll still get off scot-free, even though your testimony was worthless." He turned to face the prosecution table. "I don't think you were put in that cell next to Father Beale by accident. I think the cops knew you were a career snitch, and that's why they put you there and gave you access to the phone and newspapers and let you educate yourself. So you would be tempted to fabricate false testimony to shore up their failing case. Which, like the pathetic loser you are, you did."

Sammie leaned forward, screaming. "Don't let him tell these lies about me!"

Canelli hit the floor running. "Your honor, these accusations are unconscionable!"

Pitcock appeared unimpressed. "Are they, counsel?"

"Your honor, I can assure the court that we would never do anything improper or—"

Judge Pitcock waved him to silence. "Don't waste your energy, sir. You called this witness to the stand knowing full well what she was and what she was going to do. I've watched these past years as the use of dubious snitch testimony has become increasingly common—even though it's inherently unreliable."

"Your honor," Ben said, "I move that this woman's entire testimony be stricken from the record and that the jury be instructed to disregard every word of it."

Canelli was outraged. "The prosecution opposes this motion in the strongest possible terms."

Judge Pitcock drew in his breath. "I suppose there are some instances in which informer testimony could be reliably presented. Where the witness has no prior history of snitching. Where the witness is not a recidivist. Where the testimony can be corroborated. Where the circumstances suggest reliability. Where the deals made with the prosecutor are written and all conversations pertaining thereto have been recorded. Where the scenario does not appear to have been engineered by the law enforcement officers involved." He peered down harshly at Canelli. "But none of those circumstances are present here, are they?"

For once, Canelli was speechless.

Pitcock addressed the courtroom. "The defense motion is granted. This witness's testimony will be stricken from the record. The jury is instructed—in fact, the jury is ordered—to disregard every word she has said." He lowered his eyes to the man standing just before him. "And Mr. Canelli, if you ever bring another witness like this into my court, I will have your license."

He banged his gavel with uncommon gravity. "We're in recess. I'm going to lunch."

31

"CHAMPAGNE IS ON its way!" Christina announced as she bounced into the conference room. "Three cheers for Ben the Magnificent!"

Loving followed her lead. "High fives for the master!" he bellowed.

Ben slapped him back, but there was a scowl on his face. "This is way premature, guys."

"*Au contraire,*" Christina countered. "You were brilliant in there today. Brilliant!"

Loving agreed. "You tore that snitch to shreds, Skipper. I almost felt sorry for her."

"Is that why you asked for her phone number?" Christina inquired.

Loving's face flushed. "Wuh . . . yeah . . . I mean . . . I wanted to 'spress my condolences."

Christina hugged his shoulder. "You don't have to pretend for me, Loving. I know you're a crazy man for tattoos."

Jones entered carrying an ice bucket and bottle. "Is this where the celebration is taking place?"

Ben held up his hands. "Just in case you didn't hear me the first time, it's too soon to be celebrating. Canelli still has at least a day's worth of witnesses. Anything could happen."

"We're not celebrating winning the trial," Christina informed him. "We're celebrating the sheer joy of watching you dismember that witness. I mean, you've been on a roll this whole trial. But what you did to that snitch! That was like—unprecedented in the annals of legal history."

"She was just a stupid desperate woman telling a big lie to salvage herself. Hardly like matching wits with a chess grand master."

"And then," Christina continued, "just to make it better, you got her entire worthless testimony struck from the record. I've never seen that in all the years I've been in the courtroom."

Ben shrugged. "It's Canelli's fault. He should never have called that woman to the stand. He's normally too smart to make such stupid mistakes. My guess is his boss forced this prosecution after the second murder got so much publicity, even though the proof really wasn't there. His case wasn't good to begin with, and he's been hurting ever since."

"Yeah. And today his case exploded in his face," Loving said. "Three cheers for Kincaid, King of the Courtroom!"

All three staff members lifted their glasses and hooted and hollered.

"Will you people stop?" Ben said. "I'm just glad Father Beale isn't here. He might think this means he's home free. And he isn't. Not by a long shot."

"What a party pooper," Christina said. "Look, Ben, I don't know if this case is in the bag or not, but I know this. You've come a long way since the days when you couldn't open your briefcase without doing something silly."

There was a knock on the door, and a well-pierced face poked through the opening. "Excuse me. Mr. Kincaid?"

Ben was pleased to see Marco Ellison, his new star defense witness. He had managed to get the kid's name added to the witness list (Canelli could hardly object after naming his own last-minute witness). He'd asked the kid to stop by the office tonight to prepare.

"Thanks for coming, Marco." Ben excused himself from the conference room, then led Marco into his private office.

"Hey, nice place," Marco said. "You do all the decorating yourself?"

This was sarcasm, of course, because excepting his framed diploma and a potted plant Christina had given him for Christmas, there was no decoration at all.

"I really appreciate your coming forward," Ben said. "Your testimony could save an innocent man's life."

"Hey, I'm looking forward to it." Marco grinned, revealing the metallic stud piercing his tongue. "My friends still can't believe I was in a church where some chick got wiped. I've been beer guzzling on that story for weeks."

Ben couldn't believe this guy could be in the church without overshadowing the bride, but that was neither here nor there. "Your testimony is critical, Marco, because you establish that Father Beale was not in his office at the time of the murder. If you saw him for a good five minutes after the wedding, he can't be the killer."

"Hey, I'm happy to help out." He grinned, jabbed Ben in the ribs. "Want me to make it ten?"

"I'm—sorry?"

"Well, I'm just thinking, if five minutes is good, ten would be better, right?"

Ben's smile faded. "Well, no, actually it wouldn't, because ten minutes after the wedding, dozens of people saw him leaving the crime scene. If you make it ten minutes, you'll get destroyed on cross."

"Aw well. Just trying to help. Maybe I could say I asked him a question at the reception and we went out to the garden to talk and he was never out of my sight."

Ben felt as if the tiny candle burning in his heart since this kid turned up had been snuffed out by a tornado. "Marco . . . your job here is not to make up the best story. Your job is to tell the jury what you saw and heard."

"Oh, right, right. I getcha." Marco winked. "I'll just tell them what I saw and heard."

"I'm serious, Marco. I can't—" Ben choked. Just thinking about it was painful. "I can't put you on the stand if I know you're going to lie. It's unethical."

"Don't worry. I won't let you down. I'm a drama major—did I tell you that?"

"I'm serious, Marco."

"Hey, I'm hip. I watch Court TV. I know it's all just a game you lawyers play. They get a witness, you get a witness. I can really help you out here."

"I have to know the truth, Marco. Tell me what you really saw."

"I'm thinking I could get some really good coverage out of this trial. You know, the press has been swarming all over that courtroom."

Ben felt his teeth clenching. "Marco, were you even there? Were you at the church at all?"

Again he gave Ben his broad charismatic grim. "Who's to say I wasn't? I mean, was someone taking roll?"

Ben crossed the room and opened the door. "Get out of here, Marco."

"Hey, chill, man. We can still work something out."

"No, we can't. Go."

"I can help your guy—"

"Maybe. If you don't get caught lying. On the other hand, if you do, Father Beale will go down in flames. At any rate, I'm not putting you on. If I did, I'd be no better than any other lawyer who puts liars in the witness box."

"Hey, that's harsh. Don't treat me like this."

"Go."

"You'll be sorry, man."

"*Go.*"

Marco gave a lopsided shrug, then ambled out of the office.

Ben slumped into his chair. Damn this job anyway. Trial practice was making him manic-depressive. Just a few minutes ago, he was actually staring to feel good about the way the trial was going. And now . . .

He'd been counting on that kid to keep Father Beale off the stand. True, Canelli was fumbling and Ben had done some real damage to his witnesses. But he also knew the worst was yet to come, and they would have to put on some kind of case if they expected to persuade the jury.

Christina poked her head through the door. "I saw your star witness leave. Everything okay?"

"Definitely not," Ben grumbled. "Strike his name from the list. With indelible ink."

"That bad, huh?"

"Worse."

She walked behind him and began massaging his shoulders. "Don't worry. You'll think of something."

Ben wished he shared her confidence, but he didn't. But he hoped she was right. Because if she wasn't, Father Beale would have to go forth and testify, a Christian soldier marching as to war. And Canelli would tear him apart.

MANLY TRUSSELL RETURNED to his apartment, his fists covered with blood.

His friend was waiting for him. "Have a good time?"

Manly glanced at his hands, then walked to the sink. "You could say that."

"I do admire a man who loves his work. Success?"

Manly let the water stream over his hands, watching the thin red streaks swirl around the basin. "I think it's fair to say there's one more babykiller who won't be gabbing much in the near future. Not till his jaw reattaches, anyway."

"And he didn't identify you?"

"Nope. Learned my lesson last time. I wore the mask."

"Good. Very good." The slowed articulation and slight pursing of the lips suggested what the speaker didn't wish to say. "So . . . you just hurt him?"

"Yeah, I hurt him. Bad. Whaddaya mean, *just?*"

"I wonder if maybe it's time to . . . elevate the initiative. Take it to the next level."

Manly shut off the water and grabbed a towel. "What's that s'posed to mean?"

"I think you know."

"No, I don't. What?"

"Well . . . they're never really going to take you seriously. Not while you're just wounding them."

"I think that creep tonight is going to take his wounding very seriously." Manly slung his towel back against the rack. "Are you saying you want me to kill these people?"

"Death does have a way of driving a point home. As you well know."

"Yeah, but I—"

"I don't want to pressure you, Manly. You do what you think is right. Not everyone has the courage to . . . go the distance."

"Now, wait just a goddamn minute. I got plenty of courage. But you're talking about murder."

"Four thousand aborted babies are murdered in this country every year, Manly. Is that right?"

"That's different."

"It isn't different. It's the whole point. More murders happen every day. The question is what you're going to do about it."

Manly ran his fingers through his sandy hair. "I guess. But still . . ." He exhaled slowly. "Jesus. I don't know what to think."

"Then don't, Manly." His friend laid a hand on Manly's shoulder. "It isn't exactly your strong suit. Just leave the thinking to me. I'll take care of you. I'll take care of everything."

"You sure?"

"Absolutely. Cross my heart. In fact . . . I already have a good idea what we should do next. Something so . . . impressive, they'll have to listen to you. Something this town will never forget."

32

BEN KNEW IT had to happen—eventually Canelli was bound to put on a good witness. And he knew that the evidence was compelling and that fingerprints, alas, could not be dismissed as junk science. Thus, it stood to reason that the fingerprint expert would be the low part of the trial—or one of them, at any rate. As a result, Ben prepared for it, prepared Father Beale for it, worried about it, anticipated it.

But somehow, the anticipation is never as bad as the real thing.

BEN LISTENED AS Canelli led Dr. Emilio Fisher through his description of the painstaking methodology he had followed during his examination. They were treated to a detailed discourse on the thirty-seven primary characteristics of fingerprints, the difference between dusting powders, how fingerprints were lifted, how they were preserved, and how points of similarity are used to match prints. Canelli took him step-by-step through the chain of custody followed to preserve and protect the evidence, leaving absolutely no opportunity for tampering.

"There are three basic types of fingerprints," Fisher explained. "Visible, plastic, and latent. Visible prints are left when the fingers, palms, or feet of the suspect come into contact with any clean, smooth surface. Some type of substrate is required to capture the friction ridge detail. Dust is the most common, but we've also successfully taken prints from blood, ink, grease, paint and other similar substances."

"What about plastic prints?"

"Those occur when contact is made with a pliable surface or substance—wax, putty, gum, that sort of thing. You get a negative impression of the print, since the ridges of the skin are reproduced as indentations in the capturing substance."

"And latent prints?"

"Those occur when natural skin secretions—perspiration and body oil, principally—are mixed with dust or dirt and left on a surface suitable for recovery of the print, paper, glass or, as in this case, a smooth polished acrylic. Many forms of development are possible—light sources, sprays, chemicals—but here we used a simple dusting powder to create a color contrast between the print and its background. Once the print is found, photography and mechanical lifting methods are employed to record the image and preserve it for future analysis."

"What, if anything, did you find at the scene of the crime?" Canelli asked.

"Latents. On the smooth acrylic desk object—the St. Crispin's Award. The prints were clear and unmistakable. Of all the different types of prints, latents are the most hardy. They can last for years."

"Is there any way to date a print?"

"Not reliably. There are some who claim to have discovered techniques for judging the age of a fingerprint, but in my professional opinion, they are not reliable."

What? Ben wondered. Some junk science to which the jury will not be subjected? Wonders never cease.

"Were you able to lift the prints found on the award?"

"Yes. Very reliably. And we matched them against the fingerprint exemplar taken from the defendant upon his arrest."

"And your conclusion, if any?"

"They matched. The prints were left by Daniel Beale."

"You're certain about this?"

"I'm certain. Everyone who has ever seen the prints is certain. Even an amateur viewing the prints would realize that they match. The points of similarity are overwhelming. There is simply no question about it. Those prints were made by the defendant. And no one else."

When it was Ben's turn to cross, he felt like Don Quixote riding in to tilt at the windmills. This was a mission impossible and then some. The science of fingerprints was beyond reproach; worse, it was, unlike DNA, a matter of common knowledge to all, easily understood even by the densest of jurors.

Moreover, Dr. Fisher was a good witness. He had looked rather ordinary, in his cotton J.C. Penney's jacket and polyester slacks, but he sounded convincing on the stand, knowledgeable and confident, without seeming like a prosecution pawn willing to take any position or ram anything down the jurors' collective throats.

Ben wondered about the attire, though; it was almost as if all police experts took their outfits from the same very bad costume closet. Was it symptomatic of the fact that police salaries were so poor, or was it a matter of taste (also poor)? Or could it be the prosecutors thought if a police witness looked too good he might lose credibility? It was an imponderable Ben promised to give some serious thought. Another time.

"Now, Doctor," Ben said evenly, "when you say there were no fingerprints on the weapon other than Father Beale's, what you're actually saying is that you didn't *find* any fingerprints other than Father Beale's, right?"

"In part." Fisher was taking the cross in stride, neither disturbed nor obnoxiously unruffled. "But the reason I didn't find any others is because they weren't there."

"As far as you could detect."

"And if they had been there, I would have detected them."

Ben rubbed his forehead. This was going to be a tough nut. "Now Doctor, be honest with the jury. Is it possible to touch an object without leaving a fingerprint?"

"It's possible to brush your finger against an object and not leave a print. Possibly to sustain a more prolonged touching on a surface that is not particularly conducive to prints. But in this case, we're dealing with a clear acrylic—a substance highly conducive to leaving prints. And we know the killer didn't just lightly touch the object, either. In order to muster the force necessary to deliver the blow, he or she would've had to grip the award firmly, for an extended period of time. Given those parameters, it is in my opinion absolutely impossible that the assailant would not leave a print behind."

"Maybe the print was smeared by the force or impact."

"In which case I would've detected the smear. But I didn't. Some of Father Beale's prints were smeared, but there was nothing that could be attributed to a third party."

"What about unresolved latents?"

"There weren't any."

"Maybe the killer wiped it clean after the murder."

"He would've eliminated Beale's prints, as well as his own. Unless Daniel Beale picked it up afterward. And didn't mention it to the police. That doesn't seem likely to me."

Ben tried a new approach. "Isn't it true that some people leave prints more easily than others?"

"Yes." Fisher fingered his glasses absently. "Print residues do vary, depending principally upon the oiliness of the skin. But everyone on earth has ridges on their fingertips. And there is no way anyone could've held that award with the strength necessary to deliver that blow to the victim's head without leaving a print. It is simply impossible."

Ben glanced back at Christina. A quick look from her was all he needed to tell him he was doing just as badly as he thought he was doing. If this didn't improve quickly, the trial was going to take a major turnaround. For the worse.

"Perhaps the assailant was wearing gloves," Ben suggested.

"Admittedly, that would've explained the absence of fingerprints."

Ben smiled, glad to see the doctor was a reasonable man.

"But the police searched the church and the people present for hours and hours, literally leaving no stone or pocket unturned. They found no gloves, much less gloves splattered with blood."

"There must be other ways the killer could hold that award without leaving a print. Perhaps the killer wrapped a towel or cloth around his hand. Maybe a handkerchief."

"But if so, where is it? Again, the police searched the premises and all possible suspects with uncommon thoroughness almost immediately after the body was discovered. Any such cloth or towel would be covered with blood. It should've been easy to find, therefore—after all, there was no time to run down to the local dry cleaners. If your hypothesis were true, the implement would've been discovered—quickly and easily. But it wasn't." He turned toward the jury. "And from that, as a man of science, I can make only one logical inference. That it wasn't found because it didn't exist."

Ben knew he was getting nowhere; worse, by rehashing the evidence and giving Fisher countless opportunities to restate his conclusions, he was drilling it ever more firmly into the jurors' consciousnesses.

He glanced back at counsel table. Father Beale was losing the poker face they had crafted during all those pretrial prep sessions. The impact of this evidence was hitting him hard.

Well, better to make some point, however unhelpful, than to make no point at all, he supposed. "Granted, we don't know all the ins and outs of how it was done in this case. Nonetheless, it is possible to hold an object without leaving a print, right?"

Dr. Fisher wasn't having any. "In general, or in this case?"

"In general."

"In general, yes. But in this—"

"And if it can be done, then it is possible that it was done here, and we just haven't figured out how, right?"

"Objection," Canelli said. "Your honor, it's not relevant what's possible—only what happened."

"I'm allowed to explore alternative theories," Ben rejoined.

"But this is not a serious theory. This is pure speculation!"

Judge Pitcock pondered a moment. "I'll allow you to go a bit further, Mr. Kincaid, but I'm more interested in facts than guesswork, and I think the jury will be, too."

Ben continued. "Dr. Fisher, isn't it true that it is possible that the assailant held that award without leaving a print and we just haven't figured out how?"

"No, I'm sorry, but I can't agree with that. If that were done, I *would've* figured out how. You would probably be spouting a dozen different ways it could've been done—if you could think of any. But you can't. No one can. And as a man of science, I must conclude that if there are no viable explanations of how another person could've held that weapon—then there was no other person."

"But even if you can't explain it, it's possible—"

"If you want to take that position, Mr. Kincaid, I suppose it's possible that a ghost floated into the church and clubbed the poor victim on the head, and that's why there were no prints. But I don't believe in ghosts. Do you?"

Ben didn't answer. What was there to say?

"And I don't believe football-size awards hurl themselves into people's heads. And I don't believe that blow could've been caused by anyone on earth—except Daniel Beale."

As BEN SAT down, he tried not to let his feelings show. It was important that it seem to the jury—and to his client—as if nothing major had happened. But he knew better. He knew he had just come up against the first witness he couldn't crack, not in the least, on cross. The first witness to really make the jury suspect Father Beale might be guilty.

Juries were unpredictable, but before, Ben sensed that they were winning, at least a little bit. That the trial was, for the most part, going their way. But he didn't have that sense any longer. Now he knew better.

What he didn't know was that it was only going to get worse.

CHAPTER

33

DURING THE BREAK, Christina flipped her trial notebook to the witness list and showed Ben the score.

"By my count, we've run through all the prosecution's technical or expert types, all the cop witnesses, and all the actual eyewitnesses. All that's left are a few St. Benedict's members. So the worst should be over."

Ben shook his head. "It doesn't figure. Canelli's a savvy prosecutor, and he has a great flair for the dramatic. He'll want to go out with a bang. He must be saving something."

"But what? More disgruntled vestry members? Who cares? We've heard that tune to death."

"Which is what worries me." Ben drummed a finger against his lips. "Could it be one of them is singing a song we haven't heard yet?"

"How could there be anything we haven't heard?"

"I'd put my money on Ernestine Rupert," Father Beale said, joining the discussion. "I don't think she'll be able to resist the opportunity to trash me in public."

"Let her do her worst," Ben murmured. "She'll go down in flames as soon as I reveal she's been blackmailing half the church."

"Maybe it's this other St. Benedict's member, Carol Mason," Christina suggested. "The Sunday school teacher. Maybe she has a complaint we didn't hear about in our pretrial interview."

The discussion continued for a good ten minutes, until Judge Pitcock returned and the trial resumed. But despite all the analysis and contemplation, none of them were prepared for what happened next.

* * *

"THE STATE CALLS Marco Ellison to the stand," Canelli announced.

Ben rose out of his chair, gaping as if he'd witnessed a train wreck. What the—?

"Bench conference," Ben said, but by that time, he was already halfway there. Canelli fell into place behind him.

"Your honor," Ben began, "this witness is not on the prosecution's list."

"He's on *their* list," Canelli rejoined. "He's the one they went to all the trouble to add a few days ago, remember? Then they tried to have him yanked. They know all about him. They can hardly claim unfair surprise."

"It *is* unfair surprise, your honor. We had no idea the prosecution intended to call him. What's more, the man is a terminal liar."

"Which I suppose explains what he was doing on your list in the first place," Canelli replied.

"No," Ben said, "it explains why we decided we couldn't call him. He offered me testimony that would help my client, but I turned it down because I knew it wasn't true."

"That's funny. I don't think his testimony is going to help you at all."

"Because he's changed it! When I wouldn't put him on the stand, he must've changed his story around so that you would!" Ben appealed to the judge. "Your honor, this witness didn't see anything. He just wants a piece of the action. He wants to be on television. I think he has some crazy idea that being in this highly publicized trial will jump-start his acting career."

Canelli turned to the judge. "Obviously, your honor, in the course of preparing the witness they realized he had information that would damage their client's case, so they decided not to put him on the stand. But because Mr. Ellison is a civic-minded gentleman who only wants to see justice done, he came to the prosecution with his information."

"Civic-minded gentleman? We're talking about a punk with a pierced tongue!"

"Gentlemen, please!" Judge Pitcock looked at them sternly, his left hand covering the microphone. "I appreciate your concerns, Mr.

Kincaid, but what do you want me to do? Given the circumstances, you can't claim unfair surprise, and I can't preclude the prosecution from calling a witness who could have relevant information."

"But he doesn't, sir. He's a liar. He's making it up as he goes along. He told me one story one day, then wanted to change it all around the next."

"You'll have an opportunity to demonstrate that on cross."

"How? There were no witnesses to our conversations other than myself."

Pitcock shook his head. "I can't tell you how to try your case, Mr. Kincaid."

"Fine. Then I'll testify."

"The defense attorney testifying on behalf of his client? You know perfectly well I can't permit that."

"Then I'll step down from the case. Ms. McCall can handle the remainder."

The judge's head was still shaking. "Same firm, same lawyer."

"Then we'll both resign. I'll find a replacement to defend Father Beale."

"Change lawyers in the middle of a murder trial? You can't be serious."

Ben was about ready to tear out his hair. Or Judge Pitcock's. "Your honor—this witness is a liar!"

"Then you may cross-examine him and attempt to prove that. If you need more time to prepare, I'll give it to you. But that's the best I can do. I've bent over backwards to give your client a fair shake, Mr. Kincaid. But I can't exclude pertinent witnesses just because you don't like what they're going to say." He turned his head. "Mr. Canelli, call your witness."

Ben returned to counsel table and watched as Marco Ellison took the stand. Canelli had outfitted him in a dress shirt and pants, which was a definite improvement, although the Sunday school outfit was a bizarre contrast to the punk haircut and piercings.

Canelli quickly established that Marco had been at the wedding, had left early, had wandered out into the prayer garden, and had seen Father Beale after he left the sanctuary.

"How long did he remain in the prayer garden?" Canelli asked.

"Not long at all. Barely fifteen seconds. He checked his watch, as if he had an appointment or something, then headed to the rear doors of the church."

"The ones closest to the offices."

"That's right. He would've gotten there . . . at most maybe a minute after the wedding concluded."

"Which means he was there at the time the murder occurred," Canelli summed up. "Thank you for your testimony. I pass the witness."

Ben didn't waste a beat before launching his attack. "Mr. Ellison, isn't it true you approached me not five days ago and told me you had testimony to offer the defense?"

Marco seemed undisturbed. "That's true."

"And isn't it true you told me you had information that could help Father Beale?"

"That's what I said."

"And isn't it also true that on the next day you offered to 'improve' your story? Which is why I took you off my witness list."

"I don't know what you mean by 'improve.' "

"Then let me put it bluntly. You offered to lie to make your story better. So I'd put you on the stand."

"Now wait a minute. That isn't so."

"Didn't you say, 'Hey, I know it's all a game'?"

Marco edged forward. "Are you kidding? You were the one who said that."

"Me?" Ben's eyes widened. "Why would I—?"

"You told me trials were just a game and everyone knew it and tried to get me to change my testimony to help your client."

Ben felt his pulse racing. There were few things more frustrating than hearing someone sit in that chair and say things you knew were lies—especially when you had no means of proving it.

Marco continued. "You told me something I didn't really understand about the time of death—you wanted me to say the priest had been in the prayer garden longer than he really had. But I wouldn't do it. So you told me you wouldn't use me at trial."

Ben tried to control himself. "Mr. Ellison, I've been practicing law for many years now. I have never encouraged a witness to say something that wasn't true, and I'm not likely to start on a podunk liar like you."

"Your honor!" Canelli said. "I object!"

"The objection is sustained." Judge Pitcock's voice was considerably colder than usual. "Restrain yourself, Mr. Kincaid, or there will be repercussions."

Repercuss away, Ben thought silently. It was important that the jury knew how he felt about these accusations in no uncertain terms.

"Mr. Ellison, were you even at that wedding?"

"Of course I was. I said—"

"You've said a lot of things, and most of them were lies. I was at that wedding, and I don't remember seeing you. Were you there?"

"Yes!"

"Why?"

"Why?" He seemed startled by the question. "To—to see the wedding."

"But why? Do you go to all the weddings at St. Benedict's?"

"I . . . knew some of the people involved."

"Some of the people involved? You mean some of the people getting married?"

"Yeah. Right."

"Who was getting married? Do you even know?"

Marco was beginning to twist uncomfortably. "Of course I know. There was . . . that guy who works with you. I've seen him in the courtroom."

"Do you know his name?"

Canelli rose. "Your honor, I object. This quiz show about the wedding is not relevant."

Judge Pitcock didn't wait for Ben to respond. "I think I'll allow it."

"Jones!" Marco said triumphantly. "That's his name. I don't know his first name."

Well, no one does. "And is that why you were there? Because you know Jones? Because he sure as heck doesn't know you, and I can call him to the stand to say so, if necessary."

"Uh, no. I was there for . . . the other one. The woman."

"Patty?"

"Yeah, Patty. That's right."

Ben stepped away from the podium and faced the jury. "Her name is Paula."

Now it was Marco's turn to be angry. "He tricked me!" He turned toward the judge. "He tricked me!"

The judge nodded. "He certainly did."

"I knew it was Paula. I just got confused."

"Tell us the truth, Marco," Ben said. "You weren't there. You don't even know who was getting married."

"I *was* there. I was there because my girlfriend wanted to be there, okay? She knew one of the bridesmaids and she wanted to see the dresses and so we went there together."

Ben didn't let up. "So now you're spinning a brand-new story for the jury. You certainly are an inventive fellow, Marco. You think well on your feet."

"It's true!"

"Then why didn't you mention it before?"

"I had no reason to. Who cares why I was there?" He leaned forward, his arm outstretched. "Look, you can play your little games all you want. But I was at that wedding. And I saw that priest go to his office, just when I said I did. You're calling me a liar because you know your client is a murderer!"

"Mr. Ellison!" Judge Pitcock pounded his gavel. "You will silence yourself immediately. You're here to answer questions, not to make speeches." He turned toward Ben. "Do you have anything more for this witness?"

Ben thought a long moment. He was never going to get this clown to admit he was lying. More questions would just lead to more impassioned diatribes, more insisting on Father Beale's guilt. His trial lawyer instincts told him the smartest thing would be to stop now and go out on a good moment.

"No, your honor. I have no more use for this so-called witness."

Judge Pitcock excused Marco from the stand, and Ben huddled with his co-counsel.

"What do you think?"

"What do I think?" Christina said. "I think he's a lying, amoral piece of—"

"But the jury. Did they buy it?"

Christina turned her eyes back toward the fourteen faces she had been scrutinizing carefully throughout the testimony. "I just don't know, Ben. You spun Marco around a little and made him look stupid, but I'm afraid they'll just write that off as lawyer . . ."

"Games?"

"Well, yes. It's what they expect to see on cross-ex. But it doesn't really affect the substance of his testimony. If they believe he was there—"

"Then they'll believe Father Beale was in his office at the time of the murder."

"That's what I'm afraid of." She glanced toward their client, who was staring straight ahead, his hands clasped, his expression fixed. "I think that's what he's afraid of, too."

Marco's testimony, Ben realized, following on the heels of the fingerprint evidence, had dealt them a serious blow. Every juror, whatever his or her disposition before, had to now be seriously contemplating the possibility that Father Beale was guilty.

And what Judge Pitcock had said during the bench conference was true. He had bent over backwards to give Father Beale a fair trial. Ben couldn't remember a time when he'd had a fairer judge overseeing a capital case. Sometimes, they were so preposterously biased that the whole trial became a stacked battle more against the judge than the prosecutor. But not this time. There'd been no unfairness, no error. And if there was no procedural error, there could be no successful appeal.

Which meant Ben had to win this case at the trial. There would be no second chances.

34

DURING THE LUNCH break, Ben had the courtroom to himself. Which was fine—he liked it that way. All the other lawyers went to lunch; even Ben's crew insisted on crossing the plaza to the cafeteria and ingesting high cholesterol foods in the name of nourishment. Certainly the clients went to lunch. But Ben remained in the courtroom, preparing for the afternoon ahead.

Being in trial was like nothing else. Ben sometimes compared it to being submerged in a bathysphere; the pressure of the trial pounded down on all sides at all times, while the world outside became increasingly distant and remote. One caught echoes from time to time, but it didn't seem real. While a trial was on, only the courtroom was real, only the judge and the jury and anyone else you needed to get the job done. Everyone and everything else was too far removed to matter.

Which might explain why most people went to lunch—to recapture a tiny measure of the real world, if only for a brief time. But Ben wouldn't allow it to himself, especially not during this case. Until the final rap of the gavel, his mind had to stay totally focused on the matter at hand. If he had fifteen spare minutes, that was fifteen minutes he'd spend preparing for whatever came next. Which in this case, was Ernestine. And he had lots to say to Ernestine. So he made sure he was ready. While the rest of the world went on without him.

Well, not entirely.

"I brought you back a sandwich," Christina said, hovering over his shoulder. "Turkey wrap."

Ben's head remained buried in his papers. "No thanks."

"I got it just for you."

"Throw it away. Give it to the poor. Eat it yourself."

"Well . . . no. It is rather disgusting. I also brought some tomato soup."

"Thanks, but no."

She placed her hand on his shoulder. "Ben, you have to keep your strength up."

"Chocolate milk. Caffeine high. Adrenaline surge."

"I'm serious, Ben."

"Me too. No soup."

"Then at least eat a few Fritos. I don't want you to end up like my uncle Freddie. Did I ever tell you what happened to my uncle Freddie?"

He looked up from his papers. "If I say yes, will you not tell the story?"

She gave him a wry expression. "We worry about you, Ben, when you do your ascetic trial-addict routine." Her voice dropped a notch. "I worry about you."

"Don't waste your energy. If you want to worry about something, worry about the case."

"You're doing enough of that for both of us. What is it about this one, anyway? Why are you so personally involved?"

"I told you. I've known Father Beale for years."

"Don't kid a kidder, Ben. There's more to it than that."

He returned his nose to his notebook. "I'm trying to help a man I know isn't guilty."

"How do you know?"

"I just . . . know, okay?"

Christina let him return to his work. But she slipped a half-full bag of Fritos into his attaché, just in case.

ERNESTINE RUPERT TOTTERED to the witness stand and performed exactly as Ben had expected, only better. For the prosecution, that is. Ben had hoped she would come off as a biased old biddy with an agenda, but instead, she seemed reasonable, tempered, even compassionate. Chalk one up for Canelli, or whoever was prepping his witnesses.

Canelli spent a good deal of time establishing that Ernestine was a respected member of the community, well-to-do widow, and the founder and chairman of the PCSC—an important civic organization. He didn't mention that it was a pro-choice organization; that was too potentially controversial. Eventually, Canelli led her to the subject of the strife at St. Benedict's.

"We tried to make the new priest work," Ernestine explained patiently. "Tried every way we knew how. We didn't want his ministry to fail. But no matter what we tried, it didn't work, and no amount of effort was going to change that. Tensions grew and, in time, matured into outright hostility."

"That must have been very painful."

The blue-haired lady nodded. "I can't tell you what a strain his hostility created, not only on myself, but the entire parish. I consider the people at St. Benedict's my family. I love them all like brothers and sisters. It was as if some outsider had married into the family and begun systematically tearing it apart."

"How was this hostility manifested?" Canelli asked. This was Ernestine's cue to recount each and every outburst, every confrontation since Father Beale came to the church. Which she did. In detail. Some of them the jury had heard before, but it didn't matter. Father Beale came off as an irrational, egomaniacal, uncaring man with an explosive temper he couldn't control.

"At the last meeting before the murder, he totally lost control. He pounded on the table, his face red with rage, and shouted, 'I won't take this anymore!' Shouted it as loud as he could, right in Kate's face. And of course, soon after, she was dead."

Canelli wrapped it up by bringing Ernestine to the fateful wedding and the confrontation in the corridor. Ernestine's version had a few new wrinkles.

"I just happened to be in an alcove between the offices and the main corridor when the argument started. At first, I couldn't help but listen and didn't think anything of it. Then it became embarrassing. The fight just kept getting worse and worse, and I couldn't come out without making it obvious I'd been there all along. I had to stay put."

"So you heard the whole thing."

Ernestine nodded. "Whether I liked it or not. And believe me, I didn't like it. His language was grossly offensive. I've never heard such words—certainly not from a priest."

"What was Kate McGuire saying?"

"She was telling him he was evil, or what he was doing was evil. She didn't want it to continue. And he just kept on yelling at her. Finally, he threatened her. 'I won't put up with this,' he said. 'This isn't over.' "

Canelli paused, allowing the grim words to sink in with the jury. "And the next time you saw Daniel Beale?" he asked finally.

"Was after the wedding. I was in the alcove again, and I saw him rush by, down the corridor toward the bathroom. His hands were red." She paused, and her voice wavered slightly. "They were covered with blood."

"Thank you, Mrs. Rupert," Canelli said gravely. "No more questions."

BEN SCRUTINIZED HIS opponent as he approached the podium. She sat prim and nearly motionless, poised in the chair with her handbag in her lap and her hands crossed over it. She was a sympathetic, somewhat vulnerable appearing woman, and Ben knew if he came down too hard on her, it might alienate some of the jurors. But in this case, that was just too damn bad.

"You must be awfully fond of that alcove," Ben said, first off the bat. He let the declarative sentence hang in the air, giving everyone time to turn it around, consider it, guess where he was going.

"I don't know what you mean."

"Well," Ben explained, "twice you said you were hanging around in there by yourself, for no apparent reason. What gives? Have they got closed circuit TV in there?"

Ernestine ran her tongue along her teeth before answering. "No."

"Then why were you in the alcove?"

Ernestine drew in a tiny breath, giving herself a moment to think. "I find it a quiet spot, somewhat secluded. A good place to gather my thoughts, meditate, pray."

"Come now, Mrs. Rupert. I've seen the alcove. There's not even a chair in there."

"Nonetheless, I—"

"That's where you meet your blackmail victims, isn't it?"

Her head turned, at a small but unnatural angle. "Excuse me?"

"That's where you meet the multitude of parishioners—the ones you love like brothers and sisters—who you're blackmailing!" He said the word nice and loud, so everyone could hear it. "Right?"

"I—I sometimes meet people there. But I certainly never—"

"Don't tell me you're going to deny that you're blackmailing several members of the church."

"I—I do deny it. I would never—"

"I have witnesses, Mrs. Rupert." Out the corner of his eye, he could see the jury leaning forward, craning their necks with interest. "Two members of my staff have observed you shaking someone down. I've witnessed it. I've seen you running off after services, or during choir practice, clutching your little blue account book. Where is that, anyway?"

She had reflexively glanced down at her lap before she could stop herself. "I don't know what you mean."

"It's in your purse, isn't it? I figured as much; as far as I can tell you never go anywhere without it. Show it to the jury, Mrs. Rupert."

"I have to object," Canelli said. "These groundless accusations have nothing to do with the murder."

"I think the relevance will be clear soon," Ben replied, "if it isn't already."

Judge Pitcock nodded. "I'll allow defense counsel some latitude. Proceed."

"So what about it, Mrs. Rupert? Do you have your account book in your purse?"

She hesitated, obviously unsure what to say. "I . . . don't really know. . . ."

"Well, why don't you take a look and see? I'm betting you do."

She glanced at the judge. "No one told me my . . . purse would be searched. Can he do this?"

"I'm afraid he can, ma'am. If you brought it into the courtroom, it's fair game."

A frown settled on her face. She looked down, looked up, looked down again. Slowly her hand crept toward her handbag.

And emerged a few moments later holding the little blue book.

"May I approach?" Ben asked. The judge nodded. Ben strode forward, snatched the book, and began rifling through the pages.

"Lots of accounts in here, I see. Labeled by initials, rather than names. How discreet." He held the pages up so the jury could see. "Looks to me like you've collected ten, maybe fifteen thousand dollars over the last few years." He placed the book on the barrier between himself and the jury. "Are you still going to try to deny your blackmail operation, Mrs. Rupert?"

"It's isn't blackmail. I just—I like to lend money to people when they need it. To help out."

"Oh, so this is a charitable operation, is it?"

"Well . . . not exactly. They pay back the money over time."

"And then some, judging from this book."

"Charging interest is traditional. That doesn't make it blackmail."

Ben moved in closer. "So if I call Alvin Greene or Paul Masterson to the stand, they'll testify that you lent them money out of the kindness of your heart?"

She didn't answer immediately.

"Shall we test that theory?"

Her eyes darted around the courtroom. Ben could see the wheels turning inside her head. Could he make good his threat? What would happen if he did?

"Tell the truth, Mrs. Rupert. Because I'm prepared to call everyone in your book to the stand if necessary. And now that the secret's out, someone's likely to tell the truth."

Ernestine licked her lips pensively. She still didn't answer.

"This didn't have anything to do with lending money, did it? Much less charity. These aren't interest payments you're keeping track of. It's blackmail! Admit it!"

Ernestine shifted uncomfortably in her chair. "Make him stop," she said quietly. "Won't someone make him stop?"

"You spent your whole time at that church collecting information you could use to extract your blood money. You'd go to church socials and teas and dig around and gossip till you learned what you needed. Some tidbit about somebody's past, or sexual preference, or whatever dark secret they didn't want revealed, especially at church. And you'd use that to milk them dry."

"It isn't true." She was talking more to herself than anyone else. "It isn't."

She was visibly shaken. Now was the time to tie it all back to the case. "But you know what initials I don't see in this book? *D.B.* And that's why you hated Father Beale, isn't it? You couldn't control him like you did the others. He wasn't in the club. What's more, if he ever found out about it, you knew he'd put an end to it. And you'd be without this lovely little income stream. So he became the enemy."

Ernestine's face was blotching. "It isn't so. That isn't—"

"And that's why you're testifying against him now, isn't it? That's why you're so bound and determined to say whatever it takes to get him out and get in some other priest you can control. That's what it's all about, isn't it? You're protecting your dirty little extortion racket."

Ernestine twisted around, breathing rapidly. "You're wrong. That isn't why."

"So says the blackmailer. But how can we believe anything you say? You're a major felon."

"I—I don't—"

"Tell us the truth, Ernestine. You hate Father Beale, don't you? You hate him so much you'll do or say anything to get rid of him."

"Yes!" she said, with a sudden shattering intensity. "Yes, I hate him!"

"Because you were afraid he'd quash your dirty blackmail scheme."

"Because he destroyed our church!"

"Because you couldn't control him."

"Because he's had sex with every woman he could get his filthy hands on!" Her voice echoed through the courtroom, leaving only stunned silence in its wake.

Ben took a step back. "Because—what—"

"You heard what I said. He's been with all of them. All the women who died. And many more."

Ben moved fast to control the damage. "If you think you can exonerate yourself by telling more lies, you've—"

"It isn't a lie. It's the truth."

"Your honor," Ben said, "I move to strike. The witness is not being responsive. This is just character assassination!"

Judge Pitcock shook his head. "Sorry, counsel. You opened the door to this. Overruled."

Ben redirected his fury at the witness. "Do you have any proof of your scurrilous accusations?"

"I don't need proof."

"If you don't have any proof, then keep your—"

"Ask anyone. *Anyone!*"

"Is this something you've actually witnessed, or are you just circulating more ugly gossip? Maybe you're hoping you can add Father Beale to your blackmail list after all."

"Ask Carol!" she said, pointing to a woman in the rear of the gallery. "Ask anyone!" She was leaning forward, screaming. "We don't talk about it, because everyone's involved. Because he's had sex with so many of them. And he's dragged everyone else down into his dirty game."

Ben could feel the trial spiraling out of his control. How had this happened?

He glanced back at Father Beale. His face was expressionless, but there were crinkles around his eyes that Ben didn't know how to read.

And behind him, in the gallery, his wife, Andrea, sat, her face covered with tears. She bent forward and buried her face in her hands.

"It's true," Ernestine repeated unbidden. "Ask anyone. Anyone at all."

Ben had to get rid of this woman, and quick. Whatever good he may have done before was unraveling at the speed of light. "No more questions, your honor."

"It's true! Ask anyone!"

"No more questions!"

Judge Pitcock excused Ernestine from the witness stand, but even after she was gone, Ben could hear her words echoing in his brain. And he was certain they were rattling around in the jurors' brains as well.

It's true! Ask anyone! He wanted to ask Father Beale, but he couldn't talk to him, not now, not while the jury was watching. He had to act as if this were no great surprise, as if he already knew there was nothing to it. Even though the cold chill creeping up his spine told him this trial had just hit a snag he wasn't going to be able to finesse his way around.

CHAPTER

35

The Gospel According to Daniel

I SUPPOSE, UPON reflection, what happened at this stage of the proceedings could be viewed as a classic example of an age-old philosophical problem. Certainly since the earliest stages of introspective thought, the subject of self-examination, of scrutinizing one's own soul, has been discussed and debated. Know thyself, Socrates said. That is the first step toward knowledge. But most readers have missed the point of the statement. Socrates was not saying that self-knowledge was the first step toward genius. Socrates' point was that no one ever really knows themselves, and thus, all attempts at higher knowledge are inherently flawed by the faulty foundation upon which the search is based.

At this point in the trial, I realized how right Socrates was. I had considered these issues a million or more times. I had weighed and examined; I had debated time and again—with myself. But there comes a time when one has to move beyond that, when one must take the next step. Expose your analysis to peer review, the academics would say. Or as the more tough-minded souls in my youth group might phrase it—face up to your own bullshit.

The irony of the situation was not lost on me, even as it was happening, even as our defense was crumbling right before my eyes. Hours and hours we had spent bracing ourselves for the worst, but when the worst came, it was from a quarter no one expected. We had worked to confront the enemies; we were prepared to meet the attacks of the prosecution. We were ready to counter and thrust, to expose and embarrass, to do whatever was necessary to defeat these opponents. But when the killing stroke was finally delivered, it came from an enemy for whom none of us were prepared—not Ben, not Christina, and not me. When the end finally came, I had no one to blame.

Because the enemy who finally destroyed me was myself.

"WIFE-SWAPPING?" CANELLI said, repeating an attention-grabbing word Ben had never expected to hear in this murder trial—or any other, for that matter. Funny how these things sometimes took directions that were totally unexpected, that for all your preparation you couldn't possibly anticipate. Except that it wasn't funny. Not at all.

"That was what it amounted to," Carol Mason replied. She was a thin woman, but she seemed even thinner on the stand, flimsy and vulnerable, without visible means of support. Ben had admired her beauty before, but all that seemed flattened out now, submerged by the misery that overwhelmed her. "They don't use that terminology. They prefer to call themselves *lifestyle couples*. But it's the same thing."

"And how many people in the church were involved in this?"

"The count varied. But almost everyone in the thirty-to-fifty age range tried it at one time or another. And the few who didn't knew about it. We were pretty good about containment; the knowledge stayed within the church. New members had to be with the church for at least a year before they were invited to . . . participate."

"Why were so many people involved?"

"Because our priest wanted us to be. He was the mastermind."

Canelli stepped back from the podium, a shocked expression on his face. Ben couldn't tell how much was show. Had he anticipated the way this juicy tidbit might slip out during Ernestine's cross? If he had tried to broach this subject on direct, their family values–minded judge would've shut him down. It had to come in through the back door. Was that why Canelli saved Ernestine and Carol for the end?

Ben supposed he would never be certain. And what did it matter? Planned or not, the testimony was devastating. Ben had fought and argued, hauled out precedent after precedent, but the judge didn't rule in his favor, as indeed Ben knew he couldn't. Ben had opened the door to this testimony during the cross of Ernestine Rupert. Anything the prosecution did with it now was fair game. It related not only to credibility and character and truthfulness—but to the very issue of motive itself. It was coming in.

"How did it start?" Canelli finally asked.

"It may seem bizarre—and I suppose it was—but Father Beale introduced this . . . concept soon after he came to St. Benedict's, no differently than he would any other Christian education program."

Canelli blinked. "Christian education?"

Carol nodded. "That's how he saw it. Liberated Christians, that's what he called us. He had this whole spiel. I couldn't repeat it all, but the basic idea was that sex was separate from morals, that sex could be recreational without impugning any moral truths, that people had misinterpreted the Bible to lock sex up in a closet where it was never supposed to be. Jesus was not a prude, that's what he kept saying. It was like a slogan for him—a higher truth."

Ben felt the eyes in the courtroom burning across counsel table, scrutinizing Father Beale. A priest on trial for his beliefs was a potentially sympathetic situation. But a blasphemer and sex fiend was something else altogether.

"And so people joined this . . . Liberated Christians group?"

"Oh, yes. At first just a few. But then word got around and more joined. And then more and more. Husbands would bring their wives, wives would force their husbands."

"And you also joined?"

"Yes." Carol's hand rose to her face; she bit down on her knuckle. "I didn't want to. It was my husband, Bobby. He was keen to give it a try. I guess he's . . . more adventurous than I am. 'What can it hurt?' he kept saying. 'Everyone's doing it. Let's just give it a go and see if we like it.' "

"So you consented."

"He kept pushing and pushing and he wouldn't stop. After a while, I couldn't say no anymore. But I still wasn't . . . ready. Especially for what went on at those meetings. Bobby would encourage me to dress differently, like some of the other women did. 'Come on, show off your tits and ass.' That's what he'd say. And I did it. God knows, I did it. I felt so debased. So humiliated."

"You didn't like it?"

"No." The knuckle, braced against her mouth, began to tremble. "I didn't like it at all. I thought it was evil. Sinful and evil. It disgusted me. And I wasn't the only one, either. I knew other women who felt the same way. They went along with it, but they suffered afterward. They were led to evil, tempted by the man who came to us as our spiritual leader."

"Objection," Ben said quietly. No reason to make a bigger fuss than necessary; the jury's sympathies had to be with this obviously distraught woman. "The witness is characterizing, not testifying."

Judge Pitcock nodded. "Mrs. Mason, please restrict yourself to recounting what you've actually seen or heard."

"Yes, your honor."

Canelli jumped in to guide her back on course. "Mrs. Mason, could you please describe . . . what took place at these meetings?"

Carol closed her eyes for a long moment, as if gathering her strength. Then, slowly and deliberately, she began. "They weren't all the same. We had several different types of meetings. At the church meetings, on Wednesday nights, we just talked, believe it or not. Father Beale would lead us in a discussion of the supposed philosophical and even Biblical underpinnings of what we were doing. His theory was that recreational sex was a healthy thing and when practiced by couples—here's the bizarre part—that it would actually strengthen our marriages. In his twisted mind, this was marriage counseling." She paused. "Other times, we would meet at someone's house or, twice a year, we'd have a retreat, usually at a somewhat secluded motel in another state."

"And why did you need privacy?"

Her voice dropped off. "I would think that was obvious."

"What did you do on these retreats?"

Carol seemed tired, without energy, like a rag doll with her stuffings ripped out. "Imagine the worst. Mix a nudist camp with an orgy scene from some Roman gladiator movie, and you've just about got it."

"You didn't wear clothes?"

"That was left to the individual, but when we were in our private meetings, most people wore . . . well, less than they normally would. Or nothing at all. Booze flowed freely; that made it easier for some people. We'd do nude swimming. Messing around in hot tubs. Sometimes we'd all watch porn videos, just to get worked up. Sometimes we would play little games."

"Games?"

"Icebreakers. You know, to get to know one another."

"Such as?"

"Oh, God." She pressed a hand against a temple. "We played one that was kind of like spin the bottle, only instead of giving kisses, if the bottle pointed to you, you'd have to . . . perform oral gratification. We had a sundae party, where people smeared whipped cream and toppings on themselves and you had to lick it off. The men had a contest once to see who had the longest tongue, for . . . obvious reasons. One night we lined up in a big chain, like a bunny hop, except we were naked and the music was Ravel's *Boléro*, and we all performed massages on one another."

"The purpose of these games, I suppose, was to . . . stimulate sexual interest?"

"Yes. And help decide who was going off with whom."

"And once the pairing was complete?"

"It varied. Sometimes, we'd do private encounters in separate rooms. And sometimes . . . not." She drew in her breath, steeling herself. "Some people liked to watch—they'd stand there and observe while their spouse made love to another person. Sometimes we'd all do it in the same big living room. Together. Me and the Altar Guild ladies and the preschool teachers and whoever else." Her voice choked, like a gagging reflex was kicking in. "One big Christian orgy."

"You're telling us that . . . sexual intercourse took place?"

"In every way, shape and form that you can imagine. Wanna do it a little differently from the way your spouse does it? Here's your big chance. You like bondage? There'd be somebody there with your taste. Into pain? Someone's waiting for you."

"And you took part in this activity?"

Carol closed her eyes tightly, but a tear still crept through. "Yes. I did. To my eternal shame. Me and all my friends, all the people I loved most in the world."

"And Father Beale also took part in this sexual activity?"

"Took part? He was the main man."

Again, Ben could feel the heat of the jury's eyes. He was only glad

Andrea had excused herself from the courtroom—at Ben's suggestion. Ben knew the jury would notice she was gone, but it was better that they see the empty seat than that they see the priest's wife break down in open court.

"He had sex with other women in the church?"

"Anyone. Anyone he could get."

"Including . . ."

"Yes," she said, speaking more quietly than before. "Even me."

"And his wife knew about this?"

"Of course she did. She was there. This was a couples event, remember? I don't think she ever enjoyed it. I don't think she derived pleasure from watching her husband-the-priest prance around like a great big stud horse. But she certainly knew. We all knew."

"How long did this last?"

Carol considered. "I would guess it ran for close to three years without any serious problems. Then everything started to unravel. I wasn't the only one who was getting sickened by it. Helen Conrad was the first to admit it. She got a group of the women together and we talked. Helen was so racked with guilt I thought she might be suicidal. She prayed for forgiveness all day long—but never found any relief. After she was killed, I think we all secretly wondered if she had been punished for what she had done. And which one of us might be next. We wanted it to stop, or at the very least, to stop having the official imprimatur of our church. But Father Beale wouldn't hear of it. He thought we were doing something important, something progressive. He was really into it. And he didn't want it to end."

"What was the result?"

"The result was that Father Beale began having problems with the church, the vestry, the parishioners. First it was just a few of us, but it grew beyond that. There was definitely a backlash on all fronts. It was like, Okay, we've had our fun. Let's end this before we get caught. But Father Beale wouldn't consent. He wouldn't—or couldn't—quit. He was totally addicted to it—the sex, the power, the women."

"Was this when the vestry began to have serious disagreements with Father Beale?"

"Yes. I mean, we never said, 'Hey, this is because we want the orgies to stop.' We couldn't put that in the minutes, could we? Especially not when copies go to the bishop. We never publicly acknowledged what we were doing, not outside the Liberated Christian meetings. But that's what the dissension was all about."

"Had some of the vestry members been . . . involved?"

"Yeah, all of them, I think. Except Ruth O'Connell and Ernestine Rupert, and they certainly knew about it. By the time last year rolled around, Father Beale was confronted by a vestry that was almost uniformly opposed to him. We talked about politics and liturgical issues, but that wasn't what was in our hearts. What we wanted most. We all knew it wasn't about . . . gay rights, or whatever. It was about getting rid of the priest who had turned our sweet little church into a whorehouse."

"Was Kate McGuire one of the women who had been with Father Beale?"

"Oh, yes. Many times. And so were the other two women who were killed."

"And was she one of the women who wanted Father Beale to stop these sexual activities? To leave?"

"One of the strongest. Kate got into some major fights with him. She was having a breakdown, truth be told. She couldn't handle it any more. She was undergoing a major guilt attack. She was engaged to be married, you know, even while this was going on. She felt dirty all the time, couldn't get clean. She'd shower three times a day, but it didn't help. And she couldn't get any help from her spiritual advisor—because he was the one who had dirtied her."

"Was she doing anything other than fighting with him?"

"Yes. She made threats—we all heard them. She said if he didn't stop it, she'd report him to the ecclesiastical court." She let out a wry, bitter chuckle. "He kept saying there was nothing wrong with what we were doing. Fine then—let's hear it from the bishop." She lowered her eyes. "I suspect he would've had a different viewpoint."

"So she threatened to expose him?"

"She threatened to blow the whole thing wide open. Father Beale would never have worked again—if she hadn't been killed. In his office."

The leaden silence that blanketed the courtroom was almost unbearable. Ben tried to shake it off, tried not to let these stunning revelations prevent his brain from functioning.

"Why have you come forward now?"

Carol thought several moments before answering. "I feel bad

about it. I feel like I'm betraying everyone in the church. Exposing everyone's secrets. But—that's why we couldn't get anything done. Because everything was a secret. No one wanted to talk about it." She lowered her head. "I just thought—if someone doesn't talk about it someday, it will never stop. Never. And I couldn't stand that. I just . . . couldn't stand it."

"I think we all know what you're saying," Canelli murmured.

"You can't understand what it was like," Carol said, her voice cracking. "St. Benedict's meant so much to me. When I first came here, I was a mess, but the people at St. Benedict's helped me find my way. Helped me find my center. I used to say that church must've been built on holy ground—that's how much it meant to me. And now, to have all that taken away, stolen, and transformed into something grotesque and horrible and . . . dirty." Tears poured down her face. She braced herself against the railing, barely able to hold herself up. "I couldn't bear it. None of us could."

"Thank you," Canelli said quietly. He turned toward Ben. "Your witness."

BEN PUSHED HIMSELF to his feet, his brain racing at the speed of light. What could he do with her? Her delicate emotional state made any rough tactics impossible. What could he hope to accomplish? She didn't testify that Father Beale had committed the murder, not exactly. She had just supplied the motive, the emotional prop for the eyewitness and physical evidence that was already incriminating him.

Father Beale had remained silent throughout her testimony—no quizzical expressions, no outbursts, no scribbled notes. Ben leaned close to him and whispered one question.

"Is she lying?"

It took him a moment to respond, but when he did, what he said was unequivocal. "No."

"Mr. Kincaid," Judge Pitcock said. "The witness is yours."

"No questions," Ben answered. "Nothing for this witness."

The judge's double-take lasted barely a second; he was too seasoned a pro to let his thoughts show. "This is your last chance, Mr. Kincaid. To examine this witness on behalf of your . . . client." Even without an accompanying facial expression, the simple way he said the word was enough to tell Ben what Judge Pitcock thought of his client now. The jurist whose decisions were driven by a respect for family values was not likely to be a fan of the wife-swapping priest. There would be no more favors from him.

"No questions, your honor."

"Very well. Mr. Canelli?"

"That's all we have, your honor. The prosecution rests."

Pitcock glanced at his watch. "Very well. I think we've had enough for today. We'll start tomorrow morning at nine with the first witness for the defense." He gave the jury the usual instructions, then adjourned.

Ben didn't waste any time. "Everyone leaves by the rear exit. Conference at the office in thirty minutes."

He looked down at Father Beale, trying not to let what he was thinking and feeling show in his face. "That includes you."

"I'll be there," Beale replied. "I'll have the marshals take me directly. No dinner stop."

"Good." Ben turned toward Christina. "Order in food. We're going to be working late."

"Understood."

"No talking to the press. Not one word. Nothing they can use on the ten o'clock news. Not even a 'no comment.' "

"Got it."

"Good. Now let's get the hell out of here."

For once, Ben did not mentally rehash the day's trial as he left the courtroom. Far from it—he tried to put it out of his mind. He knew what had just happened—far too well. In a few short minutes, everything had changed. The problems he confronted now were not the same ones that had faced him before. The trial he was working now was not the same trial he had been working before. And the man he was defending was not the same person he had been defending a few moments before—and never would be to Ben again.

CHAPTER

36

*"WHY DIDN'T YOU **tell me?**"* Ben demanded.

Father Beale wasn't making eye contact. "It isn't the sort of thing that comes up in casual conversation."

"I told you that you had to tell me everything. Everything that could possibly be relevant to the trial."

"I didn't see that it was relevant."

"You didn't? The real reason there's so much antipathy against you in that church, and you didn't think it mattered?"

"I didn't think it would come up. I didn't think anyone would talk. We made a promise to one another, a solemn oath. How was I to know that Carol would—"

"You weren't supposed to guess what witnesses might do. That's my job! But I can't do it if I don't know everything there is to know about them. I was blindsided in there! Canelli destroyed us, and there wasn't a damn thing I could do about it because I didn't know what the hell was going on!"

Ben braced himself against the conference table. He knew this tirade wasn't going to get them anywhere. But he couldn't help himself. Part of it was despair—he knew what had happened to their case in the courtroom today. But there was more. Irrational or not, he also felt a sense of . . . betrayal.

"Let's all calm down for a moment and figure out what we need to do next," Christina said. She was the only other person in the room, and given the delicate matters to be discussed, Ben suspected Father Beale would probably prefer she weren't around. Too damn bad. Ben needed her—now more than ever. "What's happened has happened. We need a plan."

Ben threw his hands up. "A plan? As if we had a choice. Here's our plan. Father Beale has to take the witness stand."

Beale looked up. "I thought you were opposed to that."

"I was opposed to it! I'm still opposed to it. Don't you understand? We don't have any choice!"

"Ben," Christina said, "we have other people we could call. Character witnesses and such."

"And believe me, we will. But that's not going to cut it. Because at this point, the only thing the jurors are going to care about is the Great St. Benedict's Wife-Swap-A-Rama. And who are we going to get to testify about that? Dr. Ruth?"

"Actually," Father Beale said, "*wife-swapping* is a rather sexist term. We prefer to call ourselves lifestyle couples."

"Don't give me your little PC lecture. I don't care what you call yourselves!"

"Ben . . ." Christina said.

"Well, I don't!"

"Ben . . . you're acting out. You're personalizing this. I don't know why, but—"

"I'm not personalizing. I'm just sorry to see a trial we've all worked so hard on fall apart at the seams."

There. He'd said it. Everyone knew it already, but now he'd said it. It was on the table. Probably not an ABA-approved technique for counseling your client, but at least now they all knew where they stood.

"Fine," Father Beale said. "I'll testify. I always wanted to."

"Well, you get your wish," Ben said angrily. "And you'd better be good, because frankly—you're your only hope."

"I'll do whatever you tell me."

"You're going to have to give the jury some credible explanation for all this lifestyle couple crap. Something that seems rational, if not acceptable. Make it sound as if you really thought you were accomplishing something, as opposed to just being a horny old man trying to get some."

Beale's neck stiffened. "I'll . . . do my best."

"You're never going to get an Oklahoma jury to agree that wife-swapping is a good, healthy thing. But at least you can try to convince them it wasn't a motive for murder."

"I understand."

"And make no mistake—Canelli will be gunning for you. He's found your weakness. He'll try to use it to bury you."

"Understood."

"Good." Ben pushed away from the table, walked to the window, and stared out at the horizon.

"So . . ." Christina said, ". . . are we ready to proceed? We're going to have to map out this direct. We have to cover a lot of bases. We want to make sure we don't leave anything out."

"Damn straight."

"We still have a few advantages. Canelli will want to cross on the lifestyle stuff, but if we volunteer it on direct, that'll undercut him. And so long as we don't introduce evidence regarding Father Beale's propensity for honesty or truthfulness, Canelli won't be able to use past acts to incriminate him."

"Yes," Ben said, still gazing out the window. "We'll map out the perfect direct examination, and we'll practice it, and we'll practice it again, and we'll practice it again, until we all know it so well we could do it in our sleep." He slowly returned to the table. "But I have one question for you first, Father. One little question. And I'd better like the answer."

Father Beale sat up straight. "Yes?"

Ben leaned across the table like a vulture. He stared directly into his client's eyes. "Is there anything else?"

Beale did not need clarification. "No. Nothing else. No more secrets. Nothing I haven't told you."

"You're sure?"

"I'm sure. I'm . . . absolutely positive."

"You'd damn well better be." Ben yanked a chair out from under the table and thought he finally might be able to sit down. "Now let's get to work."

"IS SHE DEAD?"

"Not yet. But she will be."

Manly gazed down at her prostrate figure, head tilted to one side, legs bent back at an unnatural angle. "Put up a pretty good fight. Better than you'd expect. Till I clubbed her on the back of the head."

"You sound as if you admire her."

Manly paused, uncommonly reflective for once. "I admire conviction. I may not agree with her. She was, after all, part of the conspiracy to kill helpless children. But I think she at least believed in what she was doing. And she didn't give up easily."

"I thought you weren't going to . . . advance the program this early on."

"She was getting away. And she'd seen me. I had no choice."

No choice, his friend thought, because you bungled everything in your usual stupid way.

"Do you think she's dreaming?" Manly asked.

"I don't know. If you'd like, I'll club you over the head. Then you can report back to me."

"Pass. Still, she seems so peaceful."

"Not as peaceful as she'll seem . . . after you finish."

"True," Manly said, nodding. "All too true." He reached out with his hands, his fingers curled like claws.

"You're going to strangle her? Like the others?"

Manly's face twisted around until, finally, it resolved itself in a strange sort of smile. "Yes," he said, as his hands clenched her throat. "Like the others."

Bad Faith

◆ ◆ ◆

CHAPTER

37

The Gospel According to Daniel

BE CAREFUL WHAT you wish for, says the old axiom, which I believe is actually derived from St. Augustine. You may get it. Wise words indeed.

I had wanted to take the stand in my own defense all along. Although I was intellectually cognizant of my attorney's reasons for advising against it, I still wished for the opportunity. It held an irresistible attraction for me. I fantasized about telling my story with such persuasion and eloquence that the prosecution's case simply melted away. In my mind, a jury might well suspect me when all they heard were the words of my enemies, but once they heard me testify, once they heard my story told from my own lips, they would be unable to see me in any light but positive.

And it was not my plan to dissemble or fabricate. I would tell the story and tell it straight, to adapt the words of Dickinson. I would tell them the good and the bad, but I would tell it with clarity and sincerity. Confession is good for the soul, after all. While we may not be as driven to confession as our Catholic brethren, even an Episcopalian could see the merits, both therapeutic and judicial, in telling the story as it happened, warts and all. I would impress them with my forthrightness. I would dazzle them with my purity.

In retrospect, of course, I recognize this for the hubris that it was. If this were a Greek tragedy with me as the star—and indeed, many of the key elements are present—then my fatal flaw, my downfall, came from the sin of pride. I was in love with myself, my ideas and philosophies, my theological daring and innovation—when I should have been in love with God. I should have trusted Him in all respects instead of trying to do an end run around Him, trying to act as if He weren't really necessary because I was so astonishingly brilliant on my own. I never lost faith, but too much of my faith was tainted, was a bad faith, because it was invested in the spirit of man rather than the Holy Spirit of God.

All of which is easy to say now. At the time, I couldn't see it. I still perceived the opportunity to testify as a positive development. I still thought I could save myself.

How powerfully, unimaginably, stunningly wrong I was would become apparent with the speed and immediacy of a lightning bolt. A bolt, one might say, cast down from the heavens.

"HOW LONG HAVE you served as a priest?" Christina asked him, sticking faithfully to her notes. Every word, every placement of a question, had been carefully worked out the night before. Served, not worked. Priest, not rector. Establish the length to make the point that he has had successful parishes in the past.

"Thirty-four years," Father Beale replied.

"And how long have you been at St. Benedict's?"

"More than three years. The bishop recommended my transfer, and the vestry accepted the recommendation. The parish had many problems finding a rector after the retirement of a longtime founding priest, and the bishop felt I might be able to get the church back on track."

"Is that what happened?"

"No. Not even close." Father Beale was doing well, Ben thought, watching from counsel table. Good thing. If he couldn't handle himself on these softball questions, there was no hope for what would come later. His witness stand demeanor was good; he seemed cool, poised, and smart, without coming off as pompous. He still had a tendency to overintellectualize—Ben and Christina had coached him to use simple, direct words—but it wasn't so extreme that it seemed arrogant. "From the outset, there was opposition to me and almost everything I did. It got worse, as time progressed, but it was there all along."

"Why do you think that was?"

Beale stroked his beard thoughtfully. "I think there were many reasons. St. Benedict's had benefited from an extended relationship with its previous priest, Father Raymond Ostler. It's not unusual, after a situation such as that, for parishioners to have a difficult time making adjustments, accepting a new leader with his own way of doing things. In my field, the first priest after a long-termer is often referred to as the 'sacrifice priest,' because everyone knows that it probably won't work, but that some buffer is needed, some interim rector who, despite his apparent failure, in fact helps the parish make the sometimes difficult adjustment to a new leader."

"So you were St. Benedict's 'sacrifice priest'?"

"You could see it that way, and in fact, I know that the bishop did. I still had hopes that I could make it work. And at first, it was working. Although there were difficulties."

"Such as?"

"I've always been openly political; I feel that religion and politics are inextricably intertwined. You can't call yourself a Christian, in my view, and stand idly by while people are mistreated and discriminated against, whether it's people of other races, or women, or people of different sexual preferences."

"Did this create disharmony in the church?"

"Of course it did. The people of St. Benedict's may be Episcopalians, but we still live in the Bible Belt, and it shows. Still, I felt I could make people come to see my viewpoint and, if not agree, at least respect my need and right to do what I was called to do."

"Were there other problems?"

"Yes. When I first arrived, the church was deeply in debt. Pledges had fallen off, but the budget had not been adjusted accordingly. In order to stabilize the budget and put us on a firmer financial footing, I pressed for the elimination of some of our member-oriented programs. I didn't like doing it, but I thought it better to eliminate that than to do away with the outreach programs I considered the most important part of our ministry. Nonetheless, as I'm sure you can imagine, anytime you eliminate someone's pet program, you create an adversary."

"What other problems did you have?"

Beale proceeded, in the same open, candid manner. "There was an initial conflict with the music minister, Paul Masterson, who had been at St. Benedict's several years longer than I had. I think he was threatened by my arrival, and he soon began marshaling his adherents to his support, and against me. He seemed to think I was encroaching on his turf."

"Were you?"

Beale tilted his head. "To some extent, I suppose I was. But you must understand, our church's worship is governed by the Book of Common Prayer, and our policy by the Episcopal Constitution and Canons. They say the rector runs the show, plain and simple. I tried to give Paul as much autonomy as possible, but when there were liturgical issues of importance involved, such as when choosing the proper hymn to accompany and amplify the readings, I had to intervene. That was, bottom line, my job."

Christina nodded. "Was there anything else, Father Beale, that contributed to your problems at the church?"

"Yes." His head lowered, and for the first time, there was a sense of regret, a perforation of his resilient, intellectual stance. "I . . . have a temper. A bad one. I'm aware of it, and I have sought counseling for it." He shook his head. "But these are excuses. Far too often I allowed my ardor to be expressed in anger. Yelling, shouting, even threatening. Unforgivable in any human being, but especially in a parish priest."

"How many times did these temper outbursts occur?"

"Too many to count. Toward the end, barely a vestry meeting went by without some expression of hostility by me, often returned by others. It was a bad situation all around." His hands, resting on the railing, tightened into fists. "And yet, I can't express to you how intensely . . . frustrating this was for me. I felt I was doing what was right for the church and for God. I was answering a call, a bishopric appointment. I had thought and considered and weighed every decision. And despite all that, to be met with opposition at almost every point, no matter how trivial, for no better reason than that you've had the audacity to do things differently than the last priest did—" His hands began to tremble. "My frustration and disappointment was uncommonly . . . palpable. I simply can't describe it in a way that gives any indication how strongly and passionately I felt."

And Ben didn't particularly want to hear about how passionately he felt, either. Looking at his hands and face, Ben worried that they might witness a temper tantrum right on the stand, which would sink their case once and for all. Fortunately, Christina changed the subject.

"Father Beale," Christina said, slowly and deliberately, "much has been said by the prosecution witnesses about the Liberated Christians group. Including your somewhat unusual theories regarding sexual activity by consenting adults. I know this may be somewhat uncomfortable for you, but would you please explain this to the jury?"

"Of course," he said. "I don't mind at all." And indeed, to look at him, he didn't seem to. His body loosened, his hands fell, his face relaxed. "Liberated Christians is, quite simply, a group of adult couples who are trying to move beyond—to liberate themselves from—the oppressive and negative images of human sexuality that are promulgated by our society, and especially by religious groups, even though, for the most part, they have no basis in the Bible whatsoever."

And they were off. Ben knew Christina wasn't looking forward to this frank discussion of aberrant sexual practices before a jury of middle- and lower-class Oklahomans, many of them members of one Bible-thumping church or another. But in preparation, she and Ben had both eventually realized that it would be better if she handled this all-important direct examination. Coming from Ben, there was a chance it might come off too good-ol'-boy sounding, like locker-room talk. Two guys swapping stories about all the hot chicks they bagged down at the Episcopal Church.

With Christina in charge, there was no chance of that happening. With Christina asking the questions, Father Beale would be forced to be delicate. There was also a chance her presence might soften the juror response to the subject, sort of on the theory that if she's not repulsed . . .

"Is this a philosophy you invented yourself, Father?"

"Oh, heavens no. There are many such groups, all across the country. The world, in fact. Lifestyle couples—that's the preferred term at present. *Wife-swapping*, obviously, is a sexist phrase, and implies some unspoken impropriety. *Swingers* suggests a casual decadence that ignores the strong philosophical underpinnings. In fact,

there are over three hundred formally affiliated clubs for lifestyle couples in at least twenty different countries. Millions of couples are
active participants. They have their own travel industry, arranging
vacations and seminars catering to their special interests. There are
hundreds of magazines published on the subject, and I couldn't even
guess how many Web sites. I know of eleven major conventions held
for lifestyle couples every year in major U.S. cities, including the
largest, the three-day Lifestyles convention in San Diego that draws
over thirty-five hundred people a year. Oh, no—this clearly did not
start with me."

"What kind of people are these . . . lifestyle couples?"

"In the main, they are no different from you or me. They do tend to
be well-educated—over two-thirds have college degrees. They tend
to be somewhat affluent. But beyond that, they cover all walks of life.
There are even some Republicans."

Nice try, but there was nary a titter in the jury box. As Ben had
muttered on more than one previous occasion—God save me from
witnesses who want to be comedians.

"Is this a relatively recent phenomenon?"   ✓

"Not remotely. After all, the Bible tells us that erotic rites were
common in Canaan when God made His covenant with Abraham—
the great Hebrew leader chosen by God, who would later prostitute
his wife Sarah and have an adulterous fling with Hagar. The fertility
goddess Asherah welcomed orgies in her temples; it was not until she
was destroyed by the Hebrews that a new morality was established.
For the early Hebrews, you must understand, reproduction was sur-
vival; hence, they disfavored or outlawed any form of nonreproduc-
tive sexual activity—masturbation, homosexuality, abortion, sex during
menstruation. Sex outside marriage was similarly outlawed. This re-
strictive morality, formulated by primitives over four thousand years
ago, would come to dominate the lives of the world's more than 2.3
billion Christians, Muslims, and Jews.

"Still and all, that isn't the whole world. According to a recent an-
thropological survey, even well into the twentieth century, 'extra-
mateship liaison' was an approved custom in thirty-nine percent of all
world cultures. Think of that—thirty-nine percent! And though it's
kept a low profile, it's becoming increasingly common in this coun-

try, too. Through these lifestyle organizations, millions of married Americans are able to express their erotic fantasies, and in the process, strengthen their marriages."

Erotic fantasies. Somehow, Ben was willing to wager, the entire time she sweated through law school, Christina never envisioned that she would be standing in a courtroom talking about erotic fantasies. "I'm sure many people would imagine that these unusual practices would have just the opposite effect on a marriage. Would you please explain that last statement, Father?"

"Certainly. Lifestyle couples are firm believers in family values." He'd been coached not to look at the judge as he said it; that would just be too obvious. "We believe we live in a manner that melds responsible family values—like matrimony, children, and emotional monogamy—with the erotic cultivation of marriage through the practice of rites we find fun and natural. After all, the most important thing for a family is the marriage; how can anything that strengthens the marriage be bad?"

"I would imagine there are some people who would disagree with what you've said. Who would find these practices disturbing—or even sinful."

"And you would be right." Beale straightened, adopting an almost professorial pose. "Let's face it—the world is still plagued with morality squads, people who spend their lives running around passing judgment on the activities of others. But every psychological study on the subject has shown that lifestyle couples are quite normal, not at all deviant. Indeed, some have suggested that sexual monogamy may be the more deviant, more unnatural lifestyle."

Enough already. He'd either made his point or he never would. Time to move on to the nitty-gritty. "Father Beale, whether we agree or not, I think we understand your viewpoint now. What people may not yet understand yet, though, is—What does this have to do with a church?"

Beale nodded thoughtfully. "First and foremost, strengthening and preserving marriages is very much the business of a church. The problem is—people have twisted around what Christianity was about in the first place. The teachings of Christ are about love, about kindness to those around you. Not about sex. We have no reason to believe

Jesus was a starched shirt. According to the gospels, Jesus lived with and was even supported by prostitutes. He publicly defended an adulteress. He even dined with tax collectors, for Pete's sake."

This time, to Ben's surprise, there actually was some laughter in the jury box. But did that mean they were with him, that they were buying any of this? Ben couldn't tell.

"Whatever else Jesus may have been, he was not a prude. He didn't pass judgment on other people, not based upon their sexual practices or anything else. And yet, to listen to some preachers today, you'd think that the word 'morals' refers to nothing but sex. It has come to absolutely dominate so-called morality. Why? Why is sexual denial always perceived as superior to sexual indulgence? Why is organized religion so determined to control our sex lives? Why do we feel the need to disenfranchise homosexuals and masturbaters and . . . and swingers? Jesus didn't prioritize these items. Why do they obsess us so?"

He was well spoken—Ben had to give him that. Whether the jury was buying it, whether in the long run it would even matter, he couldn't know.

"Still and all, Father," Christina said, "we know that some people in your church did not accept your arguments. They were . . . disturbed by all this."

"Yes. To my disappointment, that was true. Especially toward the end." His head bowed; he seemed sincerely regretful. "Of course, any time you introduce a radically different idea, you must expect objections. But there was more to it than that. Some people, whether due to their upbringing, lack of education, bad religious instruction, whatever, believe that if we are freed from society's oppressive sexual constraints and moral censure and are allowed to indulge ourselves naturally, we will become animals, slaves to our basest desires, incapable of ethical behavior. Others, I suspect, believe that if women were freed from the sexual stereotypes that restrict them, it would liberate them from the oppression by men that is still all too real an element of our society."

"Susan Marino was one of those people, wasn't she?"

"Yes." Tiny lines crept across his forehead. "I knew she was disturbed, that she was experiencing the guilt that male-dominated society told her she should . . . but I didn't realize how profoundly she felt it, how much it traumatized her. And I hold myself responsible for that. I feel the same way about Carol Mason. It's clear to me now that she simply can't live with what she has done, can't reconcile herself to it and, at least subconsciously, sees eliminating me as the only means of eradicating her guilt." He paused. "I can only wonder how many others at the church feel the same way."

"And Kate McGuire?"

"Much the same, I think. I didn't know it until the day of the wedding. The day she died. As others have reported, she met me in the corridor and told me how she felt. How upset she was. 'It's evil,' that's what she said. What we were doing was evil."

"Was that all she said?"

"No. She threatened to report what we were doing to the bishop."

"Would that be bad?"

Beale almost smiled. "Bishop Goodwin is a progressive man, and the Episcopal Convention is a progressive church. But not that progressive."

"So what did you do?"

"I'm afraid I lost my temper. I shouted and yelled and . . . threatened."

"What did you say?"

"To be honest, I don't remember. That often happens during these extreme flashes of temper. After they've subsided, I can't even recall what occurred. But I have no reason to think that the accounts we've heard of what I said are inaccurate."

"Did you plan to see her again?"

"I did. I remember that clearly. I knew we couldn't resolve this in the few minutes remaining before the wedding began, so I asked her to meet me afterward in my office."

"And did she?"

"I assume so. All I know is when I got there—she was dead."

"Who else knew she was meeting you in your office?"

"A lot of people, apparently. I didn't realize it at the time, but a good many overheard our disagreement."

"What did you do when you discovered the body?"

"At first—nothing. I was stunned. Immobile. I mean, there she was, sprawled across my desk, blood covering the side of her head. I didn't know what to do. And then, all of a sudden, it was as if an emotional dam inside me burst. I raced forward and ran to her side. I lifted her up and pressed her close to me. That's when I got her blood all over myself. It's probably when the hair got in the wound, too. I wanted her to know that she was loved, that I loved her. But of course, it was too late."

Christina nodded, pausing for a moment to allow him to collect himself. "Then what did you do?"

"I put her down gently, administered the last rites, and started to leave the office. Then I noticed that my hands and clothes were soaked with blood. I walked to the bathroom to wash myself."

"Why didn't you call the police?"

"Well, I should've, of course, but I just wasn't thinking clearly. The shock of seeing her like that, in my office—" He shook his head, rubbed his hand over his beard. "Unless you've had something like that happen to you, you can't conceive of what it does to your brain. Eventually I realized I should phone the authorities, but by that time, her body had been discovered by others. Still, I tried to make up for it. I cooperated with the police in every possible way. I made no attempt to flee, even though I knew perfectly well I would be a suspect."

He stopped for a long moment. "You have to understand—I'm a priest. A horrible tragedy befell our church. I naturally wanted to help in any way possible. I did not believe I had done anything improper, and I wanted to do the right thing. For Kate, if for no other reason."

"Is that why you remained with the church—even after you were arrested?"

"Jesus was arrested, too, but he didn't give up his ministry. Not that I'm Jesus, by any means. But in our denomination, we believe that when you're called to a church, you're not just called by the parishioners, or the bishop—you're called by God. And if I've been called by God, if God wants me to be there—how can I quit? Whatever the circumstances."

Christina turned a page in her outline. "I have only a few more questions, Father, and then we'll be finished. They're not pleasant questions. But they have to be asked. Have you had sexual relations with Susan Marino?"

His lips pursed slightly. "Yes."

"And Kate McGuire?"

"On many occasions. We were favorite partners. We always enjoyed one another's company. Or so I thought."

"Were those the only two parishioners with whom you've . . . been?"

"No. Not even close. But I do resent the suggestion that this was all some depraved scheme employed by a dirty old man. I believed in the Liberated Christians group. What I was saying, what we were doing. And it worked. I saw the benefits right before my eyes. I saw people freed from sexual chains that had bound them all their lives. Experiencing sexual pleasure for the first time. I saw marriages healed and strengthened. It wasn't ugly or dirty. While it worked, it was beautiful."

"And what did your wife think of all this?" Not that it was relevant. But if the jury believed he'd been playing around behind her back, they'd be much more likely to hang him. And if they thought she was behind him . . . well, that was something, anyway.

"My wife, Andrea, has always been supportive of my ministry, and this was no exception. Admittedly, she was hesitant at first, and even now often prefers to watch rather than to participate. But she's behind me one hundred percent."

Both figuratively and literally, because she was back in her seat on the first row of the gallery. She was, in reality, not at all happy about it. Regardless of what she believed, being present while her husband publicly discussed his relationships with other women couldn't be fun. But Ben thought her presence was critical. She lent credibility to everything Father Beale said. If she didn't object to what he was doing, what right had anyone else?

"Do you have any regrets?"

Father Beale paused, thinking. "I still believe what I advocate. I think what we did was right, and I think most people would be better off if they followed our lead. But I wonder if . . . I wonder if maybe I pushed too hard. Particularly some of the women. Perhaps it was too much too fast. Of course, no one was forced against their will. But I may have underestimated the power and influence of a priest. I may have induced some of them to proceed . . . before they were ready."

He turned, craning his head toward the heavens. "I don't know. I just don't know. But if anyone was hurt—and it seems they were—I regret that most sincerely."

"Father Beale," Christina said finally, "did you kill Kate McGuire?"

"No." He turned, peering straight at the jury as he spoke. "I did not. Not her, and not anyone else. I cared deeply for Kate." He hesitated, then added, just under his breath. "I still do."

"Thank you, Father. No more questions."

CHAPTER

38

CANELLI HAD BEEN strangely quiet throughout the direct of Father Beale; Ben almost wondered if he was beginning to believe him. But that whim soon passed. Once cross started, it was no holds barred. Undoubtedly, Canelli thought the verdict would hinge on what happened during this cross—because Ben thought so, too.

"First of all, Mr. Beale," Canelli said as he strode across the courtroom, "I'd like to thank you for that fascinating excursion into the wonderful world of situational ethics."

Father Beale sat like a rock, staring back at Canelli, not saying a word.

Good boy, Ben thought. Just keep it up. As many times as Ben had prepped witnesses for trial, he was all too aware that most of them forgot everything he had told them when they actually took the stand. Including the most important rule of all: Don't take the bait. If he doesn't ask a question, keep your mouth closed.

"I mean, I'm being genuine," Canelli said. "How many times in your life do you get to hear someone express a complex, philosophical excuse for screwing around?"

"Your honor," Ben said wearily.

Judge Pitcock looked at Canelli harshly. "Mr. Prosecutor, I don't like that kind of talk in my courtroom."

"Sorry, sir." He wasn't.

"If this is any indication of how you intend to conduct this cross-examination, I'll shut it down right here and now."

"That won't be necessary, sir." Canelli returned his attention to the witness. "So, Father Beale . . . do you consider yourself a holy man?"

Ben rose to his feet, but he wasn't fast enough to prevent Beale from answering. "Of course I do."

Canelli shifted his gaze back to the bench. "Your honor, I ask leave of court at this time to introduce past acts evidence."

"No way," Ben cried. "Bench conference."

Ben raced Canelli to the judge, while Father Beale and the jury watched in silence.

"Your honor, he cannot introduce evidence of past acts to imply or suggest conformity during the incidents at issue. The case law on this is a mile long. It's absolutely not permitted."

"Unless," Canelli added, "the witness opens the door."

"He hasn't opened any doors. He's barely spoken."

"He said he was a holy man."

"He is!"

"Your honor," Canelli said, "this is no different from the many cases in which a witness testifies that he is honest or truthful. It opens the door to evidence of past incidents in which he was not honest or truthful. Here, we have a witness who claims that his behavior is holy. I'm now entitled to show otherwise."

"That's ridiculous," Ben said. "You set a trap for him."

Canelli shrugged. "The man said what he said."

"He's a priest, for God's sake. Saying he's holy isn't bragging. It's more like . . . a job description."

"Nonetheless," Judge Pitcock said gravely, "the man did say it."

"Only when he was directly questioned by opposing counsel," Ben said.

"It's in the record." Pitcock spread his hands. "My hands are tied."

Ben knew the judge was right, but he still hated the result, not only because it couldn't possibly help Father Beale's case, but because he knew the whole mess was his own damn fault. "Your honor, in this case, where matters of faith and religion are so intricately intertwined with criminal issues, this kind of questioning could have a prejudicial effect that far outweighs its limited probative value. I must ask the court to reconsider."

"Sorry, Mr. Kincaid. I hear what you're saying. But the law is clear." He addressed Canelli. "You may continue."

"Thank you, your honor." Canelli went into full attack-dog mode. "Tell me, Father Beale, since you got this great gig at St. Benedict's, exactly how many Liberated Christian women have you had?"

"Objection!" Ben bellowed.

"Overruled."

"I'm . . . not sure what you mean," Beale said stonily.

"Well, let me rephrase," Canelli continued. "How often did the Liberated Christians group meet?"

"Once a week. But they weren't all—"

"And I assume you had a different woman every week."

"Most of those meetings were discussional in nature."

"Well, how many weren't, sir? How many went past talking and involved coupling?"

Beale's face was tight as a drum. "Usually we had interactive sessions once a month."

"Interactive sessions. I like that. Sounds a lot better than 'we all piled into a room and had sex with one another.' "

"It wasn't like that."

"Really. What was it like? We all want to know."

"You're making it sound so . . . nasty."

"Wasn't it?"

"No, it wasn't!" Beale's voice rose sharply. He was starting to lose his temper, which, Ben knew, was exactly what Canelli wanted. "Sex is a beautiful thing. It's a gift from God. It's these narrow-minded puritans who have transformed this gift into something base and ugly."

"Uh-huh. Right." Canelli paced back and forth in front of the witness box, his tall frame hunched forward. He looked like a tiger preparing to pounce. "So, you had sex once a month, and this went on for at least three years. My goodness, Father Beale—you've had sex with, what? Thirty-six different parishioners?"

"It wasn't always someone different."

"Oh? Did you have favorites?"

"Some people will inevitably turn out to be more compatible than others."

"So you would have a return bout with the same woman."

"Sometimes."

"You know, Father, this is starting to sound less like recreational sex and more like having an affair."

"It wasn't an affair."

"I don't see the difference."

"Then you're not trying. The difference is huge. My wife knew all about it."

"Did she know about your favorites?"

Inevitably, every eye in the courtroom clocked back to the gallery to check Andrea's expression. Ben thought she was holding up well, given the circumstances. But she wasn't enjoying it; that was obvious enough.

"I don't think she kept track of who I was with or when. It wasn't important to her."

"Says you. Tell me this—was Susan Marino one of your favorites?"

Beale's breathing became deep and heavy. "We partnered together on more than one occasion."

"You were a busy man, Father. The Don Juan of the Episcopal Church."

"Don't you see what you're doing?" Beale's voice boomed across the courtroom. "You're condemning me because my sexual practices are different from yours. This is blatant prejudice. It's no different than condemning someone because they aren't chaste, or because they're homosexual, or they . . . they . . . don't use the missionary position!"

"This is different, sir," Canelli said firmly. "There's a big difference. Because here, someone got murdered."

"That had nothing to do with the Liberated Christian activities."

"I think it did. I think that's, in part, why Kate McGuire was murdered. Tell me, was she another of your favorites?"

Beale hesitated. "I have already said that we had been together on several occasions. I'd probably been with her more often than anyone else."

"You enjoyed being with her."

"Yes."

"But she didn't enjoy being with you, did she?"

"At the time, I thought—"

"When she talked to you the day of the wedding, didn't she express regret and remorse about what she had done with you?"

"Yes. I've already said—"

"She told you she wanted out, right? In fact, she wanted the whole program shut down."

"That was what she said."

"She called it evil. Wasn't that her word? Evil?"

"Yes," Beale said quietly.

The tiger whirled on him. "Looks like liberation didn't turn out so well for her, huh? And that's why you killed her, isn't it?"

Beale spoke through clenched teeth. "I did not kill her!"

Canelli didn't let up. "What would've happened if she had reported what was going on to the bishop?"

"I . . . can't be entirely sure. . . ."

"But it wouldn't have been good, huh?"

"There would have been an ecclesiastical review."

"Oh, come clean, Father. You would've lost your job."

"Very likely."

"In fact, you'd probably never work as a priest again."

"It's possible that some other penance might be arranged. . . ."

"With your record?"

"Record? I've been arrested twice. Once during a rally in support of the Equal Rights Amendment at the state capital. Once when I was marching in opposition to the Black Fox nuclear power plant."

Ben knew Beale was trying to soften the blow by being forthcoming with details that weren't harmful anyway. But that wasn't what Canelli was after. "I'm not talking about your criminal record, sir. I'm talking about your record of sexual impropriety."

Beale's lips pressed together, his face the picture of barely suppressed rage. "I don't have any such record."

Canelli's head sprang up like a cobra's. "Your honor? Past acts?"

Pitcock nodded. "You may proceed."

Ben was on his feet, once again just a beat too late. "Your honor, I object. He didn't—"

"Don't bother, Mr. Kincaid. The witness made the statement. The prosecutor is allowed to inquire."

"But your honor—"

"Sit down, Mr. Kincaid. Mr. Canelli, please proceed."

Canelli didn't need urging. "This isn't the first time your libido has gotten you into trouble with a church, is it, Father?"

Ben tumbled back into his chair, feeling like his stomach had just dropped to his knees.

"I'm not sure to what you're referring."

"Your previous church, in Oklahoma City. St. Gregory's. You had to leave because you were messing around."

Beale's voice cracked. "There was no lifestyle group in Oklahoma City."

"No, this was just a flat-out affair, wasn't it? With a married woman. Marilee Eddings. A member of your flock."

Beale spoke in a slow and controlled voice. "It was a counseling situation. Our feelings got out of hand."

"Is that supposed to make it better?"

"It was a mistake. I've acknowledged that. I confessed what happened to the bishop—"

"And that's why you lost your job."

"The bishop thought it would be best if I relocated to another parish."

"Where you wouldn't be hitting on the women?"

Beale's jaw locked up tight. Veins were visible in his neck. "If the bishop thought I was not trustworthy, he wouldn't have given me a new church."

"Your bishop seems to be very understanding about your shortcomings."

"He believes in forgiveness and redemption, as should all Christians."

"He gave you another church after you'd engaged in sexual impropriety at the last one."

Beale's voice was growing louder. "It was an isolated incident with a woman who—"

"Of course, at the church before that, it was a little girl."

One of the female jurors gasped, so loudly it could be heard throughout the courtroom. Two of the others covered their faces with their hands. Several were shaking their heads.

"I don't know what you can possibly—"

"St. John's. In Choctaw. You were brought up on charges for molesting a nine-year-old girl."

Ben felt his blood run cold. Beale's defense was disintegrating and there was nothing he could do to stop it.

"That was a misunderstanding."

"Oh, no doubt."

"It was!" Beale shouted. His face was hard and red. He gripped the banister, trying to retain control. "I was at a summer camp, as a counselor. A group of girls were playing a game. Soccer, I think it was. One of the girls scored a point, and everyone was shouting and hugging and congratulating her. I swatted her on the backside with the back of my hand."

"You touched her buttocks?"

"It's a common thing to do."

"To a nine-year-old girl?"

"In the sports world!" Beale shouted. "I know I shouldn't have done it. I just wasn't thinking."

"You seem to have a problem in that department."

"It was a mistake! The girl barely noticed. But some old busybody saw it and reported it to the girl's mother, and she brought the charges. Which were soon dropped."

"Was that because your partner-in-crime, the bishop, intervened for you again?"

"It's because there was nothing to it!" Beale teetered forward, almost rising out of his seat. "I made a mistake and learned from it. It never happened again!"

"Well, not with a nine-year-old." Canelli brought his full height to bear, hovering over the witness stand. "But you've got a history of sexual impropriety that spans your entire career."

"There are only three incidents—"

"That I was able to uncover. But before you claimed there were none at all. And three is a lot for a . . . *holy* man, wouldn't you say?"

Father Beale fell silent.

"Here's how I see it, Father. When Kate McGuire confronted you, you saw the whole thing blowing up in your face. Again. If she squealed to the bishop, and word got out about what you were doing, no one could save you. You'd be finished as a priest. You'd be publicly exposed as a sex pervert. And that's why you killed her."

"I did not kill her!" Beale roared. He jumped to his feet. "I did not kill her!"

Ben and Christina exchanged a pained look. He'd lost it. Canelli had gotten what he wanted—and the jury was watching.

"You did," Canelli said. "You killed her in cold blood. To save yourself!"

"I did not!" Beale's face flushed crimson. His entire body trembled with rage. "I did not!"

"Then who did? The invisible man? The only person whose fingerprints were on that weapon was you! How do you explain that?"

"I . . . can't."

"Because *you* killed her, didn't you? You had sex with her, time and time again, and when she didn't like it anymore, you killed her!"

"No!" Beale's face was contorted by vivid, almost tangible anger. He leaned against the railing, virtually snarling. He looked like a monster.

Judge Pitcock pounded his gavel. "The witness will sit down and control himself!"

"I did not kill her!" Beale continued, oblivious to the judge, the jury, everything. "I couldn't kill anyone!"

Which he could shout all day, Ben realized, and it wouldn't matter. Because in the courtroom, actions speak louder than words. And at the moment, he looked like a man who could kill. Could and would. And did.

Canelli gave the jury one more long look, shook his head sadly, then closed his notebook. "No more questions, your honor."

39

AFTER A MUCH needed recess, Christina spent the better part of an hour redirecting, trying to salvage some semblance of Father Beale's credibility. She took him back through all the incidents Canelli had raised on cross, eliciting his side of the story. Most important, she took him back to the scene of the crime itself, step by step, establishing where he was and why he wasn't in the office at the time of the murder. It went well—better than Ben expected. But how much difference would it make with the jury? What they had witnessed would weigh heavily on each and every one of them. What they had seen in the courtroom today they couldn't possibly forget.

"IS SHE DEAD?"

"Oh, yes," Manly said. "She's dead. Well and truly."

"You're certain."

"Absolutely. Not a doubt about it." He was feeling a mix of emotions so complex he had difficulty expressing them even to himself. He knew that he had struck a great blow for the cause. But at the same time . . . something else was buzzing through his brain. Or perhaps it was his heart. Something . . . less certain.

But that was nonsense. He'd done what he'd meant to do, and he was proud of it. He wasn't going to let any weak-kneed sentiment bring him down. He was a Crusader, after all. He'd done the right thing. He knew he had.

"I said, are you certain?"

"Absolutely. Dead as a doornail. Limp as a mackerel. Pick your cliché. She's gone."

"Good."

"You seem happy about it."

"I'm happy to see . . . to see our plan brought to fruition."

Something about his friend's answer didn't strike Manly right. "There wasn't something more, was there? You were somewhat adamant that she be the one."

"She was the perfect choice. We discussed it over and over."

"I know. I just wondered if maybe there was something more."

"Well, there wasn't. So stop being stupid. We have to remain focused. And we have to do something with the body."

What was it about that answer that didn't seem quite convincing? Manly wondered. He shouldn't be suspicious. It was just guilt creeping up on him. It was stupid. He wouldn't descend to that level.

And yet . . .

"So, are you going to help or not?"

Manly snapped out of it. "Yeah, yeah. I'm helping." He hesitated. "Look . . . don't call me stupid. I don't like it."

"Sorry. It just slipped out. It won't happen again. You know I have nothing but the highest regard for you. You're a hero in my book."

Yeah, I think I probably am, Manly thought, as he positioned himself around the corpse. But maybe not for the reason I thought.

He gazed one last time at the old woman's remains. She did look tranquil now; more than she ever had when she was living. Maybe there was a peace in the afterlife, even for babykillers and those who support them. Who knew? He took the top half, and his friend took the bottom, and together, they lifted the lifeless body of Ernestine Rupert, founder of Tulsa's top pro-choice group, late of the vestry of St. Benedict's church, into the truck.

"MR. PROSECUTOR," JUDGE Pitcock asked, "would you like to make a closing statement?"

Canelli nodded and approached the jury. "I've been in the DA's office for fourteen years now. Most of them good ones. I've won a lot of cases, and I've lost some, too. But I can tell you this, and I mean it sincerely—this has been the hardest case I've had to try in my entire career. I don't imagine there will ever be a tougher one."

Ben's eyebrows rose. This was an unusual opening, especially coming from Canelli. Unusually soft, and unusually honest.

"It isn't because I have the slightest doubt about Daniel Beale's guilt. I don't. The evidence against him is overwhelming, irrefutable. But that hasn't made my job easier. Because at heart, I'm still a good Catholic boy from the Sunday school classes of St. Thomas More's of Broken Arrow, and prosecuting a man of the cloth has not been a pleasure. And I've had to do more than that. I've had to expose him as a man who could not control his temper, and worse, could not control his sexual appetites. I've had to reveal that a man who acted as a counselor to many was in fact a sexual deviant, engaging in numerous liaisons with the women who trusted him. I've had to reveal that he had inappropriate relationships with married women and even small children. And that, you can take my word for it, has been no pleasure."

A snazzy way of reminding the jury of all the most salacious moments of the trial without seeming salacious as he did it, Ben thought. And yet, he had to admit, there was something undeniably genuine, something truly regretful, about Canelli's tone and manner.

"I kept telling myself, perhaps I was simply being inflexible. Perhaps I was too resistant to new ideas, to anything that deviated from what I grew up believing. Perhaps I had become so locked into the role of the prosecutor that I saw evil everywhere—even where it didn't exist."

Christina shot Ben a pointed look. What was this, closing argument or Canelli's private soul search? And yet, as he looked into the eyes of the jurors, he saw that they were hanging on every word. Some of them were even nodding in agreement. Whatever it was Canelli was doing, it seemed to be effective.

"I don't know," Canelli continued. "I don't know all the answers. I don't pretend to. Let's face it—the courtroom is no place for questions of faith. We are simply ill-equipped to handle such profound and mysterious matters. But here's the one thing I do know—Father Daniel Beale killed Kate McGuire. You don't need faith to recognize that truth. You don't need to approve or disapprove of his politics or his sexual practices. All you need to do is look at the unequivocal evidence.

"Daniel Beale had a long history of violent, uncontrolled temper, something you unfortunately witnessed right here in this courtroom. He was seen by numerous witnesses in a protracted argument with the victim minutes before she was killed. He threatened her. He arranged a rendezvous with her. She kept the meeting, and an eyewitness saw him keep it—placing him at the scene of the murder at the time of the murder. He was seen shortly thereafter with blood on his hands and clothes—worse, he was seen trying to wash it off, trying to remove the evidence of his crime before the police arrived. And his fingerprints were on the weapon found in his office—his and no one else's.

"In prosecution circles, this is what's called a perfect case—we've established motive and opportunity, and there is both physical and eyewitness testimony pointing unequivocally to the defendant. There is simply no doubt about this one—he's guilty. Of murder in the first degree."

The handsome DA moved slowly from one end of the jury box to the other. He paused, peering reflectively at the jurors. "When this case is over, I suspect you will not soon forget it. I suspect that you, like me, will have many questions that you will ponder for days, perhaps even longer. Questions about politics, sex, the proper role of a minister. Even questions of faith. But you mustn't let those blind you to the core truth of this trial. This is a murder trial, and the only question you are being asked to resolve is: Who killed Kate McGuire? You may have reservations about everything else, but about that there is no doubt. Daniel Beale committed the murder. No one else could have. He committed a crime against Kate McGuire, her family, the state—and against God. And as unpleasant as the duty may be, you have an obligation to punish him for that crime, in the manner prescribed by the laws of this state. It is the job you accepted when you took your seat in that box. And now I call upon you to do it."

THAT WAS, BEN mused as he walked to the jury box, perhaps the most thoughtful, introspective, low-key closing argument he had heard in his life—and probably three times as effective as a fiery impassioned diatribe would've been. Canelli, for whatever reason, had chosen to play it smart—which made Ben's job all the more difficult.

"Let's make one thing clear up front. I don't care for this business of recreational spouse swapping any better than you do. Maybe I'm just too old-fashioned, maybe I'm just too scared, I don't know. But it doesn't seem right to me and I don't like it. You probably don't, either."

He leaned across the rail separating him from the jurors. "Does that make Father Beale a murderer? No. Does this have anything to do with the murder? No."

He paused, letting the words steep and percolate in the jurors' brains. "Oh, I know what the prosecution is saying. They're trying to twist it into a motive, trying to say it created disharmony with the vestry, that Kate McGuire was upset about it. But the fact is, we already knew there was disharmony in the vestry, and we already knew that Father Beale had a big fight with Kate McGuire in the corridor at the wedding. He told you that himself, up front. What did the protracted testimony about the Liberated Christians group add to our knowledge? Nothing. Not a thing.

"So why did the prosecutor spend so much time on it? Because it's evidence of criminal intent? Hardly. He wants you to be appalled. He wants you to find Father Beale guilty because he's a bad man who did an ugly thing. Because the actual evidence of murder is thin and entirely circumstantial. So what the prosecutor can't accomplish by direct evidence he's trying to accomplish indirectly by turning you against the defendant. By trotting out every mistake he's ever made in his entire life so you will want to punish him.

"But that's not how it works, ladies and gentlemen. If you bring a verdict against my client, it can be for one reason and one reason only—because the prosecution has proved beyond a reasonable doubt that he is guilty of the crime of first-degree murder. And they haven't done it. They haven't even come close."

Ben paused, collecting his thoughts. He knew this trial had gone on long enough; he wasn't going to add several more hours of him gabbing. He had to make his point, make it well—and sit down.

"So let's clear away the debris and character assassination and look at the actual evidence that relates to the murder. What is there? Not much, truth be told. Yes, Father Beale was at the church at the time.

So were about two hundred other people. Yes, he had a fight with Kate McGuire before the wedding in front of witnesses—but that should be proof that he wasn't the murderer. Unless you think Father Beale is a total idiot, and I think it's clear that he isn't, he wouldn't be stupid enough to kill someone—in his own office—minutes after numerous people saw him having a big argument with her."

Ben continued, rattling through the prosecution evidence. "Only two witnesses attempted to put Father Beale in his office at the time of the murder—a severely nearsighted elderly woman, and a pathetic liar who first offered his testimony to the defense and then, when I wouldn't use him—because he was obviously lying—offered his services to the prosecution. The kid got his fifteen minutes of fame, but did that make what he said true? Far from it. There's not even any proof that punk was at the wedding, much less that he saw anything important. His word is worse than worthless."

Ben thought he was making his points and expressing himself well, but he'd be happier if he got some indication of that from the jury. Instead, all he saw were stony, unresponsive faces. They were listening. But he saw no evidence that they were agreeing.

"I think we can all agree to disregard the testimony of the so-called hair expert. That testimony was so weak I notice the prosecutor didn't even mention it in his summation. The single piece of physical evidence upon which the prosecutor now hangs his hat is the fingerprints on the St. Crispin's Award. He thinks it's very incriminating that Father Beale's fingerprints were on that thing. But let's think about that for a moment. It was Father Beale's award, after all. It was on his desk. He'd had it for over ten years." Ben's voice swelled. "Of course his fingerprints were on it!

"I don't know why the killer's fingerprints weren't on it. Frankly, I just haven't figured out how that was done. But I know that somehow, some way, the killer held that thing in his hands without leaving a mark. I wish I could explain it to you, but the truth is, I don't have to, because the burden of proof is on the prosecution, not the defense. I don't have to prove anything. The question before you now is whether the presence of Father Beale's fingerprints on his own desk ornament proves he's a murderer. And the answer is—no. Not remotely. And certainly not beyond a reasonable doubt."

Ben stepped back from the rail and clasped his hands. "I know all of you probably have many unanswered questions, many conundrums to contemplate. But I must remind you, as you go into that deliberation room, that it is not your job, and it would be inappropriate for you to attempt, to debate issues of sexual propriety. This is not a referendum on monogamy, on matters of faith, on whether Father Beale was a good priest, or on whether his personal philosophies are sound. This is only about murder, about whether the prosecution has proved to you that Father Beale is a murderer. He isn't. But you know what? Even if you disagree with that, even if you kind of sort of suspect he might be—that isn't good enough. Because you aren't being asked whether you think the man is guilty. You're being asked whether the prosecution has *proved* that he is guilty—beyond a reasonable doubt. That's the only question before you."

He stopped and slowly looked at each of the jurors in turn. "And the only possible answer to that question is no."

40

The Gospel According to Daniel

WE ARE TOLD, by those who read the Book of Revelations as a series of apocalyptic prophesies, that at the end of days we will each of
us face judgment.

Mine came early.

It is an extraordinary experience. Of course, we all know that we
are judged on a daily basis. The opinions of others—friends, family,
and acquaintances—are constantly shaped and reshaped. We find
ourselves on a sliding scale of public opinion, one that too often fluc-
tuates based upon what we did last, what we said, what we wrote. It is
a reality of life that any of us who works in the public eye must face.
We are quite simply judged all the time.

But not like this. And not with such grave consequences. How
many times in one's life does one realize with cold and stark immediacy that the next few moments will determine the rest of your life—
or even curtail that life? Not often. And thank God for that, because
the stress of the moment, the grave weight on the human heart, cannot be borne for long. It is not possible to describe accurately what
it's like, waiting for the jury to return and seal your fate. The incipi-
ent panic that results from the realization that your life could be sig-
nificantly foreshortened.

It was, to be certain, not pleasant, seeing all my secrets exposed,
reading about them in the newspaper, hearing about them on television, knowing that the opinions of others regarding me would be forever altered. Even with secrets that should not have been secrets, even
with bits of shame that should not have been shameful, with posi-

tions and decisions I could ably defend, I found this to be a demeaning and ultimately terrifying process. It caused me to reexamine everything, to rethink, to reconsider. To face up to the stark reality that in some respects—I may well have been wrong.

And when all is said and done, that is the most painful experience of all—to be judged according to the coarse scrutiny of your own soul. And found wanting.

BEN AND CHRISTINA and Father Beale sat at a table in the small waiting area near the courtroom as they had done more or less continuously since the judge instructed the jury and sent them away to deliberate. They'd had some Vietnamese takeout from Ri Le's and some strongly flavored dessert coffee. But no one's spirits were lifted. They sat in silence only occasionally broken by abortive attempts at small talk that never went anywhere.

"I'm going to get some regular coffee," Ben said, excusing himself. He thought he would have to go downstairs and see Charlie at the snack bar. To his surprise, he found something waiting for him right outside the door.

"Regular or decaf?" Judy said, holding a thermos in each hand.

"Judy? What in the world—?"

"We also have one filled with chocolate milk. Show him, Maura." Behind her, Maura held up a silver thermos, giggling. "I know it's your secret favorite."

"Not at times like this." He took the regular and grunted his thanks. "What are you two girls doing here?"

"You didn't think we were going to leave before we knew the verdict, did you?"

"It could be days before the jury returns."

"I don't think so."

Ben raised his eyebrows. "Is that based on your years of trial experience?"

"No. It's based on my years of watching Court TV. Long deliberations occur when the jury is confused, when the lawyers haven't done a good job of identifying the key issues. You, of course, did a brilliant job. Your closing gave me chill bumps."

"Well, thanks."

"Mind you, I'm not saying you're going to win. But I do think the jury understands the issues. They'll resolve it one way or the other. Soon."

Words of wisdom from the fifteen-year-old jury consultant. But young as she was, she was probably right.

"Thanks for the coffee. Now go home. I'll have someone call you if the jury returns." He reentered the conference room and poured the coffee. No one took much.

"How long has it been?" Christina asked.

Ben checked his watch. "Too long."

"How much longer will it take?" Father Beale asked.

"The judge will make them deliberate until ten, at least," Ben explained. "If he can possibly get it resolved today, he'll try to do it. If not, he'll dismiss them and they'll start up again tomorrow morning."

"And if they don't finish today, how long could it go?"

"There's no set limit. But given how many days the trial took, Judge Pitcock will not accept a hung jury readily. It could go on for weeks. Even months."

"Months?" Beale squeezed his temples. "Months."

"But that probably won't happen," Christina added hastily. "Most juries finish up the first day."

"And what does that mean? If they finish quickly."

"Some trial lawyers say it means a guilty verdict, but I've heard others argue exactly the opposite. The truth is—no one knows. Juries are, ultimately, unknowable and unpredictable."

"Days. Weeks. Months." Beale shook his head with despair. "I can't handle this. At least not alone." He pushed himself out of his chair. "If you two will excuse me, I'd like to find a quiet place where I can pray."

Ben's eyes narrowed. "You're going to . . . pray?"

"You think that's an unusual thing for a priest to do?"

"Well, no, but—"

"But now that you know I have a sex life, you've decided that I'm not really religious."

"I didn't mean that—"

"Uh-huh." Beale walked to the door, then stopped. "I'm a servant of God, Ben. I always have been. That's not self-aggrandizement—

that's just a statement of fact. My faith is what sustains me. And right now—I need all the sustenance I can get."

Thoroughly ashamed of himself, Ben watched Father Beale leave the room. He knew what kind of person Father Beale was as well as anyone, better than most. He had known since he was twelve years old. How could he possibly forget?

WHEN BEN SAW what he had done to the stained glass window, all those years ago, he knew he was doomed. Conner and Landon and the others had predictably vanished. But his father hadn't. He could see Edward Kincaid making his way to the scene of the crime, not running, but walking with determination and alacrity, as he always did when he had something on his mind. His father had never needed much of an excuse to disapprove of Ben, or to express his disapproval in stringent and immediate terms. The fact that this was an accident would cut no weight with him. *You must learn to act responsibly,* he would say. *And if you can't learn it on your own, then I will teach it to you.* It had happened before. And the memories were all too sharp, too recent, and too painful.

But Ben had never done anything like this before. He'd never done anything so horrible. He knew his father would view this as a public humiliation. And his father did not like to be publicly humiliated.

Ben's father was a big man, a sharp contrast to Ben's slight physique. He had always been able to intimidate Ben, but today he seemed to tower over him.

"Did you do this?" his father asked, in short, clipped tones.

In a split second, Ben considered all his options. He couldn't blame anyone else, and he certainly couldn't deny that it had happened. Trying to explain about Valerie Beth and Conner and the robing room would only make it worse.

To Ben's embarrassment, his voice squeaked as he spoke. "Yes, sir."

"You irresponsible little—" His father's fists balled up. "Haven't I told you to act more maturely? Haven't I told you to be wise?"

"Yes, sir."

"Your mother coddles you, of course. I've tried to talk to her, but she never listens."

"Yes, sir."

"You've always had every little thing you wanted. Always."

Baloney—but this was not the time to disagree. "Yes, sir."

"She lets you live in a dream world, with your books and reading all the time. You have no idea what it's like to be out in the real world, how hard it is to get by. And then you turn around and do something like this—destroying a treasure others have worked so hard for."

"I know, Father, and I'm really sorry—"

"Sorry is for losers, Ben." He grabbed his son roughly by the collar. "We're leaving." His dark expression left Ben no doubt about what would happen when they arrived home.

His father spun around so fast he almost collided with Father Beale, who was standing just behind them.

Father Beale smiled. "Is there a problem, Edward?"

"I'm afraid so, Father. My nitwit son has broken your stained glass window."

"Yes, I know. I asked him to do it."

Ben's lips parted. What—?

Edward Kincaid's eyes widened. "You *asked* him to do it?"

"Yes. Unfortunately, there was a flaw in the bottom half of the glass. Has to be replaced. We had to knock out that whole section so it could be repaired."

A line creased Ben's father's forehead. "Couldn't workmen do that?"

"Of course they could. But they would charge for it, wouldn't they? And I think this little indulgence of mine has cost the church quite enough already."

"But why Ben—?"

"Because I couldn't bear to do it myself. Weak, I know. But there you have it. I couldn't, so I asked Ben to help. Which he did. He's a fine boy, you know, Edward. You should be very proud of him."

Ben stared at the priest wordlessly. He didn't know what to say—and thought it best he not try to say anything at all.

His father cleared his throat. "Yes. Well . . . I didn't know. . . . I didn't realize . . ." His fists slowly unclenched. He released Ben's collar. The blood began to drain out of his face. "That's different, of course."

"How is the work on the parish profile coming, Edward?"

"Oh, slow. Like all committees. It takes about three meetings to write one sentence."

"I appreciate your hard work. If we're going to hire a top-notch curate, we need a strong and appealing profile. Just remember—the most important thing to emphasize is not the physical plant, or the rites practiced, or the plethora of programming. Christianity isn't about a new roof, or pledges, or Wednesday-night supper. It's about helping other people in need. That's the most important thing." He turned his head slightly. "Did you know that, Ben?"

"I do now," Ben said quietly.

"Well, I don't mean to lecture. You know how we priests are once we get wound up. I should probably arrange for the new glass, now that we've got the demolition completed. I just wanted to say hello, Edward, and to thank you again, Ben, for helping me."

"My pleasure," Ben mumbled.

"Oh, and—I'll see you Saturday at nine?"

"Saturday morning?"

Father Beale smiled. "For acolyte class. We should get started right away, I think."

Even though it was wildly inappropriate, given all that had happened, Ben couldn't help returning his smile. "I'll be there."

EVEN AFTER ALL these years, Ben remembered that day as if it were yesterday. Father Beale took a lot of grief from the vestry for destroying the window, but he never once told anyone what had really happened. When Ben heard that Beale was at odds with the vestry at St. Benedict's, his first thought was—Who is he saving this time?

That was a day everything changed for Ben. His goals and priorities. His sense of what was important. How he should live his life. Father Beale had been an intercessor for him, and many years later, Ben had chosen a career as an intercessor for others. Father Beale had given him a great gift, but the implicit understanding was that Ben would use that gift—would use his life—in a way that mattered.

"Ben?"

He looked up abruptly. "What? Yes?"

Christina stared at him strangely. "You looked as if you were sleeping."

"Oh, no. Just . . . daydreaming. What is it?"

"What do you think?" She glanced at Father Beale, then took his hand and clasped it firmly between hers. "The jury's back."

IN THE COURTROOM, Ben thought, no one can hear you scream. He wanted to rear back his head and cut loose with a big one. But Judge Pitcock would not be amused, and it would only make a hideously bad situation all the worse.

He watched as the twelve jurors (the alternates having been dismissed) filed solemnly into the courtroom. They did not look at Father Beale, did not even glance at counsel table. But that was not uncommon, Ben thought, trying to calm himself. Whether it was the influence of television, or just that they'd been working so long they wanted their big moment not to be spoiled, Ben had observed that most jurors tried not to give away the result. At least not this soon. Later, when the verdict was being read out, they would look at Father Beale. If they had acquitted him.

"The defendant will rise."

Ben and Christina and Father Beale all stood. Ben noticed that Beale's knees were shaking, so profoundly that it had to be apparent to everyone.

"Madame Foreperson, have you reached a verdict?"

The middle-aged, somewhat heavy-set woman at the left end of the first row spoke. "We have, your honor."

She passed the all-important piece of paper to the bailiff, who carried it to the judge. Pitcock glanced at it expressionlessly, then returned it to the bailiff. "Proceed."

Madame Foreperson cleared her throat. She's not looking at us, Ben thought, not me, or Christina or Father Beale. *She's not looking at us, damn it!*

"In the matter of the State of Oklahoma versus Daniel Samuel Beale, on the count of murder in the first degree, we find the defendant . . ."

Why did they always pause there? Haven't we waited long enough?

". . . we find the defendant guilty as charged."

There was a gasp somewhere in the gallery, and a moment later,

Father Beale crumbled. Ben wrapped an arm around him, trying to prop him up.

The gallery went crazy. Reporters leaped out of their seats, rushing out of the courtroom so they could switch on their cell phones and report the news. Everyone seemed to be speaking at once. Andrea had her arms stretched out toward her husband. She was sobbing and wailing and looked just as stunned as he did.

"My God, my God . . ." Beale murmured. Tears appeared in the corners of his eyes.

The sentencing phase was a blur. Both sides called witnesses, but everything Ben did was drowned in the despair that came from too much knowledge. He'd been around long enough to know that if the jury had been inclined to mitigate, they would not have gone for Murder One.

All too soon, they heard once again from Madame Foreperson. "Pursuant to the guidelines set forth in the court's instructions to the jury, we recommend that the defendant, having been found guilty of the crime of murder in the first degree by a jury of his peers, should be sentenced to execution by lethal injection."

"No," Father Beale cried. "My God, no."

"The jury's recommendation will be accepted by the court," Judge Pitcock answered.

Another tumult ensued. "No!" Andrea screamed. She collapsed into her seat.

Amidst the clamor and confusion, the sheriff's marshals appeared. "We'll take custody of the prisoner."

"My God," Beale continued, his eyes wide and unbelieving. "My God, my God, why hast thou forsaken me?"

The judge was thanking and dismissing the jury, but Ben didn't hear any of it. Never before had he felt a grown man absolutely crumble into his arms. Beale was like a baby; he couldn't walk, couldn't support his own weight.

One of the marshals inched closer. "I'm sorry. We have to take him back to the jail now."

Christina looked angry enough to tear his eyes out. "Couldn't you give us one minute alone with him?"

"I'm sorry," the marshal said, unblinking. "No."

"Daniel!" Andrea rushed forward, trying to embrace her husband, but one of the marshals held her back while they cuffed their prisoner. It took both of them to hold him upright, but they eventually managed to carry Father Beale away.

"This isn't over," Ben said as they departed. "We'll do everything we can. You can count on it."

But even as he said it, Ben knew it was balderdash. All they could do—what *could* they possibly do? Threaten to appeal? Ben knew how futile that would be. The case was over, and they had lost.

Father Beale had given Ben so much, had in a very real sense given him his mission, his life. And now, all these years later, Ben had held Father Beale's life in his hands . . . and had let it slip through his fingers.

41

"BAD NEWS?" MANLY asked as his friend hung up the phone.

"You could say that. Father Beale has been convicted."

"Convicted?"

"Murder one. He's getting the needle."

Manly nodded solemnly. "And vengeance is mine, saith the Lord."

"Evidently."

"What are we going to do with this corpse? We have to think of the right place to put it. So people will know we've punished the babykillers."

"Yeah, right. That's it," his friend said, but of course that wasn't it at all. He couldn't care less about the goddamn abortion cause; that was just a blind he'd used to persuade this simpleminded zealot to do his dirty work for him, to accomplish his end—the death of one Ernestine Rupert. Manly targeted her because she founded and chaired the pro-choice PCSC. But he had far more personal reasons for wanting her dead.

They could just hide the corpse. Bury it. Keep it out of sight. That would be safest—but it didn't help him any. The whole thing wasn't worth a damn thing if no one knew she was dead. Because as long as no one knew she was dead—

He couldn't inherit her money.

The problem was, with Beale convicted and behind bars, they couldn't pin this murder on him. They would have to contrive some other explanation.

"Do you think people will be suspicious? About another murder victim from the same church?"

"After what people have heard was going on in that church, I don't think anything will surprise them." What a fool Manly was. A twisted simpleton with a taste for violence. The most useful devils were the ones who thought they were angels.

"We'll wait a while," he said finally. "Then we'll plant the body."

"But . . . that's a long time to have a stiff lying around, isn't it?"

"What's the matter, Manly? Getting creeped out by your own work?"

"No—I just—you know. She might start to smell or something."

"We'll get her out in plenty of time. You can Lysol the house afterward. I'll help."

But he wouldn't, of course. After the body was moved and the work was completed, Grady Gilliland would disappear. No more wig, no more fake glasses and mustache, no more silly accent. There would be no need for him anymore. After all this planning and effort, the work would be done. And all that would remain was Bruce Ashour, devoted nephew of the late Ernestine Rupert, the poor sap she treated and mistreated like a miserable servant.

A miserable servant now in line for roughly 10.6 million dollars.

CHAPTER

42

"BEN, OPEN THE door. Do you hear me? Open up!"

Ben heard him, but he didn't say anything. Didn't answer. Didn't move.

"Come on, Ben, snap out of it. This is Mike. Let me in!"

The pounding on the door grew louder and more insistent, but Ben didn't budge. Rude, he knew. Self-indulgent, self-pitying. But he still didn't move.

"Christina says you've been sitting around your apartment moping for . . . way too long. She's worried about you."

He pounded the door some more, but it didn't get him anywhere.

"I'm worried about you, too. And unlike Christina, I'm not inclined to let you sit around stewing in your own juices."

What exactly did that mean? Ben wondered as he sat on the sofa, not moving. What juices? And how exactly did one stew them?

"Fine. Don't say I didn't warn you." A few seconds passed, then there was a thundering crash at the front door. Mike spilled through the entry, shoulder first.

This time, Ben responded. "You broke the door down! You splintered the jamb!"

"Sorry. Complain to the landlord."

"*I'm* the landlord!"

"Well, next time, answer the damn door." Without waiting for an invitation he knew wouldn't come, Mike threw himself into the chair facing the sofa.

"Don't you have any . . . like, real police work to be doing?"

"As a matter of fact, I'm swamped. I've got two fresh homicides, plus some nutcase who's running around beating up people connected to pro-choice organizations and abortion clinics. And despite that, please notice, I'm here with you."

"If I'm supposed to be grateful, I'm not."

"What's shaking, Ben? You're not planning to off yourself or anything, are you?"

"No. Is that all you wanted to know?"

"No, but it seemed like a good starting place. Look—I'm sorry the jury turned on you in the Beale case."

"It wasn't the jury's fault." Ben's eyes were like tiny dots of black. "The jury only did what any jury would do, given what they saw. I blew it. I lost the case."

"Ben, come on . . ."

"I did. I threw Father Beale's life away."

"You tried everything possible—"

"It wasn't enough. And now he's going to spend years of misery in jail. Then he's going to be executed. And he's innocent."

"I'm not convinced of that. I think our case against Beale was pretty damn tight."

"He's innocent. I know he is."

"But what about—"

"They're talking about sending him to McAlester, did you know that? Can you imagine? Father Beale, one of the most educated, sensitive men I've ever known, rotting away in that penitentiary? How long will he last in there?"

"Ben, I don't know why you're taking this so hard. You've lost cases before."

"Not like this. Not—not—" He couldn't finish the sentence.

"I guess there's nothing I could say that would persuade you to give yourself a break?"

"Father Beale was my friend," Ben said quietly. "And inspiration. He was there when I needed a friend. But when he needed a friend— I failed him. It's as simple as that."

The phone rang. Ben stared at it a while, seriously considering not answering it. And indeed, if Mike hadn't been there, he probably would've let it alone.

"Yes?"

"Ben? This is Ruth O'Connell."

Ruth was calling him? After she'd done everything possible to convict Father Beale?

"I'm worried about Ernestine. She's gone missing."

"And you're calling me?"

"I didn't know who else to call." The tremor in her voice told Ben she was genuinely concerned. "The police said she had to be missing longer before they could do anything. You've always helped when we have problems at the church."

"I'm sure she just got sick or fell asleep or something."

"I'm telling you, it's serious. She and I have gotten together for lunch every Friday for the last twenty-two years. She's never missed once. Not once. And even if she were going to miss, she'd call. It's not as if she could just forget, not after all these years."

Ben frowned. That did sound unusual. But what could he do?

"I'm just afraid, when we've had all those murders, and then she disappears . . ."

The full impact of what she was saying struck Ben like a hammer. Could there have been another killing? While Father Beale was behind bars? Because if there was, that would mean . . .

"I'll look into it, Ruth."

"I'd be so grateful."

"I'll get the police on the case. They'll start checking it out immediately."

"But I've called the police."

Ben looked across the room at his friend and smiled. "I may have a few connections you don't."

CHAPTER

43

BEN HAD WANTED to come, but Mike wouldn't allow it. Mike didn't believe for a minute that there was still a killer out there; the killer had been locked up good and tight. Still, if there was any chance of danger, Ben didn't need to be in the thick of it. Ben was like a danger magnet; it always seemed to gravitate toward him, and he was pathetically ill equipped to deal with it.

After issuing the APB, he drove to Ernestine's house. There was no sign of her and no sign of any struggle or violence. But Ben had told Mike she had a nephew who was with her frequently, one she treated more like a handmaiden than a relative. So that seemed like the logical next stop.

After he knocked on the door, Mike could hear hushed muttering inside. Two voices talking in subdued tones.

Mike pressed his ear against the door. He heard a shushing noise. Then the voices stopped.

Could be nothing, of course. But something about this was making the short hairs on the back of his neck stand at attention. And when you'd been a cop as long as Mike had, you learned to listen to those little short hairs.

The door swung open, but the man standing on the other side was not Bruce, the nephew. He didn't match the description Ben had given him. He was sandy-haired and muscular and . . . well, not very well-to-do or bright-looking.

"Yeah?"

Mike pulled out his badge. "I'm Major Mike Morelli. Tulsa PD."

The man looked at the badge, looked at Mike, then sort of levitated, as if unable to decide what to do next. Mike had seen the look before—but only from people who had something to hide.

"I'd just like a few words."

"Yeah." The man's eyes darted all around. "Can you just . . . give me a moment?"

"Sure," Mike said, since he had no choice, and the man closed the door.

Mike pressed his ear against the door again. More talking, footsteps, some kind of commotion. A metallic swinging noise. Something was being opened—a window, or maybe a screen door.

"Open up!" Mike shouted. "Now!"

All he heard in response were footsteps, and they were growing fainter.

Soon they would be gone, whoever they were. The question was whether Mike had the legal right to do anything about it. And it was a question he pondered for, oh, half a second, because there just wasn't time.

"Freeze!" Mike shouted, kicking the door. The flimsy lock gave and the door swung open. At the back end of the house, he saw two men scurrying through a patio door. One of them was almost instantly out of sight. The other, the man who had opened the door, would be soon. "Freeze! Police!"

Did he have the right to enter the house in pursuit? Oh, hell. Leave it for the lawyers. He raced inside—

And that's when he saw her, sprawled across a blanket lying on the floor. It didn't take him two seconds to realize Ernestine Rupert was dead—and had been for some while.

"Stop where you are!" he repeated as he raced toward the back. He unholstered his weapon. "You're under arrest! Stop or I will shoot!"

He blazed through the back patio door. The sandy-haired man was rapidly descending a series of steps that led to a sunken garage. And from there? Mike could only imagine. He'd be long gone, that much was sure.

Mike leaped off the top of the stairs. He landed on the lawn a split second later, so hard it drove his knees into his chin. It hurt, and his lip was bleeding, but he blocked the pain out of his mind. He

scrambled to his feet, raced to the garage, and dived toward the fleeing suspect.

He flew just far enough to tackle the man around the knees. A little lower than he wanted, but it would do. The man tumbled down
onto the pavement just outside the garage, banging his head against
the back wall.

Ouch. That had to sting.

"You're under arrest," Mike said, gasping. He whipped out his
handcuffs and grabbed the man's right arm. Inside the garage, he
heard a car engine starting. "Damn. Where is that—?"

The man's boot came out of nowhere. It blindsided Mike, knocking him sideways and loosening a tooth. The cuffs went jangling to
the ground. The suspect crawled out from under him and fled.

Evidently the blow to the head hadn't been as incapacitating as it
looked, Mike realized. Damn, damn, damn. Why had he been so
sloppy? He should've seen that coming. He scrabbled to his feet, trying to get his bearings, which was no small accomplishment. He
loped toward the garage door just in time to see the sandy-haired
man dive into the passenger seat. The driver—who matched the description Ben had given of the nephew—peeled out, making it from
garage to street in less than a second.

Mike slapped himself on the side of the face twice, hard. If it was
going to be a freaking car chase, he was going to need his wits about
him. He raced to his car, watching to see which way they were headed.
They had a lead of several seconds, he realized as he thrust his key
into the ignition. But he also noticed that poor Brucie was driving
some crappy boxy foreign car, a Yugo or something. Mike, of course,
was driving his trusty silver TransAm.

The odds were evening.

HALF A MINUTE later, Mike had them. They were cruising down
Memorial, which unfortunately was the busiest street in the city.
They were trying to make it to the highway, no doubt. If they could
get to I-44, they could get anywhere. Mike didn't have a license plate
number or even a competent description of the car. So he had to
make sure that didn't happen.

He got on his cell phone and requested backup, notifying them that a high-speed chase was in progress. He hated car chases; they were inherently dangerous and ended up harming civilians more often than they captured bad guys. But he wasn't going to let these two get away. Not with a corpse lying in their living room.

"Get as many black-and-whites out as possible," he barked. "Kill the stoplights. Try to block off the street before these clowns hurt someone!"

The getaway car's speed continued to increase. Mike knew it was only a matter of time before they hurt or killed an innocent motorist or pedestrian. He had to bring this to a conclusion. Fast.

He floored it, speeding by two other drivers (one of whom shot him the finger) and rammed Bruce from behind. The little foreign car lurched forward like a billiard ball. But it didn't stop.

Brucie had to be sweating it now, Mike reasoned. He was probably flooring his accelerator, too, but in his crappy car, the floor came a lot sooner than in Mike's TransAm. And to think Ben gave him grief about driving a teenager car. What did Ben know? Eternal youth had its advantages.

They made it through the traffic light at Forty-first by a whisker. Mike reached through the driver's side window and attached his portable siren, turned it on, and rammed Bruce's car again, this time all the harder. Probably crumpled his bumper a bit in the process, a thought that nearly brought tears to Mike's eyes. He'd have to petition Chief Blackwell to make good for the repairs. Which meant he'd better bring these two killers in.

He swerved into the right-hand lane, pulled up beside them, and activated the car's built-in bullhorn. "Police!" he announced, as if they didn't know that already. "You are under arrest. Pull your vehicle over immediately."

They did pull over, but not in the manner that Mike intended. Bruce suddenly swerved to the right, broadsiding Mike's TransAm. Mike cringed as he heard the painful scraping of metal that told him his beloved car had been seriously damaged. He was knocked into the next lane, barely avoiding an elderly woman in a pink Cadillac.

His teeth clenched together. Now you've done it, you aunt-murdering little bastard. Now you've made me mad. Mike pulled back into the lane beside them, cutting off an oncoming pickup truck. Fortunately the driver didn't have a rifle in the back, because he looked mad enough to fire it if he had. Mike pulled beside Bruce and slammed him sideways, giving as good as he got and then some. For a moment, Bruce totally lost control of his car. The back end rocked back and forth, threatening to spin out at any moment. Bruce worked the wheel frantically, barely preventing the car from colliding with the neighboring traffic.

"Pull over immediately," Mike repeated into the bullhorn. "You are under arrest."

Bruce did not pull over. Instead, he did something Mike wouldn't have thought possible. He drove faster.

Mike saw they were fast approaching the traffic light at Thirty-first. It was a four-way stop, the light was already yellow, and they were still a good hundred feet away from it.

Don't do it, you stupid fool, Mike thought as he applied his own brakes.

Bruce chose the other pedal. He poured it on, trying to rocket through the intersection. The light turned red several seconds before he got there, but he kept on blazing through. . . .

He never saw the electric blue pickup until it was on top of him. It plowed over the Yugo like it was a Matchbox toy, smashing the hood, shattering the glass.

My God, Mike thought, looking away. My God, my God.

He punched his cell phone and called headquarters. "We're going to need an ambulance out here," he said. "Fast." But even as he said it, he knew it wouldn't help. There wasn't enough left of that car to put on a microscope slide.

Mike banged his fist against the steering wheel, furious. He'd told them to stop, damn it. Why didn't anyone ever listen to him?

"SO BRUCE AND this Manly Trussell creep were behind the murders?" Ben asked.

"Absolutely." Mike was hunched over his desk, assiduously engaged in a complex endeavor involving paper, glue, staples, and file folders. "We found more than enough evidence in Bruce's home to prove he and his pal offed his aunt."

"That doesn't prove they did the others."

"Exactly how many killers do you think there are in your church, Ben? Jeez, small wonder I'm an agnostic." He fumbled around with the office supplies, accidentally stapling his hand. "Give me another day or two. We'll turn up some evidence to connect them to the previous murders."

"It's a shame we can't interrogate them."

"Shame isn't the word for it. That car was obliterated." He lifted the brush out of the paste pot, stringing a trail of glue across his desk blotter. "They tell me the guy in the pickup is going to be all right. Of course, he was in a pickup. Pays to be a redneck, I guess."

"I just—" Ben paused, searching for the right words. "I can't quite make it all fit in my brain. What did Bruce have against Helen Conrad? Or Kate McGuire? Or Susan Marino?"

"Nothing. That's my theory, anyway. All he wanted was the demise of his dear aunt Ernestine. But he was smart enough to realize that if she turned up murdered, no matter how good his alibi, the sole heir to her millions would be Suspect Numero Uno. He had to create another motive. Presumably he didn't know she was a blackmailer. So he enlisted this wacko Manly to start knocking off members of the vestry, leading everyone to believe that Father Beale was doing it."

"So that when he got around to Ernestine—"

"Everyone would just think it was another one of the same. It's the only way his aunt could be killed without immediately throwing suspicion on him."

"And this Manly character—?"

"Rabid pro-life activist. Of the shoot-the-docs-at-the-clinic variety. Mind you, I tend to be pro-life myself—I think anyone who cares about the sanctity of human life must be. But I've got no sympathy for these creeps who think it gives them an excuse to commit crimes, much less murder. Bruce played on Manly's pro-life leanings, ostensibly targeting Ernestine because she founded the city's most successful pro-choice outfit. Manly had a history of violence and had been institutionalized at least twice. In other words, he was just what Bruce needed."

Ben shook his head. "What a twisted scheme. Killing four people, including his aunt, and framing an innocent person for murder, just to get some money."

"Yeah. Unbelievable. And it was only ten million bucks." He winked. "Barely five, after taxes."

"I wish they'd survived, though. I need written statements to take to the judge. Show him what a hideous mistake the jury made convicting Father Beale."

"You seem to be assuming that if those two scumbags were alive they would confess, just to help you out—something I very seriously doubt. Your only hope lies with the physical evidence, which I have two crack teams working 24/7 to collect. We'll get what you need."

"Thanks. I appreciate it. This is really above and beyond—"

"Hey, I don't like being wrong, but when I am, at least I can admit it. I thought your priest was guilty as sin. So to speak." Mike tried to close the file, but everything had been inserted so clumsily it wouldn't close. "And I was wrong. So I need to make amends."

"You won't hear me complaining." Ben stared at the mess—a file that looked as if it had been compiled by a kindergartner, glue covering Mike's hands and desk, shreds of paper and staples everywhere. "This is just a guess, but—is Penelope on vacation?"

"Yes, damn it, and I'm helpless without her. I can't handle all this paperwork."

"It does look trying."

"It's awful. Who uses these paste pots anymore?"

"Penelope, apparently."

"And everything has to be attached just so and in the right order, and if you do it wrong the snobs in Records just send it back."

"Well, I've always heard police work is a high-stress occupation."

"Paperwork sucks."

"Not to mention car chases, stakeouts, gunplay . . ."

Mike tried to wipe the glue off his hands with a wet towel. "Yeah. But that's the fun part."

The World Is Not Conclusion

◆ ◆ ◆

CHAPTER

44

The Gospel According to Daniel

THERE ARE SIMPLY no words to describe the utter degradation and despair I experienced during my first days of posttrial incarceration. True, I had been in jail before, but now, with the trial completed, with all realistic hope of reprieve removed, the full horror of my situation penetrated my consciousness with an almost incapacitating impact. The filth, the loss of freedom, the intellectual stagnation—all of it assaulted my heart and my soul with an intensity that increased with every passing moment. My attorney praised me for holding on to my faith under such dire circumstances, but the truth is, I had no choice. I was like a shipwrecked castaway clinging to the only scrap of timber that hadn't submerged. Holding on to the only thing you have left is not an act of courage; it's an act of desperation.

Of course, my attorney visited regularly, being the good-hearted soul he is, and tried to lighten my spirits. We're doing everything we can, he would say. We're mounting a major appeal. But I am not a child. I can separate reality from fantasy. I knew when the forewoman read the verdict that my fate was sealed, now and for the remainder of my time on earth.

I have always believed that God has a plan for our lives. But I must confess that I have been utterly unable to discern the plan in the events that have befallen me now. I pray at night for guidance, but it does not come. What am I to do? I ask. What is my mission? I rarely have an opportunity to talk to other people, and when I do, they don't listen. The prison has denied me writing materials, except those provided by my attorney for my defense. My phone calls are restricted. I would like to think I am meant to have some impact somewhere—but how? How can I be a force for good when I have been deprived of all means of contact with the world? Is this not the true definition of hell—separation from God, from everything that matters?

And if I have already been cast into hell, here on earth, on death row—what awaits me on the other side?

HOW CAN YOU communicate effectively with someone who isn't even in the same room? Ben wondered, not for the first time. How can you comfort someone you can't touch? How can you discuss private personal matters when you're surrounded by unfriendly faces?

You can't. But when you're visiting someone on death row, those are the only choices you get.

Ben sat on the opposite side of an acrylic panel, staring at the gaunt, drawn face of Father Beale. He had shaved his beard, or it had been shaved for him. His hair was cut shorter, and he was wearing orange coveralls in place of his white collar. They talked to one another through telephones even though they were only a few feet apart.

"We're doing everything we can," Ben said. "Everything possible."

"I know you are," Father Beale replied. His voice sounded shrill and tinny over the phone. "But don't neglect your other cases. You have to make a living."

"We're mounting a major appeal," Ben continued. "Hitting the Court of Criminal Appeals with everything imaginable. And if that doesn't work, we'll go for habeas corpus."

"Don't bankrupt yourself, Ben. Andrea tells me you haven't even sent bills for the last—"

"It's just so frustrating!" Ben stared down at the tacky linoleum floor, because he knew if he looked at his client he would begin to weep. "Mike caught the killers red-handed. With a corpse in their living room, no less. But the DA's office won't buy it. They agree that Bruce and his assassin pal killed Ernestine, but won't concede that they killed the others."

"I suppose it's hard to imagine two people could be so cruel."

"They just don't want to admit they made a mistake," Ben said. "If they joined my appeal and asked for your release, they would have to acknowledge that they prosecuted an innocent man—sent him to death row, even. They're not going to do that unless they have no choice. Until Bruce and Manly's guilt is absolutely beyond question. And unfortunately, I haven't come up with any physical evidence conclusively tying them to the first three murders."

"It troubles me, about Bruce," Father Beale said. "I talked with him many times, of course. I knew he resented the way his aunt treated him—who wouldn't? But I never suspected the depth of his resentment. If only he had come to me. Talked about it." He shook his head. "What a troubled soul the poor man must've had."

Ben supposed he should be sympathetic, but what Beale said only magnified his frustration. Stop being a priest already! he wanted to shout. Look after yourself for a change!

"The problem is the fingerprints," Ben said, intentionally changing the subject. "That's the red flag the DA keeps waving in my face. If Manly committed the first three murders, why weren't his fingerprints on your St. Crispin's Award? That's the question I still can't answer. If I could, I might be able to make some progress. I was in my friend Mike Morelli's office earlier, and I told him that I—I—"

Ben stopped midsentence. A strange expression came over his face. "I was saying that—that—"

Father Beale frowned. "Ben? Is there something wrong?"

Ben seemed to be lost in some internal thought process. "I was staring at him, and I said—" His voice cut off again, and this time he let out a small gasp. "Oh, my God."

"What?" Beale leaned closer to the glass. "Is something wrong?"

"No," Ben said quietly. "No. Except—oh, my God—"

"What?" Beale bellowed into the receiver. "Would you stop talking in riddles? What is it?"

Ben spoke slowly and deliberately, barely able to believe he was saying it as he spoke. "I think I know who killed the three women at the church, including Kate McGuire. I think I know who did it—and how." He glanced at his watch. "I've got to get out of here."

"Just a minute! You can't leave me hanging like this!"

"I can't stop to talk now."

"Why? Where are you going?"

Ben drew in his breath. "To see the killer."

Beale could barely contain himself. "Who is it? Who are you going to see?"

It was not an answer Ben wanted to give, but it had to be said sometime. Was there any sense in waiting?

"Answer me!" Beale repeated. "Who are you going to see?"

Ben looked at him solemnly. "Your wife."

45

"YOU'VE FIGURED IT out, haven't you?" Andrea Beale said when she saw Ben on her doorstep.

Ben nodded his head slowly. "I think so."

"It was bound to happen." She closed her eyes. "Just a matter of time, I suppose."

She widened the door, implicitly inviting Ben to enter.

It was a nice home, tastefully decorated on what must have been a limited income. But Ben wasn't here to admire the furniture. "Will you tell me about it?"

She nodded sadly, then walked into the living room. Ben followed.

He had considered calling Mike, or maybe Loving. For all he knew, she might try to run. Or might even try to hurt him. But Ben saw no evidence of either reaction. She seemed entirely resigned, unresisting. Or maybe it was more that she was . . . out of breath. Emotionally winded. At any rate, she wasn't putting up a struggle, and Ben couldn't imagine that she ever would.

"Will you do one thing for me first?" she asked after they were both seated.

"Well, I don't know if—"

"It's a little thing. Indulge me."

Ben pressed his lips together. "Okay. What?"

"Tell me how you figured it out."

Ben nodded. Fair enough. "I've been assuming that Bruce persuaded his thug Manly to kill the three church women to set the stage for killing Ernestine, and to pin the blame on your husband. But there were problems with that theory. Bruce persuaded Manly to kill by playing on his pro-life sympathies, but Kate McGuire and Susan Marino had no connection to that cause at all. And how could Daniel be blamed for the murder of Ernestine after his bail was revoked?"

"I can see where that would present a problem."

"I've known all along the key was the absence of fingerprints on the St. Crispin's Award. There had to be some explanation—I just couldn't figure out what it was. And then, as I was speaking to your husband today, I thought back to when I last saw my friend Mike. He was messing around with some files, trying to assemble them properly, and he got glue all over himself. That's when I realized."

"Yes?"

"I remember reading somewhere about how you can coat your fingertips with a thin layer of glue. I don't remember where. One of Mike's magazines, maybe. Dick Tracy, perhaps. Who knows? It makes sense, though. One of the prosecution witnesses explained that latent prints are the result of skin secretions left on receptive surfaces. Cover your fingers with glue, and presto. No skin secretions. And it's easy to do. Any kind of glue will work. You just roll a thin layer over your hands and fingers and let it dry. Kind of like kids do in grade school. A thin transparent layer of glue will be virtually invisible to anyone else—but it will prevent you from leaving fingerprints."

"And that's when you remembered the wedding reception."

"Yes," Ben answered. "And I remembered seeing you there, carrying all those decorations and supplies—with glue all over your hands."

Andrea's eyes wandered down to the carpet. "I must hand it to you, Ben—you have a marvelous memory."

"May I ask a question now?"

The woman nodded.

"*Why?*"

She looked at him strangely. "I don't know what you mean."

"Why did you kill Kate McGuire? And the other women?"

Her eyes widened, like slowly inflated balloons. "You think I did it?"

"Well—but—you said—"

"You think I killed those women?"

"But—you had the glue on your hands!"

"Ben, I was just cleaning up, remember? I told you that at the time. I wasn't the one who made the decorations. By the time I got to the glue, Kate was already dead."

"But you said—"

"I didn't get it at first, either, not till you called just now and said you wanted to talk about glue. That's when I started thinking about it, and I realized what must've happened."

Ben's brain was in overdrive trying to take everything in. "What—but then—you're not—?"

Andrea stared at him. "You don't know who it was, do you?"

"No, evidently I don't. Could you please fill me in?"

Andrea pressed a hand against her breast. "You won't believe it," she said quietly. "You just won't believe it."

"HE LIVES RIGHT over there, you know," Judy said.

"Who? Ben?"

"Yup. That-a-way." She pointed across the Tulsa skyline. "He's not home at the moment. Probably with Mike."

"Who's Mike?"

"Homicide detective. They've known each other since college. Met their freshman year."

Maura stared at her friend. "Do you know everything about this guy? I mean, this is getting a little spooky."

"There are no secrets these days, Maura. Not to anyone with a computer and a modem. I can find out anything about anybody."

The two girls sat perched atop St. Benedict's bell tower. Not an authorized play area, but they had learned years ago how to pick the lock on the door, climb the stairs, and crawl beneath the bell to the edge of the tower. It was more than three stories high, and since the church was on the crest of a hill, it afforded a lovely view of Tulsa's rolling green landscape.

Maura opened a small handbag and withdrew a long elegant necklace. Diamonds glistened in the reflecting light of the setting sun. She held it against her neck. "Do you think it looks good on me?"

"Better than it ever did on Susan Marino, anyway."

"Or do you prefer this one?" She pulled out a much simpler piece of jewelry, a gold chain with a single heart-shaped pendant. "Understated and elegant. What do you think? Better?"

"Not even close. Kate didn't have Susan's taste. Or her money, for that matter."

"You're probably right." She threw the pendant off the edge of the tower, deep into the prayer garden. "Some of this stuff we took off Helen looks positively ratty. But I did get that lovely pocket knife, remember?" She reached into her purse and withdrew a knife about the length of her hand. She pulled out some of the blades, then lightly ran her finger down the sharp edges. "It's a lovely knife."

"Yes, and we put it to good use, didn't we?"

Both girls giggled. Maura put the knife and the jewelry back into her purse.

Maura leaned back, propping herself up with her arms. "Now Ernestine—she must've had some fabulous jewelry."

"No doubt."

"Are you as irritated about that as I am? Having her snatched away from us like that?"

Judy shrugged. "I'm not nuts for jewelry like you are."

"I'm not nuts for it."

"You dug up a grave because you heard a rumor that Natalie Bragg's wedding ring had been buried with her ashes."

"But I'm not *nuts* for it." She sighed. "Still. I would've liked to have a fourth."

Judy turned to face her friend, so simple, so unaffectedly naïve. "And what's to stop us?"

"I just thought, now that Father Beale is going to prison . . ."

"Why should that matter?" She paused, gazing reflectively at the orange sun. "I like being up here, watching all the people scurry about. They're like ants. Little ants running through their paces, doing whatever I want them to do."

"Whatever *you* want them to do? I'm part of this team, too, remember?"

"Of course I do." She patted Maura's hand. "Do you remember that rhyme from the wedding? Something old, something new, something borrowed, something blue?"

"Yes."

"Well, I figure we've had something old—that was Helen. And we've had new—Susan."

"Kate can be the blue—she had blue eyes."

"Exactly. But what about something borrowed?"

"Alvin Greene!" Maura said gleefully. "Because he was loaned to us from St. John's."

"Brilliant." Judy took her friend's hand and gave it a squeeze. "But a man? We haven't done that before. He'll struggle more."

"I think we're ready for it."

"I do, too," Judy said, and a wonderful, contented smile spread across her face. "You're a good friend, Maura," she said. "You're a good friend, and I love you."

"I love you, too, Judy. You know I do."

Judy released her hand, then returned her attention to the horizon. "It's a beautiful sunset, isn't it?"

"Beautiful," Maura echoed. Her eyelashes fluttered, and she laid her head gently on her friend's soft shoulder. "Absolutely beautiful."

46

"YOU'RE KIDDING!" MIKE'S voice was so loud Ben had to move the cell phone away from his ear.

"I'm not, Mike. I'm dead serious."

"But it couldn't be—"

"It's the only explanation."

"But *why?*"

"We'll sort that out later." Ben was speeding across town, his phone in one hand, the steering wheel in the other—not the optimal conditions for high-speed driving. "Can you meet me at the church?"

"Now? I've got a million things—"

"There will be a lot of people there tonight, Mike. And the last time a lot of people were there, someone got killed."

Ben heard a deep intake of breath on the other end of the line. "Give me ten minutes."

"You can't possibly get there in ten minutes."

Ben heard a soft chuckle. "With an eight-cylinder TransAm and a portable police siren, I can do anything I want."

"MR. GREENE, COULD you please help me?"

Alvin put down his wrench. "I'm kinda busy at the moment, little miss. Gotta get this place ready for the big concert."

Judy and Maura stood beside the altar looking down at him. Judy put on her sweetest smile. "We'd only need you for a little while."

"Still . . ." He checked his watch. "I've just got half an hour."

"Please." Her forehead crinkled, making her look sweetly frightened and irresistible. "I really really *really* need your help."

"What is it?"

"I—I think I saw a spider."

"Honey, we got spiders all over the—"

"A fiddleback."

"A fiddleback! Those are poisonous. Are you sure?"

Judy swung her head up and down. "I studied all about them in Girl Scouts."

"Where was it?"

"In the fourth-grade Sunday school room."

"Way in the back of the church?"

"Uh-huh. Please hurry. I'm so scared."

"Is anyone else around?"

"Oh no, not now." Her eyes glistened a bit. She reached out and took his hand. "It'll just be you and me and Maura back there. Just you and me and Maura."

As HE PULLED up to the church, Ben saw that, as he had feared, the parking lot was filled. Masterson's choir concert was today; both the adult and the youth choirs were performing, and Masterson had been promoting it hard and heavy as an organ fund-raiser.

Ben parked his car and ran to the front entrance, hoping against hope that he wasn't too late.

Just as he hit the front door, he saw a familiar silver TransAm barreling up the drive. Mike, and he'd brought Lieutenant Tomlinson with him. All the better.

"Where are they?" Mike asked just a few seconds later.

"Follow me." Ben led them through the narthex into the sanctuary, where the recital was already under way. The youth choir was singing an anthem: "Even When God Is Silent." The pews were filled. Whether due to excitement over the music program or relief that the Father Beale ordeal was over, the parish had turned out in large numbers. Which could make Ben and Mike's task all the more difficult.

Ben saw Alvin Greene standing near the door. "Any problems?"

"No," the short man answered. "Why?"

"Just wondered. No . . . disturbances? Excitement?"

"Not to speak of. One of the choir girls thought she saw a spider."

"Which one?"

He chuckled. "The tall one with all the spunk. Judy. Said she saw a fiddleback in the Sunday school room and wanted me to come kill it. I told her she'd have to wait until after the concert. Felt bad, but I had too much to do."

"Don't feel bad," Ben murmured. "It's the smartest thing you ever did in your life."

"Which ones are they?" Mike asked.

"Maura's on the back row. The short girl with the dark hair, second from the end."

"Jesus Christ. How old is she? Sixteen?"

"Not even."

"Where's the other one?"

"I don't know. I don't see her."

They waited until the song was over. During the applause, Ben and Mike walked as unobtrusively as possible to the choir section.

"Maura," Ben said quietly, "you need to come with me."

Maura frowned. "What? Why?"

The applause was dying out. "Just come. Now."

"What's going on here?" Masterson had left the organ to investigate. "We're in the middle of a performance."

Ben tried to keep his voice down, to attract as little attention as possible. "I need Maura."

"Can't it wait until later?"

"No."

Maura looked at Masterson with big wide eyes. "I don't want to go with him."

"Look, Kincaid, I don't know what this is all about, but I'm not letting you drag her off in the middle of my concert."

The applause was over. Everyone present was watching, listening, trying to figure out what on earth was going on.

"Let's not make a scene," Ben hissed.

"I agree," Masterson shot back. "Please leave so that we can get on with the concert!"

Mike's limited patience had reached an end. He pulled out his badge and flipped it open. "Major Morelli. Tulsa PD. I want to talk to the girl, now."

Maura took a step back—but Ben clamped his hand on her shoulder, holding her in place.

Masterson was obviously startled, but he didn't back down. "What's this all about?"

"We just need a few words with her."

"I'll have to talk to her mother."

"No, you won't." Mike stepped forward and took Maura by the hand. "Come along, miss."

"But I don't want to go!" Unable to flee, Maura had obviously realized the value of creating a public scene. "Don't let him take me away!"

"No one's going to harm you."

"Stop! *Please!* Won't someone help me? Don't let him hurt me!"

By this time, the church was in an uproar. Adults rose out of their seats, heading down the aisle to assist the poor defenseless girl. Maura wailed at the top of her lungs.

"What's going on here?" one of the men said.

"We're not going to put up with this!" said another.

Mike flashed his badge. "Look, people, I'm the police and you *are* going to put up with it or I'll have my lieutenant put you under arrest."

"Doesn't she get a lawyer? I think she should call her parents."

"Tomlinson." The lieutenant stepped forward, brandishing his handcuffs. "Anyone tries to stop me, lock 'em up."

He nodded. "Make way. Clear the area."

Tomlinson could act as tough as he was able, but Ben could see they were vastly outnumbered, and if they didn't get the girls out of here soon, they were going to have a riot on their hands.

"Where's Judy?" Ben asked Maura.

"I don't know."

"I think you do."

"I don't, and I wouldn't tell you if I did. I want to see a lawyer."

"Maura, listen to me—"

"Judy! Run!"

Ben whipped around. A small figure had emerged from the robing room in the back of the sanctuary. She took one look at what was happening, heard Maura scream, and bolted.

"Run, Judy! Run!" While he was watching the fleeing girl, Maura

stomped down on Mike's toe, hard. She broke away, then plunged into the crowd, heading for the front doors.

"Blast!" Mike started after her, but the mass of bodies around him was dense and was intentionally not cooperating with him.

"I'll go after Judy," Ben shouted. "I know the church better than you do."

"Damn, damn, damn." Mike unholstered his weapon. "You people will clear out!" he bellowed. "Understand?"

The crowd began to back off. For the most part. Ruth O'Connell couldn't restrain herself. "You leave that girl alone, you big bully. She's a wonderful child. She hasn't hurt anyone."

"Yeah," Mike muttered as he beat his way through the masses. "Except for the three women she helped murder, that is."

Mike shoved his gun back into his holster and started after her.

BEN KNEW THE interior corridors that linked the robing and choir rooms to the back offices were like a maze winding through the interior of the church. Judy, being an acolyte, undoubtedly knew them better than he did, but he pounded along, weaving around corners and tearing down corridors.

"Judy! Stop! You can't get away!"

"Leave me alone!" she shouted back.

He was closing in, only about twenty feet or so behind her. She would soon be at the other end of the church. She'd have to either go outside, where she'd be exposed, or she'd have to stop running. Either way, he was likely to get her.

"You're only making it worse, Judy."

"Go away!"

She reached the end of the corridor. She turned to face him, crouching down like a hunted animal waiting to fight off a predator. Her eyes were fierce and angry.

"Stay back! I'll hurt you!"

Ben couldn't believe his eyes. She was a fifteen-year-old girl—but this was like staring down the face of a barracuda.

"I will! I'll hurt you!"

"Judy . . . please. You can't escape. Come peacefully."

Judy ripped the fire extinguisher off the wall and threw it at him.

Ben ducked. The extinguisher missed him, but flew over his head and crashed into a plate glass window in the office behind. Shards of glass shattered and flew. Ben ducked and covered his eyes as it rained down all around him.

"For God's sake, Judy!" He brushed himself off and uncovered his eyes. "You could've—"

He didn't bother finishing.

Judy was gone.

"FREEZE!" MIKE SHOUTED. He blew through the front doors, trailing a pudgy teenage girl Ben told him had committed horrible crimes. Could it be possible?

"Police! I'm ordering you to stop!"

Maura kept on running. She veered to the left, into the prayer garden. There was a tall bell tower in the center, and she seemed to be making straight for it.

"Keep away from me!" she screamed. She wheeled around on one foot and threw something at him. Mike ducked, and her pink hand-bag flew past him.

Mike plucked it out of a bed of azaleas. Right away he saw two long elegant necklaces. He was no expert on jewelry, but he knew enough to realize they were too expensive to belong to this young girl.

"You can't get away!" Mike called out. But where had she gone? He darted down the cobbled sidewalk that wound through the gar-den, calling and shouting to no avail. Had she slipped through a rab-bit hole? Where was she?

BEN FOUND JUDY outside the church, weaving through the cars in the packed parking lot. Some of the attendees were leaving, appar-ently too traumatized by the latest bizarre happening at St. Benedict's to hang around any longer. The traffic only made the chase all the more difficult—and dangerous.

"Stop her!" Ben shouted as he darted between moving cars. "Don't let her get away!" He yelled as loud as he could, but Judy didn't slow, and no one helped. And why would they? They didn't know what was going on. They probably sympathized with their choir girl, not the pain-in-the-butt lawyer who was always causing trouble.

"You can't get away, Judy. Give it up!" She was running toward a car at the far end of the lot—her car, no doubt, or her mother's. She could probably drive, even if she wasn't licensed. God knows she could do everything else. If she had a key and she got there in time . . .

Ben poured on all the speed he could muster. He dived around a parked car, rocking up on one hand and foot. A moving car pulled out in front of him. Ben didn't slow a beat. He leaped up onto the hood and kept on running.

"Gotcha!" Ben cried. He flew down and grabbed Judy just before she slid into her car.

"Let go of me!" She struggled, pounding his chest with her fists.

"I will not. You've got a date with the police." He grabbed her wrists and twisted them behind her back. "Come on."

"Let go of me! Someone help me!"

"Give it a rest, Judy. It's all over. Now you're going to—"

Ben didn't see it coming until it was right in his face. A huge and heavy purse collided with his nose.

"Oww!" Ben fell sideways, clutching his face. Judy broke away and ran.

Ben touched his nose delicately. "I think you broke it!"

He looked up, lightbulbs exploding before his eyes. A middle-aged woman stood over him, a baby in one arm and the lethal leather in the other.

"Why the hell did you do that?"

The woman looked down at him unrepentantly. "Because I'm her mother."

SHE MUST BE in the bell tower, Mike reasoned. It was the only possible explanation.

He ran to the base of the tower and pulled at the wooden door. It was locked—from the inside, no doubt. He pulled and pulled, but it didn't budge. The door was thick and reinforced with metal. Mike didn't care to try his shoulder on it. And he didn't have to, not with his trusty Sig Sauer at the ready.

He pulled out the gun and fired. It took two shots, but the lock blew apart.

He stepped inside. It was dark, but a spiral staircase in the center of the tower was the only place to go. He started making his way up.

"We've got you dead to rights, Maura," Mike called, shouting up into the darkness. "It'll go better for you if you cooperate."

He continued climbing the stairs. It was damn creepy, moving in the darkness, not knowing what the little brat might throw at him next. This whole damn church was like a house of horrors.

He reached the top of the stairs. There was a wooden plank overhead that no doubt provided access to the bell chamber. While he climbed through, though, he knew he would be totally vulnerable.

"I'm coming in, Maura," he said loudly, "and I don't want any trouble. I've got my gun and I'm not afraid to use it." In truth, he couldn't climb while he held a gun, and if he used it on a fifteen-year-old girl, however murderous, he'd be crucified in the press and probably in the department. But she didn't have to know that.

"I'm coming through!" He pushed the panel up. It flipped over and thudded, making a resounding noise. Nothing happened.

"Here I come!"

He placed his hands on the edge and pulled as hard and fast as he could. There was no resistance. A moment later, he was in the bell chamber. The large cast iron bell hung so low he couldn't stand, so he crawled beneath it.

"Maura?"

"Don't come any closer!"

She was standing on the edge of the tower, the very edge. One short step and she would tumble to her death three stories below. Her face was red and puffy; her hands were tucked behind her back. She was crying.

"She did it," Maura said, her voice racked with sobs. "Judy did. She did all the killing. I knew about it, but I didn't help."

Mike held out his hand. "Come away from the edge, Maura."

"Don't come near me! I'll jump!" Tears streamed from her eyes. "I didn't want anything to do with it. I thought it was horrible. But she made me. She told me I had to come and I didn't know what to do."

"We can sort this out later, Maura." Mike inched closer. "For now, just come away from the edge."

"I know I shouldn't have kept the jewelry Judy gave me. I know she took it from the women after she killed them. But I didn't hurt anyone. I could never hurt anyone!"

"Just come with me, Maura." Mike was barely a foot away from her now. "Come down from there and we'll talk everything out. You don't want to hurt yourself."

"*I didn't know what to do!*" Maura was near hysterical now, screaming and flinging her head around, her hands still locked behind her back. "I'm so confused. I didn't want to hurt anyone. I just want to go home!"

"Come on now," Mike said gently. "I won't let anyone hurt you. Just come with me."

Mike gently laid his hand on her arm. The instant he did, her other arm swung out from behind her back, a brown pocket knife clenched in the fist. She plunged it into Mike's hand.

Mike screamed.

"I told you to leave me alone," Maura snarled. She shoved him backwards off the edge of the tower. "You should've listened."

"MAURA DID IT! Maura did everything!"

Even though his nose felt as if it were broken, Ben managed to limp through the parking lot and around the church until he caught up to Judy again, this time near the storage shed in the back. She was making a run for the apartment complex behind the rear fence. Ben was determined that she wasn't going to make it.

"If Maura did it, you have no reason to run!" Ben shouted after her.

"She made me watch. I didn't like it! I hated it!" She was only about a hundred feet away from the fence. Give the girl fifteen more seconds, and she'd have it. His chances of catching her would be minuscule.

"Judy, you know how the law works. It's no good running. Give yourself up. I promise I'll see that you're taken care of!"

"Maura did it! Maura did it all!"

She was even closer to the fence now. Ben gave it everything he had, but at this point, his top speed wasn't much. It looked as if she was going to make it. . . .

When Tomlinson appeared on the other side of the fence. Her head nearly collided with his.

"Going somewhere, miss?"

Judy changed course, but Ben managed to catch her on the rebound. He held her down while Tomlinson snapped the cuffs around her wrists.

"Thanks for the assist," Ben muttered. "You were great."

Tomlinson grinned. "Years of training." He looked down at the girl. "You are under arrest. Anything you say can and will be used—"

"Don't let them take me away!" Judy flung herself at Ben. She pressed her head against his chest. "I love you, Ben."

Ben pushed her away. "Don't make me sick."

"But I do! Will you represent me?"

"Not a chance."

The air around them was split by the sound of a low-pitched scream.

"What the hell was that?" Tomlinson asked.

Ben took off and answered while in motion. "Mike."

MIKE DANGLED FROM the edge of the bell tower. Two hands—one of them severely lacerated—were all that kept him from plunging three stories down onto the concrete sidewalk.

"How long can you hold on?" Maura asked, leaning over the edge, grinning. "Not long, I bet."

Mike gritted his teeth. "You sorry little witch."

"Don't call me names. I don't like it when people call me names." She jabbed the knife into his hand again.

Mike cried out in agony. He clenched his eyes shut, trying to focus all his energy into his one strong hand. You must not let go, he told himself. No matter what she does to you. You must not let go.

"Would you hurry up and fall already?" Maura said. "I need to get out of here." She came closer again with the knife. "Maybe I can speed things up." She brought the blade back down toward him—

But this time he was ready for her. As soon as she came close, he used his good hand to knock the knife against the wooden railing. Maura swore. The knife tumbled over the edge, down into the prayer garden.

Mike swung his legs around and managed to get a foot up over the edge. Mustering all his strength, he pushed himself over the precipice.

Maura was already halfway to the hatch. Mike put the pain out of his mind and flew after her. He grabbed her around the waist and knocked her to the wooden floor.

They wrestled back and forth, Maura trying to get free, Mike trying to hold on for dear life. He was at a great disadvantage, especially since his right hand was virtually useless. He managed to get one of her arms pinned behind her back, but she got a swift knee into his groin at the same instant. While he was out of commission, she climbed on top of him, kicking his ribs and pounding his ears. Mike tried to push her away, but the pain in his right hand was too great. Goddamn it, he thought, I'm losing a fight with a fifteen-year-old girl!

He tried to grab her hand, but Maura avoided him and scratched his face with her fingernails.

"You little monster!" Somehow, the additional pain gave him a new swell of energy. Mike pushed forward, flinging her back against the bell. It clanged, sending a tremulous reverberation through the wood of the tower.

He pulled himself to his feet. "Now I'm mad."

Maura tried to scramble to the hatch, but Mike was too quick for her. He grabbed the back of her dress and held tight. He gave her a sudden sharp yank, and she spun into his arms.

"Give it up," Mike grunted, as he wrapped his arms around her, holding her tight.

"Go to hell," she answered. She took his hand—the one she had stabbed twice—and bit down on it.

Pain exploded inside his brain. He felt nauseated. "Damn!" He brought his left hand around—hard—and slapped her across the face.

Ben and Tomlinson came racing through the hatch. "What's going on? Are you all right?"

Mike pushed the girl to Tomlinson, who promptly snapped cuffs over her wrists. "I'll live."

"He beat me up!" Maura cried. Once again, tears flowed from her eyes. "See the bruises? He tried to rape me!"

Mike glared at her. "You know, I don't know whether to take you down or throw you over the edge."

"Help me!" she continued screeching. "Someone please help me!"

"Give it up, Maura. It's over." With his good hand, Mike un-clipped his cell phone from his belt. "Maxine? I need two patrol cars at St. Benedict's, Seventy-first and Yale. As soon as possible. I think we've just bagged a couple of murderers."

DOWN ON THE ground, Mike and Tomlinson worked to keep the madding crowd at bay while they waited for the black-and-whites to arrive. Everyone was shouting at once, wanting to know what was go-ing on, what they thought they were doing, why they were hurting those poor innocent girls. Judy and Maura continued to scream accu-sations and cry and wail, which only made matters worse. It was a madhouse, all in the parking lot of St. Benedict's Episcopal Church.

Finally, the patrol cars arrived. Mike let the uniforms take custody of the prisoners.

"Where are they going?" It was Judy's mother, still brandishing the baby and the purse, trying to intervene for about the tenth time. "Where are they taking my baby girl?"

"Downtown," Mike answered. "Police headquarters."

"I won't let them!"

"I'm afraid it's out of your hands, ma'am. You can go downtown and meet her, if you like."

Judy's mother looked at him indignantly. "I'm calling a lawyer. You'll be sorry about this!"

Mike grimaced. "Probably."

As the uniforms dragged their prisoners past Ben, Judy threw her-self at him. "Don't let them take me away, Ben. I love you!"

"Judy, just . . . go away. I don't want to see you. Like, ever again."

"That's not what you said last night!" she screamed, loud enough for everyone to hear. "When you made love to me. You said you loved me. I was a virgin before you, Ben."

Ben's eyes narrowed. "You lying little—"

Mike held him back. "Just ignore her, Ben."

"It's true. He raped me! He gave me one of those drugs and raped me!"

The uniforms dragged the screaming girls to the patrol cars. "Don't let them take us away!" Judy and Maura cried. "We're just girls!"

"Just girls?" Ben muttered. "You're frigging Leopold and Loeb."

He watched as they were packed into the cars and driven away. He didn't know what to think. Nothing seemed to make sense anymore.

Mike was getting his hand disinfected and bandaged, and as usual, he was behaving like a perfect baby. "Be sure to give him a lollipop when it's all done," Ben told the nurse. "I think he's earned it."

"I earn it every time I get involved in one of your miserable cases," Mike groaned. "Can someone please explain to me what just happened? How two teenage girls who sing in the church choir can be multiple murderers?"

"No, I can't," Ben said sadly. "And right now, I don't even want to try."

47

MURRAY WAS ASLEEP. Again.

Ben supposed manning the reception desk was not the most exciting job in the world, but had he ever arrived when the man was awake? Was he a major party hound, Ben wondered, or was there just something about this job that induced instant narcolepsy? It was annoying, and worse, made Ben feel guilty about waking him. He looked so peaceful there, arms wrapped around himself, eyes darting back and forth beneath the lids, a soft snoring sound fluttering from his lips . . .

"Wake up, Murray."

To his credit, he came around with amazing speed and resiliency. But then, he'd done this before.

"Oh—Ben—!" He straightened, twisted a kink out of his neck. "I didn't see you there."

And for good reason. "Is this a bad time?"

"No, no . . ." He shuffled papers around on his desk. "I was just resting my eyes. Those fluorescent lights are a killer. You here to see Beale?"

"Smart man."

"Well, I knew he'd been transferred back to county pending the habeas corpus hearing. I'll have him around in ten."

"Thanks. And Murray?"

"Yeah?"

"No catnaps along the way, okay?"

Murray gave him a squinty look, then disappeared behind the interior gate.

Ben had been waiting barely a minute when, to his surprise, he saw Assistant DA Antony Canelli emerge from behind the barred door.

"I always thought you should be behind bars," Ben said as the man approached. "I just didn't expect it to happen so soon. What did they get you for? Aggravated good looks?"

"Ha ha." He walked up to Ben and set down his briefcase. "You here to see the priest?"

"Yes. And you?"

"Interviewing a potential witness."

"Not another jailhouse snitch, I hope."

Canelli shifted his weight awkwardly from one foot to the other. "Look, Kincaid, I . . . I heard about the arrest. Those two girls."

"And how did that make you feel?"

"I don't know. I mean, officially, of course, our position is that nothing has changed. But as a practical matter, I have to acknowledge . . ." He licked his lips, then started again. "If we had known about the girls before the trial, things might've gone differently."

"I would hope so."

"It's just—" Canelli paused, struggling for words. This all seemed very strange to Ben. But the man apparently had something he really wanted to say. "When you work at the DA's office, you get wrapped up in winning, you know? And you have to, because the odds are stacked so high against us that if you didn't, no one would ever get convicted of anything. So you assume everyone arrested is guilty. If there's any evidence at all, and especially if the press is covering the case, the pressure is always on to prosecute. Of course, if you prosecute and lose, you get crucified. So you gotta win. You gotta win to please everyone, and you gotta win to keep your job. I know the boss claims they don't keep win-loss records, but believe me, they do."

"So you do anything you can think of to win. No matter how sleazy."

"I don't agree with the sleazy part, but yeah, we want to convict."

"So you use snitches and junk science and liars and—"

"The point is," Canelli interrupted, "that I recognize there's a problem here. Innocent people do get convicted, way more frequently than anyone ever imagined. DNA evidence has proved it.

And that makes me feel really . . . bad." He paused. "I just don't know what to do about it."

"A DA with a conscience? Do my eyes deceive me?"

Canelli's lips pursed. "You know, you don't do yourself any favors with those kind of remarks."

"It was just a joke. . . ."

"But you do it a lot. I think, just as I go into a case assuming guilt, you go into a case assuming the prosecutor is a monomaniacal hardass willing to pull any dirty trick to get a conviction."

"I've seen it, Canelli, way too often."

"And I've seen defense attorneys who lied and helped their clients lie to get them off. Does that mean I should hate all defense attorneys?"

Ben took a step back. "You're right, of course. I'm sorry."

"I don't mean to get all soppy on you. I just think, somehow, we've got to change things. The system isn't working, let's face it. Not like it should, anyway. We know we make mistakes, but we're not doing anything about it. We just keep going through the motions, and nothing gets any better. *We* don't get any better. And that includes me. I need to get out of this zealotlike, lockstep thinking. I need to be more . . . flexible. And you need to have more . . ."

Faith? Ben wondered.

"Understanding. Being a prosecutor is a hell of a hard job."

"I know it is."

"Anyway." Canelli picked up his briefcase. "I just wanted to get that off my chest."

"I'm glad you did." Ben extended his hand. "Friends?"

Canelli took his hand and flashed his brilliant smile. "Well, friendly rivals, anyway."

"JUDY AND MAURA?" Father Beale ran his hand through his hair. "I can't believe it."

"That's pretty much everyone's reaction," Ben said. "But it's the truth."

Beale shook his head as if dazed. "Why?"

"Don't ask me. I'm not a shrink. But there are a fleet of them working over those two girls right now, trying to come up with some answers."

"Surely it wasn't just for the jewelry."

"No. I think that was a perk, not a cause." Ben shrugged. "You want to hear my best guess? I think they did it because they could. Because they wanted to see if they could get away with it. It was a deadly combination of personalities—Judy's capable aggressiveness, Maura's quiet cruel streak. Their devotion to one another. Apart, probably neither of them would've been anything remarkable. But together—they were deadly."

"But there was more to it than just the murders. I was framed. Deliberately."

"I'm not sure they meant to do that initially. But after they saw how well it worked the first time, after they saw how brilliantly it diverted suspicion from themselves, they made it a regular part of the program. Killing the second victim in your office. Rigging the lights to go out during the vestry meeting so you would go to the utility room to investigate and find the body."

"I had a talk with Judy, maybe six or eight months ago. She told me that—well, I think she had a crush on me."

"Yes, I've had a similar experience. And you probably explained that you were too old for her, not to mention married."

"Something like that." His eyes widened. "My God! You don't suppose—"

"That's why she framed you for murder? Revenge for being spurned? Or maybe it was because she knew it would bring me around to defend you?" He shook his head. "Who knows? Who could possibly understand minds like those?"

Beale fell back against the thin plywood-backed chair. Ben hated seeing him like this. The coveralls were bad enough, but the other sure signs of time spent in prison were evident as well—pasty complexion, stubbled chin, red eyes, generally unclean appearance. To see a man of his education, his compassion, reduced to this was horrifying.

"Enough about those two unfortunates," Beale said at last. "When do I get out of here?"

This was the moment Ben had been dreading. "I . . . I don't know."

"You don't know? But—if they've caught the true killers—"

"I know those girls are the murderers, but try convincing anybody else. They aren't confessing; they've got lawyers who refuse to let them say anything to anybody. The DA's office isn't buying it; they don't want to admit they mistakenly sent someone to death row."

"But the jewelry in Maura's purse—"

"Is the best thing we've got going for us. But it isn't conclusive. What's more—it only links the girls to the first and third murder—not the one for which you were convicted. As far as the DA is concerned, the only evidence they have regarding the murder of Kate McGuire points to you."

"That's absurd."

"I agree. But that's what they're saying."

"You'll use this new information in our appeal, right?"

Ben laced his fingers together, trying to give himself strength. "I already have. But here's the thing. 'Actual innocence' is not grounds for appeal. It doesn't raise any constitutional issues, at least not according to Chief Justice Rehnquist. To succeed on appeal, you need to show that there was an important procedural error in the trial court—and quite frankly, Father—there weren't any. I mean, I made some arguments, but the truth is Judge Pitcock ran a fair trial and didn't make any major mistakes. And he gave us a lot of breaks."

"Isn't there anything else we can do?"

"We're trying the federal courts. To get you out through habeas corpus petition. But as you know, the feds have severely curtailed postconviction appeals."

"There must be something else."

"We can ask the governor to pardon you."

"Then do it!"

"I have. But . . ." Ben's eyes lowered. "As you know, our current governor is a Republican. Very Republican. And this is an election year. The last thing he wants to do is appear soft on crime—or worse, create a Willie Horton scenario by releasing someone who subsequently commits another crime. Especially not on a case that has gotten as much publicity as yours. Even if you didn't do anything after you got out, releasing you could cost him some support in archconservative circles. He doesn't want to take the risk."

"I can't believe my life has become some sort of . . . political football!"

"If we had some DNA evidence or something irrefutable, it might make a difference with the governor. But the sad truth is—we don't."

"And that's it?"

"That's not it," Ben said firmly. "Christina and I are continuing to work this case. Daily. We're going to do everything there is to do and then some."

"But as for now . . . I'm stuck in prison."

Ben tried not to let his voice crack. "I'm afraid so."

"And you don't know when or if I'll ever be able to get out."

"Father, there have been defendants whose innocence was proved beyond doubt by DNA evidence who still spent additional years in jail. There are no guarantees."

"Is there anything I can do?"

"Yes." Ben motioned to the guard standing at the door. "I've arranged for you to have paper and pencils brought to your cell. Told them it was a necessary part of your defense. Tried to get you a type-writer . . . but anyway. I want you to write down everything that's happened. Everything since this whole mess started. The gospel according to Daniel. Don't leave anything out."

"And then?"

"And then, when I read it, and reread it, and reread it, I'm hoping I'll see something, think of something, remember something—something that will help me get you out of prison."

Beale nodded. All in all, Ben thought he was taking this hideous news extraordinarily well. "I'll start immediately." He looked up at Ben. "You'll think of something. I know you will."

"Don't say that."

"Why not?" He paused. "I have faith in you."

"Remember when I told you about Christina's contract case? About bad faith?"

"There's no such thing."

"There is. It's possible to have too much faith, or to misplace it."

Beale shook his head firmly. "I have faith in you, Ben. Just as I have faith in God."

Ben was incredulous. "How can you still have faith in God . . . when you're behind bars?"

"I believe in the sun even when it is not shining."

"Your God put you in prison for a crime you didn't commit."

"Yes, and I don't know why, either. But I know there is a reason. And I know in time it will be revealed to me."

Ben couldn't restrain himself. "If your God is so damn powerful, why didn't He save you? Why did He let those women be murdered? Why does He allow children to become murderers? Why didn't He save the victims of the Holocaust?"

"God doesn't do room service. He's not a fairy godfather, floating around granting wishes. He's something greater than that."

"If He's something greater, I wish to hell I knew what it was."

Beale fell silent. His finger touched his lips and he sat for a moment, watching Ben.

"You didn't bring Christina with you today?"

"No. She's doing habeas corpus research. Why?"

"Just wondered. I've . . ." He paused another moment, smiled slightly, then continued. "I've seen how she looks at you, when you're not watching. And I've seen how you look at her, when your guard is down."

"Christina and I are good friends," Ben said, very quickly.

"Uh-huh."

"What does this have to do with God, anyway?"

"Have you read Victor Hugo?"

"On occasion."

"Les Misérables?"

"Long time ago. Why?"

"Do you remember what the priest says to Jean Valjean? After he rescues him from the police by pretending that he gave Jean the candlesticks he actually stole? After he tells Jean his life now belongs to God, so act accordingly? And Jean doesn't know what to do. How to go about it."

"I'm lousy with quotes. What does he say?"

Father Beale smiled. " 'To love another person is to see the face of God.' "

48

The Gospel According to Daniel

THIS WILL BE the final entry in this heretical gospel, this renegade account of a priest whose life was turned upside down for reasons he couldn't begin to understand. I've recorded it all, every word, thought, and deed. And I tried to tell it true, although I'm sure that at times, to paraphrase Emily Dickinson once more, I told it slant. I don't know that I revealed any great secrets, any startling insights. And I don't know what use this will be to my attorney, or to anyone else. But I was asked to prepare it, and I did. It is what it is.

I don't know what will happen next. Perhaps my attorney will succeed and I will be released. Perhaps he will fail and I will be executed. Or perhaps he will only manage to have my sentence reduced to life imprisonment and I will spend the rest of my days behind these cold walls. That, I think, would be the worst result of all, and yet I cannot deny that it is possible that is God's will. I have seen much work that needs to be done since I came to this horrible place. Many souls in need of salvation. Many hearts in anguish, without hope. This is not the future I would've chosen for myself, but if this is God's plan, then so be it.

Anne Frank still believed there was good in the world, even when her short life was at its darkest moment. And so must I. I have already had so much more than she, that if it is time for the quality of my life to be drastically altered, then I must accept that with grace. But I am still amazed, even in this dire place, at the tiny acts of kindness I see everywhere. The brief moments of consideration, of unselfishness, even in the grimmest of circumstances. Sharing food. Reading letters for those who cannot. Comforting the lost and forgotten. I know there is evil in the world, true palpable evil, in men, women—even in something as seemingly innocent as a young girl. But I also know there is great good. Perhaps its rarity is what makes it so special—and what ultimately gives us our greatest indication of the divine nature of the human spirit.

I still have my faith. And while I don't think retaining that is any great act of courage, it is a comfort to me. I can sleep nights, sometimes, with the knowledge that regardless of what horrors I am forced to undergo—it is for a reason. I do believe that. I must believe that. Because if it were not so—life at this point would simply not be worth living. And I want to go on living. I want to believe. And so I shall.

THE HOMILY WAS finished, the anthem had been sung, and the new interim priest, Father Doner, had chanted and sung through the Sanctus and the Lord's Prayer and the Agnus Dei. Soon it would be time for the choir to rise and take communion; they were always among the first to go, so they could be back in the choir loft singing while the congregation took theirs.

Ben wished his choir robe had pockets, but it didn't. They wore big bulky Anglican-looking things, white shifts on a dark, full-length, bulky, hot and heavy gown—with no pockets. Who designed these, anyway? Probably some monk five hundred years ago, and people have irrationally been copying it ever since, even though it's bulky, hot, heavy . . . et cetera. And had no pockets.

He had tried to concentrate on the homily, but his mind was elsewhere. In the courtroom, replaying his every move, wondering if he could've done something differently. Better. In the jailhouse, trying to bring comfort to the man who had brought so much to him, knowing that he had failed him. And at the juvenile detention center, burrowing into the minds of two young girls, trying to understand what to him was simply unknowable. It was too much for his puny brain. It was, as Father Beale would say, greater than him.

Is that why people turned to God? Ben wondered. When all was said and done, was it just the desire to make sense of it all, or to believe that someone, somewhere could make sense of it? He couldn't say, but if that was it, he could sympathize.

But could he believe? That was the sticking point. He had seen too much, had known too intimately all the bad, the crooked, the grimy, the depraved, the flat-out evil that lurked in the world. He had seen the worst of everyone—even a beloved priest. And yet, it seemed clear to Ben now that Father Beale's flaws did not make him a fraud—they made him a man. And humanity, with all its imperfections, was still capable of achieving greatness. And occasionally did.

The time had come. All around him, the rest of the choir rose to its feet, and before he really understood when or why, Ben rose also. He followed them as they filed down the nave and knelt with them at the altar rail.

"The body of Christ," Father Doner said as he passed Ben the wafer. And Ben took it and ate it.

Did he believe? It was too hard a question to answer. But I want to believe, he thought, as he brought the silver chalice to his lips and sipped the wine. I want to believe. And for now, that's enough.

ACKNOWLEDGMENTS

UNFORTUNATELY, FATHER BEALE'S fate in this novel is all too real. *Actual Innocence,* a book by Pulitzer Prize–winning journalist Jim Dwyer with Peter Neufeld and Barry Schreck, provides horrifying details about sixty-five convicts who were sent to prison or death row—after being convicted by a unanimous jury—before DNA testing produced stone-cold proof of their innocence. Unfortunately, even after these convicts' guiltlessness was established, many of them were not freed, because under current appellate law, "actual innocence" is not necessarily grounds for release from prison. Worse, because post-conviction appeals have been sharply truncated, many innocent convicts found themselves without legal recourse before the DNA technology to exonerate them even existed. A recent report produced by Equal Justice USA, a project of the Hyattsville-based Quixote Center, found that sixteen men in seven states had been executed despite "compelling evidence of their innocence." How does this happen? Eyewitnesses are often mistaken, snitches lie, confessions are coerced or fabricated, junk science is permitted, and lawyers fail. If all this is true, how many Father Beales must there be in our American prisons?

To help correct this injustice, lawyer Peter Neufeld has founded the pro bono Innocence Project at the Benjamin N. Cardozo School of Law. The Innocence Project is a nonprofit organization dedicated to using DNA evidence to seek releases in the hundreds of remaining cases of wrongly convicted persons. They have also proposed a bipartisan Innocence Protection Act, which would give inmates the right to DNA tests to prove their innocence and would require the preservation of evidence after conviction. There have been more than one hundred post-conviction exonerations based upon DNA evidence in the last few years—but there is still much work to be done. Persons wanting to know more about this endeavor can visit: http://www. cardozo.yu.edu/innocence_project/.

Once again, I want to thank my editor, Joe Blades, and my agents, Robert Gottlieb and Matt Bialer, for their guidance and support. I want to thank Arlene Joplin, my criminal law expert, and William Mc-Connell, my Episcopal church expert, for reading and commenting on an early draft of the book. And I want to thank my family, Kirsten and Harry and Alice and Ralph, for keeping me relatively sane.

Readers are invited to E-mail me at: wb@williambernhardt.com. You can also visit my Web site and sign up for my E-mail newsletter: www.williambernhardt.com.